THE SIGN OF LOVE

Duron Books by Barbara Cartland

The Marquis Who Hated Women
Look, Listen and Love
The Curse of the Clan
Punishment of a Vixen
The Outrageous Lady
A Touch of Love
The Dragon and the Pearl
The Love Pirate
The Temptation of Torilla
Love and the Loathsome Leopard
The Naked Battle
The Hell-Cat and the King
No Escape from Love
The Sign of Love
The Castle Made for Love

BARBARA CARTLAND

The Sign of Love

DURON BOOKS

Library of Congress Cataloging in Publication Data

Cartland, Barbara, 1902–
The sign of love.

I.   Title.
PZ3.C247Si   1977   [PR6005.A765]   823'.9'12   77–17353
ISBN 0–87272–032–2

THE SIGN OF LOVE
A Duron Book / December 1977

Duron Books are published by Brodart, Inc., Williamsport, Pa. Its trademark, consisting of the words "Duron Books" is registered in the United
States Patent Office and in other countries.

PRINTED IN THE UNITED STATES OF AMERICA

THE SIGN OF LOVE

Author's Note

My grandfather as an undergraduate at Oxford was at the Opening of the Suez Canal. The description of the ceremony, the Royal guests, and the magnificent party given by the Khedive at Ismailia are all accurate.

The building of the Canal combined with the personal extravagance of Ismail Pasha bankrupted Egypt in 1875.

Mr. Benjamin Disraeli, Prime Minister of Britain, was able to buy the Khedive's shares for four million pounds.

Whatever the cost, the achievement of Ferdinand de Lesseps, whose dream came true after he had spent a life-time surmounting incredible difficulties in raising money and obstructions in the Canal itself, is one of the great adventure stories of the world.

His bronze statue at the entrance to the Canal was destroyed by a hostile mob in 1956 but his name lives on in the pages of history.

After his life-long struggle had been acclaimed, Ferdinand de Lesseps married his second wife, a young French girl, in a little Chapel at Ismailia. She was to bear him twelve children.

Chapter One
1869

The passengers from the steamer which had crossed the English Channel from Calais hurried onto the Quay at Dover.

It was raining lightly, but on their faces there were expressions of relief and almost of joy as they realised that the crossing was over and their feet were on firm ground again.

Coming slowly down the gangway and helping an elderly woman was a girl with an anxious expression in her large grey eyes.

It took them a long time to reach the Quay and the girl was conscious that the passengers behind them were muttering at their slowness and doing everything possible to hasten their progress.

Finally, as they stepped onto the wet, stone pier, the elderly woman seemed to stagger, and it was with difficulty that the girl supported her to an empty porter's truck on which she could sit.

The woman gave a groan and put her hands up to her face.

"*Je suis malade, très malade.*"

"I know, *Mademoiselle*," the girl said, "but if you will make a last effort we can reach the train and then there will be no need for you to move until we arrive in London."

In response the Frenchwoman merely groaned.

"Come along," the girl urged. "It is not very far. Lean on me, *Mademoiselle,* or better still, I will put my arms round you."

She tried to pull the elderly woman to her feet but the Frenchwoman resisted her.

"*Non, c'est impossible!*" she murmured.

"But we cannot miss the train," the girl urged again. "Please, *Mademoiselle,* you must try!"

She pulled the woman to her feet, but as she did so the woman suddenly collapsed and fell down to the ground in a crumpled heap.

The girl looked at her in horror.

She realised now that *Mademoiselle's* protests of illness had been quite real, and not due, as she had thought, merely to sea-sickness.

It had been a very rough crossing, the majority of the passengers had succumbed almost before they left Calais harbour, and *Mademoiselle* Bouvais had warned her before they arrived at the port that she was a very bad sailor.

But Bettina had not known how bad that was likely to be until the steamer had rolled, pitched, tossed, and done everything but stand on its head before they reached the shelter of Dover harbour.

Now she thought again, as actually she had thought in the first place, that it had been madness to send anyone so old to escort her, even though she knew that *Mademoiselle* Bouvais was the most easily spared of the teachers in the school.

Bettina looked round wildly for help.

But the passengers and the porters hurrying by did not even give the collapsed woman a glance.

Desperately she spoke to an elderly lady who she thought looked kind.

"Please, can you help me?" she asked. "My companion . . "

She was brushed to one side almost roughly, and the lady, rustling in her silk skirts and warm fur cape, swept away from her towards the waiting train.

"Porter! Porter!" Bettina cried, but all the porters were too busy.

Their trucks were piled high with luggage, while the passengers who employed them were giving complicated orders as to where they wished to sit—"First Class, facing the engine"; "A corner of the Second Class"; " 'Ladies Only' "; "The Restaurant Car."

"What am I to do?" Bettina asked herself.

She looked at *Mademoiselle* Bouvais and saw that her eyes were closed, her face ashen pale.

It struck her suddenly that she might be dead, and now she turned frantically, with a note of sheer desperation in her voice, to a gentleman who was walking alone.

"You must help me!" she cried. "This lady is dead or dying and no-one will do anything to assist her."

The gentleman looked at Bettina, then at the *Mademoiselle* lying in the mud on the ground, the rain soaking her bonnet and under it her grey hair.

Without speaking he bent down, and lifting the Frenchwoman in his arms he carried her under cover.

"Oh, thank you, thank you!" Bettina said. "She was very sea-sick coming across the Channel and now I am afraid that it has been too much for her heart."

"I think that is very likely," the gentleman replied, "and it is important that she should have medical attention immediately."

"Do you mean here in Dover?" Bettina enquired.

"There will be a Hospital," the gentleman said. "I will make enquiries."

As he spoke they reached the door of the Waiting-Room and Bettina hurriedly opened it for him so that he could carry his burden inside.

She looked very small and pathetic in his arms, and it seemed to Bettina that the blood had left her face entirely and her skin was so white and transparent that she was already a corpse.

But when he had laid her down on the black

leather seat which stood along one wall of the room,
the gentleman put a finger on the Frenchwoman's
pulse and said quietly:

"She is alive."

"Thank God!" Bettina breathed a sigh of relief.
"I was afraid . . . terribly . . . afraid."

"I can understand you feeling like that," the gentleman replied, "because the lady is very old."

"She was the only mistress the school could spare
to escort me to London."

His lips smiled faintly at her explanation before
he said:

"Wait here. I will see what I can find out about a
Doctor and the Hospital."

He went from the Waiting-Room and Bettina
pulled down her escort's skirt so that it did not reveal
her buttoned boots, then loosened the ribbons of her
bonnet under her chin.

Mademoiselle seemed so limp and motionless
that, as if Bettina needed to be reassured about what
she had been told, she put her own fingers on the
Frenchwoman's wrist.

The pulse was beating very, very faintly, so
faintly that at first she thought she was only imagin-
ing it.

Fortunately the Waiting-Room was warm because there was a fire in the grate, and it was also
empty.

She could hear the noise on the platform outside
and knew it must be getting on towards the time
when the train would leave for London.

She supposed that by now their porter would
have put their luggage in the Guard's Van and was
looking for them to receive his tip.

He had gone ahead when they left the ship,
blithely confident that they would be following him.

'If Papa intended meeting me, he will be worried,' Bettina thought.

Then she told herself that that was the least
of her troubles. She had to see to *Mademoiselle* first,
and if possible save her life.

She had a sudden fear that the gentleman who had been so kind might now have abandoned them, because he too wished to catch the train, he would leave them to their fate.

Then, just as she heard the whistle blow and knew that the Boat Express was steaming out of the station, the door of the Waiting-Room opened.

Bettina gave a sigh of relief as she saw that the gentleman had returned and with him was a middle-aged man who she thought must be the Doctor.

The latter bustled across the Waiting-Room towards *Mademoiselle.*

He looked down at her, took her pulse, then drew a stethoscope from the black bag he carried and listened to her heart.

Bettina was silent until he said:

"I think you are right, My Lord. It is a case of a heart-attack brought on by violent sea-sickness. It is not an uncommon occurrence, I can assure you."

"Can we get her to the Hospital?" the gentleman asked.

"Of course, My Lord. There is no difficulty about that. If you will excuse me, I will send someone immediately for an ambulance."

"Thank you, Doctor. That is very kind of you."

For the first time the Doctor looked at Bettina.

"I understand from IIis Lordship that this lady is your teacher and chaperone," he said.

"Yes," Bettina replied. "Her name is *Mademoiselle* Bouvais. She was very reluctant to come on the journey and told me she had always been a bad sailor."

The Doctor nodded his head as if that was what he had expected to hear.

"I will take all the particulars you can give me when we reach the Hospital," he said.

With a polite bow to the gentleman whom he had addressed as "My Lord," he hurried from the Waiting-Room.

"I am afraid you have lost your train on our ac-

count," Bettina said softly, "but I am grateful, very
. . . very grateful, for your help."

"I am glad I could be of service. But when you
have *Mademoiselle* Bouvais safely in the Hospital,
what will you do?"

"I suppose I shall have to catch the next train to
London," Bettina replied. "My father will doubtless be
worried when I do not arrive on the Boat Train."

"What is your name?" the gentleman enquired.

"Bettina Charlwood."

"And I am Eustace Veston—Lord Eustace Veston."

"Thank you so very much for being so kind and
helpful. No-one else would listen to me."

"Few people behave like Good Samaritans when
they are rushing about in a railway station," Lord
Eustace replied.

"That is true," Bettina said. "I think it must be
because really they are frightened of trains. They
are so big and noisy and everybody seems to be
intimidated by them."

"I will find out when the next train will leave
for London," Lord Eustace said. "I suppose your luggage has already gone ahead?"

"I expect so," Bettina answered. "I shall somehow have to get *Mademoiselle's* returned to her."

"I do not think you need worry about that," he
replied. "They will provide her with everything she
needs at the Hospital."

He glanced at the Frenchwoman as he spoke,
then he bent forward once again to take her wrist in
his fingers.

Bettina saw him feeling for the pulse, then held
her breath as she realised the truth of what he feared.

He stood for what seemed a long time, holding
the thin, blue-veined wrist showing beneath the black
taffeta of her sleeve, then he put it down very gently
and looked at Bettina.

"I am sorry," he said quietly, "but I am afraid we
are too late."

"Oh no!"

The exclamation come from Bettina's lips with a little cry and she knelt down beside the Frenchwoman, looking into her face as if she expected her eyes to open and prove Lord Eustace wrong.

"She cannot be dead ... she cannot!" she cried.

"She suffered no pain," Lord Eustace said, "and knew nothing about it. I think it is the way most people would wish to die."

"Yes ... of course," Bettina agreed.

She felt she ought to be more upset than she actually was, but all she felt was that the dead woman looked very, very old and that the life which flickered within her had not been very strong at any time.

'I ought to say a prayer,' Bettina thought to herself, then felt embarrassed about kneeling on the floor in the Waiting-Room with a man she had only just met standing beside her.

'May you rest in peace,' she whispered in her heart, then rose a little awkwardly to her feet.

"There is nothing more you can do now," Lord Eustace said, "and when the Doctor returns I will find out how soon there is another train to London."

"But ought I to ... leave her?" Bettina asked. "And what about the funeral? She was a Catholic."

"I imagined that," Lord Eustace replied, "and I think we can leave everything in the hands of the Doctor, who seems to be a sensible man, and I understand he has a large practise in Dover."

Bettina looked at him uncertainly and Lord Eustace said:

"Leave it all to me. I am sure your father would wish you to get home as soon as possible."

"He would understand that in a way I am ... responsible for *Mademoiselle* Bouvais," Bettina said.

"But she was meant to be responsible for you."

Bettina gave a little shiver, and he said:

"Come nearer to the fire. Something like this is always a shock. Shall I see if I can get you a cup of tea?"

"No, I am quite all right; but thank you very much," Bettina said. "You have been so kind already. I do not like to impose upon you further."

"As I have already said, I am only too glad to be of help," Lord Eustace replied.

She moved towards the fire and when she reached it she held out her hands to the flickering flames.

"Do you think the Doctor's fees and the funeral will be very expensive?" she asked. "I am afraid I have very little money with me, but I know that Papa will send a cheque as soon as I reach London."

"I will explain that to the Doctor," Lord Eustace said. "And now I think you should sit down. This has been, I know, very upsetting for you."

"It would have been much worse if you had not been here," Bettina answered.

However, she sat down, as he had suggested, because she felt as if her legs could no longer support her.

She had never before seen anyone dead and now she thought that it was frightening how quickly someone could die.

One moment *Mademoiselle* had been moaning and groaning about her sea-sickness, complaining with all the volubility of a Frenchwoman, and the next minute she was silent—still!

Somehow, she now seemed very small and ineffectual, and one wondered why any child had ever obeyed her or how she had ever exercised any authority in the school.

Dead!

It was a horrid word, Bettina thought. There was something so final about it, and it was hard for the moment to think, as a Catholic would, that *Mademoiselle*'s soul had gone to Paradise and that because she was a good woman the Gates of Heaven would be open to her.

"I am going to find you a cup of tea," Lord Eustace said, his voice breaking in on Bettina's train of thought.

He left the Waiting-Room, and Bettina, from her

chair near the fire, looked across at *Mademoiselle* lying on the bench.

'I must pray for her, because there is no-one else to do so,' she thought.

She wondered if perhaps she could have been kinder and more considerate than she had been during the Channel crossing.

Mademoiselle in fact had not been the sort of woman to inspire consideration, let alone affection or love.

None of the girls in the school had ever liked her, and perhaps because she was small of stature she had always seemed to be aggressively domineering, ordering everyone about, usually unnecessarily, and invariably being full of complaints.

'Poor *Mademoiselle*,' Bettina thought to herself.

She wondered if the Frenchwoman was in fact happier now than she had been in what must have been a long-drawn and tedious life at the school.

The other teachers had always had pupils ready to wait on them slavishly in return for a smile of encouragement or a compliment. But *Madame* de Vesarie had chosen her teachers with care.

They all contributed to her famous school, which was acknowledged to be the best *Seminary pour les Jeunes Filles* in France.

"In fact," *Madame* had often said, "in the whole of Europe there is no other school of equal importance."

Mademoiselle Bouvais had been there for so many years that she knew more about the history of the school than did *Madame* herself.

That, Bettina thought, was why even though she had become far too old to teach she had remained, while other mistresses came and went.

Bettina knew that her death would mean very little to the school or to *Madame* de Vesarie.

The girls would be told the sad news after Prayers, and they would all go down on their knees and pray for *Mademoiselle*'s departed soul. Then she would be forgotten.

It somehow seemed terrible that a long life should end with one prayer and then forgetfulness, and Bettina wished that she could find herself crying or at least feeling acutely unhappy because *Mademoiselle* was dead.

Then with a sudden lifting of her chin she said to herself:

"I will not cry! I really did not like her when she was alive. Why should I pretend, now that she is dead?"

She remembered that once, long ago, someone —it might have been her father—had said about a funeral:

"A mass of expensive flowers now that she is dead, and you can be sure she didn't get so much as a faded daisy when she was alive."

"That is what is wrong," Bettina told herself. "We should be kinder to the living and less inclined to put on a show when they are no longer here to see it."

She remembered the flowers that had filled the Church at her mother's funeral. Many of the wreaths had come from people her mother had not liked and had always refused to have inside the house.

"I wonder why they bothered to send them?" Bettina had asked herself at the time.

Her mother would have been amused because she would have known, although she would never have said so, that the senders wished to "keep in" with Sir Charles because he was frequently in the company of the Prince of Wales and all his friends were very smart and influential.

As her thoughts went back to her mother's funeral, Bettina remembered how broken-hearted her father had seemed at the time, but how quickly he had recovered.

"Life has to go on, Bettina," he had said while his daughter's eyes were still red with tears.

She had missed her mother so intolerably that she could not even think about her without crying.

"Yes, I know, Papa," she had managed to say, because she knew he was waiting for an answer.

"What I am going to do now," her father said, "is go to see your Godmother, Lady Buxton. She has always taken an interest in you, and I feel she is the one person who can help us at this particular moment."

"In what way, Papa?"

"I am not quite certain," her father replied, "but I am sure Sheila Buxton will know what to do."

She had indeed known, Bettina thought, and almost before she realised what was happening she had been sent off to France to *Madame* de Vesarie's school, where she was to remain for the next three years.

She had turned eighteen this summer, and she thought that she would be allowed to leave in April and make her début as all her friends of the same age were to do.

However, when she had written to her father about it she had learnt that Lady Buxton was ill. Her father had written:

> Stay where you are. I cannot trouble your Godmother at the moment and, quite frankly, there is no chance of her "bringing you out" this year while she is laid up.

It had been hard to find herself the oldest girl in the school and to receive letters from her friends describing the Balls, Theatres, and entertainments they were attending while she had to have special lessons on her own because she was too advanced for the top form.

Then suddenly, two weeks ago, she had learnt that her Godmother was dead and that she was to come home immediately.

It had been a complete surprise both to herself and to *Madame* de Vesarie.

"I should have thought, Bettina, that your father

would have wished you to complete this term, at least," *Madame* said.

"Yes, I would have thought so too, *Madame*," Bettina replied.

"You might remind him, dear, that we have not yet received the fees, which are always payable in advance. Of course, we can make some reduction, but you will please point out to him that the term started on the first of September."

"Yes, *Madame*."

Bettina had known then, without being told, the reason why she had been summoned home.

Her Godmother had always paid her school fees, and with her death this arrangement had to come to an end.

Ever since she could remember, her father and mother had always been hard up, but nothing prevented her father from associating with his rich friends and taking part in all their interests, whatever the cost.

He hunted, he shot, he raced, he did all the things which contributed to the amusement of the "Marlborough House Set," which centred round the Prince and Princess of Wales.

Bettina knew with a sinking of her heart that there would be little money left for her, and now that Lady Buxton was dead it was doubtful if she would have even one new gown in which to attend a Ball, should she be invited to one.

Her thoughts were so far away that it gave her quite a start when Lord Eustace came back into the Waiting-Room, accompanied by a steward from the Buffet carrying a tray containing a pot of tea and some rather thick ham sandwiches.

The steward set them down on a chair beside Bettina, thanked Lord Eustace for what was obviously a generous tip, and hurried away.

"You will feel better when you have had something to eat and drink," Lord Eustace said.

"You are so kind," Bettina answered.

"There is a train in another half an hour," he

said. "I have arranged for a tea-basket for you, and have reserved for you a seat in a 'Ladies Only' compartment!"

Bettina murmured her thanks and poured out the tea.

Lord Eustace had been right. She did feel better—so much better, in fact, that she picked up one of the ham sandwiches, and realised as she bit into it that she was quite hungry.

No-one had wanted to eat anything on board the ship and she had felt too shy to eat alone.

The ham sandwiches tasted good and when she had eaten one she started on another.

She had taken only a few bites of it when the Doctor returned, and she rose hastily to her feet.

"Sit down," Lord Eustace said, "and leave everything to me."

He drew the Doctor into a corner of the room and they talked in low voices so that Bettina could not hear what they were saying.

She did not like to go on eating and drinking and suddenly became acutely conscious again of the dead body of *Mademoiselle*

Ambulance-men came in to lift her onto a stretcher and cover her completely with a blanket.

Bettina felt that she ought in some way to say good-bye to her, but the ambulance-men moved from the room in an impersonal, professional manner and the door was shut behind them.

The Doctor was still talking to Lord Eustace and now Bettina saw that they had in their hands *Mademoiselle*'s papers, which they had taken from her hand-bag.

Then as if their conversation was finished the Doctor walked towards Bettina.

"The address here is that of *Madame* de Vesarie's school," he said. "This is where we should write to give notification of the death of this lady?"

"Yes, that is right," Bettina answered. "If she had a home or relations, I do not know anything about them."

"I can understand that," the Doctor said. "And you may rest assured, Miss Charlwood, that everything will be done as her Priest would require. I have already sent someone from the Hospital to inform him that a Roman Catholic was extremely ill. He will be expecting to give her the Last Rites, but as it is he will of course arrange her funeral in a Catholic cemetery."

"Thank you very much," Bettina said. "I am very grateful for all the trouble you have gone to."

"I am only sorry that we could not save her life," the Doctor replied.

He shook Bettina's hand. She felt that she ought to mention something about payment, then remembered that Lord Eustace had said he would see to everything.

'Papa must pay him,' she thought.

Then she realised it was very likely that Lord Eustace would know her father, who always seemed to know every member of the aristocracy.

When the Doctor had gone, Lord Eustace came to sit down in a chair by the fireside.

"I had better give you my father's address," Bettina said. "I was wondering if perhaps you know him?"

Lord Eustace did not reply, and she added:

"He is Sir Charles Charlwood, a friend of the Prince of Wales."

To her surprise, Lord Eustace seemed to stiffen before he replied:

"I have heard of your father, but I do not move in the same set that he does."

"No?" Bettina quesioned, puzzled.

"If you want the truth," Lord Eustace said, "I disapprove of the Prince and most of the people with whom he associates."

As if he felt he had been rude, he added quickly:

"Please, do not think I am disparaging your father, whom I do not know. But the Prince's behaviour causes a great deal of gossip which can only be deprecated at a time when there is so much suffering and misery in the country."

"They admire His Royal Highness very much in France," Bettina replied. "In fact they always speak as if they love him."

"I understand that His Royal Highness made a good impression in Paris," Lord Eustace conceded. "At the same time, his extravagance and that of his friends and the luxurious parties they give contrast badly with the starvation and the unemployment amongst the lower classes."

"Is it . . . very bad?" Bettina questioned.

"Terrible!" Lord Eustace said. "And I am appalled—yes, appalled, Miss Charlwood—at the indifference, the lack of interest, amongst those who should be gravely troubled by the terrible problems that one can see in every major city in Britain."

There was an unmistakable note of sincerity in his voice and Bettina said after a moment:

"I feel that you want to try to help the poor."

"I do indeed," Lord Eustace replied, "but it is not easy. I assure you, Miss Charlwood, one is up against not only apathy but sheer selfish ignorance on the part of those whose duty it is to know better."

"The poor are lucky to have you as their champion," Bettina said with a little smile.

"One day I would like to show you what I am trying to do to help the less fortunate members of the community," Lord Eustace said. "But it is merely a drop in the ocean—an ocean of despondency, misery, and despair."

He spoke almost dramatically and Bettina looked at him with a new interest.

She had hardly had time, with the horror of what was happening to *Mademoiselle,* to look at the man who had befriended her.

Now she saw that while he was good-looking, with clear-cut features and a square, intelligent-looking forehead, he also looked sombre and at the same time almost grim.

He was fashionably yet soberly dressed, and she

thought that he had chosen such clothes to be un-obtrusive even though he obviously went to a good tailor.

'He is always ready to be kind to those in trouble,' Bettina thought, 'and that is why he helped me.'

Lord Eustace looked at his watch.

"Our train should be in at any moment now," he said. "Wait here while I go and look for a porter to find our seats for us."

As he walked across the Waiting-Room, Bettina realised that he had broad shoulders and although he was not particularly tall he was well-built.

"He is certainly a very unusual person," she told herself. "Quite different from the other men I have met."

She remembered how jovial and full of laughter her father's friends always were as they smoked their cigars and invariably seemed to have a glass in their hands.

There was something about them, Bettina thought in retrospect, that made them seem frivolous and concerned with nothing but their own enjoyment.

How very different they were from this serious young man who cared so deeply about the poor.

"I am sure I am very lucky to have met him just at this moment," she told herself.

Then she added with a little sigh:

"I wish he were travelling in the same carriage to London and we could go on talking."

＊   ＊   ＊

A gust of wind swept down Park Lane and caught the top-hat of the gentleman who was stepping out of his barouche at Alveston House.

He held on to it with difficulty, and walked in through the impressive front door to hand it to a white-wigged, liveried servant.

"It's a very blustery day, M'Lord," the Butler said as he helped him off with his coat.

"It is growing cold, too," Lord Milthorpe replied, "but we must expect that in October."

"We must indeed, M'Lord," the Butler agreed respectfully.

Then, going ahead, he opened the large mahogany doors at the end of the huge marble-floored hall and announced:

"Lord Milthorpe, Your Grace!"

The Duke, who was sitting in front of the fire at the end of the room, looked up with a smile on his face.

"You are late, George!" he remarked. "Charles and I were wondering what had happened to you."

"The Prince kept me," Lord Milthorpe replied.

He settled himself in a deep, comfortable armchair near the other two gentlemen in the room and accepted a glass of sherry from the silver salver proffered him by a flunkey.

"I thought that must be the reason," the Duke said. "How is His Royal Highness?"

"Extremely discomfitted," Lord Milthorpe replied, "and very frustrated."

"What has happened now?" Sir Charles Charlwood asked.

A footman was refilling his glass and as he took it from the tray he added:

"It is always the same where poor old Bertie is concerned. I suppose the Queen has refused to let him do yet another thing on which he had set his heart."

"Right first guess!" Lord Milthorpe exclaimed.

"It is not a competition for which I would offer a prize," the Duke of Alveston remarked laconically.

"You know, Varien, it really is disgraceful," Lord Milthorpe remarked. "In fact I consider it a scandal that the only person who is going to represent us at the Opening of the Suez Canal is our Ambassador in Constantinople."

"Good God!" Sir Charles exclaimed. "The Prince was certain he would be able to go. He was looking forward to it after the magnificent way the Khedive of Egypt entertained him and the Princess last year."

"The edict from Buckingham Palace is the invariable 'no,' " Lord Milthorpe said.

"It is indeed a scandal!" Sir Charles exclaimed. "I was just reading about the Opening of the Canal in *The Times*. The Empress Eugénie is to be the Guest of Honour, the Emperor of Austria is to be present, and also the Crown Prince of Prussia! My God—how will Britain look with a mere Ambassador to grace such a throng?"

"All the Queen cares about is stopping the Prince from being in a position of any real importance," Lord Milthorpe said. "She just wants him to sit about the Palace at her beck and call, and I swear if there is a good notice about him in the newspapers, which is rare, she tears it up in a temper."

"Who shall blame him for finding his amusements where he can?" Sir Charles asked.

"Who indeed," Lord Milthorpe agreed.

"But it certainly seems an extraordinary decision as regards the Opening of the Canal," the Duke said slowly.

He was younger than either of his companions, but his air of authority made him seem older than he was.

An extraordinarily good-looking man, he was outstanding in any company in which he appeared. At the same time, his reputation, like that of the Prince of Wales, was continually in question.

Not that it troubled him in the slightest.

The Duke was a law unto himself, and, as he was exceedingly wealthy—one of the largest landowners in the country—and his title graced the history of England, no-one was prepared to remonstrate with him no matter what he wished to do.

He was a close friend of the heir to the throne, but at the same time he did not consider himself one of the "Marlborough House Set" for the simple reason that the "Alveston House Set" rivalled and in fact surpassed it in every way.

The Prince himself always complained that the

most beautiful women, the best dinners, the finest entertainment, and the most luxurious parties were given at Alveston House.

"Dammit all, Varien!" he had said more than once. "It is not only that you can afford such extravagance—it is, I suspect, that your taste is better than anyone else's, and you have more original ideas."

"You flatter me, Sir!" the Duke had replied. But while he spoke politely there was a cynical twist to his lips.

He often found that the pace the Prince set, simply because he was bored and irritated by the restrictions his mother laid upon him, was too contrived to have the spontaneity that he himself enjoyed so freely.

"You know what we are, Varien?" the Prince had once said jovially. "We are the Kings of Society, and because I am fond of you I do not really mind sharing my throne."

The Duke had murmured something complimentary. At the same time, he himself had no intention of sharing a throne with anyone.

He knew that he was envied by most of his contemporaries, that he had only to lift his little finger to have them grovelling slavishly at his feet.

He was so rich that he could indulge all his whims, and so generous that his friends never lacked for any need of which he was aware.

At the same time, he was more aloof in his bearing than the Prince of Wales himself, and any onlooker might have said he was more kingly.

There was something imperious about him, something which kept even those who loved him at arm's length.

There were women in his life, of course. They came and they went, and he had only to enter a Ball-Room for every female heart to flutter and hundreds of pairs of eyes to look towards him beguilingly, with an unmistakable invitation in them.

"He is like a Greek God," one of the beauties of Marlborough House had murmured to another.

"How many do you know, dearest?" her friend had enquired.

"One is enough," had been the reply, "yet not as intimately as I would wish!"

"As a matter of fact," Sir Charles was saying, "the Grand Duke Michael of Russia, when I saw him three months ago, told me he had every intention of attending the Opening of the Canal, so that is one more 'Royal' who will be there."

"I suppose the real truth is that we, as a country, are sulking because we would not support the scheme to start with," Lord Milthorpe said. "Palmerston was against it, and of course Stratford de Redcliffe did everything he could to prevent De Lesseps from putting his plan into operation from the very beginning."

"One cannot help admiring the man," Sir Charles remarked. "It took him years of frustration before he had got the thing begun and enough money to even start digging."

"Well, now it is a *fait accompli*," Lord Milthorpe said, "and Britain is determined not to participate in his triumph."

"I see no reason why all Britons should stay at home," the Duke remarked slowly, almost drawling his words.

His two friends turned towards him with a look of surprise.

"What are you suggesting, Varien?" Sir Charles enquired.

"Simply that what the Prince is unable to do—we can!" the Duke replied.

"You mean—go to the Opening?"

"Of course! Why not?"

"Why not indeed!" Lord Milthorpe exclaimed. "God, Varien, you always have had a sense of what is important! Of course you must go. A Duke is always a Duke, and you know as well as I do that you have always got on well with the Empress."

"Varien has always 'got on,' as you put it, with every pretty woman," Sir Charles remarked, "and Paris abounds with broken hearts every time he stays there."

"The Empress's heart is very much intact," the Duke said. "At the same time, I think she will be glad that we should support De Lesseps, who actually is married to a cousin of hers. Although I find Franz Josef rather a 'dull stick,' the Grand Duke Michael is always fun."

"Then you will go!" Lord Milthorpe exclaimed. "And if you leave me behind, Varien, I swear I shall cut my throat!"

"Of course I have no intention of leaving you behind, George," the Duke replied, "and while we have luncheon we will plan our party. There is plenty of room aboard the *Jupiter* for all our special friends."

"I had forgotten that you have your new steam yacht," Lord Milthorpe replied. "And what could be a better christening for her than a voyage to the Suez Canal?"

"The Prince will die of envy," Sir Charles said. "I hear that the Khedive of Egypt is giving fantastic parties."

"Fantastic is the right word when it comes to a series of 'Arabian Nights'!" Lord Milthorpe said with a smile.

"Well, it is settled," the Duke said, with just a touch of boredom in his voice, as if the enthusiasm of his friends grated on him. "You must both tell me who you particularly wish to ask, and my secretary will get out the invitations right away."

He spoke almost as if the subject were closed, but Sir Charles said:

"I have just remembered something, Varien. I do not think I shall be able to come."

"Not come, Charles? Why not? You're not going to tell me you prefer hunting to being in Egypt?

Besides, I dare say we can arrange a gazelle-hunt for you, which is rather amusing if you have not taken part in one before."

"There is nothing I would prefer more than to be on board the *Jupiter,* as you well know, Varien."

"Then what is the obstruction?" the Duke enquired.

There was a pause before Sir Charles replied:

"My daughter arrives home from abroad tomorrow and I have not yet made any arrangements for her to be chaperoned. I could hardly leave her alone in London."

"Your daughter?" Lord Milthorpe exclaimed. "I had almost forgotten you had one!"

"Bettina has been at school in France," Sir Charles replied. "She should really have made her début this year, but her Godmother, Sheila Buxton, was ill. And now she has died."

"Yes, of course," Lord Milthorpe answered. "A damn fine woman. I was always fond of her."

"So, that leaves you with a daughter on your hands, Charles," the Duke said slowly.

"It does," Sir Charles agreed, with a heavy note in his voice.

"Then she must come along on the trip," the Duke said, "because, quite frankly, Charles, we cannot do without you to keep us all amused and in good temper."

Sir Charles's eyes lit up.

"Do you really mean that?"

"Of course I mean it! What does one more matter? Indeed, I will ask a young man for your girl— why not my heir presumptive?"

"Do you mean Eustace?" Lord Milthorpe enquired.

"Of course I mean Eustace," the Duke replied. "It will do my half-brother good to get away from his sermonising and eternal lobbying of my friends in the House of Lords. They keep complaining about him, saying he tries to make their flesh creep and at the same time blackmails them into emptying their pockets."

Neither of the two gentlemen to whom he was speaking answered.

The Duke knew it was because they were not prepared to criticise his half-brother to his face, and were trying to find something pleasant to say about him.

"It is very kind of you to have Bettina, Varien," Sir Charles remarked after a moment, breaking the silence. "I only hope the child will not be a bore, but she used to have plenty to say for herself."

"If she is anything like her father, she will be the life and soul of the party," Lord Milthorpe remarked.

"Thank you, George," Sir Charles said. "I do my best to sing for my supper."

The Duke laughed.

"And you do it very effectively, Charles. You know as well as I do that no party is complete without you."

Sir Charles was just about to reply when the Butler announced:

"Lady Daisy Sheridan, Your Grace, and the Honourable Mrs. Dimsdale!"

The two women, both exceptionally beautiful, stepped into the room, and as the Duke walked forward to welcome them there was no doubt from the look in Lady Daisy's eyes and the expression in his that they meant something special to each other.

She gave him both her gloved hands and he raised them to his lips.

"I am sorry we are late," Lady Daisy said. "Kitty insisted on buying a profusion of new bonnets which neither of us can afford, but we do so hope you will think we look dazzling in them."

"Could I think anything else?" the Duke asked.

There was an amused twist to his lips and a cynical note in his voice.

He knew quite well who would be expected to

pay for the bonnets, and it would, he knew, have
been inconceivable for Daisy and Kitty to come to
luncheon without some request which would involve
him in opening his purse.

He knew Daisy's little ways too well.

Married to a hard-gambling man, she would
have found it impossible to keep up her reputation
of being one of the best-dressed women in London
if her lovers had not met the bills.

The Duke was only too willing to do what was
required of him. At the same time, he thought it a
pity, as he had thought before, that Daisy made it
quite so obvious.

As if she knew that he had acquiesced to her
demand, he felt her fingers tighten on his for a moment. Then, with a grace that made her move like a
swan over a lake, she held out her hand to Lord
Milthorpe.

"Dear George," she said, "I knew you would be
here, and it is lovely to see you."

"I hope you have not been tempting Kitty into
new depths of extravagance," he said. "I have just
bought two exceedingly fine hunters and have not yet
been able to pay for them."

"Nonsense!" Lady Daisy retorted. "You are as rich
as Croesus, and the only trouble is that you cannot
count your shekels."

"That is something no-one can say about me,"
said Sir Charles, smiling.

"No, indeed," Lady Daisy replied, "but we all
know how much you would give us if you could."

"I think," Sir Charles said after a moment, "that
is one of the nicest things anyone has ever said to me."

"You deserve it, Charles," Lady Daisy replied.
"Now, tell me what you three musketeers were talking about before we arrived."

"The answer should be obvious, but it is not," Sir
Charles answered.

"Not talking about us?" Lady Daisy questioned.
"I have never heard anything so outrageous! Varien,
are you being untrue to me? I cannot bear it!"

"On the contrary," the Duke said, "we have thought of something that will amuse you far more than the Hunt-Balls, the pheasant-shoots, and the dreary round of house-parties which fill your diary at the moment."

"What can you be suggesting?" Lady Daisy enquired.

"That we should all attend the Opening of the Suez Canal!" the Duke replied, and waited for the shriek of excitement which followed his words.

Chapter Two

As the train drew into the station, Bettina looked out the window and saw her father.

She thought it would be impossible to miss him even in the largest crowd imaginable.

No-one else looked so smart, so dashing; indeed, he was exactly what his friends called "a regular swell."

With his top-hat on the side of his head and a carnation in his buttonhole, he was leaning on his malacca cane, looking somewhat anxiously at the incoming train.

Bettina opened the door of her carriage and jumped onto the platform to run towards him.

"Papa! Papa!" she cried. "I knew you would be here waiting for me."

She flung her arms round his neck, and as she kissed him he asked:

"What the devil happened to you? I was getting worried."

"I was afraid you would be," Bettina answered.

"When your luggage arrived alone, I imagined all sorts of terrible things," Sir Charles said.

But he was smiling and his eyes were twinkling as he looked at his daughter and exclaimed:

"Good God, you have become a beauty! I was expecting the little girl I remembered, not someone who looks like your mother when I first met her."

"Thank you, Papa!" Bettina laughed. "And I want

you to thank the gentleman who has been very kind
to me, very kind indeed. The mistress who was es-
corting me to England had a heart-attack and died
at Dover."

"So that is why you are late!" Sir Charles exclaimed.

"You can imagine how terrible it was," Bettina
said. "I would not have known what to do if it
had not been for Lord Eustace Veston."

She looked round as she spoke and saw the
young man in question advancing towards her down
the platform.

"Here he is, Papa," she went on before Sir Charles
could speak. "Please tell him how grateful you are."

Sir Charles's gratitude was very sincere and
Lord Eustace's sombre face seemed to relax a little as
he accepted Sir Charles's thanks and told him what
arrangements he had made about the dead woman.

"It was a pleasure to do what I could for your
daughter, Sir Charles," he said at length, "and may I
say that she behaved calmly and with great dignity
under extremely distressing circumstances."

"I am glad to hear it," Sir Charles replied; then
as if he had nothing more to say to Lord Eustace he
turned to his daughter and added:

"We must find your luggage, Bettina. I told a
porter to look after it until the next train came in."

"It was clever of you, Papa, to think that that was
when I would arrive," Bettina said as she smiled at
him.

Then she held out her hand to Lord Eustace.

"Thank you again so very much," she said softly.
"I do not know what I would have done without
your help."

"I am glad that you have found your father and
are now in safe hands," Lord Eustace replied.

He took her hand for a moment, then raised his
hat and walked away.

Bettina looked after him a little wistfully. She
had somehow hoped that he would say they must
meet again.

Then, at the delight of seeing her father, she forgot everything but the joy of being home.

She had so much to tell him, so many questions to ask, that they had reached the house in Eaton Place before she remembered with a little pang in her heart that her mother would not be there to greet her.

It struck her as soon as she entered the small hall that the atmosphere had changed and the house did not look the same.

There were none of the little touches with which Lady Charlwood had made the house so charming and which had always seemed a perfect background for her and her happiness.

In the first place, there were no flowers, and Bettina saw that the lace curtains needed washing and the covers in the Drawing-Room were faded and shabby.

But her father, she thought, looked as prosperous as he always had. His clothes fitted him as if he had been poured into them, and naturally they were in the very latest fashion set by the Prince of Wales.

Sir Charles had married young and now was only just forty, but he had the figure and looks of a much younger man.

"If I have grown up, Papa," Bettina said impulsively, "you have not grown a day older; in fact I think you look younger!"

"You flatter me," Sir Charles protested, but she saw that he was pleased.

"What have you been doing, Papa?" she went on. "What exciting house-parties have you attended? And is the Prince of Wales still your greatest friend?"

Sir Charles laughed.

"What a lot of questions all at once! Yes, the Prince still honours me with his friendship and I spend a great deal of time at Marlborough House. But perhaps I enjoy even more the company of the Duke of Alveston."

Bettina wrinkled her brow.

"I seem to remember you speaking about him. Yes, of course—I remember that Mama did not approve of him."

"Your mother disapproved of a great number of my friends," Sir Charles said, "but Alveston is a very good chap, though perhaps his reputation is somewhat on a par with the Prince's."

He paused; then, looking at Bettina, he said:

"In fact, the Duke is the half-brother of your new young man."

"My new young man?" Bettina repeated in bewilderment.

"Lord Eustace Veston."

"So that's who he is!" Bettina exclaimed. "In which case why did he say he had never met you?"

Sir Charles poured himself a glass of sherry from the grog-tray without asking his daughter if she would like one.

"The Duke and his half-brother do not get on," he answered. "But he intends to ask him to come on this trip on which I am taking you. That you have already met him in such romantic circumstances is, I consider, a very useful introduction."

"What trip?" Bettina asked.

"You have been invited, Bettina," Sir Charles said slowly and dramatically, "to join the Duke's party for the Opening of the Suez Canal!"

Bettina stared at him for a moment, incredulous, then she said in a voice that seemed to catch in her throat:

"Do you . . . really mean that . . . Papa?"

"Of course I mean it," Sir Charles replied. "When I told the Duke you were coming home from France, he said I could bring you with me."

"I can hardly believe it!" Bettina exclaimed. "As you can imagine, they talked of nothing else in France. It all sounds so thrilling and fabulous. The Empress will be there!"

"And a great number of other people," Sir Charles said, "including us!"

As he spoke, he sat down in an arm-chair and

crossed his legs, and as Bettina stood in front of him
he looked her up and down, appraising her, she felt,
almost as if she were a horse which he was considering buying.

"You have exactly three days," Sir Charles said at
length, "in which to dress yourself in suitable clothes
as befits a Lady of Fashion."

"Papa!"

Bettina's exclamation was a cry of horror.

"It is impossible!" she said. "I have nothing . . .
nothing to wear at all! I expected you would let me
come home last April for the Season, so I was waiting
until then, and made do with the clothes I had at
school."

She paused and drew in her breath.

"When you said it was impossible because God-
mama was ill, it seemed such a waste of money to
buy new gowns for just a few more months at school.
So, everything that is not too small for me is in rags."

"I rather anticipated something like that," Sir
Charles said, "and, knowing women as I do, I was
quite certain your first request on crossing the threshold would be for a trousseau."

"Not a trousseau, Papa," Bettina expostulated,
"just a few evening-gowns, and of course some dresses
for daytime."

"It is going to be a rush," Sir Charles conceded,
"but you will have to buy what you can. Your mother's
clothes are all upstairs. They will be too old for you,
but perhaps the shop she always went to—what was
it called?—perhaps they can alter them, especially
if you buy some new gowns at the same time."

Bettina's eyes lit up, then she said in a hesitating
voice:

"Can we . . . afford it . . . Papa?"

"No," Sir Charles replied, "we cannot afford it,
and to tell the truth, Bettina, I have at the moment
not a penny to my name. Nothing but debts, damn
them!"

Bettina gave a deep sigh.

"Well, perhaps, Papa, I had better not join the

Duke's party. I could not bear that you should ... be ashamed of me."

Sir Charles rose to his feet.

"Do not be a fool, child!" he said. "This is your big chance. You will meet more eligible men with Alveston than you are ever likely to meet being paraded round the Ball-Rooms with a lot of other unfledged débutantes."

He paused before he added:

"Besides, who could be a more suitable parti than Lord Eustace Veston?"

Bettina looked at him with startled eyes.

"Surely ... you are not ... suggesting, Papa ..."

"Why not?" Sir Charles enquired. "Lord Eustace may not be a Duke, and he is in my opinion very unlikely to inherit his half-brother's title and his fortune. At the same time, he is well-heeled and you could not marry into a better family or a more aristocratic one."

Bettina looked away from her father, then moved across the room to stand holding on to the back of what had been her mother's favourite chair.

"I had not ... thought to be ... married so quickly," she said in a low voice.

"You are over eighteen," Sir Charles replied, "and the sooner you have a wedding-ring on your finger, the better! Besides, quite frankly, Bettina, I cannot afford to keep you."

"Oh ... Papa!"

The words were hardly audible, but he heard them.

"It is not that I do not want to," Sir Charles said quickly. "You know that. I like having you with me. We have always been friends, you and I. The truth is, I cannot afford to keep myself unless I make money by gambling, but the cards have been running against me lately."

"You know how it upset Mama when you played for high stakes," Bettina said.

"There is nothing else I can do in the company I keep," Sir Charles answered, "and to be honest, Bettina, I enjoy it. At the same time ..."

He paused, and Bettina knew he was thinking of those anxious moments at the end of the month when the tradesmen's bills came in and the servants expected their wages.

In the old days her mother used to look at him with apprehensive eyes, knowing there was never enough money for all their needs.

Sir Charles walked across the room and back.

"It is like this, Bettina," he said. "I have a damned good life. I receive more invitations than I can accept, and people like the Prince and Alveston honour me with their friendship. They always say that no party would be complete without me."

There was just a touch of boastfulness in his voice before he went on:

"But it all costs money. It may give me a roof over my head and all I can eat and drink, and even mount me when I want to hunt. But I still must have the clothes in which to do it and a valet to look after me."

Bettina was listening attentively as he went on:

"I also have to have this house to come back to when I am in London. There is no question of my making any further economies."

"I can understand that, Papa."

"Then you realise that I am not being unkind when I say that, much as I would like to, I cannot afford the expense of a daughter."

Bettina gave a little sigh.

"I meant to be very economical and cost you practically nothing."

"Do you think I would want you to stay at home as some kind of drudge and not take your rightful place in society?" Sir Charles asked almost angrily. "I am proud of you, Bettina, especially now that I see how pretty you have grown. When you are well-dressed you will be a sensation! And, dammit, that is what I intend you to be!"

"But how, Papa? How can we do it?"

Bettina had the idea that her father was feeling for words, and after a moment he said:

"When your mother died I had to sell her jewellery to pay for the funeral, the Doctors' bills, and various other things."

Bettina stiffened for a moment.

She had half-hoped that the pearls her mother had always worn, as well as the turquoise-and-diamond earrings that she remembered ever since she was a child and the ring that went with them, would one day be hers.

"There was nothing else I could do," Sir Charles was saying, "but I kept back one piece—a diamond star that she particularly wanted you to have."

"I love that star!" Bettina exclaimed. "When Mama wore it in her hair I always thought she looked like a fairy on a Christmas-tree."

"I sold it this morning!" Sir Charles said abruptly.

"You ... sold it ... Papa?"

"So that you could have the clothes you need to wear when you are the Duke's guest."

For a moment Bettina wanted to tell him he had no right to sell the jewel which her mother had left her, but because she loved her father she bit back the words.

"I expect that was ... what Mama would ... have wanted you to do," she said, "and I know she would wish you to be ... proud of me."

She felt that her father relaxed, as if he had actually been afraid that she would be angry with him. Then as the sparkle came back into her eyes he said:

"There is no fear of my not being that, but remember, the person you want to admire you is Lord Eustace."

*   *   *

Travelling in the Duke's private train, which was carrying them to Southampton, Bettina thought that if she had dressed to please Lord Eustace she would have chosen a very different gown from the one she was wearing.

During her years in France, the pupils in *Ma-*

dame de Vesarie's fashionable school had taught her a great deal about clothes, and she was intelligent enough to adapt what was fashionable to suit her looks.

The beauty of her fair hair, which was so pale as to look in some lights almost white, would have been eclipsed by the brilliant colours which were affected by the ladies in the Duke's party.

They wore gowns of scarlet, peacock blue, or emerald green, with ostrich-feathers to match in their small bonnets.

Their bustles bristled with frills and the huge satin bows with which they were weighted down.

There were frills round the hems of their skirts, round their necks, and round their wrists, which, combined with the glitter of their expensive jewels, made the Drawing-Room of the Duke's special train look like an aviary of parakeets.

In contrast, Bettina's travelling-gown was of the blue of love-in-a-mist, so soft that it was a perfect complement for her pale hair.

The ribbons of her bonnet encircled her small chin and made the translucence of her skin more obvious than it would have been otherwise.

Because there had been so little time Bettina had been able to buy only a very few gowns for the trip, but she was grateful that because she was so slim, many that had been made merely for display fitted her with very little alteration.

She found it impossible to buy any summer-gowns, which her father told her she would need when they reached Ismailia, but fortunately her mother had had several that were of pretty materials and the same gentle, pastel colours which suited her.

It was an excitement which she could not repress to know that now, after many years in the dreary, dull clothes she had worn at school, she was to blossom out like a butterfly emerging from its chrysalis.

She had known by the expression on her father's face that she looked exactly as he had hoped she would, and she would have been very stupid if she had not been aware when she saw her reflection in the mirror that she was in fact very attractive.

But still she was a bit nervous, and as they drove towards the station she had slipped her hand into her father's.

"You are quite certain that I look all right, Papa?" she had asked. "And you will help me not to make any social errors? I am sure the Duke is very frightening and all your smart society friends who love you will find me a terrible bore."

"They will do nothing of the sort," Sir Charles said reassuringly, "but concentrate on Lord Eustace. He will feel like a fish out of water—I am certain of that."

"Why does he not get on with his half-brother, the Duke, if he is as charming as you say?" Bettina asked.

"The old Duke married for the second time when he was getting old," Sir Charles answered. "For some unknown reason, he chose a dull, sanctimonious woman who was given to good words and despised the social life which her husband had always enjoyed."

Bettina thought that that would account for Lord Eustace's preoccupation with the sufferings of the poor.

"She was not bad-looking," Sir Charles went on, "and she came from a good family, but when the old Duke died she refused to have anything to do with his son, and she and her son, Eustace, lived on one of Alveston's estates in the North."

"It sounds as if Lord Eustace never had a chance of having any fun," Bettina said.

"He does not enjoy any, and he tries to make sure that nobody else does," her father remarked.

Then, as if he regretted his words, which might put Lord Eustace in a bad light, he added quickly:

"All the same, I understand he is a good chap and serious-minded, which of course one should be these days if one is young and ambitious."

"Ambitious in what way, Papa?"

"I suppose to make his mark rather as Lord Shaftesbury has done—fighting for the underdog, taking up causes of injustice, and all that sort of thing."

"It certainly sounds very creditable," Bettina said.

"It is. It is indeed," Sir Charles averred. "You ask him to tell you what interests him, Bettina. That is always the quickest way to a man's heart."

When they joined the Duke's special train, Bettina fancied that when Lord Eustace saw her there was a faint expression of pleasure on his face.

"We meet again, Miss Charlwood," he said.

"But in very different circumstances, My Lord," Bettina replied, curtseying.

"Very different indeed," Lord Eustace agreed.

She thought he cast a disparaging glance on the other guests, who were chattering and laughing round them.

Bettina remembered what her father had told her, and when they had seated themselves in the comfortable arm-chairs and footmen wearing the Alveston livery were handing round the drinks and delicious things to eat, she said:

"I was so hoping, My Lord, that we could meet again and you would tell me about the work that interests you, which you spoke of when we were at Dover."

"I have brought several pamphlets with me which have already been published," Lord Eustace replied, "and some I am in the process of writing. I shall be glad to read them to you, Miss Charlwood, and I am sure I shall have time while we are at sea."

"That would be delightful!" Bettina cried.

At the same time, she could not help wondering what the other members of the party would be doing.

She hoped that no-one, not even Lord Eustace, would stop her from looking at the scenery in the Mediterranean and enjoying the sunshine.

It was like having a very special dream come true, she thought, to be going to the Opening of the

Suez Canal, which in France had occupied the minds of everybody for so long.

Because *Madame* de Vesarie had been very interested in the De Lesseps family, with whom she had had an acquaintance, her pupils had heard every detail of Ferdinand de Lesseps's desperate struggle to build a Canal through the Isthmus, which would join the two great seas.

It was in fact, Bettina learnt, Napoleon Bonaparte who had first seriously thought it possible to change the geography of the world.

Madame de Vesarie had described graphically how in 1798 Napoleon had stood above Suez on a shallow reach of marshy ground and found what he was looking for—the bed of the ancient canal of the Pharaohs, which had not been used for thousands of years.

It was the summer during which Napoleon had invaded and occupied Egypt and was in possession of Cairo.

"To destroy England," he had declared previously, "we must get command of Egypt."

It was Egypt that commanded the Mediterranean and the passage to India, and Napoleon intended to strike at his enemy not at home but through her Eastern Empire.

But after Waterloo the idea of the Canal had been forgotten, until Ferdinand de Lesseps saw the feasibility of it and decided, as *Madame* de Vesarie had said dramatically, to become "the Vasco da Gama of Suez."

The girls had listened, entranced, to *Madame's* stories of the enormous difficulties encountered by the French Vice-Consul to Egypt.

First he had to enthuse Mohammed Ali, the Ruler of Egypt, with his idea, but fortunately he was an old man, and his son Prince Mohammed Said succeeded him.

Bettina had been fascinated by the story of how the Prince had already been a friend of Ferdinand de Lesseps.

When the Prince was only eleven, his father, anxious at that time to develop his Navy, was having him trained as a seaman.

The boy was, however, enormously fat, and although he was made to jump over ropes, trot round the walls of Alexandria, row, and climb masts for two hours a day, he grew no slimmer.

His father put him on a drastic diet, strictly limiting his eating and ordering him to be weighed each week, with the results being transmitted to him in Cairo.

It was really far too strict a régime for a growing boy who in fact had some glandular trouble, so Mohammed Said would visit De Lesseps every day.

In the Consulate's private quarters he would throw himself down on a divan, tired and famished, while the servants brought him plates of spaghetti and French pastries to relieve his hunger.

Because Ferdinand de Lesseps was so kind, the young Prince became deeply attached to the older man, who also took him for rides in the desert and taught him fencing and other activities of the French culture.

It was Prince Said who, as Viceroy of Egypt, was to support Ferdinand de Lesseps and finance him when in 1854 he began his great campaign to join the waters of the Mediterranean with those of the Red Sea.

"Why did he have so many difficulties?" Bettina had asked when *Madame* de Vesarie paused in her story.

"The English were against him and did everything they could to stop him from succeeding in his ambition," *Madame* had replied sharply. "The British Prime Minister in particular, Lord Palmerston, was afraid of seeing the commercial and maritime relations of Great Britain upset by the opening of a new route."

Madame's voice sharpened as she went on:

"What is more, Lord Palmerston actually said that it was the greatest financial swindle ever imposed on the credibility and stupidity of the people of Great Britain."

"How short-sighted!" Bettina exclaimed.

"The English often are," *Madame* snapped.

"If England went against him, how did he get started?" one of the other pupils asked.

Madame smiled.

"*Monsieur* de Lesseps remembered that Prince Said's father, Mohammed Ali, had said many years before: 'Always keep this in mind, my young friend— if you have any important scheme on hand, depend upon yourself alone.' "

"And did he?" someone asked.

"He depended on himself even for raising the money he needed to start digging in the sand. He raised it by public subscription in stock for the Canal Company, and from the French public alone he received something over a hundred million francs— four million pounds!"

The pupils had clapped their hands.

"They believed in him," a pretty French girl said.

"Of course," *Madame* answered. "We always trust and believe in our own people, especially when they are right."

Madame's elation, however, was modified by a little sigh.

"Unfortunately, the money was not enough, but by the time *Monsieur* de Lesseps realised this, he had, on the morning of April twenty-fifth, 1859, picked up a shovel himself and dug into the sand beside the Bay of Pelusium."

"What happened then?" Bettina enquired.

"He passed the shovel to his engineering staff and to each of the one hundred workmen standing by. One by one they each turned over a shovelful of sand and quietly and without much drama the Suez Canal was begun!"

Madame told the tale not once but a hundred times, and with the rest of the French nation Bettina followed all the difficulties, the problems, and the

heartbreaks which occurred during the great under-
taking of one idealistic Frenchman.

There were many set-backs. At one moment the
digging stopped and all the Egyptian labourers were
withdrawn.

Then at last, with the help of Napoleon III,
Emperor of France, the digging began again, and this
time it entered an entirely new phase.

The primitive days of pick and shovel were over
and during the next four years the professionals with
heavy machinery moved in to complete the job.

Unfortunately, Prince Mohammed Said died
and his throne was taken by his nephew Ismail Pasha,
who became the Khedive.

This year on August 15 Bettina had read the
huge, triumphant headlines in the French newspapers announcing that the Red Sea had flowed along
the channel from Suez and poured into the Bitter
Lakes to blend with the waters of the Mediterranean.

The two seas had been joined, and East and
West were one!

She had been so interested, so thrilled, with the
whole project that now she felt as if it was inevitable
that she should by some magic that she had never
anticipated be present at the Opening Ceremony itself.

She was so excited at the thought that it was
hard that first evening to listen to the chatter and
gossip of the other ladies, or even to attend to the
grave tones of Lord Eustace.

Apart from the fact that she was journeying towards Egypt, she knew that she had entered a world
that was like a fairy-land after the austerity of school.

Never had she known that such luxury and comfort was possible, or that the creatures who inhabited
such a world should be so beautiful, so elegant, so
different in every way from anyone she had ever
known except her father.

It was fascinating for Bettina to see him surrounded by his friends, who were laughing at his

jokes, patting him on the back, applauding, congratulating, encouraging him.

Now she could understand, she thought, why he had no wish to relinquish this world in which he shone, and she knew he must stay in it whatever the cost to herself, or in the past to her mother.

She could understand now so many things that had been difficult to accept in the past—the first of them being her mother's insistence that everything her father wore must be of the best.

Only Bettina knew how often her mother economised personally so that her father could have new suits, new riding-breeches, new boots, new shoes, and innumerable white stocks which appeared more immaculate and smarter in the hunting-field than those worn by any other rider.

It was almost, she told herself, as if her father were on a stage and held the attention of the audience so that he could make them laugh or cry as he wished.

"No wonder everyone wants Papa to be their guest," she told herself as the evening drew on and Sir Charles was undeniably "the life and soul of the party."

She expected the Duke to join them for dinner, which was served in another coach adjoining the Drawing-Room, with footmen waiting on them with professional dexterity despite the moving train.

The menu consisted of such delicious food that Bettina thought the Chef must be a genius to produce such a meal in what must inevitably be cramped circumstances.

There was no doubt that the Duke did everything in style. There were silver candelabra on the table, half a dozen different wines besides champagne, and a corsage of orchids for every lady in the party.

They were the first orchids that Bettina had ever received, and because they were white and star-shaped she wondered if perhaps they had been especially chosen for her.

Then she told herself she was just being imaginative. It must be merely chance that she had received flowers that were particularly suitable—while Lady Daisy Sheridan had been given huge mauve cattleyas which toned with an elaborate gown sparkling with amethysts.

"Where is Varien?" a guest asked Lady Daisy when she appeared. "Surely he is dining with us this evening? Or have you forbidden him to do so and intend keeping him all to yourself?"

There was a spiteful note in the other woman's voice which told Bettina that Lady Daisy had some special relationship with the Duke and that the other woman resented it.

"Varien is tired and wants to be alone this evening," Lady Daisy replied.

"Alone?" another beauty questioned. "That does not include you, of course, dearest?"

There was some laughter at this, but Lady Daisy seemed quite unperturbed.

"We should all retire early," she said. "It is sure to be rough once we leave harbour, and anyway I loathe the sea!"

But when Bettina retired to her Sleeping-Carriage she knew that the gentlemen at least had no intention of taking Lady Daisy's advice.

Her father had settled down at one of the cardtables which had been set up in the Drawing-Room while they were at dinner.

The train had been shunted into a siding so that they could sleep undisturbed during the night and proceed on their journey early the next morning.

Sir Charles looked up as Bettina stood beside him.

"I hope you are not going to watch me play, my dear," he said. "It would make me nervous."

"I can hardly believe that, Charlie," a man said jokingly from the other side of the table. "I have never known a pretty woman to make you nervous yet!"

"My daughter is different," Sir Charles replied.

"And I for one will drink to the difference!" another player remarked. "She is a very lovely girl, and just the sort of daughter you should have, Charles."

"I think so too!" Sir Charles replied, smiling. "You are going to bed, my dear?"

"Yes, Papa."

Bettina bent and kissed him on the cheek.

"Do I get a kiss?" his partner asked.

Bettina smiled at him and dropped a curtsey.

"I keep my kisses for my father," she murmured.

There was a roar of laughter as if she had said something witty.

"You will not be saying that this time next year," someone remarked as she moved away.

A lady who had already been pleasant to her walked with her into the next coach where their sleeping compartments were.

They were exquisitely furnished with comfortable beds, plenty of mirrors, and wash-basins framed with red Morocco leather.

Each one, Bettina thought, was like a small doll's house and when she went to bed she found herself thinking how exciting it all was.

She had not said good-night to Lord Eustace, for she had noticed as she left the Drawing-Room that he was seated in a corner at the far end of it, reading a book.

"Why does he not join in with the others?" she questioned.

He had sat next to her at dinner, but after they had exchanged a few words she found it impossible not to listen to the amusing things the other guests were saying, especially her father.

A great deal of the conversation of course was quite incomprehensible to Bettina, because it concerned other people and she had no idea who they were.

Even so, it seemed to her that everyone was as sparkling as the champagne they drank, and only Lord Eustace sat tight-lipped and scowling, making no effort even to be pleasant.

'He is deliberately ostracizing himself!' Bettina thought.

❁   ❁   ❁

Because she did not wish to miss a moment of the excitement ahead, Bettina was awake as soon as the train began to move smoothly on its journey to Southampton.

She pulled aside the curtains over the window, saw it was still dark, and forced herself to lie down again until, when the dawn came, she could no longer stay in bed.

She washed and dressed herself. She had put the white orchids she had worn the night before in a glass on her wash-stand. They looked so lovely that she detached one and pinned it at her neck.

"I may never be able to be so grand again," she told her reflection with a little smile.

She went into the Drawing-Room to find that the servants had tidied away the card-tables and placed the morning newspapers ready for anyone who required them.

There were flowers in heavy vases clamped down to prevent them from being upset by the movement of the train.

There were satin cushions in the comfortable arm-chairs and on the damask-covered sofa. There were pictures on the walls, and the curtains that ornamented the windows were of crimson velvet and very attractive.

Bettina looked round.

'How lovely to be as rich as this,' she thought, 'and to have everything one wants.'

There was a writing-table and she walked towards it to look at the profusion of things laid on it which might be required for writing a letter.

The blotter, the pen-holder, the pen-tray, the letter-opener, the magnifying-glass, the stamp-container —all were ornamented with the Alveston crest.

There was also a leather box containing writing-

paper and envelopes engraved with the same crest, a
griffon with a sheaf of wheat in its hand and a crown
on its head.

"Someone has thought out every detail," Bettina
told herself, then hearing a step behind her she looked
round.

For a moment she could only stare at the man
who had just entered. If she thought her father was
impressive, it was nothing to the magnificence of the
newcomer.

He was tall—taller than any other man in the
party—broad-shouldered, and he had, she thought,
the most arresting and at the same time the most unusual face she had ever seen on a man.

There was something about him that was awe-
inspiring.

He had such authority, such an air of consequence, that she felt it enveloped him like an aura,
and it would be impossible not to look at him however
many other men there might be in the room.

For a moment it seemed as if he too was surprised to see her, then he said:

"I think you must be Bettina Charlwood."

A little belatedly Bettina curtseyed.

"I am ... Your Grace."

There was no doubt in her mind who the newcomer was.

"Then let me welcome you to my party," the
Duke said. "I think I would have guessed you were
your father's daughter even if I had not met and admired your mother."

"Thank you," Bettina said.

"You are up very early. I did not expect to find
any of my guests awake at this hour."

"I was too excited to sleep," Bettina explained,
"and I was admiring the carriage. It was difficult to
see it properly yesterday when there were so many
people in it."

"And doubtless an irresistible distraction," the
Duke said.

He spoke in a slightly dry manner with just a touch of cynicism and she looked at him enquiringly.

"I believe this is your first party since you left school," he said.

"I would like to thank you very much for inviting me," Bettina replied. "I never dreamt, I never imagined for a moment, that I should have the privilege of attending the Opening of the Suez Canal."

"It is something which interests you?" the Duke enquired.

"I have been living in France, Your Grace."

"Of course!" he said. "And I suppose they are very proud of their achievement."

"They are indeed proud and triumphant, especially as they have proved the British wrong," Bettina answered.

The Duke laughed.

"We can only admit that in this instance we were wrong," he said, "completely and absolutely. But personally I have always believed the Suez Canal was a possibility."

"Were you brave enough to say so to Lord Palmerston?" Bettina asked.

The Duke glanced at her sharply as if he was surprised that she should know of the former Prime Minister's opposition to the project. Then he answered:

"As a matter of fact, I did make a speech in the House of Lords four or five years ago supporting the scheme. Not surprisingly, no-one listened."

Bettina thought it was in fact very surprising that no-one would listen to anyone so impressive, but she was too shy to say so.

The Duke picked up one of the newspapers and she realised that this was his reason for coming to the carriage.

Thinking she must not make a nuisance of herself when he wanted to read, she resolutely sat down at the writing-table.

The only person she could think of who would be

really thrilled to know that she was to be at the Opening of the Canal was *Madame* de Vesarie.

Accordingly, she started a letter to her schoolmistress, very conscious as she did so that behind her, sitting back in an arm-chair with his legs crossed, the Duke was reading *The Times*.

'He is magnificent to look at,' Bettina thought.

She thought perhaps one of the reasons why Lord Eustace disliked his half-brother was that he so easily eclipsed the Duke not only in social importance but also in looks.

She was just finishing her letter when Lord Eustace came into the carriage.

"Good-morning, Varien!" he said with an unmistakably cold note in his voice.

"Good-morning, Eustace," the Duke replied. "I hope you spent a comfortable night."

"Very comfortable, thank you. It made me think of one of the subjects I wish to discuss with you when you can spare the time."

"If you intend boring me with your heart-rending stories of the 'down-and-outs' or the rabble who sleep under the arches by the river, you can spare your breath," the Duke answered sharply. "I have my own charities, Eustace, as you have yours, and I have no money to spare at the moment."

"How can you say anything like that?" Lord Eustace asked scornfully. "What you are spending on this trip to Egypt, or, if you like, what we ate and drank at dinner last night, would keep a hundred people in comfort for a year!"

"I hope, Eustace," the Duke said in a tired voice, "you are not going to begrudge every piece of food I and my guests put into our mouths or every drop of wine we raise to our lips. And if you think I intend to nearly bankrupt myself as Shaftesbury has done in giving all I have to the poor, you are very much mistaken!"

"You make me ashamed," Lord Eustace said, "ashamed that as a family we do so little for those who suffer through no fault of their own."

"Little!" the Duke said in a voice of thunder. "If you call . . ."

He stopped.

"Listen, Eustace, I do not intend to lose my temper with you, nor to reiterate, as I have done so often, that charity should not be indiscriminate, nor money expended profligately."

The Duke's voice was like a whip-lash as he finished:

"You are my guest and you will behave as one, with propriety both towards me and my friends. I want no more of the begging-bowl and no sanctimonious sermonising—do you understand?"

In answer Lord Eustace walked out of the carriage and without turning round Bettina heard the rustle of the newspaper as the Duke opened his copy of *The Times* again.

She felt her heart thumping and she knew that listening to the row between the two brothers had both been embarrassing and had left her tense in a manner she could not explain to herself.

She had often heard girls quarrelling—there was plenty of that at school—but she had never before heard two men speaking to each other harshly and bitterly, nor had she felt an animosity that filled the air because it was obvious they disliked each other.

Then, to her relief, her father came into the carriage.

"Good-morning, Varien!" he said to the Duke, and as he passed the desk he bent to kiss Bettina's cheek.

"You are early, my poppet. That proves you could not sleep out of sheer excitement."

"That is true, Papa," Bettina replied. "I awoke as soon as the train started to move."

"I did the same," Sir Charles said, "and I did not get to bed until late."

"Gambling again, Charles?" the Duke enquired. "You know you cannot afford it."

"I can afford last night," Sir Charles said with satisfaction. "I won a packet from Downshire."

"He can certainly afford it." The Duke smiled. "But he will never rest until he wins it all back."

"The possibility of which I shall do my best to circumvent," Sir Charles answered, and they both laughed.

"Let us have breakfast," the Duke suggested. "I feel in need of it."

There was something in his tone that made Sir Charles look at him sharply.

"Has something upset you?" he enquired.

"Only Eustace," the Duke replied.

"Oh, Eustace," Sir Charles ejaculated; then, glancing towards Bettina, he added: "A young man who needs the inspiring hand of an understanding woman."

Bettina knew that the last sentence was added entirely for her benefit.

What she did not see was that as her father spoke he winked at the Duke.

Chapter Three

Bettina struggled along the deck towards a secluded spot she had discovered where she could be alone and which no-one else seemed to know about.

It was difficult to keep her balance because the *Jupiter* had run into a rough sea.

There were glints of sunshine between the clouds, but the yacht was pitching and rolling uncomfortably, although a sailor would have said that she rode the sea royally.

Never had Bettina imagined that a yacht could be so comfortable or so luxurious.

The *Jupiter* had only recently been delivered and was a screw-propeller steamer of the type that had just been made fashionable by the Cunard and the Peninsular and Oriental lines.

The latter had built the *Himalaya*, which was the largest vessel of its type in the world—its trunk engines had given it, on trial, a speed of almost fourteen knots.

The Duke had announced as they left Southampton that he intended to exceed this record by at least two to three knots.

His words instantly started his guests betting on each day's run, and Bettina soon realised that the gentlemen in fact would bet on anything as long as it provided a challenge amongst them.

She had as they moved out to sea begun to learn

51

a little about the rest of the party, but at first she had
been fascinated by the *Jupiter* herself.

She was told that the Duke had chosen every
inch of the decorations and they were entirely his own
taste.

She was amazed that a man could have such brilliant ideas of colour, space, and furnishings.

There was nothing over-ornate or superfluous in
the Saloon or in the amazingly comfortable bed-cab-
ins, and to Bettina everything was not only luxurious
but beautiful.

She loved the Adam green with which the Saloon
was painted and the white and gold of the Dining-
Room, beyond which was a red-walled Card-Room
where the gentlemen could smoke and gamble.

There was also a small Writing-Room where
anyone could be alone and quiet, but, more important, this contained shelves of books which brought
Bettina inexpressible delight.

She loved reading and was quite content while
the other ladies gossiped to slip away by herself to
read the books from the Duke's Library, which
opened new horizons she had never known before.

Although she was well educated in English and
French Literature and in the Classics, *Madame* de
Vesarie had been very particular about the novels
which fell into her pupils' hands.

Now Bettina found herself entranced by Dumas
and by Gustave Flaubert, besides other French au-
thors and a number of English ones.

However, this morning as she struggled down
the deck, although she carried a book protected by
her oil-skins, she wanted to think.

She hoped no-one would see her, because she
made a strange figure.

She wore over her gown a thick warm coat, which
had belonged to her mother, because the wind in the
Bay of Biscay already had the November chill in it,
and over it she had put on an oil-skin coat which was
intended to be worn by a man.

She had had some difficulty in getting it, but she

knew it was a sensible thing to wear and had asked the maid who looked after her if such a thing was obtainable on board.

"I'm sure it is, Miss," Rose had answered, "and as everything's new you won't mind wearing it."

"I do not think I would mind sharing an oil-skin anyway," Bettina answered.

She knew however that Rose would be shocked at the idea of her putting on anything that had been previously worn by a "common sailor."

There were twelve guests aboard the *Jupiter* and as many personal servants to look after them.

Every gentleman had brought a valet with him, and if Rose was unable to find what she wanted, Bettina had every intention of asking her father's man, Higgins, who was adept at getting anything that might be required, however unusual.

But Rose, who, Bettina learnt, was employed in the Duke's ancestral home in the country, came back with a brand-new oil-skin that had not even been taken out of its wrappings.

"Here you are, Miss," she said. "It's very strange you'll look in it."

"It will be better than getting soaked to the skin," Bettina said with a smile.

"You shouldn't be going out on deck, Miss, and that's a fact! None of the other ladies have left their cabins since the storm began."

"Are they all sea-sick?" Bettina enquired.

"They wouldn't like to admit it, Miss!"

Bettina laughed.

"It is certainly undignified and very unromantic," she said, "and I am glad I am a good sailor."

"You are indeed, Miss," Rose said admiringly. "You're the only person I'm looking after that has eaten any breakfast, and some of the other maids have been up all night attending to their ladies."

Bettina felt quite guilty at having slept so peacefully through the storm, but she felt it would be lovely to get out in the air and she had no desire either to stay in her cabin or sit alone in the Saloon.

It was also a relief to be free of the drama that was taking place between Lady Daisy and Lady Tatham.

While they were on the train and on the first day at sea, Bettina had been so beguiled by the dazzling beauty of Lady Daisy and two of the other female guests that she had not really noticed Lady Tatham. When she did so she found her as beautiful, if not more beautiful, than Lady Daisy.

They were of very different types; Lady Daisy with her fair hair, blue eyes, and Junoesque figure, was the prototype of the English rose which the women's magazines extolled in glowing phraseology and which Bettina was certain was the ideal of most men.

Lady Tatham—"Enid" to her friends—was dark, with hair that contained blue lights and green eyes that had a slight slant to them at the corners.

They gave her a mysterious, enigmatic expression which had earned her the nickname of "the Sphinx," and her red lips curved provocatively against a dazzling magnolia skin that somehow made Lady Daisy's pink-and-white complexion look insipid.

There could be no doubt in anyone's mind before they left Southampton that the two ladies were rivals for the attention of the Duke.

They sat on either side of him at meals and vied with each other to keep him laughing and amused.

But when after dinner the ladies withdrew to the Saloon or were alone at other times, there was a note in their voices of steel meeting steel.

Bettina learnt that Lady Tatham was married but that her husband preferred the country. She swept like a meteor through London Society, followed by a host of admirers but not by the man whose name she bore.

The rest of the ladies were amused by the battle taking place and seemed quite content with the gentlemen with whom they were obviously paired for the voyage.

The nicest of these, Bettina decided, was the Honourable Mrs. Dimsdale, who had been kind to her from the moment she arrived.

"I love your father, Bettina," she said, "in fact everybody loves Charles Charlwood, and we have all tried our best to prevent him from being lonely since he lost your mother."

"That is very kind of you!" Bettina exclaimed.

"When we get back to London I will try to be kind to you too," Mrs. Dimsdale went on. "I have a niece who is about your age and I know my sister would be only too delighted to chaperone you to some of the Balls this winter."

"Thank you very, very much," Bettina said.

She would have felt "out of it" with the rest of the party if Mrs. Dimsdale had not always appeared to be pleased to see her when she joined the ladies in the Saloon after dinner.

She would call her to her side and talk to her while Lady Daisy and Lady Tatham were scratching at each other.

Last night when the sea was just beginning to get rough and Bettina knew that the ladies' nerves were on edge, there had been an explosion.

Perhaps because they too were afraid of feeling sea-sick, the gentlemen had appeared to drink more than usual of the vintage wines that were served at dinner.

Bettina suspected that Lord Milthorpe at any rate was rather unsteady on his feet when they all came into the Saloon.

Of course it may have been the motion of the yacht, but all the gentlemen, with the exception of her father, the Duke, and of course Lord Eustace Veston, seemed unusually red in the face and had a kind of swimmy look about their eyes which gave them a somewhat stupid appearance.

But, whatever it was, Lord Ivan Walsham walked up to Lady Daisy and put his arm round her waist.

"You are in damned good looks tonight, Daisy," he said. "Let us go out into the moonlight and I will make love to you."

Lady Daisy escaped from his clutches with practiced dexterity and replied laughingly:

"Do not dare to touch me, Ivan! You know that I belong to Varien, and he belongs to me."

"Are you so sure of that?" Lady Tatham had enquired.

There was a challenge in her voice and an expression in her green eyes that was unmistakable.

Perhaps if the wine at dinner had not been so plentiful Lady Daisy would have made a witty retort. Instead she asked fiercely:

"May I enquire what you mean by that?"

"Do you really want me to tell you—and in public?" Lady Tatham asked.

Now her eyes slanted mysteriously and the twist of her lips was undeniably provocative.

"You will tell me what you mean," Lady Daisy said furiously, "or I will shake it out of you!"

As she spoke, she walked forward in such a determined way that everyone gave a little gasp.

Then as the Duke, who had been behind the other gentlemen, came into the Saloon, Lady Tatham ran towards him in pretended distress.

"Save me! Save me, Varien!" she cried, flinging herself against him. "Save me from this—this Medusa with snakes in her hair!"

The Duke, who had not heard what had just been said, looked surprised.

Because the ship was rolling he was forced through sheer courtesy to put his arm round Lady Tatham to prevent her from falling.

It was then that Lady Daisy slapped her rival in the face and went into hysterics.

All the ladies present hustled round her while, apparently quite unperturbed by what had happened, the Duke sat down at the card-table and asked Sir Charles and two other men to join him.

Both Lady Daisy and Lady Tatham retired immediately to their cabins and because she felt the episode was extremely embarrassing Bettina went to hers.

She was reading in bed when an hour or so later there was a knock on her door and when she called out: "Come in!" her father entered.

"Is anything the matter, Papa?" she asked, surprised to see him.

"Not exactly," Sir Charles answered. "I wanted to talk to you."

He sat down on the side of the bed, having to hang on to the brass end to reach it because the *Jupiter* was now rolling uncomfortably.

Bettina put down her book and looked at him, wide-eyed.

"I felt, after that regrettable scene this evening, that we ought to have a little talk," Sir Charles said.

"Was it wrong of me to come to bed?" Bettina asked quickly.

"No, not at all—it was extremely sensible," Sir Charles answered, "but I realised when those two women were making fools of themselves that you are really too young for that sort of thing."

He paused, then he said in a low voice:

"Your mother would not have approved of your being here, you know that."

Bettina said nothing, for she was not certain what she should say.

"You see, my poppet," Sir Charles went on after a moment, "the Duke, as I think I have told you before, has a reputation for fast living and is known to be what historians call a Rake."

"He is very magnificent, Papa!"

"Too good-looking, too rich, too everything that attracts women," her father said, "and that, Bettina, is the truth in a nut-shell."

"You mean that women always behave like that about him?" Bettina asked, wide-eyed.

"Fairly frequently, I am afraid," Sir Charles answered, "and I cannot imagine, unless it was out of pure devilment, why he asked Daisy and Enid together in the same party."

"Which one of them is he in love with, Papa?"

Sir Charles was silent, then he said:

"It is not exactly a question of love, Bettina. I do not think Varien has really been in love with anyone for years, if ever."

"Then . . . I do not . . . understand."

"It is not expected that you should," Sir Charles said. "I am well aware that I should not have brought you straight from school into a set-up of this sort, but there was no alternative if I was to attend the Opening of the Canal, which I longed to do."

"You know how wonderful it will be for me too to be there," Bettina said.

Her father smiled.

"No-one else was likely to ask us."

Bettina smiled back.

"No, of course not, Papa. So we must not criticise, must we?"

"You are a very sensible child, Bettina," Sir Charles said, patting her hand, "and I am very proud of you. At the same time, I feel rather guilty about it all."

"Please do not do that, Papa," Bettina pleaded. "Everyone has been so kind to me, and I am enjoying every moment of the voyage. As long as no-one quarrels with me or slaps my face, I do not mind what they do to each other."

"But it is wrong. It is not the sort of thing you should be mixed up in," Sir Charles said heavily. "Daisy should know better, but then Enid Tatham is doing her damnedest to make trouble."

"Is she very much in love with the Duke?" Bettina asked.

"She wants him doubtless as a man, but very much more so because he is a Duke," Sir Charles answered frankly.

"You mean it would be a feather in her cap if the

Duke was talked of as her beau?" Bettina asked. "But what I do not . . . understand, Papa, is . . ."

She paused.

"Well?" Sir Charles prompted.

"It is what they ultimately expect to get out of having the Duke interested in them. After all, Lady Daisy and Lady Tatham are both married and have husbands. He cannot marry either of them."

Sir Charles was silent for a moment and Bettina thought he was choosing his words with care.

"Of course Varien cannot marry either of the ladies in question," he said after what seemed a long pause, "and frankly, I do not think he will marry anybody. In fact he has always said he intends to remain a bachelor and Eustace can have the title for all he cares."

"He does not want a son?" Bettina enquired.

"Not enough to give up his freedom for it," Sir Charles replied. "As a matter of fact, he was married once."

"He was?" Bettina exclaimed in surprise. "No-one has ever mentioned it."

"It happened so long ago that everybody except Varien himself has forgotten what happened."

"Tell me about it, Papa," Bettina pleaded.

"He was married when he was twenty-one, long before I knew him well," Sir Charles said, "but I do remember the newspapers were full of the festivities that were given to celebrate both his wedding and his twenty-first birthday, a huge dinner for the tenants on the Alveston estate, with fireworks and all that sort of thing."

"What happened?" Bettina asked, curiously.

"Alveston's bride was about the same age as himself. It was an arranged marriage, of course, between the fathers on both sides. Their estates marched together and they thought that nothing could be more advantageous for the families than that their lands, like their children, should be joined together."

Bettina waited, her eyes on her father's face.

"Unfortunately," Sir Charles continued, "human nature being what it is, the bride and bridegroom loathed each other almost on sight."

"Then why did they get married?" Bettina enquired.

"I suppose paternal pressure was too strong to resist, and most marriages amongst the aristocracy are based on good, sound economic grounds!" Sir Charles answered.

"Go on, Papa."

"They were married for nearly a year, and Varien's wife was expecting a child. He has never talked about what happened, but rumour has it that they had a seething row, one of the many which had taken place after they married, and she went out hunting when he told her not to and had a fall which killed both herself and the unborn child."

Bettina gave a little exclamation.

"Oh, Papa, how horrifying!"

"It certainly soured Varien's attitude towards marriage," Sir Charles said, "and when a few years later he became the Duke, he did exactly what he wanted. He had many of what the French call *affaires de coeur*, but always with married women."

"Do . . . do the husbands never mind or become . . . jealous?" Bettina asked in a hesitating voice.

She was not quite certain exactly what happened when a man had an *affaire de coeur*.

But she knew that the Prince of Wales had caused a great deal of excitement in France two years ago when the newspapers publicised his relationship with the actress Hortense Schneider.

The girls at school had come back after the holidays sniggering and giggling about the Prince and Hortense, and later they had a great deal more to say about the Prince and the Princess de Sagan.

The De Sagan Château was where the Prince stayed when he took his trips abroad, which were always *en garçon*, while Princess Alexandra visited her parents in Copenhagen.

The French pupils were not being rude or crit-

ical of *le Prince de Galles* when they described his
love-affairs or criticised his behaviour.

It was actually what they admired about him,
and Bettina found that she was envied because she
was English and her father was a friend of the
Prince's.

In a way, some of the glitter and glamour of the
Prince himself rubbed off on her.

Therefore, it did not surprise her that the Duke
should have love-affairs. It was only that the behaviour of the two women he admired made them seem
less romantic and less glamorous than she had expected.

She felt that the Duke was so magnificent and
so splendid in appearance that the women on whom
he bestowed his favours should be his equal.

Sir Charles's eyes were on Bettina's face as she
thought over what he had told her, and now because
she realised he was really perturbed about her she
took his hand in both of hers and said:

"You are not to worry about me, Papa. I am so
happy to be with you, and it is so exciting to be
going to Egypt, that nothing else matters . . . really
nothing!"

Sir Charles gave a sigh of relief. Then as if it was
always at the back of his mind he asked:

"How are you getting along with Eustace?"

"He has read me two of his pamphlets, Papa."

"Encourage him," Sir Charles admonished, "make
him talk to you about his ambitions for the future.
You could help him, Bettina, and, quite frankly, I
think he needs help."

"He is so very serious-minded, Papa, and I am
afraid he dislikes the Duke."

"You must try to persuade him to take a more human view of life," Sir Charles said lightly. "And now I
must be getting back."

"Are you still playing cards, Papa?"

"Yes, Walsham cut in while I came to talk to you,
but they are expecting me back."

"And they miss you," Bettina added with a smile.

"Everyone loves you, Papa. You never quarrel with anyone."

"It is a luxury I cannot afford," Sir Charles replied jokingly.

As they both laughed he bent down and kissed her cheek.

"Good-night, Bettina. You are very pretty, and if Varien keeps to his vow of remaining a bachelor, I may see you a Duchess yet."

Bettina did not reply. She watched her father walk carefully to the door and heard him move away down the passage.

Then she sat staring ahead of her, but she was thinking of the Duke and his disastrous marriage.

*   *   *

Now with the sea-wind in her face her thoughts returned to what her father had said to her and she knew that if she were doing what he wanted she would have waited in the Saloon in the hope that Lord Eustace would join her.

She had listened to his pamphlets and he had explained to her in some detail the work he was doing amongst the "down-and-outs" in the slums of London.

It was rather difficult to understand how they all could be saved or their lives changed.

But she thought it was very commendable that a young man should spent so much time worrying over what she was certain most people would consider "riff-raff" and not worth a second thought.

She only wished that Lord Eustace need not be so sombre and gloomy about everything.

"Surely something has been done?" she had asked.

"Very little," he replied. "The Government is not interested in spending money on such poverty-stricken creatures."

"Why do you not go into Parliament?"

Lord Eustace had paused for a moment before he replied:

"One day I hope to be in the House of Lords!"

She knew that by this he meant he hoped he would one day succeed to his half-brother's place as the Duke of Alveston.

Because his was only a courtesy title he was not eligible for the Lords, but could enter the House of Commons as an ordinary elected Member.

There could be, Bettina reckoned, only eleven or twelve years between the brothers, so surely that did not entitle Lord Eustace to expect that the Duke would die so early that he could inherit while still young enough to lead an active political life.

She was, however, too shy to ask further questions, but merely forced herself to listen attentively as he read her the notes he had made for another pamphlet.

This one, on slum clearance, was to be distributed to Members of Parliament and all rich men whom he thought might give him money for his charities.

She had the feeling, although she did not like to say so, that the pamphlets were written in a hectoring, dictatorial manner which would discourage rather than evoke sympathy for the causes for which he pleaded.

She wondered if she could suggest that a more conciliatory tone might more effectively produce the funds which, it was obvious, he so urgently needed.

Then she told herself that while Lord Eustace was willing for her to be an appreciative audience, he was not asking her to be a critic.

Bettina found her sheltered spot at the stern of the ship, and although the spray from the waves had splashed over her while getting there, the water had rolled off her oil-skins.

She sat down and made herself comfortable, but she did not open her book.

Instead, she looked at the rolling sea and the shafts of sunshine coming between the clouds, and she thought it was all exquisitely beautiful, like a painting by Turner.

There was a sense of freedom in the open sea which she had never felt anywhere else.

She had found it hard these past years to be confined at school and confined also during the holidays.

Her father had never suggested that she should return to England for the holidays, and she had either remained at school with two or three other girls whose homes were far away, or had stayed with her French friends who had invited her to their houses.

She had been interested in seeing the way the French people lived, and with one friend she had been able to ride, and with another to attend some of the Operas in Paris and visit the Museums and Art Galleries.

French girls lived very sheltered lives, always chaperoned, never taking part in the entertainments of their parents until they were grown up, and at times Bettina had missed her mother and father unbearably.

But now, when everything could have been different, she found that she had to exchange one secluded life for another.

If she married, as her father had told her was imperative, then she would be under the jurisdiction of a husband who might prove even more stringent than *Madame* de Vesarie.

She gave a deep sigh at the thought of what the future might hold for her, and as she did so a voice said:

"So this is where you are hiding yourself! I thought I saw someone struggling along the deck, but I could not believe that any woman in my party would be so adventurous."

She looked up to see the Duke standing in front of her and she thought involuntarily that his yachting-coat with its brass buttons and his peaked cap became him, as did everything else he wore.

He sat down beside her and she made room for him on the seat, which had really been intended for only one person.

She had taken off her oil-skin cap, although she still wore the coat, and her head was bare, the wind whipping small tendrils of her pale hair round her cheeks.

She made no attempt to tidy them and the Duke thought she was quite unaware that she looked like a sea-nymph.

"Why are you hiding here?" he asked.

"I wanted to look at the sea," Bettina answered. "It is so majestic."

"You are obviously a good sailor!"

"I am very lucky," Bettina replied with a smile.

"At the same time, you must be careful when you are moving about the deck and the ship is rolling like this," the Duke admonished. "Otherwise you may be swept overboard."

"Oh! Not before I have seen the Opening of the Suez Canal!" Bettina exclaimed.

He laughed.

"Surely it would matter whenever it happened?"

"I am . . . trying to let the . . . future take care of . . . itself," Bettina said without choosing her words.

"Trying?" the Duke questioned.

"There is nothing else I can do."

There was a hint of dismay in her voice which he did not miss. Then he asked:

"Are you enjoying yourself?"

"More than I have ever enjoyed anything in my whole life!" Bettina answered. "Your yacht is wonderful, and there is so much to see, so much to absorb, so much to think about."

"And what do you think about?"

She was surprised that he was interested.

"I was thinking this morning," she said after a moment, realising he was waiting for an answer, "of the rainbow Ferdinand de Lesseps saw which convinced him that it had appeared on the luckiest day of his life."

"I do not remember that story," the Duke said. "Tell me about it."

"It was when he returned to Egypt twenty years

after the beginning of his dream of a Canal," Bettina began. "His friend Prince Said had by this time become the Viceroy and welcomed him as his guest."

The Duke nodded his head as if he remembered that that was what had happened, and Bettina went on:

"It was on November fifteenth, 1854, that *Monsieur* de Lesseps made up his mind to approach the Viceroy on the matter of the Suez Canal. They were camping outside Alexandria and at five o'clock in the morning he rose and stood outside his tent."

The Duke was listening attentively and she continued:

"The first light of the sun was beginning to outline the horizon, yet the day promised to be overcast. Then suddenly something happened!"

"What was it?" the Duke asked.

"There appeared in the West a brilliant rainbow running from the East to the West," Bettina answered.

She smiled as she went on:

"The rainbow was exactly what *Monsieur* de Lesseps needed to convince himself it would be the luckiest day of his life. He dressed and at five o'clock mounted his Arabian pony and galloped through the camp to the Viceroy's tent."

Bettina's eyes were shining as she spoke, as if she saw it all happening.

"In front of the Royal tent a large barrier had been erected. Ferdinand de Lesseps, always an exceptional horseman, jumped it. The Viceroy saw him and so did his Generals and they cheered and applauded."

"The Arabs always appreciate good horsemanship," the Duke remarked.

"I think he knew that," Bettina answered, "and as he dismounted and went into the Viceroy's tent, his heart was full of confidence."

"An interesting story," the Duke said. "And do you believe in signs and omens?"

"Yes, of course!"

She looked at the Duke and thought his expression was cynical.

"There have been so many in history," she explained. "The Star of Bethlehem, for one."

The Duke smiled and the cynicism went from his eyes.

"I was thinking the other day," Bettina went on, "that most of what you call 'signs and omens' consist of some kind of light: a star, a burning bush, a rainbow, the light that came from people themselves which afterwards was immortalised in the Christian idea of a halo."

There was silence for a moment. Then the Duke said very quietly:

"Perhaps that light is what we are all looking for."

Then he rose to his feet, and without saying anything more he left her.

Only when he had gone did Bettina feel it was a very strange conversation to have had with a man, especially her host.

She wondered if she had bored him. Then somehow she knew he was not bored, but had behaved with her differently from the way he did with other women in the party.

Bettina was astute enough to know that if he had been alone with Lady Daisy or Lady Tatham, or perhaps with any other of his female guests, they would have flattered him and flirted with him, flashing their eyes at him, behaving in a manner which she could only describe to herself as being "deliberately alluring."

"I do not know how to do any of those things," she told herself, "and I only said what I thought. I wonder, was it wrong of me?"

She felt uncertain and unsure, and yet she knew it was impossible for her to be anything except what she actually was.

She wondered if the day would ever come when she would be polished and sophisticated like Lady Daisy or deliberately provocative like Lady Tatham.

Then she told herself that her mother had never

been like that. She had been sweet, gentle, and charming, and when they could afford it she had been a perfect hostess.

Bettina was certain that she would never have gone out of her way to deliberately entice a man in the way these other women did.

"Mama would not have liked them," she told herself positively, and then she knew that after all she had done the right thing.

At luncheon she was the only woman present, despite the fact that the storm was not so violent as it had been during the night and in the morning.

"The wind is abating," the Duke said, "and the Captain anticipates that we are through the worst and will soon be in calm waters."

"I shall not believe that until we reach Gibraltar," Lord Milthorpe said, "and I do not mind telling you, Varien, that when I am at sea I am always afraid of falling down and breaking a leg."

"If that happens, I have someone aboard who could set it for you," the Duke replied, and there was a roar of laughter.

"You are always prepared for every contingency, Varien," Sir Charles remarked.

"I try to be," the Duke answered, "but to save George's leg I suggest that you confine yourselves to the card-tables. I cannot believe that anyone with the exception of Miss Charlwood wants to brave the elements."

"Miss Charlwood?" someone enquired curiously.

Bettina flushed as everyone looked at her.

"I . . . like being on . . . deck," she said, looking at her father as if for his approval.

Sir Charles smiled.

"That is all right, as long as your sea-legs are sounder than George's."

"Nothing will induce me to leave the Saloon," Lord Milthorpe said positively.

Immediately after luncheon the gentlemen returned to the Card-Room and Bettina hoped that her father would not lose money.

She was just about to go to her cabin to get her coat when outside the Saloon the Duke said:

"Would it amuse you, Miss Charlwood, to come on the bridge?"

"I would love to!" Bettina exclaimed. "Will you really take me?"

"My Captain would be honoured to make your acquaintance," the Duke replied. "But put on a thick coat. It is quite cold outside."

"I know that," Bettina answered, "and I will not keep you waiting."

She ran to her cabin to put on not the heavy coat she had worn in the morning but a cape which had also belonged to her mother and which had a hood trimmed with fur.

Her mother had always looked lovely with the fur framing her face, and Bettina hoped that the Duke would think that she too looked attractive.

She was as quick as she could be, knowing that men hate to be kept waiting, but when she joined him outside the door which led to the deck he was no longer alone.

Lord Eustace was with him and she felt her heart sink.

Somehow, she thought, if there was another quarrel it would spoil the day that had been enchanted so far and so different from the tension and squabbles of the night before.

But to her relief the Duke and his half-brother were not quarrelling. Instead they stood in silence almost side by side and Bettina had the strange feeling that they were both waiting for her.

"I was looking for you, Miss Charlwood," Lord Eustace said before the Duke could speak, "because I thought you would like to hear what I have written this morning."

Bettina glanced at the Duke, but his face seemed quite expressionless, and as he said nothing she replied after a moment:

"Of course, I would like to hear it very much, but perhaps a little later? His Grace has promised to take me on the bridge and it is something I am longing to do."

"Perhaps you would like to join us, Eustace?" the Duke suggested.

"No, thank you," Lord Eustace replied in a disagreeable voice. "I will wait for Miss Charlwood in the Writing-Room."

It was where he had read to her before, and Bettina said:

"I will join you as soon as I am free."

As he turned away she looked up eagerly at the Duke.

"I am ready, and as the sea is not so rough I shall not need an oil-skin."

"I was wondering from where you had obtained one," the Duke remarked.

"Actually, it belongs to you," she said, "or rather to the ship."

"I thought perhaps I recognised it."

"That I was able to obtain it was of course another instance of your inexhaustible hospitality," she said demurely, her eyes twinkling.

"I see you are going to try and catch me out," the Duke said, "but I always have the excuse that this is a 'Maiden Voyage,' and therefore I am quite prepared at the end of it to have a long list of requirements which shall be supplied for another time."

As they moved onto the deck Bettina could not help wondering if there would ever be another time as far as she was concerned.

She had the feeling that if, as her father wished, she married Lord Eustace, she would in the future see very little of the Duke.

She was sure that Lord Eustace had asked her to listen to him reading one of his pamphlets simply because he wished to prevent her from being with his brother.

Every moment the two men were together it was obvious they had nothing in common, and Bettina suspected that Lord Eustace would now be sulking because she had preferred to go on the bridge rather than let him read to her.

'He does not own me yet,' she thought to herself.

Then she felt her heart sink at the very idea of listening for the rest of her life to a tirade against extravagance and luxury and having to concentrate almost exclusively on those who lived in what seemed in contrast a slough of despond.

'It is wrong of me to feel like that,' Bettina thought to herself. 'I must be compassionate and sympathetic.'

Then because they were climbing up onto the bridge, she swept Lord Eustace and his troubles to the back of her mind.

Everything the Duke was going to show her was new and exciting, something she had never seen before.

Sensing her excitement, the Duke looked down at her and smiled as if she were a child he was taking to a pantomime.

'He is wonderful,' she thought. 'As wonderful as a man . . . as his possessions are!'

Chapter Four

Bettina awoke very early with a feeling that something wonderful was going to happen.

It was Wednesday, November 17, and it was impossible to believe that in London there was doubtless a fog or the first snow of winter, while everything outside her port-hole was bathed in dazzling golden sunlight.

Every day that they had steamed down the Mediterranean, nearer and nearer to Suez, she had felt more thrilled, more excited with the anticipation of what lay ahead.

She had really paid little attention to what the other members of the Duke's party were doing.

All she wished to do was to look at the Mediterranean, which was like the blue of the Madonna's robe, to see sometimes a distant coastline and in the last few days to have her first glimpse of Africa.

It was all so enchanting that her face shone with excitement, and the gentlemen in the party watched her with a tenderness in their eyes, as if they were watching an excited child.

Bettina had found it increasingly difficult to listen to Lord Eustace's moanings about the slums and his harrowing tales of the neglect of the old people and the lack of education amongst the children.

She chided herself because half the time he was talking and reading to her she found it impossible to concentrate on what he was saying.

73

'I ought to be affected by these things too,' she thought.

Yet something irrepressibly joyful made her want to sing and dance, to hold out her arms to the gulls swirling round the masts or the porpoises she sometimes glimpsed turning over in the waves.

She had not had a chance of speaking to the Duke alone—Lady Daisy saw to that—until the night before last.

Then, after the ladies had retired to bed and the gentlemen lingered on at the card-tables, Bettina had slipped out on deck.

She had been afraid that Lord Eustace might see her and follow her, so she kept in the shadows of the superstructure until she reached the bow of the ship.

She leant on the rail, looking at the phosphorus in the water, which gave it a magical appearance, and at the stars overhead, so brilliant that they made the Heavens seem like a huge arc of light.

She stood there for a long time, for it was quite warm, and she felt deeply moved by the beauty of it and thought that in some secret way it had a message for her personally.

Then a voice she recognised said beside her:

"I somehow felt that you would be unable to resist this."

She did not turn her head but was vividly conscious that the Duke had joined her and was also leaning over the rail, his shoulder close to hers.

"It is wonderful!" she said in a soft voice.

"What does it mean to you?" he asked.

She did not answer and after a moment he said:

"Most people say that such a sight makes them feel insignificant and lonely."

There was a touch of cynicism in his voice, but Bettina was not to know that it was a conventional phrase by which women invariably asked for the comfort of his arms and the touch of his lips to disperse their loneliness.

"I do not feel like that," Bettina replied.

"No?"

"What it makes me feel," she said slowly, "is the wonder and privilege of being alive."

She felt he would not understand, and so she explained:

"Scientists think that perhaps in every one of the stars there is another world, other planets, and when I look up I think how wonderful it is that I am here and I too am alive."

She threw back her head as she spoke and her features were silhouetted against the darkness as the starlight turned her hair to silver.

The Duke did not move, he only watched her.

"And such a vast conclave of people does not make you feel insignificant?" he asked.

Bettina shook her head.

"It makes me think instead of the man who asked Buddha how many times he would be reborn—do you remember that tale?"

"Tell me," the Duke said.

"Lord Buddha," Bettina began, "was sitting under a huge banyan tree, and, as I expect you know, a banyan tree has more leaves than any other. A man approached him and said:

" 'Tell me, My Lord, how many lives shall I have before I reach eternal wisdom?'

"Buddha thought for a moment, then he said:

" 'As many as there are leaves on this banyan tree!'

" 'So few?' the man exclaimed in a voice of incredible joy. 'How very wonderful!' "

The Duke laughed softly.

"So you expect to have a great many more lives."

"I think one can only learn in a body. That is why it is such a privilege to have one," Bettina answered. "That is what the Buddhists believe and it seems a logical explanation of how we can advance spiritually towards the real truth."

"I hope we can," the Duke said, "if that is what we ultimately find."

He moved away as he spoke and she did not

watch him go. Her face was still turned towards the stars.

Now this morning all she wanted was sunshine.

She had been half-afraid that the festivities ahead might be spoilt by bad weather, but as she jumped out of bed and went to the port-hole she saw that it was a clear, sparkling day under an intensely blue sky.

Last night they had steamed into Port Said, where for a week other vessels had been accumulating for the great occasion.

Egypt's newest harbour, it lay on the Mediterranean side of the Isthmus of Suez, and Bettina saw that it was crowded with ships.

There were nearly eighty of them riding at anchor, with colourful pennants streaming from every mast and the flags from almost all the seafaring nations of the world fluttering in the light breeze.

She dressed quickly and hurried onto the deck, determined not to miss a moment of the spectacle which she knew would excite everyone, even Lord Eustace, however determined he might be not to be impressed.

She was soon joined by other members of the party and a few moments before eight o'clock a sleek black yacht which flew the colours of France and which Bettina knew was *L'Aigle* sailed into sight.

There was a woman on the bridge who she knew was the Empress Eugénie and beside her was an elderly man in a black frock-coat—*Monsieur* Ferdinand de Lesseps.

They steamed through the rest of the ships and cannons sounded from the shore batteries and from all the war-ships lying at anchor.

The Empress smiled and waved her handkerchief and the crowd roared out applause.

Shielding her eyes from the bright Egyptian sun, the Empress looked ashore to see the excited crowd.

There were Egyptian workers, soldiers, Bedouins, and Turkish noblemen. There were black men from the Sudan and white men from all the countries of Europe.

Greek sailors and French engineers mixed with the merchants of Syria, veiled Tuaregs from the desert, Ukrainians, men in caftans, sheiks with green turbans.

Then suddenly the air was filled with the sound of steam-whistles and wailing sirens.

The cannons sounded again and again and the Naval Bands on the war-ships began to play a military march.

L'Aigle moved ahead and passed through the entrance to the Suez Canal.

Bettina felt her heart beating with the drama and excitement of it all.

In front of the flotilla which was beginning to follow *L'Aigle* lay a hundred miles of silent desert which covered the Isthmus of Suez, but the new door had been opened, leading to India and the riches of the Far East.

At fifteen-minute intervals the other ships in the harbour entered the Canal. They had been ordered to keep to a speed of five knots an hour and the distance between them was three quarters of a mile.

In single file behind the Empress came the *Greif*, which carried the Emperor Franz Josef of Austria-Hungary, next there was a frigate with the Crown Prince of Prussia, and following it a Dutch yacht with the Prince and Princess of Holland.

The Duke, standing on the bridge of the *Jupiter*, knew every ship by sight and also knew who was aboard each one of them.

He pointed out the Russian ship of the Grand Duke Michael, who had come as a representative of the Czar, and rather scathingly the *Psyche*, in which was Mr. Henry Elliot, the British Ambassador to Constantinople.

Soon after this the *Jupiter* joined the procession and now at last Bettina could see the enchanting scene she had expected.

It was like some fantastic mirage, she thought, the silent ships that seemed almost to be travelling over the desert, watched by the white-robed Bedouins on the banks of the Canal.

It was difficult to put into words what she felt, and she was glad that everyone else was so busy chattering amongst themselves that she was left alone.

Just before six o'clock in the evening, the yacht containing the Empress and *Monsieur* Ferdinand de Lesseps steamed into Lake Timsah.

While the Canal was being dug, the Duke told his party, the workmen had built a town on the lakes of the northwestern shore. They called it "Ismailia" in honour of the Khedive of Egypt, and there was no doubt that it was an ideal place for him to give a party.

Looking at it from the yacht, Bettina could see silhouetted against the sunset the brilliant colours of the ornate buildings, the flowers, and the flags.

The lights which glittered in the town like falling stars made it really appear like a fantasy from *The Arabian Nights*.

"This has cost the Khedive a fortune!" Lord Milthorpe remarked.

"I believe the cost of his party alone will come to over one and a half million pounds!" the Duke replied.

Bettina heard Lord Eustace give an exclamation of disgust, and she quickly moved away from him.

It was all so lovely and she did not want it to be spoilt by calculating the cost. She knew that Lord Eustace was going to tell her that thousands of the Egyptians were starving and that the money which was being spent on this huge festivity should have been spent on them.

That night the ships which had moved down the Canal were all anchored in the lake.

It was hard for Bettina to leave the beautiful sight they made and not to stay up listening to the music and the noise of the crowds on shore

Finally she forced herself to go to bed, because she knew that tomorrow was going to be a very busy day.

As the Duke's party had not left England in time to arrive at Port Said before the seventeenth—the day when the ships and yachts were to pass through the Canal—they had, she found, missed the Religious Service which had taken place the previous day on the beach in the presence of the Empress Eugénie.

"It was a Religious Service," a friend of the Duke's who had come aboard told them, "which had never before been held in any Oriental country."

He explained that on one platform, to the accompaniment of gunfire, the Grand Ulema read a simple discourse followed by Moslem prayer.

"He must have looked most impressive," the Duke remarked.

"He did," his friend agreed. "On a similar platform on the right, the mitred Bishop of Alexandria officiated in a Christian Te Deum."

"I am sorry we missed it," the Duke said, "but I really only made up my mind to come to Egypt when I learnt that the Prince of Wales had been refused permission to do so."

"The Khedive was exceedingly disappointed," his friend answered, "but he is looking forward most enthusiastically to greeting you."

"I am glad to hear that," the Duke said, "and at least we are in time for his party!"

Once again the sky was bright and clear, and as Bettina hurried up onto the deck, the harbour of Ismailia presented an even more spectacular sight than that of Port Said the day before.

The Khedive's new Palace had been built by the lake and dominated the town.

The war-ships had begun firing their cannons and the noise of sirens and whistles filled the air.

The Duke had told his party to be ready to go ashore soon after breakfast, and they embarked to find flowers everywhere, triumphal arches, and trees in blossom.

The Duke was received by the Khedive and just before noon a launch brought Ferdinand de Lesseps and the Empress ashore for luncheon, after which they made a tour of the town.

Bettina thought that the Empress, dressed in yellow and wearing a large straw hat with a flowing veil, looked lovely.

There was a long procession of carriages to drive through the tree-lined boulevards between two rows of Egyptian Cavalry, one mounted on white horses, the other on bays.

They passed through the town and reached the desert-plain outside Ismailia.

Here, to Bettina's delight, there was an enormous Arab encampment, since the Khedive had invited thirty thousand Arabs in addition to his European guests.

They had put up their gaily striped tents in the desert and had brought with them their wives, their children, their camels, and their flocks of sheep.

The Duke's party joined the Empress, Ferdinand de Lesseps, and the Emperor Franz Josef, who sat with the other Royalties under the awning of a sumptuous tent.

The Duke seemed to know everybody intimately, and the Empress in particular had a very special greeting for him. Bettina thought there was a soft expression in her dark eyes when he kissed her hand.

"I had a feeling Your Grace might be here," she said with her charming smile.

"How could I stay away when I learnt that Your Majesty was to be the Guest of Honour?" the Duke replied.

She laughed in response. Then the Duke joined his party, which had been allotted a place near the Princess Sophia of Holland and the Crown Prince Frederick of Prussia.

They all chatted with the Duke and her father, but Bettina was content to look round her at the luxurious rugs that lay on the sand under their feet, and at the brass trays on wooden stands that held coffee, dates, and other delicacies.

She loved watching the Arab Chieftains, who were all dressed in flowing robes of white wool and carried jewelled daggers at their waists.

Suddenly one of the Chieftains raised his arm as a signal and the front of the tent was filled with Arab horsemen.

They galloped past, their robes flowing like wings in the wind, firing their carbines in the air as they went. They threw up great clouds of dust, which did not settle until after there was a six-mile race of dromedaries with screaming Arabs on their humps.

Then there were wild dervishes from the Sudan to entertain the Khedive's guests.

Some held red-hot coals between their teeth, while others swallowed live scorpions.

Next, fakirs took their turn with tricks of magic, and Bettina felt breathless at the wonders they produced.

It was hard to tear themselves away and return to the yacht, but they had to change for the party that was to take place in the Khedive's Palace.

By the time they reached the harbour, fireworks were being let off over the town, and rockets rose in the air while stars exploded in the sky.

Rose was waiting to help Bettina into her white gown after her bath.

She certainly needed one, for the dust of the desert had covered them all with a thin golden film.

With a sigh, Bettina looked at the pretty, comparatively simple gown she had bought in London.

She was quite sure that Lady Daisy and the other ladies would look like birds of Paradise, and she felt that in contrast her father and perhaps the Duke would think she was not smart enough.

"I suppose all the ladies are wearing jewels," she said to Rose.

"Yes, indeed, Miss," Rose answered. "His Grace

has lent Lady Daisy the Alveston tiara, which is almost like a crown."

She paused, then she said with a little smile:

"Lady Tatham is wearing the Alveston emeralds."

'And I have not even Mama's little star to wear,'
Bettina thought to herself wistfully.

There was a knock at the door and when Rose
opened it she came back with something in her hand.

Bettina looked and saw that she held a cluster of
the same star-orchids that she had worn on her first
night at sea.

"Are those for me?" she asked.

"With His Grace's compliments, Miss."

"How marvellous!" Bettina exclaimed. "They are
just what I need, Rose. Could you arrange them in my
hair?"

There were enough orchids not only for her hair
but also for a cluster to be pinned to the front of her
gown, and she felt that they were more effective than
any jewel and gave her a glamour that had not been
there previously.

When she walked into the Saloon where they
were all gathering before they went ashore, she saw
that the Duke's eyes were on her and she went to his
side.

"Thank you very much for the orchids," she
said. "It was so kind of you to think of me, and I
know it has made all the difference to my appearance."

"They are like you," he said quietly, "but you
hardly need them, for your eyes are like the stars at
which we were looking the other night."

She stared at him in astonishment, finding it hard
to comprehend that he should pay her such a compliment. Then Lady Daisy came into the Saloon blazing
with diamonds and Bettina moved to stand beside her
father.

"Enjoying yourself, my poppet?" he asked.

There was no need for her to answer him. In fact
she could not find the words, but he knew what she
was feeling.

The Palace, which the Khedive had built in less than six months, was surrounded by flower-filled gardens and there was a Pavilion where nearly a thousand people could sit down to dinner.

Palm trees were hung with Chinese lanterns, and crystal chandeliers which had been ordered from Paris dazzled the eye in every room.

There were gilt chairs and marble-topped tables, and on the walls there were costly paintings from France.

There were a thousand waiters in scarlet livery and powdered wigs, and Sir Charles told Bettina that in the kitchens five hundred cooks were preparing the feast.

It had been difficult to reach the Palace in their carriages, because of the crowds in the streets, watching the dancers, jugglers, and musicians.

In the Palace itself there was confusion. The rooms were crowded to the point of suffocation and it was almost impossible to breathe, let alone to move.

Bettina had thought the decorations the Duke was wearing on his evening-coat were dazzling, until she saw those worn by the diplomats and the Chieftains with the jewelled handles of their scimitars.

It was nearly midnight before the Empress Eugénie arrived, looking lovelier than ever in a gown of cerise satin covered in diamonds, a glittering coronet on her dark hair.

Fortunately, the Duke's party was in the Royal Dining-Room; otherwise, because of the crowd in the Pavilion, it was doubtful if they would have got anything to eat or drink.

Undoubtedly the most important person present was the man everyone wished to meet—Ferdinand de Lesseps.

Bettina thought how thrilled *Madame* de Vesarie would have been if she had had the chance of shaking his hand and congratulating him on his achievement, as everyone else was doing.

"*Merci, merci,*" he kept saying. "*Merci, mille fois.*"

And because he looked at sixty-four more like a kindly grandfather with his snow-white hair, it was difficult to realise how much he had suffered and endured to bring his dreams to fruition.

"He has given almost his entire life to the creation of the Canal," Bettina said.

She was speaking to herself and it gave her a start when Lord Eustace answered:

"It is certainly an achievement, but ruined, in my opinion, by all this extravagance. Do you realise there have been twenty-four courses served at the banquet tonight, and at least a quarter of the Khedive's subjects are suffering from malnutrition?"

"I know, and it is terrible!" Bettina said. "But please do not tell me about it tonight. I want to remember how beautiful all this is, to look at the huge candelabra on the tables, the jewels, the flowers, and the happiness on *Monsieur* de Lesseps's face."

"The Khedive will not be smiling when he realises he has bankrupted his country," Lord Eustace remarked harshly.

Because she could not bear to hear any more, Bettina turned to the gentleman on her other side, who was paying her fulsome compliments and was prepared to agree with everything she said.

All too soon for Bettina the evening was over, and when they returned to the yacht the Duke said they would begin their journey back to England not and join the convey which was to go on as far as the Red Sea.

"We shall see this route very often in the future," he said. "Do you realise it is now possible to reach India in seventeen days from England instead of taking four months?"

"It is fantastic!" Lord Milthorpe agreed. "At the same time, perhaps the world will become too small and we shall all get bored with it far too quickly."

"You are a pessimist, George!" the Duke teased. "Or it is merely because you are lazy and prefer to take things slowly?"

They had laughed at that, but as the Duke's yacht moved back towards Port Said, Bettina looked out at the desert and prayed that one day she would be able to return.

Everybody was rather tired the next day, having not got to bed until after dawn. This undoubtedly was responsible for Lady Daisy and Lady Enid being once again at each other's throat.

A row blew up over some trivial remark which afterwards it was impossible to remember, and they had snarled at each other like two tiger-cats.

Bettina slipped away after dinner to stand on deck and look at the harbour of Suez, where they were now anchored.

It was not as crowded as it had been before the opening of the Canal, but there were still the five British iron-clad war-ships which had fired a salute at the appearance of *L'Aigle*.

They looked very attractive with their lights reflected in the still water beneath them, but they and the lights ashore were eclipsed by the stars overhead and a young moon creeping up the sky.

It was very romantic and Bettina found herself wondering what it would be like to be in such a setting with someone she loved.

What was love like? she wondered. She had dreamt that she would one day find for herself the kind of love which her mother had had for her father.

Then she gave a little shiver.

She knew that if she married Lord Eustace, as her father wanted her to do, she would never have known the rapturous, spiritual love she sought, or the ecstasy which she believed a man and a woman should feel for each other before they married.

"How could I ever feel that with him?" she asked herself.

She knew that when he sat near her to read his pamphlets to her she instinctively wished to draw away.

And if ever his hand touched hers by accident

she felt a repugnance which she tried to stifle but which if she was truthful she knew was there.

"How can I marry him? Oh, Mama, how can I?" she asked the stars.

Now they seemed very far away and she felt cold despite the warmth of the night.

She went below, feeling a little despondent.

'I am tired,' she thought, 'that is all. Tomorrow I shall feel differently.'

But the words were singularly uncomforting.

She went into her cabin and a moment later Rose came in to undo her gown.

One glance at the maid told Bettina that she had been crying. Her eyes were red and swollen and there was an expression of abject misery on her usually smiling face.

"What is the matter, Rose?" Bettina asked.

"Nothing—Miss."

"That is not true," Bettina said. "You are unhappy and I want to know why."

"I can't tell—you, Miss," Rose answered.

Then she burst into tears and pulled out a handkerchief from her apron pocket to hide her face.

"I hate to see you like this," Bettina said. "Please, Rose, tell me what is the matter. Have you heard that someone you love is dead?"

"They might—as well be," Rose muttered.

"But we have had no letters from England," Bettina said. "The Duke was saying so only this morning, so you cannot have had bad news from home."

"It's not that, Miss—and you can't—you can't help me," Rose answered. "No-one can!"

Bettina looked at the cabin door to see if it was tightly shut. Then she said:

"Listen, Rose, anything you tell me in confidence I would not betray to anybody else, but I cannot bear you to be unhappy. Tell me what has happened."

"It's—His Lordship, Miss," Rose said as she sobbed.

"His Lordship?" Bettina queried.

"Lord Eustace."

"What has he done? How can he have upset you?" Bettina enquired.

"He saw me and Jack, Miss, and you wouldn't—believe the—things he said to us."

"Jack?" Bettina queried.

"Oh, Miss, I love him, and he wants to marry me. He said so. We were going to get engaged as soon as we got home and told our families, but now it'll never —happen."

"I do not understand," Bettina said. "Start from the beginning, Rose, and tell me everything."

Rose tried to pull herself together and wipe her eyes, but even so the tears continued to flow down her cheeks.

"I've fancied Jack ever since I came on board, Miss."

"Who is he?" Bettina asked.

"He's one of the sailors, Miss, and he's ever so nice. He said he liked me from the first moment he saw me—as I—liked him."

Tears choked Rose's voice. After a moment Bettina said:

"Go on, tell me what happened."

"Well, we talks nearly every evening and he never suggests anything—wrong, and never even tries to —kiss me. Behaved like a gentleman, he did."

Rose paused, then continued with difficulty:

"Until tonight—I was—standing with him under —the st-stars, and he s-says to me: 'You'll marry me, Rose, won't you, as soon as we've saved enough?' and I says: 'Oh, Jack!' It was what I'd longed for, what I'd prayed he'd say."

Rose drew in her breath, then went on:

"He puts his arms round me and kisses me—and it was the first time he'd ever touched me, Miss, I swears it!"

"I believe you," Bettina said, "and there was nothing wrong in his kissing you now that you are engaged."

"That's what I thinks, Miss, but Lord Eustace sees us, and I can't tell you what he says! He accuses

Jack of horrible things, and says he'll speak to the Captain in the morning and get him dismissed when we get back to England."

Rose burst into tears again and in between her sobs she murmured:

"And he—he says he'll—tell the Housekeeper at —h-home about my behaviour and I'll be turned away without a—reference."

Rose gave a little gasp before she added:

"That means I'll—never get another job and now J-Jack won't be able to marry me."

"I have never heard anything so outrageous!" Bettina exclaimed. "Did you tell His Lordship that you were engaged to be married?"

"He wouldn't listen, Miss. He just rants and raves at Jack and speaks to me as if I was a—fallen woman, and I'm not—I swear I'm not, Miss."

Rose put her hands over her eyes and her sobs shook her like a tempest.

Bettina put her arms round her.

"It is all right, Rose," she said. "Do not cry. I will make it all right, I promise you."

"It'll be no use talking to His Lordship, Miss. When he makes up his mind to do something—he does it!"

"What do you mean by that?" Bettina asked.

"He moved my old Granny from her home on the Alveston estate in Kensal Green. She'd lived there all her life. Loved it, she did—all her friends were round her. But Lord Eustace said the house was unsanitary and ordered it to be pulled down."

"Surely he could not make her move?" Bettina asked.

"He managed it, Miss. Got some officials to chuck her out."

"Not out into the street?" Bettina exclaimed in horror.

"Oh, no, Miss! Not as bad as that. He found her a new house somewhere on the estate. But she's never been happy there. She misses her friends and the shops she knew. She's just fading away. I shouldn't be surprised if she's dead when I gets home."

Rose paused for a moment. Then she said with another burst of tears:

"And that's what I'll be. I'd rather be dead if I can't be married to Jack! And if I lose my job and he's out of work too, what chance have we got? None! None!"

"I promise you, Rose, that will not happen," Bettina said.

She wanted to say that if all else failed she would get her father to employ Rose and find a job for Jack, but she knew there would not be enough money to pay her, so she had to think of something else.

"I promise you I will do something," she said. "This shall not happen to you. I refuse to let it!"

"I don't think as how you can help me, Miss, but it's very kind of you to want to, and you knows as well as I do I should not be telling my troubles to a lady like you."

"A lady like me should be helping you," Bettina said determinedly, "and that is what I intend to do."

Rose helped her to undress and when she left the cabin Bettina said:

"Promise me, Rose, that you will try to sleep. If you get a chance, send a message to Jack that I am going to try to put things right for you both. I expect he is pretty miserable too."

Rose was so overcome by the mention of Jack's name that she could not reply.

She closed the cabin door, and Bettina lay in bed, thinking of what she had heard.

She could hardly believe that Lord Eustace, with all his talk of helping those who were less fortunate than himself, could be so insensitive.

Yet, because she had listened to his pamphlets and thought them dictatorial and often overbearing, she could understand that he would not listen to Rose and Jack's point of view, which doubtless had been very badly expressed

It was a quite usual, in fact almost universal, rule that no maid-servant should have "followers."

But considerate employers like her mother had always made exceptions for those who were genuinely engaged to be married, or what the staff called "walking out."

'I suppose Lord Eustace thought it was just a "ship-board romance,"' Bettina thought, trying to make excuses for him.

But, because she liked and trusted Rose, she was sure that he had jumped to conclusions in thinking she was behaving wantonly.

Rose was a decent girl and her father was one of the foresters on the Alveston estate.

She had been very proud, she told Bettina, to be chosen to be one of the maids to look after the Duke's guests on this trip.

But she had added honestly that the main reason she had been allowed to come was because the other housemaids were too old or were frightened of the sea.

'She need not have told me that,' Bettina thought now, and knew it was another reason she was sure that Rose was truthful.

She was so perturbed by the story she had heard that she found it impossible to sleep.

In fact it was nearly dawn before she finally dozed off, and when she awoke she found that the ship had left port and had reached the Mediterranean.

It was then that she decided the best thing she could do for Rose was to go straight to the Duke.

"I will tell him exactly what happened," she said to herself, "and I am sure he will not let such an injustice be perpetrated amongst his servants."

She dressed herself carefully, putting on one of the summer-dresses which had belonged to her mother.

Of a very pale, spring-like green, it made her look very young.

Because she thought it would give her courage,

she took one of the orchids she had worn last night
and pinned it at the neck of her gown as she had her
first morning on board.

As she expected, none of the ladies had left their
cabins, but she heard the voices of the gentlemen
having breakfast in the Dining-Room.

She somehow guessed that the Duke would not
be amongst them. She knew that early in the morning
he took his exercise, walking alone round the deck.

She went to look for him, and saw him at the
stern of the ship as he moved briskly round the superstructure. Lifting up her skirts with one hand, she
ran after him.

She had expected him to carry on round the
deck, but obviously he had changed his direction,
for as she rounded the corner she bumped into him.

She gave a startled exclamation and he steadied
her with both his hands as he said:

"You appear to be in a hurry, Miss Charlwood,
or are you running away from someone?"

"I was looking for you, Your Grace," Bettina answered breathlessly.

"Then you have found me," the Duke replied
with a smile.

"I wanted to speak to you," Bettina said.

She felt her heart beating tumultuously and supposed it must be because she had run so quickly.

The Duke looked at her for a moment and saw
the anxiety in her grey eyes.

"I am ready to listen," he said.

Bettina looked round. Just behind them, fitted
into the superstructure, was a wooden seat where
people could sit sheltered from the wind and watch
the wake emerging from the propellers.

"Shall we sit down?" she asked.

"Why not," the Duke replied.

They sat down and Bettina turned a little side-
ways, clasping her hands together.

"You may think it very ... strange," she began
breathlessly, "that I should ... trouble you with ...
something which may seem very ... trivial."

"I would not think anything trivial if it concerned you personally, Miss Charlwood."

The Duke spoke kindly, but at the same time Bettina thought he was so grand, so overwhelming, that he might perhaps laugh at the story of Rose and Jack and think her extremely presumptuous in bringing it to his notice.

Her fingers tightened together and after a moment she said in a very small voice:

"Last night... Rose—she is the... maid who looks after me—was ... desperately unhappy."

She waited for the Duke to say he was not interested in the feelings of a mere maid-servant, but he did not speak and he appeared to be listening, so Bettina went on:

"She was in tears and I made her tell me what had upset her. She told me it was because of what... Lord Eustace had done."

"Eustace!"

The Duke repeated the name with an incredulous note in his voice.

Whatever he had expected to hear, it was not this. Then Bettina realised that the way she had phrased it might have given the Duke an entirely wrong impression.

"No, no!" she said quickly. "It is not what Lord Eustace had done to Rose personally. It is ... nothing like that."

"Then what has he done?"

Hesitatingly, and rather badly, Bettina thought, she told him what Rose had told her.

When she came to the end of the story she did not dare to look at the Duke, but instead said with a passionate sincerity in her voice:

"I trust Rose. I know she is not like ... that. She is a good girl, and while she has been dressing me we have talked of many things. I should know if she was the ... sort of girl Lord Eustace ... thought her to ... be."

The Duke still said nothing.

There was a grim line to his lips and she knew he was incensed.

"I have made you angry!" she exclaimed. "Oh, please, I am sorry if I should not have come to you, but I did not like to talk to the Captain, and Rose cannot wait and be miserable all the way back to England because she thinks she will be dismissed from your service."

"You did the right thing in telling me this," the Duke said, "and I am not angry with you nor with Rose and her young man."

Bettina gave a deep sigh of relief.

"You do understand! I thought you ... would."

"Why did you think I would understand?" the Duke asked.

"Because you are not intolerant and dictatorial like ..."

She stopped, feeling it was rude to speak as she intended about Lord Eustace.

"The 'do-gooders' in the world," the Duke said after a moment, "are often an incredible nuisance."

"They mean well," Bettina said quickly, feeling she must somehow speak a good word on Lord Eustace's behalf.

"That is 'to damn with faint praise,'" the Duke quoted.

Bettina gave a little sigh.

"I think the truth is that some people often force their own ideas of what is right and wrong on others without taking their feelings and personal inclinations into consideration."

She was thinking of Rose's grandmother as she spoke, and the Duke answered:

"That is exactly what I think, Miss Charlwood."

He paused before he added:

"Will you leave this problem to me? I promise you I will solve it and that whatever else happens, your protégées, Rose and Jack, shall have the chance of being united in matrimony if that is what they want."

Bettina looked up at him with her eyes shining.

"Do you mean that? Oh, Your Grace, thank you!
I felt you would understand . . . I was sure you would
. . . and you will make two people so very happy."

The Duke looked at her and put one hand over
hers.

"Leave everything to me," he said, and then rose
to his feet.

Bettina sped back to her own cabin as if she had
wings on her feet.

She entered to find Rose making her bed and
she burst in to fling her arms round the girl.

"It is all right, Rose! Everything is going to be
all right and you will be able to marry Jack as you
want to!"

"What are you saying, Miss?"

"I have spoken to the Duke and he said that he
will see to everything personally. Oh, Rose, he was
so kind, so wonderful about it all!"

"Do you really . . . mean that, Miss?" Rose asked.

"It is true. You do not have to worry any more,"
Bettina replied.

"Oh, Miss . . ."

Rose dissolved in tears again but this time they
were tears of joy.

*　　*　　*

When the Duke left Bettina he walked into the
Card-Room to look for his half-brother, but the only
person there was Sir Charles, looking unusually despondent.

"What is it, Charles?" the Duke asked.

"I had a damned silly wager with Downshire last
night," Sir Charles answered, "and this morning I find
that I have lost."

"I told you not to challenge him," the Duke said.
"He is one of those people who eventually always
come out on top."

"You are right, Varien. You always are," Sir
Charles said with a sigh.

"Have you seen Eustace?"

"I think he is having breakfast."

A steward came into the room with some silver ash-trays.

"Ask Lord Eustace to come here," the Duke ordered, "and do not return until I send for you."

"Very good, Your Grace."

"If you want to talk to Eustace alone, I will go," Sir Charles said.

"No, Charles, stay," the Duke answered. "I want you to hear what I have to say."

"I would really rather not," Sir Charles said, looking at the unmistakably grim expression on his host's face.

"I want an impartial referee, Charles," the Duke replied.

Sir Charles sat down again with a resigned expression on his face.

A moment later Lord Eustace came into the Smoking-Room.

"You wanted me, Varien?"

"Yes," the Duke replied. "Shut the door!"

Lord Eustace obeyed and stood looking at his half-brother questioningly.

"I understand," the Duke said slowly, "that last night you accused two of my employees of misconduct."

"That is true," Lord Eustace said. "I considered their behavior extremely reprehensible."

"You did not think that the correct thing to do was to report to me what you imagined they were doing?"

"I have every intention of seeing the Captain this morning and telling him the man's behaviour was disgraceful and he should be dismissed as soon as we reach England," Lord Eustace said.

"How dare you!" the Duke retorted. "How dare you interfere with my staff, the running of my ship? And what is more, how dare you presume to threaten my servants with punishments you are in no position to inflict?"

"When the Captain hears what I have to say he will hardly keep a man with such profligate morals on your staff," Lord Eustace replied. "As to the woman, she was doubtless emulating the behavior of some of your female guests, but that is no excuse."

"If you speak like that," the Duke stormed, "I will throw you overboard and hope you drown!"

"I can quite believe that," Lord Eustace sneered, "because you seldom hear the truth, Varien, and do not like it when you do! The morals aboard this ship are a disgrace to society and to the family name. With such an example in front of them it is not surprising that the servants are as licentious as their master."

The Duke clenched his fist and without doubt would have struck his half-brother if Sir Charles had not intervened.

He rose hastily to stand between them.

"It is a mistake to lose your temper, Varien," he said, "and, Eustace, you have no right to speak to the Duke in such a manner."

"I have every right!" Lord Eustace retorted. "Have you any idea what hell it is for me to stand by and watch him chucking his money away on women who are little better than prostitutes and on men whom he encourages to be unfaithful to their wives?"

His voice rose as he went on:

"He is content to let the Alveston estates to go rack and ruin so long as he can pay for his Casanova-like activities."

Lord Eustace almost spat the words at Sir Charles, and as he was about to answer the Duke interposed:

"What you are saying is a lie, but even if I do behave as you say, what business is it of yours? I am the head of the family and I shall do as I wish!"

"But you forget," Lord Eustace retorted, "that I am your heir and when you are dead I shall have to restore some sort of order and decency out of the mess you have made of everything."

He shouted the words at his half-brother, then turned and went out of the Smoking-Room, slamming the door behind him.

"My heir," the Duke said as if to himself.

There was silence for a moment, as both the men whom he had left stared at the closed door.

Then the Duke said very quietly:

"My heir indeed! I propose, Charles, to marry your daughter!"

Chapter Five

After Rose had left the cabin, Bettina remembered that there was a lace collar which needed mending on one of her gowns.

As Rose was so preoccupied with her own affairs and also had other ladies to look after, Bettina decided she would do it herself.

She looked for the little sewing-box that had been her mother's and which contained most of the cottons and silks she required for mending and repairs.

She slipped the silver thimble onto her finger and chose a silk to match the lace, which was old and very fragile.

She threaded her needle and darned it with small, skilful stitches, thinking as she did so of the hours she had spent at school learning to embroider under the tuition of a French nun.

Madame de Vesarie had been very insistent that her pupils should have every feminine accomplishment.

They were taught to play the pianoforte, to sketch and to paint water-colours, and to embroider with the traditional stitches which had been handed down for centuries.

Some of the older girls were allowed to cook so that when they returned to their ancestral mansions they would be able to supervise the Stillrooms, where all the pastries, jams, and special condiments were made.

Because Bettina had stayed so long at school she had learnt everything that *Madame* de Vesarie's Seminary could teach her.

She thought now with a little drooping of her spirits that if she had to marry Lord Eustace she would probably spend all her time sewing, and not fine or beautiful materials but garments for the poor.

These would undoubtedly be extremely ugly, because people who had no money were not allowed to be vain or self-conscious.

She found herself wondering why people like Lord Eustace always made the poor feel crushed and servile, allowing them no feelings or will of their own, and expecting them to obey in every way what was decided for them.

She thought Rose's story of how her grandmother had been treated was typical of what she had learnt from reading the newspapers and some reports on the objects and aims of the reformers.

They had the right idea, she realised, but they put them into operation in the wrong way.

There was too much regimentation, too much driving people into doing what those in authority thought to be right, rather than persuading them to be cooperative.

She gave a little sigh.

She was quite certain that if she put forward such ideas Lord Eustace would not listen to her!

Unexpectedly the door opened and her father came into the cabin.

She looked up at him with a smile of welcome, then as she saw the expression on his face she asked quickly:

"What has happened?"

Sir Charles shut the door behind him and walked across the small cabin to the port-hole as if he was in need of air.

He stood for a moment looking out onto the blue sea. Then he said:

"I have something to tell you, Bettina!"

"What is it, Papa?" she enquired.

Again there was a pause, and then Sir Charles said:

"I have just come from the Duke."

"From the Duke?" Bettina repeated.

She had a sudden fear that the Duke had changed his mind about Rose and Jack. Supposing after all he agreed with Lord Eustace that their behaviour was reprehensible, and that he had decided not to interfere but to let them be punished as his half-brother had suggested?

She felt almost a sharp pain at the idea. Then as she sat, her eyes wide and anxious on her father, he turned to say:

"The Duke has asked me to tell you, Bettina, that he wishes to marry you!"

For a moment Bettina thought she could not have heard her father correctly.

Then the gown she was mending fell from her hands and instinctively they moved to her breasts as if to soothe a sudden tumult.

In a voice Sir Charles could hardly hear she asked:

"Is . . . this . . . a joke, Papa?"

"No, Bettina," Sir Charles answered. "The Duke has definitely said that he would like you to be his wife. Of course, he will speak to you himself, but he asked my permission and naturally I have given it wholeheartedly."

As if what he had to say made him feel overcome, Sir Charles sat down on the bed.

"I can hardly believe this," he said. "That you should marry Varien was something I never imagined would happen even in my wildest dreams."

Bettina said nothing and after a moment he went on:

"I thought by aspiring to Eustace I was flying pretty high. After all, as you are well aware, in the social circles in which I move, aristocratic families arrange the marriages of their sons and daughters with great care."

He paused for a moment, then went on:

"To aspire to being a Duchess in England today is as easy for an ordinary girl like yourself as trying to fly to the moon!"

He drew in his breath.

"If Varien actually means to marry you, I can only believe, Bettina, that you are the luckiest girl in the world!"

For almost the first time since he had entered her cabin, Sir Charles looked at his daughter.

She was staring at him with a bemused expression in her huge grey eyes, which seemed to fill her small face.

"You are very like your mother," Sir Charles said, "and she was the loveliest person I have ever seen in my whole life."

There was now a note of deep affection in his voice, which superceded the tone of surprise mixed with triumph in which he had spoken before.

Then as he waited Bettina said slowly and clearly:

"Why ... does the Duke ... want to ... marry me?"

Sir Charles looked away from her again.

"I think you know the answer to that," he replied. "He wants an heir and he dislikes Eustace! Who shall blame him?"

"I thought you said that he had always ... sworn never to ... marry again after the ... unhappiness of his first ... marriage."

"Men change their minds, my dear," Sir Charles answered, "and you and I can thank our lucky stars that the Duke has changed his."

"I can understand that you want me to ... marry him, Papa."

"Of course I want you to marry him!" Sir Charles said positively. "There is no question about that. Do you know what it will mean for you to be the Mistress of Alveston House in Park Lane, which is second in importance only to Marlborough House? To play hostess in the country in one of the most magnificent

Castles in the whole of England? And God knows how many other possessions Varien has!"

He glanced at his daughter's face. Then in a quieter tone, with something almost coaxing and conciliatory in it, he said:

"I am not only thinking of what the Duke owns. You know that I am very fond of him. He is younger than I am, but I have always counted him as one of my best friends. Men like him, and that is important."

Bettina did not speak, but as if he knew what she was thinking Sir Charles went on:

"Of course there have been women in his life —many of them. They have fallen into his arms like over-ripe peaches, and any man would be either a Saint or a fool to refuse them! But I am sure of one thing—Varien will always treat his wife with respect and propriety."

Bettina still did not speak but she made a little movement, and as if he interpreted it as a protest Sir Charles continued:

"You need not doubt that, and I know what I am talking about. Whatever else he may be, whatever people may say about him, Varien is a gentleman, and as far as you are concerned he will always behave like one."

Bettina gave a little sign and now she bent down to pick up the gown she had been mending from where it lay on the floor.

"The Duke is waiting for you, Bettina," Sir Charles said. "You will find him in his private Sitting-Room at the other end of the yacht."

"W-what am I to . . . say to him . . . Papa?"

"What are you to say?" Sir Charles echoed. "Accept his offer of marriage with both hands! Then go down on your knees and thank the gods for your good fortune."

He gave a deep sigh that seemed to come from the very depths of his being.

"I can still hardly believe this has happened," he said. "In fact I do not mind telling you that this

morning I was in despair, Bettina. I lost a large sum
of money last night."

"Oh no, Papa!"

"I was cursing myself for a fool," Sir Charles re-
lated, "but now it does not matter—it does not matter in the least!"

There was no need for him to elaborate. Bettina
knew that as the father-in-law of the Duke of Alveston his credit would be boundless.

What was more, while he had always been welcome as a guest in every house the Duke owned,
now he would be there by right.

In a low voice Bettina said:

"I will go and ... see the Duke, Papa, but ... explain to me where I will find him."

"You go past the Smoking-Room," Sir Charles
replied, "and the Duke's private quarters are beyond
that. No-one else shares that part of the yacht with
him, and who shall blame him in wishing sometimes
to be alone?"

Bettina did not answer.

She did not even look at her reflection in the
mirror; she merely turned and went from the cabin,
shutting the door softly behind her.

She walked along the passage hoping she would
not meet any of the house-party.

She felt as if her brain was in a turmoil.

At the same time, she moved automatically, doing what she was told to do, feeling as if she were
numb and merely a puppet. Her will had suddenly
ceased to exist.

She slipped past the Dining-Room, hearing the
voice of Lord Milthorpe and the laughter of the other
male guests. Then she passed the Card-Room and
found herself in a part of the yacht she had not visited before.

A door was open at the end of the passage and
she had a glimpse of a large cabin and in the centre
of it a masculine-looking mahogany bed.

She hesitated, knowing that the Duke would not

be seeing her there. Then his valet, a middle-aged man with a kindly face, whom she had noticed before, came from an adjacent cabin.

"Good-morning, Miss," he said. "His Grace is expecting you."

He held open the door behind him and Bettina entered a smaller cabin that was golden with the sunshine coming through the port-holes.

She had a quick glimpse of a bookcase on one wall, two deep, comfortable arm-chairs in red leather, and sporting prints on the walls.

Then she had eyes only for the Duke, who had been sitting at his desk before she entered.

He rose to his feet and it seemed to Bettina as if he looked at her with a very searching expression in his eyes.

Now the feeling of numbness and of being only a puppet seemed to pass; her heart began to beat, as if in fear, with a thumping stroke, and she felt her breath constricted in her throat.

It was impossible to speak, and as if the Duke also felt tongue-tied they stood looking at each other while the sunshine turned Bettina's hair to gold.

"Will you sit down?" the Duke asked at length.

His voice seemed very low and deep and Bettina sank gratefully into the red leather arm-chair as if she was suddenly too weak to go on standing.

"Papa . . . sent me to . . . you," she said in a small voice that seemed even to herself to come from very far away.

"He has told you, Bettina, that I wish you to be my wife?"

"Yes . . . he has . . . told . . . me."

"If you will marry me," the Duke said, "I will do my best to make you happy."

"Thank . . . you," Bettina murmured in a voice little above a whisper.

Then she added:

"M-may I . . . ask you something?"

"Of course," the Duke answered.

He had been standing at the side of the desk and now he sat down in the other arm-chair, his eyes on her face.

"It is ... just that ... could this be a ... secret from everybody ... until we ... get back to ... England?"

"That is a very sensible suggestion," the Duke answered, "and actually one which your father has already made."

He did not add that Sir Charles had said:

"For God's sake, Varien, do not speak of marrying Bettina until we get home. Daisy and Enid will kill the child!"

He saw a look of relief come over Bettina's face, and he added quietly:

"We will do nothing, of course, without discussing it first between ourselves, and I think when we arrive home you would like to come to Alveston Castle for Christmas. Your father certainly wishes to ride my horses and I have a feeling you would enjoy them too."

"It would be very ... exciting," Bettina murmured.

"Then that is settled," the Duke replied. "We will both of us behave quite normally towards each other until we get to the Castle, and then we will make plans."

"Thank ... you," Bettina said. "Thank you ... very much."

Her eyes met the Duke's. Then, because she was shy, her eye-lashes lowered, and they were dark against her pale cheeks.

As if he understood her embarrassment, the Duke rose and said in a different tone:

"I will go now to see the Captain. I intend to tell him that Jack Sutton, which is the name, I understand, of your maid's young man, is to be granted special leave when we reach Southampton to meet his future wife's father and mother."

"That is kind ... very, very kind of you," Bettina said. "Rose was so happy when I told her how wonderful you had been that she burst into tears. But they were very different from the tears she was shedding last night."

"Then you can tell her," the Duke smiled, "what I am arranging, and I presume that we had better give them a wedding-present which will help them towards the furnishing of their future home."

"I would love to do . . . that," Bettina said, "but . . ."

The Duke waited.

"I am afraid I have . . . very little money," she continued, "in fact . . . if I am honest . . . I have none!"

"But I have plenty," the Duke answered, "and have you forgotten that in the Marriage Service I shall say: 'With all my worldly goods I thee endow'?"

Bettina felt he was teasing her, and because she knew that the solemnity of the way in which they had been speaking must somehow be as dismal for him as was the manner in which Lord Eustace spoke, she replied with a smile:

"You would be very . . . discomfitted if in fact I took all you . . . offered!"

The Duke laughed, and then he said:

"I think you will find that I have enough for both of us!"

Bettina heard a ship's bell ring and she said quickly:

"I think, Your Grace, I should go back to the other part of the yacht. If anyone knew I was here in your . . . private Sitting-Room, they might think it . . . strange."

"Yes, of course," the Duke agreed, "and we will keep our secret, Bettina, until we reach the Castle."

"Thank . . . you," Bettina said again.

She moved towards the door but did not realise that the Duke intended to open it for her.

As she put out her hand it touched his, which was already on the handle, and she felt something run through her which was almost like a shock.

She could not explain it, but it was a feeling she had never known before.

Then without looking at him she went out into the passage and started to hurry back the way she had come.

She had almost reached the Dining-Room when a man came out of it and stood barring her way.

Intent on her thoughts, still bemused with the strange feeling the touch of the Duke's hand had given her, Bettina did not realise he was there until she had almost collided with him.

Then she raised her eyes and found Lord Eustace glaring at her.

"Where have you been? Why are you here?" he asked harshly.

She did not answer, and he took hold of her arm, holding it tightly above the elbow, and started to pull her along with him.

"What are you doing?" Bettina asked. "Let me go!"

"I want to speak to you," Lord Eustace replied.

He dragged her towards the Writing-Room and pulled her in through the door while she was still trying to free herself from his grip.

There was no-one in the room, and releasing her he shut the door behind him and stood with his back to it.

"What were you doing in Varien's private suite?" he enquired.

Bettina put up her chin.

She was angry at the manner in which Lord Eustace spoke to her, and besides, he had hurt her arm when his fingers had tightened against the softness of her skin.

"The Duke wished to speak to me," she said. "Is there anything wrong in that?"

"Everything could be wrong as far as Varien is concerned," Lord Eustace replied, and he was sneering.

Bettina said nothing and after a moment he went on:

"I imagine you were pleading with him to show mercy towards that immoral maid-servant. Well, let me tell you, whatever Varien may say, I have every intention of reporting her behaviour to the House-keeper at the Castle and seeing that she is dismissed."

"You cannot be so cruel!" Bettina cried. "Rose is not immoral. She is engaged to her sailor, and no-one in the world, except you, would think it improper for a girl to kiss the man to whom she is engaged."

"That may be the explanation the woman gave you," Lord Eustace said, "but I believe the evidence of my own eyes. In fact the way they were behaving did not surprise me. This yacht is a hell-hole of immorality, and I will not have you mixed up in it."

"I think you . . . exaggerate," Bettina protested.

At the same time, she could not help thinking that the behaviour of Lady Daisy and Lady Tatham gave some justification for Lord Eustace to speak in such a manner.

As if by the expression on her face he knew what she was thinking, Lord Eustace said with an unpleasant smile:

"Exactly! And do you think your mother, if she were alive, would have countenanced your being here in close association with the two so-called Ladies who are nothing but a pair of harlots?"

Bettina started.

She had never heard anyone use such language and the words shocked her. Besides, there was something singularly unpleasant in the tone of Lord Eustace's voice.

"I do not wish to . . . discuss it," she replied. "I have to see Papa. Please let me pass."

She took a step towards the door but Lord Eustace did not move.

"Listen to me, Bettina," he said. "You are very young and innocent, and I consider it extremely reprehensible of your father to have brought you here in the first place. But now that you know the depths of depravity to which the so-called Social World will stoop, make up your mind that in the future you will have nothing to do with those who have such evil lives."

"I do not intend to allow you to criticise Papa," Bettina retorted.

"Sir Charles is old enough to do what he likes," Lord Eustace answered, "but you are young and, as it happens, very pretty."

He did not make it sound particularly like a compliment, and Bettina merely repeated:

"I wish to go to Papa."

"When I am ready to let you," Lord Eustace answered. "But first you have to listen to me."

"I do not wish to listen to you," Bettina said, "and if you want my opinion I think it is very bad manners to eat a man's salt and abuse him behind his back."

"Where my half-brother is concerned the rules of chivalry do not apply," Lord Eustace retorted. "I only came on this trip, which is everything I expected it to be, when I learnt that you were to be one of the guests."

She looked at him in surprise and he went on:

"When I looked after you at Dover I realised you were pure and innocent, a child who knew nothing of the world and certainly nothing of that part of it which is reigned over by my illustrious half-brother!"

His voice was spiteful. Then he added in a different tone:

"I accepted his invitation because I thought I could save you! Save you from being soiled and besmirched by the evil women with whom my half-brother associates, and with the licentious Rakes he calls his friends."

"That was . . . very kind of . . . you," Bettina said a little breathlessly, overcome by the turn the conversation had taken, "but Papa is with me and he has looked after me . . . as he always . . . has."

"Your father cannot protect you from what you

see taking place and from what you hear being said," Lord Eustace retorted. "And if you make excuses for the people with whom you have been associating on this voyage, then all I can say is that you are already contaminated, already sinking into the slime and filth in which they wallow."

It flashed through Bettina's mind that Lord Eustace was positively unhinged by his hatred of his half-brother and the life he led.

Yesterday, she thought, this would have perturbed her and she would have felt afraid.

But now with a sudden sense of freedom she knew there was no need for her to be troubled by what Lord Eustace thought or did not think.

Ever since coming on board she had been overshadowed and menaced by the thought that her father wished her to marry him.

Now, like the sunshine sweeping away the darkness of the night, her fear had gone.

Lord Eustace could hate, sneer, and denounce as much as he pleased. Once they reached England she need never see him again.

Because there was a sudden happiness in the thought, she said in a quiet, conciliatory tone:

"You are upsetting yourself, My Lord. Things are not as bad as you imagine. I am very grateful that you have tried to protect me and prevent me from being corrupted. But I assure you I am quite safe, and like Papa, I never remember the unpleasant things which happen, only the nice ones."

She smiled at Lord Eustace before she added:

"I really must go. Papa will be wondering what has happened to me."

"Your father must wait," Lord Eustace replied firmly. "I have something to ask you, Bettina, but I did not mean to do so until we reached England."

There was something in the way he spoke and the expression in his eyes that gave Bettina a sudden sense of danger.

She knew what he was going to say, and felt she must stop him before the words passed his lips.

"We will talk later, My Lord," she said quickly, "but not now. I really cannot stop now."

"You will listen to me," he said in the obstinate tone she knew so well.

He was still standing with his back to the door and there was nothing Bettina could do to move him.

She waited apprehensively, feeling frantically that she must somehow prevent him from saying the words she expected, but feeling helplessly that it was impossible.

"I want you to marry me," Lord Eustace said. "I will teach you all you need to know about life. There will be no question of your ever again coming in contact with the dregs of a dissolute aristocracy."

Bettina drew in her breath. The words were spoken, she had been unable to prevent them. Now she had to reply.

"I . . . I am very . . . honoured," she said in a hesitating little voice. "B-but I must be honest and say that while I . . . am grateful for your kindness to me . . . I cannot . . . marry you."

"Do not be so ridiculous!" Lord Eustace said sharply. "You will marry me not only because I want you to but because it is your father's wish. He has already intimated very clearly that he considers me a suitable son-in-law, which is exactly what I am."

"I am . . . sorry," Bettina said, "very sorry to . . . upset you, but I . . . I want you to know now—from the very beginning—that it is impossible for me ever to . . . marry you."

To her surprise, there was a smile on Lord Eustace's thin lips.

"You are very young," he said, "and I can understand that your first proposal of marriage would not only surprise you but seem overwhelming. Just get used to the idea, Bettina, that you will be my wife, and we will be married sometime in the next year, when I have had time to make the necessary arrangements."

"No!" Bettina cried. "No!"

Lord Eustace smiled again.

"Go and talk to your father. He will explain to you that you are unlikely to get a better offer."

He paused, then added, his eyes on her face:

"I know this makes you feel shy since you have not, unlike so many other women, thought previously of marrying me, and that is to your credit. But I am sure, Bettina, I can teach you to be the sort of wife I need, to help me with my plans for the future."

He paused significantly before he continued:

"It will of course take time, and a great deal of application on your part, but you will soon realise and appreciate that the battle into which I have thrown myself wholeheartedly is well worthwhile."

He spoke in a grandiose way and Bettina felt she could find no answer. Now at last he moved away from the door and opened it.

"Go to your father," he said. "You will find he will be delighted at your news."

Without saying anything Bettina escaped, feeling almost as if she had been buffeted unconscious by the waves of the sea.

She ran down the passage towards her cabin and burst in to find thankfully that her father was still there waiting for her.

He was sitting on the bed, reading a newspaper, and she flung herself upon him, putting her arms round his neck.

"Oh, Papa! Papa!" she said.

Sir Charles dropped the newspaper and held her close.

"I expect it has been a bit of a surprise, poppet," he said. "Never mind, you will get used to the idea of being a Duchess, and God knows I am proud of you."

"It is ... not the ... Duke," Bettina answered, "it is Lord Eustace! Oh ... Papa, he says that I ... have to marry him and that you will be so ... pleased!"

For a moment Sir Charles stared at his daughter in astonishment, then he began to laugh.

"So Eustace has come up to scratch, only to be pipped at the winning-post! It is the funniest thing

I have ever heard, and it serves him damned right!
The sanctimonious swine—he deserved a set-down!"

Bettina took her arms from round her father's
neck.

"But, Papa . . . you . . . wanted me to . . . marry
him!"

"Only before I knew you could aspire very much
higher," Sir Charles answered, quite unabashed.

"I really think," Bettina said in a low voice,
"there is . . . something in what Lord Eustace says
about . . . you and your . . . friends."

"Do not tell me what he said," Sir Charles replied. "I know Eustace's view all too well. Forget him!
It is Varien with whom we are concerned."

"Yes, I know . . . but Lord Eustace is very . . .
overpowering, and when he has made up his mind he
can be extremely . . . obstinate."

There was just a touch of fear in her voice which
Sir Charles did not miss.

"Forget him," he said again. "Eustace cannot hurt
you now and you will see very little of him once
you are married. He seldom accepts his half-brother's
invitations."

"He said he only came on this trip because he
knew I would be here."

"So that was the reason!" Sir Charles ejaculated.
"Oh, well, it shows he has good taste in one thing,
if in nothing else. You are certainly different from the
riff-raff, the gin-sodden down-and-outs on whom he
usually expends his time."

"I was thinking this morning that he has the
right ideas, but he goes about it in the wrong way,"
Bettina said.

"I am not even certain his ideas are right," Sir
Charles answered. "He abuses his half-brother but nobody knows better than I do of the generous way
in which Varien helps other people, and actually the
Alveston estate is a model of its kind."

"In what way?" Bettina asked.

"Well, you will have to ask Varien," Sir Charles
replied. "But I know he has built more orphanges and

more alms-houses than any other great landlord. He supports several Hospitals, and the charities to which he subscribes would fill a book!"

"Then why does Lord Eustace say such . . . terrible things about him?"

Sir Charles smiled.

"My dear child, you cannot have read the Ninth—or it is the Tenth?—Commandment, the one about envying your neighbour."

"Do you mean that Lord Eustace is jealous?"

"Of course he is! He loathes his half-brother because he is the Duke. His mother hated Varien because he was the heir when Eustace was born. There was nothing she could do about it except to be spiteful, disagreeable, and continually try to put his father against his son. Luckily she did not succeed."

"Now I . . . understand quite a . . . lot of things," Bettina said slowly.

"And because Varien enjoys the good things of life, because he is a sportsman, a friend of the Prince of Wales, a King among men, Eustace has gone to the other extreme."

Sir Charles continued:

"He has made his friends the poverty-stricken rabble in whom no-one was interested. At least amongst them he can shine, as his half-brother shines in a very different world."

"I am sorry for him," Bettina said.

"You need not be," her father answered. "In his own way he is eaten up with his own conceit. I can tell you one thing—it would never cross his mind that you might refuse his offer of marriage."

Remembering what Lord Eustace had said, Bettina knew this was true.

"You will have to . . . speak to him, Papa."

"I will," Sir Charles answered, "but not until we reach England."

"No, of course not," Bettina agreed quickly. "The Duke has said we will behave quite normally until we reach the Castle. I could not face the other guests if they suspected . . ."

Her voice died away.

"That is what I thought," Sir Charles said, "but there is no reason why they should suspect anything. As my old Nurse used to say, 'keep yourself to yourself,' for the rest of the journey. And that includes, where possible, keeping away from Eustace."

"I shall certainly do that, Papa," Bettina said.

It was, however, easier said than done.

As they steamed homewards up the Mediterranean she was aware that Lord Eustace was trying to get her alone and finding it increasingly frustrating when he could not manage it.

It was not easy to hide in a yacht or to be always in the company of the other guests.

On the voyage out Bettina had avoided Lady Daisy and Lady Tatham as much as possible.

If she was honest with herself, she knew that it was because they shocked her, although not quite as violently as they shocked Lord Eustace, but the manner in which they behaved towards the Duke seemed to her to be fast and at times vulgar.

Now, to see them fawning over him at meals, to hear their remarks which always had a little innuendo in them, to watch the invitation in their eyes, made Bettina feel uncomfortable and also gave her another feeling to which she could not put a name.

It also made her aware of her own insignificance.

How, she asked herself, could she ever be like them? How could she be sophisticated, witty, and at the same time deliberately, provocatively alluring?

She did not know how to be any of those things, and if that was the type of woman the Duke admired and who amused him, he would find her dull within a few hours of their marriage.

At night she tried to think things out logically and clearly for herself.

The Duke hated his half-brother, who quite obviously despised him. He had therefore come to the conclusion, against his better inclination, that he must marry again and produce an heir.

Perhaps in other circumstances he would not have chosen her, but because she had been there when he was angry with Eustace, when he resented his high-handed manner in interfering with his servants, he had decided that he might as well marry her as any other woman.

It was a very dispiriting picture and Bettina felt her heart sink as she thought it over.

The night before they left the Mediterranean and passed through the Strait of Gibraltar to leave behind the warmer weather and the calm seas for the cold and winds of the Bay of Biscay, she slipped up onto the deck when she was certain no-one would see her.

She put on her warm cloak with its fur-trimmed hood which framed her face.

There was a touch of frost in the air. At the same time, the stars were brilliant overhead and Bettina could look up at them and remember how she and the Duke had seen them together.

She thought then that he had been different, serious and understanding, ready to listen to her ideas, which, she thought humbly, must have seemed very childish to him.

Quite suddenly she knew how much she longed for her marriage to be a successful and happy one.

She wanted to bring the Duke happiness, perhaps a happiness he had never known; and this certainly must not be a marriage of quarrels and disagreeableness, such as he had endured with his first wife.

She felt only her mother would understand what she was feeling, and as she looked up at the stars she found herself praying.

"Help me, Mama. Help me to do the things he will like. Tell me how to look after him."

As she spoke, she thought it was a strange request to make about the Duke, who had hundreds of ser-

vants to pander to his every need, and yet she felt
perhaps someday he might need her.

If only her mother were there and she could talk
to her about it. If only she could be told what a man
like the Duke wanted from his wife, from the mother of his children.

She felt herself tremble because it was all so
overwhelming, and with one last look at the stars
she slipped below to lie sleepless in her cabin for a
long time.

*   *   *

Once they were in rough weather there was an
inescapable relief in knowing that Lady Daisy and
Lady Tatham had succumbed and would remain in
their cabins.

Mrs. Dimsdale appeared the first day, but then she
too retired with the other ladies and Bettina was
once again the only woman to appear at meals.

The gentlemen teased her, paid her compliments, and treated her like a rather precocious child.

Bettina actually enjoyed herself, although she
sometimes glanced apprehensively at the Duke, who
was sitting at the head of the table, in case he
thought she was not behaving in the way he would
wish her to do.

She was quite aware that Lord Eustace was
glowering at her through every meal and disapproved of every smile that curved her lips, every
laugh that came spontaneously from her throat.

The other gentlemen teased him too.

"Come on, Eustace," they would say. "How can
you be so disagreeable about it? You have to let us
share Miss Charlwood with you when she is the only
female company we have left."

Lord Eustace did not reply but only looked
more sullen and disagreeable than before.

Because Bettina felt he was suffering she allowed
him to read her one of the new pamphlets he had
composed, not in the intimacy of the Writing-Room
but in the Saloon, which they occupied alone but

where there were always servants moving in and out.

He took out the closely written sheets of paper which he intended to read to her, then he said fiercely:

"You have been avoiding me!"

Bettina did not deny it.

"You ... frightened me the way you ... spoke last time we were ... together," she replied.

"I had no wish to do that," he said. "At the same time, you will have to learn to obey me, Bettina."

Bettina did not answer and he went on:

"For it to be a happy marriage a wife must always be subservient to her husband, and let me make it clear, we shall not move in the circles where women like Lady Daisy and Lady Tatham have complaisant husbands who remain at home while they go gallivanting with their lovers."

"Please, Lord Eustace, do not let us speak of anything but the work you are doing," Bettina pleaded.

"The work I am doing for the down-and-outs concerns me just as it is impossible for me not to be concerned about the people with whom we are forced to associate at this moment."

"As I told you before," Bettina said, "I think it is wrong and extremely bad manners for you to abuse your half-brother and his guests."

"I loathe him! Do you hear me, Bettina? I loathe him!" Lord Eustace said violently. "And once we are married we will never, either of us, ever see him again!"

He looked at her with dark, glowering eyes to see if she was prepared to argue. Then he said:

"Thank God I have enough money of my own not to be dependent on the charity of that profligate."

"You are not to speak like that," Bettina replied. "This hatred will harm you. If you go on, it will twist your character and you will become abnormal."

Lord Eustace laughed unpleasantly.

"My dear child," he said, "what do you know of

abnormality, or of men for that matter? I suppose in a way you are beguiled by Varien's face and appearance and the fact that he has a coronet on his head."

He laughed again.

"All women are the same, and you are no exception, but I will teach you to appreciate the real things, the real values of life and people who are not hypocrites and do not disguise licentiousness under a smiling mask."

Bettina sighed.

"I am waiting to hear your pamphlet."

"You will hear it when I am ready to read it to you," Lord Eustace snapped. "Let me make this quite clear from the beginning, Bettina: I am your master. I decide what will and will not be done, and you will obey me."

Bettina contemplated getting up and leaving him.

Then because they were alone in the Saloon she thought he might try to stop her, and she could not bear the thought of his touching her hand or her arm.

She escaped as soon as she could and was delighted to hear the next morning that Lord Eustace as well as two other gentlemen in the party were too unwell to leave their cabins.

Once again the *Jupiter* had run into bad weather and this time they had a head sea, which made it difficult to move about.

All the same, Bettina was determined to go on deck.

She dressed herself in the warm coat she had worn before and put over it the oil-skin which had been intended for use by the sailors.

She tied the white strings of the oil-skin hat under her chin, and moving very cautiously she made her way out onto the deck.

It was certainly very rough, the waves washing over the rails, each one seeming higher and more majestic than the last.

Bettina moved a little way towards the bow, feeling it was somehow a breathless excitement to watch the yacht forging ahead in what seemed to be almost impossible circumstances.

The green waves with their curved white crests reared up in front of the vessel almost like dragons, and yet fearlessly the *Jupiter* rode them, then challenged the next.

Bettina felt that the yacht was a white Knight battling his way through hostile foes and always emerging the victor.

The wind grew stronger, the sea more turbulent, and she realised that her oil-skin was running with the spray and she was in fact feeling rather cold.

She turned to struggle back to the door and as she did so her feet slipped on the wet deck.

She gave a little cry, and would have fallen, but two arms were round her, holding her close.

She realised with a sense of relief that the Duke had been standing behind her, but the noise and tumult of the sea had stopped her from knowing it.

He held her against his chest and she looked up at him with a smile.

Then as her eyes met his she felt as though something strange happened to her heart and it turned a somersault within her breast.

For the moment everything seemed to stand still and there were only his eyes looking down into hers.

Then as the spray of the waves splashed over them both she knew that she loved him!

Chapter Six

Bettina stood on deck to watch the yacht come into port at Southampton.

She was relieved that the voyage was over.

There had been a tension that was unmistakable ever since they had reached calmer waters and Lady Daisy and Lady Tatham had risen from their sick-beds to continue fighting each other and fawning over the Duke.

Sir Charles was aware, although Bettina was not, that the main reason now for their animosity was that each of the ladies was certain that the Duke was bestowing his favours on the other.

Actually, he spent most of his time either on the bridge with the Captain or in his own Sitting-Room.

But the jealousy and suspicion between the two beautiful ladies affected the whole party, and Bettina thought she would never have believed she would welcome the end of the glamorous voyage.

She was also worried about Lord Eustace, who, every moment she spent alone with him, reiterated that they were to be married and would listen to nothing she might say to the contrary.

'Papa will have to tell him once we are back in England,' she thought.

At the same time, she could not help feeling a little ashamed that her father had encouraged Lord

Eustace to believe he would be a very acceptable
son-in-law.

Ever since she had fallen in love with the Duke
she had said a prayer every night, grateful that she
did not in fact have to marry Lord Eustace.

Every time she looked at his dark scowling face
and listened to his violent denunciation of his half-
brother and his friends, she knew she had had a very
lucky escape.

How could she have endured years of that? she
asked herself. Yet she knew that had Lord Eustace
offered for her before the Duke, she would have been
obliged to accept him whatever her feelings were in
the matter.

But now everything was different, and although
the sky overhead was dark and glowering she felt
that England was bathed in sunshine.

Once they had said their farewells to the other
members of the party, she would be alone with the
Duke and her father, and she knew that she was
looking forward to it with an eagerness which
seemed to increase with every hour that passed.

"I love him! I love him!" she had told herself
when she was in bed at night.

She knew now that although she had not acknowledged it before, she had in fact been in love
with him almost from the first moment she saw him.

He was so magnificent, so imperious, and even at
the same time a little frightening.

But when he had talked to her under the stars
and she had felt a strange sensation because his
shoulder was close to hers, it had been love, although
because she was so ignorant she had not recognised
it.

The yacht moved towards the Quay, and now,
so unexpectedly that she started, she heard a voice
say sharply:

"So this is where you have been hiding yourself!"

She had no need to turn her face to know that
Lord Eustace was standing beside her and that he

would be looking sullen and disagreeable because she had escaped him.

"We are home!" Bettina said.

"I hear from your father that you intend staying at the Castle for Christmas."

"Yes."

"I thought you were coming to London. I intended to call on you tomorrow morning."

"We are going to the Castle."

"I do not wish you to go there!"

Lord Eustace's voice was commanding.

"It is all arranged," Bettina said quickly.

"Then I will talk to your father on the train and persuade him to change his mind. We have a lot to discuss, Bettina, and the sooner we arrange our wedding-day, the better."

Bettina held on tightly to the railing in front of her.

She knew that they were all to travel in the Duke's private train towards London but that he, her father, and herself would get off at Guildford and drive from there to the Castle.

Quite suddenly she felt that if Lord Eustace made a scene in front of Lady Daisy and Lady Tatham she would not be able to bear it.

She drew in a deep breath.

"I have something to tell you," she said, "but it is a secret, and you must swear to me you will not mention it in front of the other members of the party."

"I have no intention of even speaking to them if I can help it," Lord Eustace replied. "I can only assure you that in the future neither you nor I will come in contact with Varien's friends unless it is absolutely unavoidable."

"Then you promise that what I have to say will remain a secret?" Bettina asked.

"I cannot imagine what you have to tell me, but I will give you my word if that is what you want."

Bettina drew in her breath.

"I cannot ... marry you because I am going to ... marry ... the Duke!"

The words were said and now she waited, trembling.

For a moment there was complete silence. Then Lord Eustace said:

"Are you really telling me that Varien has asked you to be his wife and you have accepted him?"

"Yes."

"I can hardly believe that you would be—" Lord Eustace began furiously, then checked himself.

"I do not suppose you really had any say in the matter," he said as if he spoke to himself. "It would be exactly what your father would wish, and Varien intends to cut me out as his heir."

Bettina did not answer. She only stared ahead, unable to move, almost afraid to think.

Then Lord Eustace said:

"I might have guessed that something like this would happen."

There was an unrepressed fury in his words as he turned and walked away, leaving her alone.

A little later Bettina saw him walk down the gangway to the Quay ahead of the rest of the party, and when they reached the private train there was no sign of him.

She heard the Duke say:

"We are ready to leave. Is Lord Eustace on the train?"

"He informed me, Your Grace, that he was not coming with us," a servant replied.

The Duke raised his eye-brows but said nothing, and Bettina felt the sudden tension ebb from her so that she was almost weak with relief that she would not see Lord Eustace again.

The servants served champagne, and Lady Daisy seated herself in one of the comfortable arm-chairs near the Duke and said:

"I hope, Varien dear, you are planning a party for Christmas and that I am to be one of your guests?"

She spoke as if it was impossible she would not be, but the Duke replied:

"I have not yet decided what I shall do over Christmas. I want to get home first and find out what has been happening while I have been away."

"If you are expecting an invitation from the Prince," Lady Daisy said, "I can tell you that he will be at Sandringham, very much *en famille,* and you know as well as I do that once they are all there it is almost impossible to squeeze many other people in the house."

She paused and added with a smile:

"You are fortunate that the Castle is so big."

The Duke rose to his feet.

"I believe my secretary has some mail for me on the train," he said, "so do not count me in if you intend to play bridge."

He walked away and Bettina saw Lady Daisy stare after him with perplexity in her eyes and a tight line to her lips.

Sir Charles, however, tactfully insisted that they should do as the Duke suggested, and they had soon made up two tables of bridge, which left Bettina free to read.

However, she found it difficult to concentrate on anything but her anticipation of what lay ahead.

Now she would be able to talk to the Duke without being afraid of being seen. Now they would discuss when they were to be married and her heart seemed to beat more quickly at the idea.

The Duke reappeared when it was time for luncheon and almost as soon as the meal was over the train drew into Guildford station.

"I had no idea that Charles was going with you to the Castle," Lady Daisy remarked.

Bettina realised that she did not mention her because she was too insignificant for it to matter.

"Charles is coming to help me exercise my horses," the Duke answered with a smile. "I am sure they have all become fat and lazy while I have been away."

"I expect the ground will be too hard for you to hunt," Lady Daisy said almost spitefully.

"There is more snow than frost," the Duke said optimistically.

"You must come up to London as soon as possible," Lady Daisy said insistently, "and do not forget my invitation for Christmas."

As if Lady Tatham realised that her rival was making somewhat of a nuisance of herself, she took a very different line.

"It has been such a marvellous trip, Varien," she cooed. "I cannot thank you enough for taking me to such a Historic Ceremony, which I shall always remember."

She looked up into his face with her slanting green eyes and said softly:

"I intend to give you something very special to commemorate the happy times we have spent together."

Bettina saw the fury on Lady Daisy's face but at that moment the train came to a stop and the Duke had every excuse to make his farewells quickly to the other members of his party.

Sir Charles and Bettina did the same. Then without waiting to see the train on its way they proceeded to where the Duke's carriages were waiting for them.

Drawn by four magnificent horses, the travelling-cabriolet with the Ducal arms emblazoned on it was more comfortable than Bettina had ever imagined a carriage could be.

There was a landau for the servants and the luggage, so they drove off at once and seemed to travel at an almost incredible speed once they were outside the town.

Now Bettina could see that the countryside was white with snow and in consequence was very beautiful.

"It was a good party, Varien," Sir Charles said, lighting a cigar, "but like most parties it went on too long."

"I agree with you," the Duke answered. "I thought afterwards that I should have sent my guests over-land from Marseilles. I do not believe anyone except you and Bettina enjoyed the Bay of Biscay."

"Bettina is as good a sailor as you are, Varien," Sir Charles said proudly.

"Which is something else we have in common," the Duke remarked to Bettina.

She wondered what the other things were, but she was too shy to ask and merely sat in silence beside the Duke on the back seat, while her father, sitting opposite them, had plenty to say.

"I wonder, might Daisy be right and it will be too hard to hunt?" Sir Charles asked.

"I hope she is wrong," the Duke replied, "but we shall know as soon as we arrive. It is extraordinary how women are always jealous of a man's sport."

Bettina made an inward resolution that this was something she would never be.

Her mother had said to her many years ago:

"I am always so glad when your Papa is out in the open air. It is so much better for him than sitting at a card-table which he cannot afford, and smoking too many cigars, which is bad for his chest."

"But he leaves you behind, Mama," Bettina had said.

Her mother smiled.

"He comes home to me, darling, to tell me of his triumphs, as well as his failures, and that is what is important."

'I wish I could remember all the things Mama said,' Bettina thought now, but then she told herself that perhaps her love and her instinct would guide her.

They drove for nearly three quarters of an hour before suddenly ahead of them she saw the Castle.

From all she had heard about it Bettina had expected it to be impressive, but it was larger, more awe-inspiring, and indeed more beautiful than she had anticipated.

The Duke's flag was flying over the huge roof with its turrets, its cupolas, and its chimneys, and it was surrounded by terraces, walls, gardens with statues, shrubberies, and woods with a stream flowing through the Parkland.

She felt that anything she could say would be inadequate and so she just sat staring at it with wide eyes.

As they arrived there seemed to be an army of liveried flunkeys to greet them in a huge marble hall with a curved oak staircase.

As they were shown into a Salon which was as large as a Ball-Room, Bettina suddenly felt afraid.

It was one thing to think of being married to the Duke when they were in the confines of the yacht, large though it was by other people's standards.

But it was quite another to imagine for one moment that she could be the mistress of this colossal edifice with its hordes of servants, its vast estates, and all the other ramifications of wealth.

'I shall be lost . . . smothered!' Bettina thought in a sudden panic.

Then she felt the Duke take her hand and say quietly in his deep voice:

"Welcome to my home, Bettina! I hope you will learn to love it as I do!"

Bettina felt a thrill run through her at the touch of his hand and the kindness in his words.

She knew at that moment that if he had asked her to live in a place the size of an Army barracks or on top of the Himalayas, she would have agreed to it; indeed, she would have agreed to do anything he asked.

"I expect you want a drink, Charles," the Duke said, "but Bettina will prefer tea and it will be ready in a few minutes."

He smiled at her as he said:

"Why not go upstairs and take off your bonnet and cape? You will be far more comfortable."

"Yes, of course," Bettina said obediently.

The Duke walked with her back into the hall and spoke to the Clerk of the Chambers.

"Tell Mrs. Kingdom that I wish Miss Charlwood to have the Garden-Room and for Sir Charles to be near her."

"Very good, Your Grace."

The Clerk of the Chambers escorted Bettina to the top of the stairs where a Housekeeper, rustling in a black dress, a silver chatelaine at her waist, was waiting.

"Miss Charlwood is to have the Garden-Room, Mrs. Kingdom."

The Housekeeper curtseyed and Bettina held out her hand.

"This is a very magnificent Castle, Mrs. Kingdom!"

"It is indeed, Miss."

The Housekeeper bustled ahead, leading Bettina down a long passage ornamented with fine pieces of furniture and gilt-framed portraits on the wall.

She longed to stop and look at them, knowing they were the Duke's ancestors, but then she remembered there would be plenty of time later to explore the whole Castle.

Finally Mrs. Kingdom opened a door into a room which was not as large nor as awe-inspiring as Bettina had expected.

In fact it was low-ceilinged, but very attractive with a Chinese wallpaper depicting flowers, and the hangings on the bed were also embroidered with flowers.

"How pretty!" Bettina exclaimed.

"This is the Elizabethan Wing, Miss, which His Grace has only recently had redecorated."

"It is lovely!" Bettina said, looking round and seeing flowers everywhere.

She felt she knew why the Duke had chosen it for her.

"It's even prettier in the summer, Miss," Mrs. Kingdom explained. "The balcony outside has steps going down into a small garden of its own and the walls are covered with wistaria."

"It sounds lovely!"

"Of course there's nothing but snow now."

"I was thinking how beautifully warm the house is," Bettina said.

The Housekeeper smiled.

"His Grace always insists that a fire is lit in every room at this time of the year."

"In every room?" Bettina echoed.

"Yes, Miss. It keeps the temperature high all the winter and we none of us have colds, sneezes, or sniffles, as happens in other houses."

"It certainly sounds very luxurious."

"We should be humiliated if our guests didn't have every comfort possible," the Housekeeper replied.

Bettina was well aware that when the staff talked of a place as being "theirs" as well as belonging to their master it was a sign of a happy household.

As she took off her bonnet and cape she thought how kind it was of the Duke to have put her in a room that he knew she would appreciate because she loved flowers.

It was then she saw that on her dressing-table there were two vases filled with white orchids, and she thought perhaps he had telegraphed ahead to order them.

Then she told herself it could only be coincidence.

A maid came to ask if she could help her, but Bettina was already prepared to go downstairs again.

She found the way to the Salon and discovered that a most elaborate tea was set out beside the fireplace. There was a profusion of silver, and cake-stands containing every sort of delicacy.

"We are waiting for you to pour out," the Duke said. "You must get used to being hostess."

Bettina blushed as she took her place, but while Sir Charles refused a cup of tea, the Duke had one and she poured one for herself.

"You look as if you have something to say," Sir

Charles said as the Duke stood with his back to the fire.

"I know what you are wanting to talk about, Charles," the Duke said with a faint smile, "but I intend to discuss our marriage with Bettina alone. Then later we will tell you what we have decided."

"You are being very high-handed," Sir Charles said as he smiled.

"Why not?" the Duke enquired. "It is Bettina's wedding-day and I think that as she is the most important person concerned, everything should be as she wishes rather than anyone else."

"I am not grumbling," Sir Charles replied. "I am only so happy that the two people I love best in the world should be together."

"I am sure Bettina wants to rest before dinner," the Duke said. "But I want to take her round the Castle myself and it would be too late tonight."

"Naturally," Sir Charles agreed, "and there is tomorrow, unless you want to do something else."

"That is what I was about to tell you," the Duke answered impatiently. "I have to go to London. It is only for the day and I shall be back in the evening, but perhaps not until after dinner."

"So you are leaving us on our own," Sir Charles said.

"I dare say you will find plenty in the stables to amuse you. Do you ride, Bettina?"

"When I have the chance of borrowing a horse," Bettina replied.

"Well, you will find you have a pretty wide choice here," the Duke said, and added to Sir Charles:

"There is no hunting tomorrow, Charles, but unless we have a very hard frost I am told it may be possible on Thursday."

"Then I will take Bettina out for a ride and see if she has forgotten all the lessons I taught her," Sir Charles answered.

"I wish I could come with you," the Duke said, "but I really have to go to London."

Bettina could not help wondering if he was in fact going to see Lady Daisy, and if he intended to tell both her and Lady Tatham that he was to be married.

Then the thought struck her that even if he was married it might make no difference in his relationship with them.

The idea was so agonising, like a physical pain, that she knew she was jealous.

"How can I help it when I love him so?" she asked herself. "He is so handsome, so attractive, that I can understand there will always be women like Lady Daisy and Lady Tatham running after him."

Suddenly the largeness of the house and her own insignificance made her feel that everything was too overpowering and she almost wished she could run away.

"I shall disappoint him," she told herself unhappily.

But when she came down to dinner and saw the Duke waiting for her in the Salon, magnificent in his evening-clothes, she felt that any agony she must suffer because she loved him was worthwhile.

She was wearing one of the simple gowns that she had taken with her in the yacht and which the maids had hurriedly pressed after they had unpacked it.

Bettina had taken two of the orchids from the vase on the dressing-table and pinned them to the front of her gown.

She saw the Duke glance at them as she curtseyed to him, and she said, touching them with her long fingers:

"They were in my bed-room, and they made me think of those which you gave me when we went to the Khedive's party. I was so thrilled to have them, as I had no jewels."

"I have not forgotten," the Duke said, "but I would in fact have sent you some to wear tonight if I had not already decided to give you something else."

As he spoke he took a box from the table by the fireplace and held it out to her.

"It belongs to the Alveston collection," he said, "but I thought you would like to wear it until I can buy you some jewellery that will be entirely your own."

Bettina opened the box and gave a little exclamation of surprise, for it contained a spray of flowers in diamonds very delicately made and so exquisite that they were an exact replica of the flowers they depicted.

"How lovely!" she said breathily.

"I knew you would think so," the Duke said. "It was made by one of the Master Craftsmen in the last century, and I thought, Bettina, it would become you."

"Thank you, thank you very much!" Bettina said. "Shall I put it on?"

"I should be very disappointed if you did not."

She took off the two orchids she had pinned to the front of her gown, but when she would have fixed the brooch herself the Duke did it for her.

He did it quickly and dexterously but Bettina felt for a moment the touch of his fingers against her skin and a little quiver went through her.

As if he felt it too, the Duke looked at her and as their eyes met Bettina felt herself quiver again.

Before either of them could speak, Sir Charles came into the Salon.

❋   ❋   ❋

The next day Bettina first inspected the stables with her father, then they rode together in the Park.

It was several months since Bettina had been on a horse and she had never been mounted on such a magnificent animal as had been suggested for her by the Duke's Chief Groom.

She had, fortunately, packed amongst the things she had taken to Egypt a riding-habit which one of her French friends had given her because her own were completely worn out.

It was very becoming but rather too elaborate for what was fashionable in England.

Her father, looking at her critically, said:

"You had better order for yourself some really smart habits from Busvines. They are the best tailors and it is a mistake to be overdressed in the hunting-field."

"I believe Busvines is very expensive, Papa."

"What does that matter?" Sir Charles replied.

Bettina looked at him enquiringly and he said after a moment:

"Varien has already told me that he will pay for your trousseau."

"Oh, Papa, I am sure that is . . . incorrect."

"It may well be," Sir Charles replied, "but you can hardly go to your wedding looking like Cinderella! Varien, as you know, is used to well-dressed women."

Bettina said nothing.

She only felt it embarrassing that the Duke should be paying for the clothes she wore before she was his wife, while Sir Charles was only too ready to accept everything he could from him.

From the way that Lady Daisy and Lady Tatham talked, she had suspected that the Duke had given them innumerable presents and had paid a number of their bills.

She instinctively wished to be different and to avoid, if possible, taking anything from him, at least until she bore his name.

She knew that her father would not understand her reluctance to behave like the other women the Duke knew, but however much she wished to pay for her own clothes, she knew her father could not afford to.

At the same time, Bettina found herself worrying as to what she should do, or at least what she could say to the Duke, to make him realise that she was not grasping at everything he could offer.

Last night when she had gone to bed and taken off the brooch he had given her, she had thought as it glittered in the lights in her bed-room that it almost had a message for her.

Then she told herself she was just being imaginative.

The Duke was being kind and considerate, and it was only something from the Alveston collection.

After all, he had loaned both Lady Daisy and Lady Tatham the jewels in which they had appeared at the Khedive's party.

It made her think that after all she would rather have had the orchids—at least they were personal and had not been worn before by anyone but herself.

Then she knew she was being ungrateful.

But when she got into bed and lay with only the firelight flickering on the beautiful flowered wallpaper, she felt she yearned and longed for something that she could not put into words.

"I should be the happiest person in the world," she said aloud, and yet there was something missing.

It began to snow after tea, and while Sir Charles dozed in front of the fire Bettina walked round the Salon, looking at the pictures, the exquisite objets d'art, and the inlaid tables.

She wished she could explore the other parts of the Castle, but the Duke had said he wanted to show it to her himself, and she started to count the hours until she could see him again.

"I want to talk to him, I want to be alone with him," she murmured beneath her breath, and wondered what he would have to say about their wedding.

'Perhaps he will want it to be a long engagement,' she thought, 'as that would give him time to adjust himself to the idea of being married again.'

It was painful to think of the wife he had once had and the unhappiness he had endured.

"I will do everything he wants," Bettina told herself, then prayed that what he wanted would not involve other women.

The idea made her unnecessarily restless and Sir Charles awoke to ask:

"Why are you prowling about? What are you
hoping to find?"

"Only more treasures." Bettina smiled. "I have
never seen so many exquisite things all in one room."

"Wait until you see the rest of the Castle," Sir
Charles said. "It has been added to by every suc-
cessive generation of Alvestons, who have all been
collectors in one way or another."

Bettina was listening intently and he went on:

"There are Temples in the garden which came
from Greece and weapons in the Armoury which
were acquired in India and Turkey. The French furniture is, I believe, a unique collection, while the pictures are all superlative."

"Papa, I want to ask you something," Bettina
said, sitting down beside him.

"What is it?" Sir Charles asked.

"Do you ... think it is ... possible for me to make
the Duke ... happy?"

Sir Charles was silent for a moment, then he said
in a different tone of voice from the one he had used
before:

"I understand what you are asking me, Bettina,
and I am going to answer you honestly: I do not
know!"

"I was afraid that was what you might say, Papa."

"I love Varien. He is a magnificent man, generous and kind. And yet there is some wall fencing
him in which no-one, not even his best friends, can
climb."

"That is ... what I ... feel," Bettina murmured.

"It is a reserve or perhaps a defence thrown up
following his first ghastly marriage," Sir Charles
said. "But, whatever it is, it makes him in some ways
unapproachable."

He rose to his feet to stand with his back to the
fireplace, before he went on:

"You are young, Bettina, and you are idealistic. I
know what you are asking me is whether Varien will
ever love you. You want a happy ending to the fairy-
story. What woman does not?"

Bettina did not speak but her eyes were on her father's face.

"All I can hope is that you will find what your mother and I found," Sir Charles continued, "perfect happiness when two people really love each other. But where Varien is concerned I have no idea whether you can break through the barrier which stands between him and those who reach for his heart."

Sir Charles threw his cigar into the fire.

"Dammit all!" he said. "I ought to have answered you in a different way. I ought to have made you believe it is possible and that you will succeed."

"I would rather know the . . . truth, Papa."

"Then all I can say is that there is an outside chance," Sir Charles said. "I have often backed an outsider and watched him gallop first past the winning-post."

Bettina rose to her feet and kissed her father's cheek.

"Thank you, Papa."

She went from the Salon and as Sir Charles watched her go there was an expression of pain in his eyes.

They went to bed early because, as Sir Charles said, it was a change for him after the late nights he had spent playing cards on board the *Jupiter*, and the snow had made him sleepy.

It had been snowing all the evening, but when Bettina looked out her bed-room window there was a full moon coming through the clouds and even a few stars to be seen in the sky.

They were of nothing like the brilliance or the size of the stars above the desert which she had looked at with the Duke, but they made her think of him and she felt herself longing for tomorrow to come quickly so that they would meet again.

"I love him!" she whispered, looking up into the Heavens, and she prayed that he would one day love her.

"Just a little, God," she said, "just a very little.

I do not ask for anything as wonderful as the love Papa had for Mama, but just a little love! Make him want to be with me and not find me a bore."

The moonlight revealed the snow-covered, enclosed garden beneath her window and beyond it she could see the trees with snow on their bare branches.

"This is a fairy-land," she told herself, "and although the Duke is undoubtedly Prince Charming, I cannot hope that I am really the Princess he has been looking for all his life."

The idea was dispiriting. She let the curtains fall and crossing the room got into bed.

The firelight flickered on the flowers on the Chinese wallpaper, on the orchids on her dressing-table, and on the curtains with their forget-me-nots, roses, and lilies-of-the-valley embroidered centuries ago by skilful fingers.

"It is all so beautiful, but it needs love," Bettina told herself.

Her eyes closed and she was just drifting into dreamland when she heard a sound at the window.

For a moment it hardly registered in her mind. Then she thought that it was a spray of ivy tapping against the glass.

It often happened in a wind, and more than once at school in France she had been awakened in such a manner because the School-House had many creepers climbing up it.

The sound came again and now Bettina heard the long French window being opened, she sat up, not for the moment afraid but surprised.

The curtains parted and Lord Eustace came into the room!

The firelight shone on his face and she stared at him in sheer astonishment before she exclaimed:

"Lord Eustace! What are you doing here?"

He came towards her, still with his hat on his head, and she saw that he was wearing a long, dark over-coat.

"Why have you come to the Castle?" she asked.

"I have come for you."

"What do you . . . mean?"

"What I say."

He reached the bed and she stared up at him in disbelief.

"I told you that I intend to marry you," Lord Eustace said, "and as I realise you are incapable of deciding such a thing for yourself, I have decided it for you."

"I do not know what you are talking about," Bettina cried. "You must go away . . . go away at once! You should not be here in my bed-room, as you well know!"

"I am certainly leaving," he answered, "but you are coming with me."

He reached out as he spoke and Bettina saw that he had a handkerchief in his hand.

She pressed herself back against the pillows, putting out her hands as she cried:

"What are you . . . doing? Go away! Do not . . . touch . . ."

Before she could say the last word, the handkerchief was over her mouth and he had gagged her.

He knotted it behind her head even while she struck out at him with her hands, realising as she did so that it was now impossible for her to scream.

She was hampered by the bed-clothes covering her, and before she could attempt to move away from him and get out of the other side of the bed, he had taken a broad strap from his coat pocket.

He put it behind her and, forcing her arms down to her sides, fastened it at her waist.

He worked so quickly and so effectively that Bettina was completely immobilised almost before she realised what was happening.

Then Lord Eustace swept back the bed-clothes, tied her ankles together with another strap, and, pulling off a blanket, wrapped it round her while she struggled ineffectively to prevent him.

She realised she was now no better than an inanimate object unable to move, unable to cry out, and when he had wrapped the blanket round her, covering even her face, she felt him lift her in his arms.

She knew then that he intended to take her away with him.

She thought despairingly that once he had done so neither the Duke nor her father would be able to find her and she would belong to Lord Eustace as he intended her to do.

"Help!" she wanted to cry, but could make no sound through her lips.

She felt Lord Eustace carry her through the French windows. Then they were descending the stone steps which led from the balcony into the walled garden.

Desperately Bettina called out in her heart to the Duke, feeling that because she loved him he must hear her, must know that she was in danger and needed him.

"Save me! Save me! Help me! Oh, God, make him help me!" she called.

Lord Eustace had reached the garden and was walking over the snow towards the iron gate which led onto the lawns.

Because the grass was thick with snow his footsteps made no sound, and with her face covered with the blanket Bettina felt the whole thing was some terrible nightmare from which it was impossible to awaken.

"Help me...oh...help me," she cried to the Duke. "He is taking me...away and you will... never find . . . me again."

Then almost as if her words had been answered by Heaven itself she heard a voice she knew ask:

"What the devil is happening? Who are you?"

Then an ejaculation that was like a pistol-shot.

"Good God, you, Eustace! What are you doing here?"

"Taking away something which belongs to me," Lord Eustace replied truculently.

Bettina was afraid that the Duke would not realise what Lord Eustace was carrying.

She wanted to scream out that she was there and that he must save her, but though she tried to move it was impossible with Lord Eustace's arms tight as a clamp round her.

"What have you got there?" the Duke demanded.

Bettina thought that they must be in the shadow of the wall, which would prevent the moonlight from revealing the bundle in his arms very clearly.

"That is my business!" Lord Eustace replied. "Let me pass, Varien!"

"Not until I see what you are stealing from my house," the Duke answered.

"I have no intention of showing it to you."

"I insist!"

The Duke must have made a move towards him, for suddenly Bettina found herself dropped roughly onto the ground and she knew that only the cushion of snow prevented it from being very painful.

The movement dislodged the blanket which covered her face and now she could see Lord Eustace, having rid himself of her, rushing at the Duke and striking at him.

He took his half-brother by surprise; the Duke's head, jerking backwards to avoid a blow, made his hat fall from his head. For a moment he staggered, then returned blow for blow.

They were fighting violently, Bettina realised, and she knew that all the pent-up hatred that Lord Eustace had for the Duke was expressed in the fury which he put into his punches.

However, the Duke was both taller and stronger, and, although Bettina did not know it until later, he was an experienced amateur pugilist.

One moment there was a scuffle, a struggle, and the dull thud of blow upon blow, and then the next it was all over.

With a sharp uppercut on the point of the chin from the Duke, Lord Eustace seemed almost to fly backwards in the air before he sprawled unconscious in the snow.

The Duke hardly waited to see him fall, then turned immediately to Bettina.

He saw the gag over her mouth but he merely lifted her in his arms, and, holding her closely against him, walked across the garden and up the stone steps, through the French window, and into her bed-room.

He carried her to the rug in front of the fire and set her down to stand as he supposed on her own feet. But when she swayed against him he realised she could not move.

He held her against his chest with one arm and undid the gag at the back of her head with the other.

She was trembling both in terror and from the cold and, turning her face against his shoulder, she burst into tears.

"It is all right," he said. "It is all right. You are safe."

The blanket had slipped to the ground and he saw the strap which held her arms, and undid it. Then he lifted her up to carry her towards the bed.

Bettina held on to him and cried incoherently through her tears:

"No—no! I c-cannot . . . sleep here! He will c-come back. He will take me . . . away!"

The Duke did not argue. Carrying her, wearing only her nightgown, he opened the door and walked along the passage outside.

Most of the lights had been put out, but there were still enough left for him to see his way and he walked for some time with Bettina still crying against him.

Then he opened a door and she knew they had entered a room which seemed to be on the other side of the Castle.

"You will be safe here," the Duke said, speaking for the first time. "You are in the room next to mine, Bettina, and I promise that no-one will ever abduct you again."

He put her down on the bed and undid the strap

round her ankles. Then he pulled the bed-clothes over her to stand looking very large and protective beside her.

She could see him silhouetted against the firelight, but because the tears blinded her eyes she could not see the expression on his face. She put out both her hands towards him.

"Do not ... leave me," she begged. "Please ... do not go ... away."

"I am going to talk to you, Bettina," he said, "and you must tell me what happened. But if I leave the door open will you allow me first to go next door and tidy myself?"

He turned as he spoke and she saw that his collar was torn, his tie was undone, and there was a gash on his cheek which was bleeding.

"You are hurt!" she cried. "Lord Eustace has ... hurt you!"

The Duke put up his fingers to the wound.

"I think it was his signet ring which cut me," he said. "It is not serious."

He smiled at her, then he went through a different door from that through which he had carried her in from the passage, and Bettina realised it led to his own bed-room.

He left it wide open and now she could hear him speak to someone and guessed his valet had been waiting up for him.

'I am ... next to him. He is ... close to me and Lord Eustace cannot ... hurt me ... again,' Bettina thought.

At the same time, her heart was still thumping frantically in her breast and it was difficult to believe the nightmare was over.

Her feet were cold and so were her hands, but the room was warm.

In the firelight she could see that it was a very large, beautiful room with a huge canopied bed on which she was lying and there were three high windows hung with blue satin damask.

But she really wanted to look at nothing except the open door through which the Duke would return to her.

How could he have saved her? How could he have known what was happening when she cried out so desperately for him?

It seemed a very long time, but it was really only a few minutes before the Duke came back into the room and closed the door behind him.

He stooped to put some more logs on the fire, then as the flames shot up, filling the room with a golden light, she saw he was wearing a velvet smoking-jacket such as he had sometimes worn on the yacht, and there was a white silk scarf round his neck.

He had washed the blood from his cheek and he looked so handsome and so reassuring that as he came towards the bed Bettina instinctively held out her hands to him.

He sat down on the side of the bed facing her.

"How could I know? How could I have guessed," he said, "that you would be involved in such a deplorable situation?"

Bettina's fingers hung on to his as if they were a life-line.

"I ... called you," she said. "I ... called to ... you in my ... heart and suddenly you were ... there!"

"I must have known instinctively that something was happening to you," the Duke said. "When I got back from London I felt worried about you, although I could not imagine why."

He smiled as he added:

"I had been thinking about you as I came down in the train and when I reached the Castle I somehow felt you wanted me."

"I did ... want you!" Bettina whispered. "I wanted you ... desperately!"

"I could hardly come to your bed-room," the Duke said, "so I thought I would walk round and look up at your window. I cannot explain even to myself why I decided to do so."

"It must have been my ... Guardian Angel who ... guided you to ... me," Bettina murmured.

"Just as I told myself I was being rather foolish," the Duke went on, "I saw there were new foot-prints in the snow and wondered whose they could be."

"I could not scream ... but I ... prayed for ... you."

"I think I knew that," the Duke answered, "and when I saw Eustace I was sure that something was very wrong."

"Did you ... know that he was ... carrying me?" Bettina asked.

"Not at first," the Duke replied. "It did not seem like a body in his arms, and it flashed through my mind that he was taking one of the tapestries which are exceedingly valuable and which he has often contended should be sold and the money given to the poor—his poor, of course!"

The Duke paused. Then he said:

"It was only when he dropped you on the ground and went for me that I realised what was happening."

Because it swept over Bettina once again how terrifying it had been she bent forward so that she could hide her face against the Duke's shoulder as she had done before.

"I thought ... he would ... take me away and I would never ... see you again," she murmured almost inaudibly.

His arms went round her to hold her close against him.

"And would that have worried you?" he asked. "I have often wondered if you would have preferred Eustace to me. He is much nearer your age."

"I ... hate him!" Bettina said. "He is ... repulsive ... horrible ... but now I know too that he is ... w-wicked!"

"It was not exactly wicked to want you," the Duke said.

"Suppose he ... tries again?" Bettina said in a very low voice.

The Duke put his arms on her shoulders and very
gently pushed her back against the pillows. Looking
down into her eyes, wide and frightened in the firelight, he said:

"We can make you sure, if you like, that it is
impossible for him to do so."

"H-how can we . . . do that?"

"By getting married as soon as possible."

Bettina gave a little gasp and he went on:

"Once you are my wife, Bettina, it will be impossible for anyone to kidnap or insult you."

"I should feel . . . safer."

"Is that all you would feel?" the Duke enquired.

She looked at him, not understanding what he
was asking, and after a moment he said:

"I want you to tell me why you called for me
when you were frightened by Eustace. After all, your
father was nearer."

There was a silence after he had spoken.

Then as Bettina dropped her eyes shyly the
Duke put his fingers under her chin to turn her face
up to his.

"Look at me, Bettina!" he said. "I want to know
the answer to my question."

"I . . . I knew that . . . you would . . . save me."

"If I was there," the Duke added. "But how did
you know I would hear your silent cry, the cry that
came from your heart?"

It was difficult to take her eyes from his. Then
almost as if he compelled her to tell the truth Bettina
whispered:

"I knew . . . you would . . . hear me because . . . I
love . . . you!"

Even as she spoke she realised that the Duke
might not wish to hear of her love for him and quickly she added:

"I . . . I will not be a . . . nuisance like those . . .
other women. I will not worry you nor make scenes
. . . but I cannot . . . help . . . loving you."

"Any more than I can help loving you!" the Duke
answered, and his lips came down on hers.

For a moment Bettina felt only an astonishment that seemed to take the breath away from her body.

Then she knew that this was what she had been longing for; this was what she had been wanting ever since she had known the Duke.

She felt something warm and wonderful seep through her cold body, sweeping away the fear, the uncertainty, and even the jealousy she had felt of the other women who had loved him.

Then it became more wonderful, more glorious than anything she had ever known. It was as if all the stars they had looked at and the desert itself were part of the wonder of his kiss and the closeness of him.

It was part of the beauty of the Castle and there was music and flowers in his kiss and a rapture that seemed to run through her like a shaft of moonlight so that she trembled.

When finally the Duke raised his head, Bettina's face was radiant in the firelight and her eyes were shining like stars.

"I love . . . you! I love . . . you!" she cried. "I did not know . . . love could be so . . . wonderful, so perfect."

"Neither did I," the Duke said.

She looked at him for a moment. Then she asked:

"Are you . . . saying that you . . . love me . . . a little?"

"I love you as I have never loved anyone before in my life," the Duke replied. "In fact I have never known love until this moment."

"Is . . . is that . . . true?"

"So true that I can hardly believe it myself," he answered. "Actually I loved you the first time I saw you, but I would not admit it."

"The . . . first time?" Bettina asked.

She remembered how he had come into the Drawing-Room on the train early in the morning and she had been alone.

"When I saw you standing by the writing-table

with the orchids at your neck," the Duke said, "it seemed as if you were enveloped by light."

"Do you mean the... light that we... said was a sign of something very... special?" Bettina asked.

"The light in this case was a sign of love," the Duke said, "the love I have never known, my darling."

"I cannot... believe it! You are so... wonderful so... magnificent, and I cannot... help loving you but... why should you love... me?"

The Duke smiled.

"Perhaps it is because you are different from any other woman I have ever known before."

He reached out his hand as he spoke to touch her hair, which was falling over her shoulders.

"I have not known many good women," he said, "and you, my darling, are very good, very pure, and very innocent."

"I want to be good for... you," Bettina said. "I have prayed that I should be, but I never thought you would really... love me, and Papa said he thought you had never really... loved anybody."

"Your father was right," the Duke said. "I thought love was an illusion, something maudlin which women called romance. But when I saw you, my darling, I realised it was life itself—the life I had never known but had always missed."

"Can I... really make you... feel like... that?" Bettina asked.

"I have felt like that, as you say, ever since I have known you," the Duke replied. "And when we stood together looking at the stars it was very difficult not to take you in my arms and kiss you, to tell you how much you already meant to me."

"W-why... did you not... do so?"

"It was not the right place and I was involved with people with whom you should never have been associating."

Bettina knew he was speaking of Lady Daisy and Lady Tatham.

"That is what Lord Eustace said."

The Duke sighed.

"Eustace was right, and you will never know how jealous I have been of him."

"Jealous?" Bettina cried.

"I knew your father wished you to marry him. He had already told me so, and I thought at first it would be a very suitable match. It might have changed Eustace from the monster he has made of himself into a human being, but then . . ."

The Duke paused.

"Tell . . . me," Bettina whispered.

"I wanted you for myself."

He sighed again.

"I told myself I was much too old for you, and that you would never be able to cope with my kind of life."

"That is . . . what I am . . . afraid of," Bettina confessed.

"I did not realise at first that what I called 'my kind of life' was over—finished!" the Duke said. "I have grown increasingly bored with it over the years, at the repetition of parties and, my darling, a succession of different women."

He saw the sudden pain in Bettina's eyes and bent forward to kiss her again.

His lips were at first gentle, then as he felt the softness of them yield to his, he became more insistent, more demanding.

When he raised his head he said:

"There are so many different things for you and me to do—things I have never done before which will be very exciting, like starting off on a new adventure together."

"I think I am . . . dreaming all . . . this," Bettina said. "It is what I have longed for you to say . . . but what I was . . . sure I would never . . . hear."

"There is so much for us to discover about each other," the Duke said, "and we will start by going round the world, finding new places, making new friends."

There was no need for Bettina to answer him.

He saw the radiance in her eyes before she said with a little catch in her breath:

"S-suppose I . . . bore you?"

"If you do," the Duke said, "and if I bore you, it will be because we are not really in love. But I have a feeling, my lovely one, that we are very much in love, as I think our hearts knew we were when we looked up at the stars."

"I only realised I was in love with . . . you when you saved me from being swept overboard," Bettina said.

"I cannot bear to think that might have happened!" the Duke exclaimed.

He bent forward to kiss both her eyes, then her cheeks and the softness of her neck.

"I love you, God, how I love you!" he exclaimed. "But, my darling, you have been through a horrible experience and I must leave you to go to sleep."

"I do not . . . want you to . . . leave me."

She was too innocent to know what she was saying and the Duke's expression was very tender as he replied:

"It will not be long before that will never happen. We shall be together all day and all night, my precious, so that I can protect you and keep you safe in my arms."

He kissed her again, then he said:

"I will leave the communicating door open between our rooms just in case you are afraid. If you call out I will hear you."

"Will you first . . . look to see that the windows are closed?" Bettina asked.

"There is a straight drop of over thirty feet outside these windows," the Duke answered. "I assure you that Eustace cannot get in unless he has changed into a spider!"

He made Bettina laugh as he had intended.

He walked across the room and saw that all three windows were locked. Then as he came back towards the bed he said:

"Tomorrow we will make plans to be married at once."

Bettina gave a little cry.

"Can I ... ask you something?"

"What is it?" he enquired.

"You will not be ... angry?"

"I promise I will never be that with you."

"Then ... please ... could we ... possibly be married ... very, very quietly?" Bettina asked.

The Duke did not answer and after a moment she went on:

"I could not ... bear to have your ... friends there hating me because I am your wife ... and also ..."

"Go on!"

"I do not want ... to think of you on my ... wedding-day as a ... Duke. I just want you to be a ... man. A man whom I love and who ... God has given to me for my ... husband."

The Duke did not speak, and afraid of what she had asked, Bettina said quickly:

"But ... of course ... if you want something ... different, I will understand and do anything ... you want."

The Duke took her hand and raised it to his lips.

"I did not answer at once, my adorable one," he said, "because I was thinking I was the most fortunate man in the world to have found you! That is exactly how I would want my wife to think of me—as a man. And as a man, my darling, may I tell you that I love you with all my heart."

"Oh ... Varien!"

Bettina reached up her arms to put them round his neck.

Then as his lips held hers captive she knew that God had answered her prayers.

Chapter Seven

Bettina awoke and for a moment wondered where she was. Then she heard the sea beating against the port-holes and felt the roll of the yacht.

Yesterday the storm had been tumultuous and the Duke had insisted that she stay in bed, but now she thought it was not as rough as it had been.

Thoughts passed drowsily through her mind.

Then she felt something resting across her body and thought it was her husband's arm.

Without opening her eyes she put out her hand to touch it and encountered something soft and woolly which was also lumpy.

A voice beside her said:

"A happy Christmas, my darling!"

She felt a glorious rapture rise within her as she opened her eyes to see the Duke looking down into her face, his lips very near to hers.

"A happy ... Christmas ... Oh, Varien! I meant to say it first."

"You were fast asleep," he answered, "and looking very beautiful."

Her hand was still exploring what lay on top of her and now she gave a little cry of excitement.

"A stocking! You have given me a stocking for Christmas!"

She sat up in bed as excited as a child.

"I have not had one since I was twelve," she

said, "and it was such a disappointment when Mama
and Papa said I was too old for one."

"I think you are still young enough to have one,"
the Duke answered.

With her fair hair falling over her shoulders Bettina indeed looked very young and very lovely as she
gazed at the stocking which lay on the bed.

She recognised it as the sort of woollen stocking
the Duke would wear out shooting, and from the top
of it protuded half a dozen red-and-gold crackers.

The Duke, resting on his elbow, watched her
with a tenderness in his eyes that no-one had ever
seen before as she took the crackers from the stocking.

"We will pull these in a moment," she said, "but
first I want to see what is inside."

As she spoke she drew out what seemed only a
pretty, ornamental box, until she found that when
opened it played music.

"A music-box is something I have always wanted,"
she exclaimed, "and it looks very old."

"It is," the Duke replied. "It is French eighteenth
century, but I knew it was something you would like."

"How did you know that?"

"I noticed all the things that particularly pleased
you when we went round the Castle together."

She gave him a smile of undiluted happiness and
to herself she thought there had never been anyone
who had observed her so closely or who understood
everything that she felt.

"It is enchanting," she said, "but I thought our
presents were to be under the Christmas-tree in the
Saloon."

"These are secret presents," the Duke replied.

"How thrilling!" she cried. "Why did I not think
of secret presents for you?"

"You gave me one last night," the Duke said
softly, and she blushed.

The tune from the music-box tinkled to a close
and she set it down on the bed and once more put
her hand inside the stocking.

She drew out a monkey on a stick. It was a child's toy and she remembered owning one once when she was very small.

"Where could you have found this?" she asked.

"Actually a street-vendor was selling them outside my Club," the Duke smiled.

"I adore it!" Bettina said, pulling the string which made the monkey climb up and down the pole.

Again she put it down and explored the stocking.

This time she drew out an apple, an orange, a little box of the most expensive comfits, and another box which was Georgian and had been designed for ladies who wore small black patches on their faces beneath their powdered wigs.

"It is so pretty," Bettina exclaimed. "I shall keep it always on my dressing-table."

The next box was velvet and obviously came from a jeweller.

The Duke put his hand over hers as she would have opened it and said:

"Guess what is inside."

"I cannot imagine what it can be."

"Then look and see if it is what you want."

Bettina opened the box. Inside was a gold bracelet with letters in coloured jewels dangling from it.

She read them aloud.

I LOVE BETTINA

She gave a little cry of delight.

"How could you have thought of anything so original?"

"It is to wear on the yacht when the Alveston diamonds are too grand."

"I shall wear it every day ... please, darling Varien, put it on for me!"

He kissed her wrist, then fastened the bracelet, and she held up her arm so that the light coming through the port-holes made it glitter.

Now she thought the stocking was empty, but

there was something else inside and when she drew out a little black leather jewel-case she looked at it curiously as if it reminded her of something she had seen before.

Then when she opened it she gave an exclamation of sheer happiness, for inside was the small diamond star that her mother had left her and which her father had sold.

"How could you have found it? How could you have given me anything that I wanted so much? Oh, clever, clever Varien, I am so happy to have it."

"Your father told me that he had to sell it to buy you gowns to wear on our trip to Egypt," the Duke said. "I went to the shop and fortunately they had not disposed of it."

Bettina looked at it with a suspicion of tears in her eyes as it reminded her so vividly of her mother.

Then she threw herself down on the pillows beside the Duke and raised her face to his.

"Thank you ... thank you for my wonderful presents," she said, "but you have given me ... so much. I ought not to ... take more."

"They are signs of my love," he answered, "and I have every intention of giving you so many more things, my beautiful wife."

It seemed to Bettina that ever since their marriage only by giving could he express what he felt for her.

When they had been married very quietly with only Sir Charles present in the Chapel at the Castle she had prayed fervently as they knelt side by side in front of the altar.

She had begged God to help her break through all the barriers that the Duke had erected round his heart and that he would love her as she loved him.

She had thought it would be impossible to love him more than she did already but her love had increased and multiplied every day, every moment, and every hour they were together.

It was as if she had walked into a glorious dream, so dazzling as to seem unreal and yet at the same time vividly alive with a spiritual intensity she had never known before.

She had only to look at the Duke to feel that every nerve in her body vibrated to him like a musical instrument.

When he touched her, thrills ran through her and he aroused sensations such as she had never imagined.

When she came down the staircase of the Castle wearing the exquisite lace veil that had been in the Alveston family for generations and a tiara on her head, she knew that the fairy-tale of which her father had spoken was in fact coming true.

The Duke had said she was the Princess for whom he had been looking all his life, and she believed him.

At the same time, she knew that the aloofness he had cultivated or which had been forced upon him for so many years could not be swept away by a magic wand.

It could only crumble slowly beneath the wonder of their love, and it was for her and her alone to find the heart he had hidden so successfully from everybody else.

A few days earlier she had been afraid.

But now when the Duke's kisses had told her how much he wanted her, she knew that his need was not only physical but was also spiritual and sacred.

She faced honestly the task which lay ahead of her.

Yet, when he put the ring on her finger, when she heard his deep voice repeating the vows of the Marriage Service, she felt that they were in truth becoming one person.

'Our love comes from God,' she thought, 'and will endure however many difficulties there may be ahead.'

It was the Duke who had arranged when their wedding should take place and who decided how they should spend their honeymoon, with a speed which left not only Bettina but also Sir Charles breathless.

"You cannot really mean to go aboard so quickly!" he had protested in astonishment.

"Bettina wants to see the end of the Suez Canal," the Duke replied, "and to reach the Red Sea."

His eyes were twinkling as he spoke and he asked Bettina:

"Is that not true?"

"Can we really go back again?" she enquired, remembering how she thought she might never return when they had come home after the party at Ismailia.

"We are going to have a very long honeymoon," the Duke said, "and when we return we shall be an old married couple, and no-one will be the slightest bit interested in us."

She thought she knew why he was running away. At the same time, she thought it the most wonderful plan she had ever heard.

"I commend your idea as good common sense," Sir Charles said quietly.

"I thought you would understand, Charles," the Duke said, his eyes meeting those of his future father-in-law.

Both men were thinking of Bettina.

She would not be in England to hear all the spiteful things the Duke's past loves would undoubtedly say when they heard he was to be married.

She would also get used to the idea of being a Duchess and the inevitable responsibilities of her position while they cruised in the sunshine and explored new parts of the world.

"All you have to do," the Duke said to Bettina, "is to pack up your luggage again."

Then he added to Sir Charles:

"I do not like to think of you having a lonely Christmas, and so, Charles, I suggest you stay at the Castle and invite some of your friends to keep you company. There will be horses for you to ride and my wine-cellars are at your disposal."

"Do you really mean that, Varien?" Sir Charles asked.

Bettina slipped her hand in his.

"You must accept, Papa, and then we shall not feel guilty at going away and leaving you at Christmas-time. When I was a little girl it was always a very special time for us all."

Sir Charles had, therefore, accepted the invitation with undisguised pleasure and when the day after their wedding Bettina and the Duke drove away through the snow she had said:

"You have been so kind to Papa. I cannot think of anything that would give him more pleasure than to act as host in the Castle."

"He will keep the horses well exercised," the Duke said and she knew that in a way he felt embarrassed by his own generosity.

When they were alone the day before they were married Bettina had asked hesitatingly:

"What ... happened ... to Lord Eustace?"

"You need not think of him for some years at any rate."

"What do you mean?"

"I have sent him to look after some land we own in western Africa. He will find a great many reforms are needed there, and there are doubtless a number of injustices over which Eustace will enjoy making a scene."

"He ... agreed ... to go?"

"He did not have much choice," the Duke replied.

His voice was grim and Bettina said accusingly:

"You forced him to ... obey you."

"Yes—I will not have you frightened or worried because he is in England."

Bettina would have said she was no longer so afraid, but before she could speak the Duke kissed her.

Because of the rapture which flooded over her it was impossible to think of Lord Eustace or of anything but the Duke and how much she loved him.

She had felt before they married that there were so many things for her to learn about him, that she was afraid.

Yet when they were once again in the *Jupiter* he did not seem so awe-inspiring as he had against the background of the Castle.

The yacht too seemed redolent with happiness, now that there were no squabbling women aboard to spoil the atmosphere or Lord Eustace glowering at her with dark eyes.

Every moment she was with the Duke and close in his arms Bettina felt as if they were on a magic vessel sailing to secret destinations of utter bliss where no-one could disturb their happiness.

Because she loved him, she knew that now, as she had prayed, the barriers he had erected within himself were crumbling and beginning to disappear.

There was no longer the dry note in his voice, the hard look in his eyes, or the cynical twist to his lips.

Instead, his eyes as well as his words spoke to her of love and she often surprised a tender expression on his face which made her heart turn over in her breast.

She did not know that to the Duke she personified the flower with which he had identified her.

He was experienced enough to know that in her youth and her innocence there were many things he must teach her, but gently, so as not to frighten or shock her.

Bettina had no idea how strictly he controlled himself so that he wooed her in a way he had never before wooed a woman.

He realised because he was so gentle and understanding and because he evoked in her an ecstasy which made their love-making part of the Divine that she was like a flower opening its petals towards the sun.

Every day he awakened her a little more until last night he had ignited in her the flame he had longed for, which complemented the raging fire within himself.

It had been so perfect that he too had been thrilled and aroused in a way he had never known before in all his numerous love-affairs.

He had known as he fell asleep that he had found the magic touch-stone of love which all men seek and so few find.

"I love you! Oh, Varien, I love you!" Bettina said now.

He kissed her eyes, then her mouth, as he drew her closer to him. Her body was very soft against the athletic hardness of his.

"I can hardly believe it is Christmas Day," she said, "and we are here alone instead of having a huge ... and rather terrifying party in the Castle."

"That was something I never had any intention of having," the Duke answered.

He knew she was thinking of Lady Daisy, who had invited herself.

"It is so exciting having Christmas just with you," Bettina said.

"There will be many Christmases when you will want to have a party." The Duke smiled.

"It depends ... whom we invite."

"We will choose our guests together, as we will do everything else," the Duke answered, "and in case you are disappointed I am quite certain you will find that the Chef will provide us with a plum-pudding and lots of other traditional things which are usually very indigestible."

"Including, I hope, a bunch of mistletoe?"

"I can kiss you without that," the Duke answered.

He found her lips as he spoke and felt a little quiver go through her.

"Can I still excite you, my darling?"

The colour rose in her cheeks, her eyes were suddenly very shy, and she hid her face against his neck.

"Last night was so ... wonderful!" she whispered. "I felt as if you ... carried me up to the stars ... the stars we shall see when we reach Suez."

"We will stand and look at them as we did that night," the Duke replied, "and you can tell me once again that you feel it a privilege to be alive."

"And a privilege to be your wife," Bettina said with a passionate note in her voice, "and very, very privileged because you ... love me a ... little."

"Do you really think it is only a little?" the Duke enquired.

"I love you with all of me, and perhaps one day you will love me with all of you."

"I am not going to say that I love you as much as is possible for me to love anyone," the Duke replied, "for the simple reason that every day I find there are new depths to my love which I did not even know existed."

He raised his head to look down at her, at the flush on her cheeks, at the first dawning of desire in her eyes, at the breath coming quickly between her parted lips, at the rise and fall of her breasts beneath the thin silk nightgown.

"What is there about you that makes you so different from everyone else?" he asked.

He swept her hair back from her forehead as he said:

"You are very beautiful, your features are perfect, but it is so much more than that. Perhaps, my precious, it is the purity of your soul shining in your eyes and which speaks to my soul and I had forgotten I had one until I met you."

Bettina's eyes widened.

He had never spoken so seriously before, then she put har arm round his neck to draw his lips close to hers again.

"We belong to each other," she said. "I am sure now that we are one person, but, my beloved husband, you are the most important part ... and I am so very privileged to be a little ... bit of you."

"The bit that matters," the Duke replied, "because I realise that it is you who have found for us the secret of happiness."

"Which is ... love?" Bettina asked.

"Of course," he answered, "the love I thought I would never find and which was, not surprisingly, completely lacking in the places where I looked for it."

She knew that he was thinking of the gaiety and at the same time the emptiness of those who congregated at Marlborough House and at his own house in London.

Then he said almost as if he was speaking to himself:

"We still have our responsibilities, my beautiful wife, towards the place to which we have been born and 'the state of life to which it has pleased God to call us.'"

She knew what he was trying to say and she said in a low voice:

"You must help me not to make ... mistakes. I realise how ... ignorant I am ... but if you are there with me I shall try to do ... everything you want me to do."

"You are very young," the Duke said, "but there is so much wisdom in that small head of yours."

He kissed her forehead and added:

"We will not anticipate today what lies ahead in the future, but only be happy because this is our honeymoon and because we are together on Christmas Day."

"That is what I want ... and there is ... something I want to ... say to you."

"What is it?" the Duke asked.

She put her head back against his shoulder, then she said in a very low little voice:

"Last night I was thinking just before I fell asleep how ... wonderful you were and how wildly ... inexpressibly happy you have made me."

The Duke's arms tightened round her and he kissed her hair as she went on:

"I thought too of all the things you have given me—my magnificent engagement ring, the fur coat to come on this voyage, the gowns that we are to pick up at Nice, and now Mama's little diamond star. Oh, Varien, there are so many, many things!"

"And so many more I want to give you," he said. "I love you so much, my darling, that I would like to take the stars from the sky and hang them round your neck."

"That is what you have done," Bettina whispered, "but you have put them in my . . . heart."

"As they are in mine."

"I have not finished what I was telling you."

"I am listening."

"I was thinking that I had nothing to give you in return."

The Duke would have spoken but she put her fingers on his lips and he kissed them but he did not speak.

"I longed to give you a sign of my love, something which could not be bought with money, because I have none, but which would tell you how much I love you and how . . . grateful I am for . . . you."

There was a little pause; then Bettina, moving even closer to the Duke and holding on to him very tightly, said:

"Then it was almost as if a voice told me what my sign of love must be."

"Tell me," the Duke said tenderly.

"I will try to give you . . . lots and lots of sons, all just like . . . you."

"And I want lots of daughters like you, my precious."

There was a note in his voice that told Bettina he was deeply moved by what she had said and there was also a flicker of fire in his eyes.

"If we have children," she went on, "they will fill the Castle and it will not seem so . . . frightening for . . . me."

"You need never be frightened while I am with you," the Duke answered.

"And if you are . . . not?"

He knew how much lay behind this simple question and he bent his head until his mouth was against hers.

"Wherever I am—you will be," he said. "You

belong to me, Bettina, and I can never live without you. My body is yours and yours is mine, but so are our minds and our thoughts and our dreams. My life is indivisibly merged with yours; now and for eternity, we are one."

As if it was the reassurance she had wanted, it swept away the last lingering doubts in her mind.

As her lips, very soft and yielding, waited for his, she knew that the last barrier the Duke had erected within himself had fallen.

He was hers completely and absolutely, as she was his.

Then he was kissing her demandingly, possessively, passionately, and as she surrendered herself to the ecstasy and rapture of love he carried her towards the stars.

ABOUT THE AUTHOR

Barbara Cartland, the celebrated romantic author, historian, playwright, lecturer, political speaker and television personality, has now written over 200 books. Miss Cartland has had a number of historical books published and several biographical ones, including that of her brother, Major Ronald Cartland, who was the first Member of Parliament to be killed in the War. This book had a Foreword by Sir Winston Churchill.

In private life, Barbara Cartland, who is a Dame of the Order of St. John of Jerusalem, has fought for better conditions and salaries for Midwives and nurses. As President of the Royal College of Midwives (Hertfordshire Branch), she has been invested with the first Badge of Office ever given in Great Britain, which was subscribed to by the Midwives themselves. She has also championed the cause for old people and founded the first Romany Gypsy Camp in the world.

Barbara Cartland is deeply interested in Vitamin Therapy and is President of the British National Association for Health.

RILEY IN THE MORNING

BANTAM

New York   Toronto   London

Sydney   Auckland

Riley in the Morning

Sandra Brown

RILEY IN THE MORNING

Bantam Loveswept edition / November 1985

Bantam hardcover edition / January 2001

All rights reserved.

Copyright © 1985 by Sandra Brown.✓

LIBRARY OF CONGRESS CATALOGING-IN-PUBLICATION DATA

Brown, Sandra, 1948–

Riley in the morning / Sandra Brown.

p.   cm.

ISBN 0-553-10414-4 (alk. paper)

1. Separated people—Fiction.   2. Parties—Fiction.   I. Title.

PS3552.R718 R55 2001

813'.54—dc21

00-059869

Fic.

Published simultaneously in the United States and Canada

Bantam Books are published by Bantam Books, a division of Random House, Inc. Its trademark,
consisting of the words "Bantam Books" and the portrayal of a rooster, is Registered in U.S. Patent
and Trademark Office and in other countries. Marca Registrada. Bantam Books, 1540 Broadway,
New York, New York 10036.

PRINTED IN THE UNITED STATES OF AMERICA

RRH   10   9   8   7   6   5   4   3   2   1

RILEY IN THE MORNING

Dear Reader,

You have my wholehearted thanks for the interest and enthusiasm you've shown for my Loveswept romances over the past decade. I'm enormously pleased that the enjoyment I derived from writing them was contagious. Obviously you share my fondness for love stories that always end happily and leave us with a warm inner glow.

Nothing quite equals the excitement one experiences when falling in love. In each romance, I tried to capture that excitement. The settings and characters and plots changed, but that was the recurring theme.

Something in all of us delights in lovers and their uneven pursuit of mutual fulfillment and happiness. Indeed, the pursuit is half the fun! I became deeply involved with each pair of lovers and their unique story. As though paying a visit to old friends for whom I played matchmaker, I often reread their stories myself.

I hope you enjoy this encore edition of one of my personal favorites.

—SANDRA BROWN

CHAPTER ONE

Ms. Cassidy, dear?"

"Yes?"

"So sorry, darling, but your table simply isn't large enough."

"Damn," Brin muttered under her breath as she struggled with the zipper at the back of her dress. She twisted around to check in the mirror what was causing it to stick. When she turned, an electric curler slid out of her hair, leaving a heavy strand to fall over her eye. She shoved it off her face, looping it around one of the hair-curler pins that radiated from her head like a space-age halo. "Arrange everything as best you can, Stewart. Has the bartender arrived yet?"

"I *have* arranged everything as best I can," he said petulantly. "You need a larger table."

Brin's arms fell heavily to her sides. Glancing at the harried image in the mirror, one eye artfully made up, the other as yet untouched, she called herself a fool for hostessing this party in the first place. She had timed everything down to the second. She didn't need any kinks in the tight schedule, such as a stuck zipper and a querulous caterer.

Turning, she flung open the bathroom door and confronted Stewart, who stood with his pale hands on his hips, wearing an expression just as sour as hers.

"I don't have a larger table," Brin said irritably. "Let's see what we can do. Is the bartender here yet?" On stocking feet she hurried through the bedroom, down the stairs, and into the dining room, where a buffet was being set up. Her dress was slipping off her shoulders, but then, there was no need to be too concerned about modesty in front of Stewart.

Two of his assistants were standing by, arms crossed idly over their chests, as though waiting for a bus. She shot them exasperated looks that didn't faze them in the slightest.

"Jackie said he'd be here by now," Stewart said of the missing bartender. "I can't imagine what's keeping him. We're *extremely* close."

"Why doesn't that make me feel better?"

Brin spoke the question under her breath as she studied the table. The food on the silver trays was attractively arranged and lavishly garnished, but the trays were jammed together, overlapping in places. Some extended over the edges of the table. Stewart might be difficult and aggravating, but he knew his stuff, and she couldn't argue with him. "You're right, we'll have to do some rearranging."

"It's that ghastly centerpiece," Stewart said, pointing with distaste. "You should have let me select the flowers. Remember I told you—"

"I remember, I remember, but I wanted to choose my own florist."

"Can't we remove the thing? Or at least let me rearrange it so it isn't so . . . so . . . ." He made a descriptive gesture with his hands.

"You're not to touch it. I paid a hundred dollars for it."

"You get what you pay for," he said snidely.

She faced him angrily, hooking the errant strand of hair around another pin when it slipped from the first. "This has nothing to do with money. The florist happens to be a friend of mine, and she's been in the business longer than you've been alive."

I must be agitated, Brin thought. *Why am I standing here arguing with smug Stewart, when I'm only half dressed and forty guests are due to arrive at any moment?*

She returned her attention to the crowded table. "Can you leave some of the trays in the kitchen and replace the ones on the table as they empty?"

Stewart's hand fluttered to his chest and his mouth fell open in horror. "Absolutely not! My darling, these dishes are planned to alternately soothe and excite the palate. They're a blend of tart and—"

"Oh, for heaven's sake!" Brin cried. "Who will know in what order their palates are supposed to be soothed or excited? These people will just want to eat. I doubt they'll pay attention to anything except whether the food tastes good or not."

Gnawing her cheek in concentration, she scanned the table again. "All right," she said, her mind made up, "set that bowl of marinated shrimp on the coffee table in the living room. Have a cup of toothpicks nearby. And you," she said, pointing to one of the indolent assistants, "move that cheese tray over there by the bar. I think there's room for that chafing dish of Swedish meatballs on the table by the sofa. That should make room on the table."

The three young men rolled their eyes at one another. "You're a gastronomical philistine of the worst sort," Stewart said snippishly.

"Just do it. And where's that bartender you promised me? Nothing's set up."

"He'll be here."

"Well, he'd better be here soon, or I'm going to start deducting from your bill."

The doorbell chimed. "See?" Stewart said loftily. "No cause for panic. That's him now." He swished toward the front door before Brin had a chance to.

"Who are *you?*" The disembodied voice asking the rude question was deep and demanding.

Brin recognized the voice immediately and felt the earth drop out from under her.

"Oh my dear, I'm positively dying!" Stewart cried

theatrically, his hands aflutter. "I can't believe it. She didn't tell me *you* would be among the party guests."

"What the hell are you talking about? What party?" the voice asked in a surly growl. "Where's Brin?"

She forced herself into motion and went toward the door, stepping in the line of vision of the man standing on the threshold. "Thank you, Stewart," she said quietly. "I believe you have work to do."

She was amazed at how calm she sounded. On the inside, chaos reigned: Her vital organs were doing backward somersaults; her knees had turned the consistency of Stewart's famous tomato aspic; all the blood had drained from her head. But outwardly she presented a facade of aloofness that should have won her an Oscar at least.

After Stewart had moved out of earshot, she looked at the man. "What are you doing here, Riley?"

"Just thought I'd drop by." He propped his shoulder against the doorjamb and let his eyes—*damn those blue eyes*— drift over her. He seemed amused by the curlers in her hair, the unfastened dress she was having a hard time keeping up, and her stockinged feet.

"Well, you should have called before you came, because you couldn't have picked a more inconvenient time. You'll have to excuse me. I have guests due to arrive in a few minutes. I haven't finished my makeup—"

"That's not a kinky new fad? Making up just one eye?"

"—or touched my hair," she finished, ignoring his teasing. "The bartender hasn't shown up yet. And the caterer is being a colossal pain."

"Sounds like you need help." He shoved his way inside before Brin could stammer a protest. "You guys have everything under control?" he asked the three caterers, who were staring at him in awe.

"Everything's perfect, absolutely perfect, Mr. Riley," Stewart gushed. "Can we get you anything?"

"Riley," Brin ground out between her teeth.

"Hmm?" He turned around, supremely unconcerned about her apparent agitation.

"May I see you alone? Please."

"What, now?"

"Now."

"Sure, honey. The bedroom?"

"The kitchen." She walked stiffly past the three gaping caterers, saying, "Carry on," in as firm a voice as she could muster.

Angrily she pushed open the swinging door and stepped into the kitchen. She usually liked this room, with its classic black-and-white-checked tile floor, its spacious countertops, and well-arranged appliances. Tonight it was cluttered with party paraphernalia, but she didn't notice any of it as she pivoted to face the man who was barely two steps behind her.

"Riley, what are you doing here?" She repeated the question with undisguised asperity.

"I wanted to see you."

"After seven months?"

"Has it been only seven months?"

"And you chose tonight by chance?"

"How was I supposed to know you were giving a party?"

"You could have called."

"It was a spur-of-the-moment decision."

"Isn't everything you do?" He frowned, and she drew a deep breath. No sense in getting unpleasant. "How did you know where I was living?"

"I knew." His eyes slowly took in the kitchen and the twilit view beyond the wide windows. "A Russian Hill address. I'm impressed."

"Don't be. I'm house-sitting. A friend of mine went to Europe for two years."

"Anybody I know?"

"No, I don't think so. She's an old school chum." Brin guarded against looking at him. When she looked at him, her eyes got greedy and wanted to take in every detail. She wouldn't punish herself that way.

"Lucky you. The day you walk out on me, your friend takes off for Europe. You couldn't have planned it better. Or did you plan it?"

Her eyes flew up to his. "Don't start this now, Riley."

"Don't you think seven months is long enough to stew about it? I want to know why my wife just checked out one day while I was at work."

Uneasy, she shifted from one foot to the other. "It wasn't like that."

"Then what was it like? Tell me. I want to know."

"Do you?"

"Yes."

"Well, you've taken your sweet time to find out. The reasons behind my leaving couldn't have been very important to you. Why did you get curious tonight, after seven months? Did one of your public appearances get canceled? Did you find yourself alone and without anything spontaneous or interesting to do?"

"Whew! Hitting below the belt, are we?" He socked her lightly in the tummy. Actually a little below the tummy. And well below the belt.

She jumped back in alarm at the effect even that touch had on her. "Will you please leave, Riley? I have guests coming. I've got to comb out my hair. I . . ."

Her voice faltered when he reached up and tugged sharply on the loose strand. He was smiling. "It's cute when it's all tumbled. Reminds me of what you look like when you first get out of bed."

"I . . . I haven't even finished dressing."

His eyes slid hotly down her body, all the way to her feet. "Your toes are so sweet."

"Riley."

"And sexy. Remember when we discovered each other's toes and what a turn-on dallying with them can be?"

"Riley!" Her fists were digging into her hips as she glared up at him. She was becoming more vexed by the moment. Vexed and aroused.

"In the hot tub, wasn't it?"

"Oh! There's just no talking to you." She spun on her heel and headed for the door. "I'm going upstairs. When I come down I expect you to be gone."

"Wait a minute." He caught her arm and drew her up short. "Your zipper's not done up all the way. No wonder that dress keeps falling off your shoulders. Not that I'm complaining. I could make a meal out of your shoulders. Are you trying to entice me with those brief glimpses of forbidden flesh?"

"Riley—"

"Hold still." His hands were at her waist. His knuckles brushed the skin of her back as he struggled to work the cloth from beneath the bite of the zipper without tearing it. "You almost mangled it."

"I was in a state even before you showed up."

"Over a zipper?"

"That was only the tip of the iceberg."

"Troubles?"

"Not 'troubles,' exactly. I just wanted everything to be nice tonight."

"So you really are having a party."

"Of course. What did you think?"

"I don't know. Maybe that you were taking up with Stewart's sort."

"Very funny. Aren't you done yet?"

With every heartbeat it was becoming more difficult to stand still. The touch of his hands was so achingly familiar. The scent of his breath as it fanned her neck was memory-stirring, and this husbandly chore of zipping her dress reminded her of other times, happy times she had tried to forget.

"Who's the party for?"

"The people I work with."

"At the radio station?"

So he knew where she was working now. Well, that hadn't taken any great detective work on his part. It had been published in all the local newspapers. In fact there had been quite a splash in media circles when Brin Cassidy left Jon Riley and his popular morning television talk show, *Riley in the Morning,* to accept a job producing a radio phone-in discussion program.

At the time there had been speculation on the future of their marriage, too. Living down the gossip columns, the published innuendos, the myriad invasions of privacy, had been hard to do. But that hadn't been the hardest thing. The hardest thing had been learning to live without Riley.

And now he was here, near, touching her again, and it took every ounce of self-discipline she had not to turn in his arms and hold him against her.

"Hurry, please, Riley."

"You still haven't told me what the occasion is."

"Mr. Winn's birthday."

"Ah-ha. That explains the cake." He nodded toward the tiered chocolate confection on the countertop.

"Haven't you fixed that zipper yet?"

"So Abel Winn himself will be here. President and CEO of the Winn Company."

"Do you know him?"

"I've met him once or twice." He finally succeeded in wresting the fabric free of the zipper and pulled it up. He fastened the hook and eye, which was a mere six inches above her waist, and bent his knees to reduce his height. He pecked a soft kiss directly between her bare shoulder blades, as had been his habit when they had shared a house, a bed, their bodies.

Brin gasped softly.

Stewart sailed through the door in time to see Brin's cheeks turning pink and Riley's grin widening as he rose to his full height again. "Well," the caterer drawled, "I take it you two know each other."

"He's . . . uh . . . he's my . . . uh . . ."

"Husband," Riley calmly supplied. "Can we help you with something?"

"Husband?" Stewart squeaked.

"Husband," Riley repeated, unruffled.

"Weeeell." Stewart gave Brin a once-over that was catty and covetous at the same time.

"What was it you wanted?" Riley asked.

His brisk tone snapped the caterer to attention. "I just came to tell Mrs. Riley that—"

"Ms. Cassidy," Brin corrected.

"Oh, certainly, Ms. *Cassidy*. I'm Stewart, by the way," he said to Riley with an ingratiating smile.

"Stewart." Riley nodded.

"A pleasure. Yes, well, Steve and Bart have done a simply *marvelous* job rearranging the trays. They'll be circulating all night to make sure they're replenished. I pinched a few of the most offensive buds—only a few, dear—from that centerpiece. It all looks quite smashing now."

"Fine," Brin said tightly, wishing with all her mind that

Riley would lift his hands off her shoulders and put space between the front of his thighs and the backs of hers. Unfortunately her heart wanted no part of that wish.

"It might get a bit crowded when I flambé the Bananas
Foster. I hope we don't set anyone on fire."

She could feel Riley's silent chuckle vibrating through
his body. "I'm sure I can trust you to be careful."

"One teeny-weeny, tiny problem," Stewart added.

"What?"

"Jackie hasn't arrived yet. I can't imagine what got into
him."

"Damned if I'd hazard a guess," Riley said for her ears
alone.

She clamped down on her lower lip to keep from laughing out loud. A few minutes ago the absence of the bartender
had sent her into a tailspin. Now that seemed a mild crisis,
too insignificant to worry about. What she had to cope with
now was the thrill that zinged through her every time she felt
the front of Riley's trousers brush against her buttocks.
"We'll make do, Stewart."

"The boys wanted me to ask, is *he* staying?" He pointed
to Riley.

"Yes." "No." They answered in unison, Riley in the af-
firmative, Brin in the negative.

"Oh, I just adore sticky little situations like this," Stewart
cooed.

"This isn't a sticky little situation. Will you please excuse
us? We'll give you back the kitchen in just a moment," Brin
said by way of dismissal.

"Of course." He left, after winking at her and blowing Riley a kiss.

Brin did an about-face with military precision. "You can't stay, Riley. I'm asking you to leave."

"You need me." She wondered if that statement carried a double meaning but decided it didn't when he added, "To tend bar."

"One of Stewart's assistants can do that."

"You heard him. Steve and Bart will be circulating all night."

"Then I'll handle it."

"The hostess? Don't be ridiculous. And Stewart is out because he'll be handling the food and pinching offensive buds. But if he tries to flambé *my* banana, I'll punch him out."

She gritted her teeth to keep from laughing. Dammit, she didn't want Riley to be funny and charming. She sure didn't want him to smile that slow, sexy smile or look at her with those eyes that were so achingly, beautifully blue.

"Face it, Brin. You haven't got a choice. Now, get your adorable tush upstairs and finish dressing. Brush out your hair. Give the lashes on your left eye a lick of the mascara wand and let me take over down here. Oh, and don't forget your shoes."

Her father had always said that a good soldier knew when to surrender with dignity. Brin recognized defeat and gave in to it graciously. "You can start getting things ready, but if Jackie shows up, I'll expect you to leave without causing a scene."

"What do I do first?" Riley shrugged off his jacket and tossed it across a chair at the kitchen table.

He was wearing a sports shirt and jeans under the poplin windbreaker. Expensive, true. Tasteful, true. The height of fashion, true. But she didn't want him to look so devastatingly gorgeous when he had seen her, for the first time in seven months, looking like the survivor of a shipwreck. "You're not even dressed for a party," she grumbled.

"California chic."

"But this is a semiformal affair."

"So I'll be an oddity." He had raised his voice, slightly but discernibly. Yet it was all honey and velvet when he added, "Besides, I could name times when you preferred me without any clothes at all." His eyes penetrated hers. "*Numerous* times."

She wet her lips. In this skirmish, he was the victor, unconditionally. "Lemons and limes are there," she said, pointing to the countertop, where the fruit was still wrapped in plastic bags. "Slice them. Drain those jars of olives, cocktail onions, and cherries. Put them in those shallow dishes. The bar's adjacent to the dining room."

"I'll find it. Glasses?"

"Dozens of them. At the bar."

"Ice?"

"Two full chests under the bar."

"Setups?"

"They're there too."

"Piece of cake," he said arrogantly. "Where's a knife?"

"Second drawer to the right of the sink."

He found one and wielded it with the flourish of a fencer. "Scat."

Before she could lunge across the kitchen and kiss him just for being so damn cute, she did exactly as he suggested. Upstairs at the marble dressing table in the bathroom, she fumbled with the eye crayons, eye-shadow wands, shading blushers, and lipstick brushes. It was a wonder she didn't end up looking like a clown-school dropout. Miraculously, the results both highlighted her best features and appeared beautifully natural.

As she was stepping into her shoes, she heard the doorbell chime. She hoped Stewart would act as temporary host while she put in her earrings, misted herself with fragrance, added a final pat to her hair, and slid a thin diamond bracelet on her wrist. She leaned down to smooth her stocking. The bracelet caught on the sheer nylon and put a run in it.

With a barrage of unladylike cursing, she rummaged in her hosiery drawer, hoping that this wasn't her last pair of near-black stockings. It wasn't, but by the time she had put on the new pair, she was in a tizzy. The doorbell continued to ring with maddening frequency.

And the hostess hadn't yet put in an appearance!

It was Riley's fault, she thought as she rushed down the stairs. How dare he sabotage her party? How dare he ruin tonight for her?

Riley, Riley, Riley.

Why had he selected tonight to seek her out? He had had seven months to contact her, seven months in which she hadn't received so much as a telephone call from him. But doing things in an ordinary, mannerly fashion wasn't Riley's style. No, no, he had picked tonight to come see her, the worst possible night for him to show up on her doorstep.

He's looking well. *Who are you kidding, Brin? He looks positively wonderful.*

Perhaps a trifle thinner. *Your imagination. God knows there are plenty of women willing to cook for him if he asked them to.*

Didn't you notice more gray hair? *It only makes his eyes look bluer.*

No matter how good he looks, or how charming he acts, he has no right to crash your party. And no matter how shaky you are, you are *not* glad to see him. *And the Golden Gate Bridge isn't in San Francisco.*

Taking a deep breath, she stepped off the bottom stair and into the friendly confusion of the party.

"Brin, we were beginning to think you'd skipped out on your own party."

"You look beautiful."

"Great dress. Why haven't you ever worn it to work?"

"Because we wouldn't have gotten any work done, you bozo."

Brin was surrounded by the guests who had already arrived. She exchanged pleasantries with them, apologizing profusely for being late coming downstairs. "Help yourselves to the buffet and bar."

"We already have. And don't think we didn't notice the celebrity guest."

Past their shoulders Brin spied Riley at the bar. He was

handling highballs and wine bottles as adroitly as a juggler. A ring of adoring females had formed around him. She was suddenly glad she had told her new colleagues that her separation from Riley was an amicable one. With any luck, no one would find his presence here tonight odd.

"Riley put in a surprise appearance," she said distantly, watching as Riley playfully ate a cherry proffered by one of his admirers. The woman giggled as his teeth closed around it and lifted it from her fingers.

"You mean he wasn't invited?"

Brin didn't like being backed into a corner, and recognized a loaded question when she heard one. Shaking herself out of her trance, she beamed a nonchalant smile and said, "Please excuse me. The caterer is still at the door welcoming my guests."

She shouldered her way through the thickening crowd, joking and smiling welcome as she went. "Thank you, Stewart," she said as she relieved him at the door. "You've gone above and beyond the call of duty."

"It'll be reflected on my bill. I've got popovers in the oven. They could have burned, you know."

Before the evening was out, she was going to smack him. It seemed destined to happen.

"Hello, so glad you could come. Let me take your coats." She turned on the charm as group after group of guests filled up the house. When she opened the door to Abel Winn, her plastic smile gave way to one of heartfelt warmth. "Our guest of honor. Happy birthday, Abel."

He was a man of indeterminate age, immaculately groomed, compactly and sturdily built. He wasn't very tall, but he exuded self-assurance and had the bearing of a born leader. His eyes reflected an intelligence that bordered on shrewdness. His smile for Brin was genuine, and softened the features of an otherwise stern, Teutonic face.

"Brin, dear, you shouldn't have done all this on my behalf." He leaned forward as he clasped her hand between both of his. "But I'm glad you did. I love parties. Especially when they're in my honor."

She laughed with him and ushered him inside. "There's food and drink aplenty. Help yourself."

"Won't you join me?"

"I still have hostess duties to carry out. Maybe later."

"I'll look forward to the time." He drew a more serious expression. "And speaking of time . . ."

"It's running out. I know. Tomorrow is the deadline you gave me."

"Have you made a decision?"

"Not yet, Abel."

"I was hoping your acceptance would be my birthday present tonight."

"It's a big decision." Inadvertently her eyes sought out Riley. She was disconcerted when she met his blue gaze from across the room. There was a crease of disapproval between his dark brows as he stared at her and Abel. "Please give me until tomorrow. I promise to give you my answer then."

"I'm certain it will be the one I want to hear. We'll talk

later." Abel patted her hand before releasing it and moving into the midst of the party.

Someone had turned on the stereo. Conversation had risen above the level of the blaring music. The party was in full swing. It might have had an inauspicious beginning, but Brin was gratified to see that it was going well.

"It's all wonderful, Brin. You've outdone yourself." The woman who sidled up to her was dressed in jade satin. Brin recognized her as a member of the sales department at the radio station.

"Thank you."

"How did you ever manage?"

"Don't ask," Brin returned with a grimace. "Right up to the last minute it was disaster with a capital *d*."

"Well, it all came together beautifully. Your idea to have Jon Riley act as bartender was inspired. You must have a *very* friendly separation. How'd you ever talk him into it?"

"Just lucky, I guess."

The woman was so busy gobbling up Riley with her eyes that she failed to catch Brin's sarcasm. Objectively, Brin tried to view him through the other woman's eyes. He was heart-stoppingly handsome. Salt-and-pepper hair, cut and arranged to look as rakish as possible. Yet boyish, with a few strands carelessly falling over his forehead. An open invitation for a woman to run her fingers through it.

His face was lean and angular, the bone structure lending itself to a television camera's most discerning angle. A strong jaw. Slender nose, slightly flared over the straight, narrow lips. Lips that had dimples in each corner as strategically placed as punctuation marks.

His eyes were a color of blue the heavens would envy. "When you look at me, it's like being raped by an angel," she had told him once during a romantic interlude. He had thought she was just flattering him. He hadn't understood, but another woman would have. When he looked at a woman in that special, private way, his eyes pierced straight through her. It was violation, but the sweetest, dearest penetration imaginable.

His physique was tall, almost lanky, but hard and muscular. He could drape a shapeless burlap sack over that rangy body and make it look like high fashion. Clothes had been invented for bodies like his. He looked good without clothes too. Six feet four inches of tanned skin. Shadowed by soft, dark body hair. Chest hair that would make a woman's mouth water.

And he knew it.

As Brin and her companion continued to watch, Stewart went behind the bar and said something to Riley, embellishing it with wild gestures. Riley said something back, something that was obviously not to Stewart's liking. The caterer put his hands on his hips and screwed his face up into a comical pucker. Riley's gaze searched the room until it landed on Brin. Since his hands were busy, he jerked his chin up, indicating that she was needed.

"Excuse me." She wended her way through the crowd to the bar. "What is it?"

"Ask him," Riley said tersely.

"Well?" She looked at Stewart.

"Some *person*," Stewart said, "a terribly crude bruiser from Oklahoma or someplace equally as barbaric, is drinking *beer*, of all the ungodly things."

"The point, Stewart, the point," Brin said.

"He asked for salted nuts. Nuts! I mean, really! And I asked *him*"—he emphasized, pointing limply at Riley—"if he had any nuts and—"

"And I told him to stay the hell away from me."

Oh, Lord. She was getting a killer of a headache, and it hurt all the way down to her toenails. "I think I have a can of nuts in the kitchen. I'll get it."

The kitchen was almost as quiet and serene as a church, in contrast to the racket and chaos beyond its door. Brin went into the butler's pantry and switched on the light. She moved aside boxes of cereal and crackers, searching for the can of cashews she remembered seeing there several days ago. A shadow fell across her. "Just a minute, Stewart, and I'll find them. I know they're in here somewhere."

"I'm sure Stewart will be glad to hear that."

"Riley!" she exclaimed, spinning around at the sound of that honey-coated voice, which was a sound technician's dream. "Where's Stewart?"

"I left him mixing a Scotch and water. I think he can handle that."

Her eyes rounded with surprise when he reached for the doorknob and closed them into the closet. It was actually a roomy pantry, but with two people closed inside it, the dimensions seemed to shrink. "What are you doing?"

"Locking you in."

"But—"

"I've missed you, Brin."

"This is—"

"And I don't intend to wait another second for a taste of you."

CHAPTER TWO

His mouth, from the instant it touched hers, was hungry and demanding. There was no preliminary investigation, no subtle teasing, no testing the waters, no time for her to protest or prepare herself for the onslaught. In a heartbeat his lips were on hers. Hotly possessive. Provocative. Persuasive.

Brin's rational self took a giant step backward, separating itself from her and leaving her defenseless and responsive. The taste, the texture, the heat of the kiss were all so familiar. She sank into it as one snuggles into an old, comfortable robe.

No other man could kiss like Riley. Oh, she remembered that thrusting pressure of his tongue. Yes, yes, just like that. Deep and swirling and greedy, as though he'd die for want of her. And that feathering caress against the roof of her mouth.

The withdrawal, slow and sensuous. A leisurely sweep against her teeth. A damp licking of her lips.

"I've missed you. So much. I couldn't stand it another day. I had to see you. Brin, Brin . . ."

He kissed her again, and she heard wanton sounds emanating from her own throat. Her body responded in that warm, fluid way that inevitably leads to making love.

He was hard.

Yes, she remembered that too. His virility.

And now she felt it against the velvet-clad softness of her belly. If she didn't stop this now, things would get out of hand and she would hate herself later. Her body's yearning was powerful, but she fought it.

"Riley, no." The command didn't carry much weight, since it was issued on a breathy sigh. Brin was amazed that she could speak at all. His lips were moving softly over her neck, taking love bites. His tongue dipped into the triangle at the base of her throat. "Ahh, Riley, no, please."

"You still like that, do you?"

"No."

"Liar."

And her whimper proved him right. His hand moved down to her breast and she trembled against him. "Stop, Riley."

"Stop what? This?"

His agile thumb did some of its best work. She groaned. "I mean it. Stop. This is crazy."

"This is beautiful." He buried his face in her neck even as his caress brought about the response he craved. "So beautiful."

Another kiss followed, less urgent than the first, but a thousand times more evocative. She went limp against him. "This is so unfair."

"Damn right. I want you naked."

"No, I mean . . . hmm . . . I could kill you for this."

His laugh was little more than a silent gust of breath in her ear. "How can you blame me? You look delectable. I always liked you in black."

The black velvet creation was a rare find, and Brin had known it the moment she saw the dress on a sale rack in Magnin's. It had long dolman sleeves that tapered to her wrist. The skirt was narrow and fit her hips to perfection. It was banded just below her knees with black satin. The neckline was high and cut straight across from the point of one shoulder to the other. Virtually backless, the dress was scooped out to mere inches above her waist.

She wished now that there were something between her skin and Riley's fingers as they lightly strummed her spine. Why was she letting him do this? She was weak, that was why. Where he was concerned, she had never exercised any willpower. She did foolish, irresponsible things; she acted rashly and paid later. Hadn't she grown up any? Hadn't she learned her lesson yet? Was she going to sacrifice her independence for the sake of a few kisses? No!

She pushed him away. He didn't release her, but lifted his head and stared down into her turbulent eyes. "Still mad at me? Why don't you tell me what I did?"

"I was never mad at you."

"Oh, I see. You left because you *weren't* mad at me."

"I don't want to play word games, Riley. And even if I did, I can't now. Do you realize I have a houseful of people who—"

"Do you still keep your secret cache of peanut M&Ms?"

"What!" Exasperation and surprise went into her exclamation.

"Now, don't pretend you don't know what I'm talking about," he chided. "That little basket of M&Ms you always hid in the pantry."

"I did not!"

"You did too," he countered, laughing and tweaking her nose. "Because you didn't want me to know you were snitching them once you'd sworn off chocolate."

"You were snitching them too!" She blushed to a bright crimson when she realized that she had admitted her own guilt.

While they were talking, Riley had been searching through the shelves of canned goods and cannisters of rice and pasta. "Uh-huh!" He gave a triumphant cry as his hand lighted on the telltale basket of candy, hidden behind two cans of grapefruit juice. He brought forth the basket and popped one of the M&Ms into his mouth. Before Brin could deflect his hand, he forced one between her lips.

"Why didn't you tell me you knew?" she asked sulkily.

"You knew I knew. Didn't you?" He asked the soft, prodding question with such an endearing grin, she couldn't resist smiling back.

"Yes. Why did we pretend it was a secret?"

"Because the game was so much fun. We didn't want to spoil it." The mischievous spark in his eyes mellowed to a steady blue flame. "We had a lot of fun, Brin."

"A lot of problems too."

"Most marriages do. I wasn't aware that we suffered an inordinate number."

"I know." She spoke quietly, lowering her gaze. "They were my problems, not yours," Brin confided.

"So you suffered in silence. Why didn't you talk to me about them?"

"I don't want to discuss it." She reached for the doorknob and pulled on it. The door didn't budge. Riley's hand was splayed wide on it, holding it closed.

"*I* want to discuss it, dammit."

"This is not the time."

"It's past time. It's been seven months! I want to know, and I want to know now, why my wife, my bride, walked out on me."

His temper flared. It frequently did. His fury might terrorize cameramen and engineers, even station managers, but Brin had learned early in their relationship not to give way. She certainly couldn't quail beneath it now. Though he dwarfed her physically, she faced him with matching belligerence. "I refuse to talk about it. It wouldn't do any good."

"This 'problem' is one we couldn't work out, is that it?"

"Yes! Something like that."

"I don't believe that."

"Take my word for it."

"Another man? Is it another man?"

"No."

"What else could it be? What else would be so final that it couldn't be worked out?"

"You're way off track, Riley."

"Abel Winn?"

"What?"

"Did you leave me for Abel Winn? Did you leave me to sleep with him?"

She slapped him. Hard. It was the first time either of them had ever struck the other. Brin was shocked to see her handprint form on his cheek. If her palm hadn't been stinging like a million pinpricks, she wouldn't have believed she had done it. A trickle of fear ran through her when she considered what Riley might do in reprisal.

But instead of getting angry, he smiled. He knew from her violent reaction that his accusation couldn't be true. He felt a vast sense of relief. A knot of misery began to unravel in his chest. The thing he had dreaded most didn't exist. Brin's reason for leaving him wasn't love for another man. He had sought her out tonight prepared to do anything to get her back. Make any compromise. Heal any hurt. But if she had loved another man, especially one as wealthy and powerful as Winn, it would have been hopeless.

His smile made her forget her momentary fear and only served to enflame her more. "How dare you say something like that to me?" she hissed. "I was faithful to you. That you could think . . . Oh!" She yanked on the doorknob, and this time he let her go. But as she left the pantry he was half a step behind her.

"You always were your most adorable when you were mad," he taunted. "You were mad the first day we met, remember?"

"No."

He gripped her upper arm and spun her around to face him. She landed against his chest, head thrown back, throat arched, breasts heaving. "The hell you don't," he growled. Then he kissed her soundly.

"Well, honestly," Stewart said from the doorway, "every time I catch you two alone you're in a clench. What's going on? Are you making it or not?"

Brin extricated herself from Riley's arms and left him to make their excuses to Stewart. She reentered the dining room and made a beeline for the bar, hastily pouring herself a glass of chilled white wine. Striving for composure, she moved away before Riley resumed his post at the bar.

That man! she fumed silently. His ego would make a case study. His nerve . . . well, it went beyond description. He thought that after seven months of separation he could just waltz into her house, lock her in a pantry, and without so much as a "How have you been, Brin?" kiss her the way he had.

She smiled placidly at her guests, who seemed not to have noticed that she had been missing. Abel had. When her eyes locked with his, they were inquiring. She suddenly wondered if her hair had been mussed by Riley's eager hands.

Were her lips as red and pulsing as they felt? Were her clothes disarranged? In just those few minutes in the pantry Riley had been able to arouse her to a feverish pitch. Was it visible on the outside?

Pasting a false smile on her face, she engaged the gregarious couple standing next to her in conversation about their three-month-old daughter.

But Brin couldn't keep her mind on feedings and diapers and pediatricians. It seemed determined to wander back to that day Riley had reminded her of, the one when she first met him. . . .

It was Brin's first day on the new job, and she was justifiably nervous as she made her way from her assigned space in the parking lot to the back door of the studio, where she would be admitted by a guard when she presented her pass.

"You've taken on a tremendous amount of responsibility," the personnel manager had warned her several days earlier. "He's not an easy man to work with. Artistic temperament, you understand."

She understood. Artistic temperament, my foot. Jon Riley was afflicted with the star syndrome. It was a unique disease that caused suffering in anyone caught in the tyrannical path of the afflicted. "I have every confidence that I can work with Mr. Riley," she had said assuredly.

The personnel manager cleared his throat. "Yes, well . . ." His expression was skeptical. "We've tried out several producers, both men and women, for *Riley in the Morning*. We haven't hit on the right combination of talents and personalities yet."

"You mean Mr. Riley's temper tantrums have scared the others off." The man's brows had jumped high in surprise at her bluntness. "I won't be so easily gotten rid of."

Brin only hoped she could maintain that level of confidence, as she made her way down the dank, dim hallway, which smelled of stale cigarette smoke and seemed characteristic of the two television studios where she had worked prior to taking this job.

She heard the shouting and weeping before she even shoved open the padded door and entered the cavernous studio. It was like stepping into the Mad Hatter's tea party without properly preparing oneself, or possibly entering the lions' cage without a whip or chair. Either way, the chances of survival seemed remote.

"Where was your head? Huh? Never mind. Let me hazard a guess." The guess that the man—Brin immediately recognized him as Jon Riley—made was obscene, and she winced when he voiced it. "You've done stupid things before, ignorant, asinine things, but this tops it! This is the great, big granddaddy of screwups!" He ran his hand through his hair and paused for breath.

The victim of this verbal flagellation was a woman who appeared to be in her early twenties. She stood in front of Riley with her face buried in her hands, shoulders hunched, sobbing wetly and noisily.

Assorted members of the crew reacted differently to the argument. One cameraman, his arm negligently flung over the end of his expensive camera while a cigarette dangled from his lips, looked for all the world like he was watching a play and enjoying it immensely.

A girl wearing jeans, sweatshirt, and sneakers was sitting on the concrete floor with her legs folded Indian fashion, chewing gum for all she was worth and occasionally blowing bubbles. Two young men were held in thrall by the pages of an issue of *Penthouse* magazine. Another, the most amazing of all, was sound asleep, his chair propped against the wall on its two back legs.

Riley paced back and forth in front of the crying young woman, shooting poison glances in her direction. He spat out his words like bullets from a machine gun. "What am I supposed to do? How do you suggest I get this straight? We've got a show to get on tape. It airs tomorrow. *Tomorrow!* And I'm surrounded by morons like you who can't even . . ." He stopped, running out of either vituperative words or breath. Brin wasn't sure which.

The young woman took advantage of his pause. "The new producer is supposed to be here today. Maybe she can calm her down."

"She, she, she. What producer? They've no doubt hired some deb whose tits are bigger than her brain. Spare me another producer. *You* were supposed to be acting as producer, and look what a fiasco you've managed to pull off."

"I'm sorry. I . . . I don't know—"

"Exactly."

The girl wailed and covered her face again. Brin had

heard all she could stand. She took the steps necessary to bring her into the pool of light in the otherwise unlit studio. "Excuse me."

The star of *Riley in the Morning* whirled around and stabbed her with the bluest eyes she'd ever seen. They were legendary. Brin could see immediately why they were worthy of every comment she'd ever heard about them.

The victim of Riley's abuse stopped crying long enough to look up at Brin, a ray of hope shining in her tear-filled eyes.

A long gray ash fell from the cameraman's cigarette as he lazily shifted it from one side of his mouth to the other.

The sleeping man's chair hit the floor as he came awake abruptly, probably because a quiet, calm voice in that studio was as jarring as a fire alarm somewhere else.

Her voice had also called attention away from the *Penthouse* centerfold. Two pairs of eyes peered at Brin over the edge of the magazine.

The girl sitting on the floor stared up at Brin over her burst bubble.

"Don't tell me. Let me guess." Riley, standing arrogantly, with his hands propped on his hips, gave her a cursory once-over.

"That's right, Mr. Riley. I'm the deb with bigger tits than brains." Someone snickered. Someone else coughed. Riley's blue gaze dropped to her chest. Brin stood her ground. "As you can see, they aren't impressively large. I assure you my gray matter is. Would anyone care to tell me what's going on?"

They all started talking at once. Brin held up both hands. "Mr. Riley first, please, since he seems to be the most upset."

"I never get upset, Miss . . . ?"

"Cassidy. If you'd seen fit to be present at my interview, you'd know my name, Mr. Riley. We could have had a production meeting then, and possibly this fiasco, as I heard you refer to it, could have been avoided." Score one for her.

"I leave at two every afternoon," he said without a flicker of warmth in his cold blue eyes. "Your interview wasn't until four. I wasn't about to hang around for two hours."

"But if you had," she said sweetly, "you wouldn't be ranting and raving this morning, would you?"

"Now, just a minute—"

"If I overheard correctly, we don't have a minute to spare," Brin snapped. "Do you want to get that show of yours on tape, or not? Tell me the problem. Let's fix it. Then if you want to tear into me you can, when we both have the time."

He gnawed the inside of his cheek, rocking back and forth slightly on the balls of his feet, looking like a man about to explode. Brin calmly stared him down. Finally he started talking in short, angry bursts.

"Dim Whit, here, told my guest—who happens to be a flaming freak with pink hair—to be here an hour before she was supposed to be. She is furious for having to wait while we set up. We've practically locked her in a room to keep her from screaming the building down. She's behaving like a lunatic, almost hysterical."

"That seems to be the general condition around here, from what I've seen so far," Brin remarked dryly.

Riley gave her a murderous look, but for the sake of time continued without comment. "The studio wasn't set up and ready for taping because *she*," he said, pointing to the cowering young woman, "forgot to put us on the schedule, which is already tight at best. In an hour we have to turn the studio over to production, because they're taping news promos this morning."

When his recital came to an end, Riley looked at her as if to say, "There. You asked for it; you got it. Now fix it." He looked almost satisfied. Smug. Daring her to respond.

Admiral Cassidy's daughter had never backed down from a dare.

Brin turned to the sniveling young woman Riley had referred to as Dim Whit. "What is your name?"

"Whitney," she said almost inaudibly.

"Whitney Stone, the sales manager's daughter, whom I've been appointed to wet-nurse through apprenticeship," Riley said.

"Shut up," Brin said, spinning around to face him. The cameraman whistled softly. The gum chewer nearly swallowed the wad in her mouth. "Your childish tirade wasn't helping much, was it?"

Before Riley could offer a rebuttal, Brin looked back at the girl. "Stop crying. That isn't doing us any good either. Now, the first thing I want you to do is get Mr. Riley a cup of coffee. I think he can use one. Then go upstairs to the control room and see if a director and sound engineer are available. If not, find them. Tell them I'm sorry the taping this morning wasn't scheduled and that I'll see to it a mistake like this never happens again. Got it?"

"Yes, ma'am." She fled the room as though escaping execution.

"You, you, and you," Brin said, pointing to three idle studio crewmen, "strike this news set and get Riley's ready."

"But the night crew's supposed to do that after the newscast. We—"

Brin glared at the objector. "Do it," she said succinctly.

They exchanged glances all around. The one who had been sleeping shrugged and pulled himself out of his chair. The others tossed down the magazine and ambled toward the news set, grumbling to each other.

"Put out that cigarette," she said to the cameraman. "You can't properly operate a camera with a cigarette either in your mouth or in your hand. No more smoking on this set. Is that understood?"

The man ignored her. "Hey, Riley, can she do that?"

Brin spoke up. "I can. I just did. If you don't like it, find yourself a job on another show. Just remember all those graduates of the video institutes who would love to fill your shoes. And you," she said looking down at the girl, who still had her legs folded beneath her, "keep the chewing gum in your mouth or you're off the set too. And while you're making up your mind, check out both Mr. Riley's microphone and one for his guest."

She turned to Riley, refusing to countenance the temper brewing behind those sapphire eyes. "Who is your guest for this show?"

"Pamela Hunn."

Pamela Hunn *did* have pink hair, and Brin was tempted to smile, but refrained, knowing that the way she played this hand might determine the outcome of the game. "Where is she?"

His chin jutted forward. "Dim Whit can show you." The young woman was just then crossing the studio, carrying the cup of steaming coffee like a peace offering. She stumbled over a cable and sloshed the coffee on the floor. Riley cursed beneath his breath. But he took the coffee from her with a gruffly spoken "Thanks."

"I suggest you put on some makeup, Mr. Riley," Brin said, hoping Whitney hadn't heard Riley's unkind epithet. "I'll come for you when we're ready. Do you have any material on Ms. Hunn?"

"Some," he replied curtly.

"Shouldn't you be studying it?"

With that terse suggestion she left the studio, asking Whitney Stone to show her where they had sequestered the enraged Pamela Hunn. She was a designer of haute couture, who had become immensely popular in recent years because her clothes were worn by the female lead of a weekly television series.

When Brin opened the door to the "green room," which in this instance was actually dirty beige, she was confronted by a woman whose face was almost as florid as her fuzzy hair. She had colorless beady eyes under a prominent brow. Her thin nose was pinched even tighter by fury.

"I demand an explanation for this outrage. I've never . . . well, I can't even begin to tell you how this has . . . Insult of the highest caliber, that's what it is."

She sputtered the words through lips that were perpetually pursed. When she realized she was speaking to someone she hadn't seen before, she stopped long enough to survey Brin haughtily. "Who are you? That's one of my blouses."

Brin thanked whatever angel was responsible for her having chosen to wear this particular blouse on this particular day. She could have chortled when Riley had told her who the offended guest was because she knew she would have an ace in the hole in dealing with her.

"My name is Brin Cassidy, and yes, this is one of your designs, Ms. Hunn. I saved my money for months to buy something with your label in it, and I can't tell you how much I love my blouse."

Pamela Hunn sniffed. "It's a gorgeous garment, of course. It would be on anybody, but you wear it exceptionally well. Size six? Four, maybe. The fabrication was inspired. The sleeve fairly flows with every movement, but it wouldn't have if I hadn't insisted that it be cut just so."

For several seconds she studied her creation with unabashed pride, then she sniffed again, as though she'd smelled something unpleasant. "You haven't said who you are in this menagerie. I'll have you know, young woman, that I have been a guest on Johnny Carson's *Tonight Show, Good Morning*

America, 60 Minutes, and *The Merv Griffin Show*. I've never, *never* been treated so shabbily. This is positively the garbage can of television shows. The armpit of—"

"You're absolutely right, Ms. Hunn. I couldn't agree with you more. If I were you, I'd refuse to do the show and storm out. Why should you subject yourself to a television interview after the way you've been treated? Why do them any favors? Imagine, you, the virtuoso of American designers, being handled like an ordinary guest, like an . . . an *actress* or something. Don't they realize you're an artist?"

Brin drew herself up as though she had had her say. In a quiet, deferential tone she asked, "Shall I call you a cab? Or did you come by limousine?"

"I . . . I . . . uh . . . drove myself. Occasionally I like to. Only occasionally, you understand. For recreation."

"Of course. Come, Ms. Hunn, let me usher you out. We've kept you entirely too long, and your time is so extremely valuable. Is that a portfolio of sketches? Don't forget it. How unfortunate that the audience will be denied seeing your designs because of the incompetence of the imbeciles around here. Stupidity is rampant on all levels of society, isn't it? Even in the fashion industry, I'll bet."

She was walking smartly at Pamela Hunn's side, praying that she was taking the right hallway toward the exit of the building. The intersecting corridors were an unfamiliar labyrinth, and she wondered what explanation she would give Pamela Hunn if she took a wrong turn straight into a broom closet. Her heart was hammering. Would her bluff work?

She smiled at the designer. "Didn't I read that you're doing an exclusive fashion show here in the Bay Area?"

"At Neiman's, yes. Tomorrow."

"How wonderful! Maybe I'll be able to attend. I only hope *someone* does."

The high heels of the designer's pointed-toe European shoes virtually screeched to a halt. "Why wouldn't they come? Why wouldn't I and my fashions draw a crowd?"

"Well, Ms. Hunn, *Riley in the Morning* has a large viewing audience, even if it is incompetently produced. But don't worry," she said, patting the other woman's rail-thin arm, "there'll probably be lots of women who'll see your fashion show publicized through another media."

"But—"

"And I didn't believe a word of what they said about Rachel Lamiel after she refused to do a local television show." She urged Pamela Hunn forward, but the woman didn't budge.

"Lamiel? She refused to do . . . What did they say?"

"Please," Brin said in a conspiratorial whisper. "You're asking me to be indiscreet."

"I won't tell anybody. What did they say about Lamiel?" Her skinny nostrils were quivering.

Brin glanced around with the wariness of someone about to impart a state secret. "They said that her designs were lousy and that she didn't want to advertise the fact before the fashion show was sold out. But as I said," she rushed to add, "*I* didn't believe that was the reason she flew into a rage and refused to go on television, as she had promised to do." She nudged the designer onward, hoping Pamela Hunn wouldn't guess that the tale she had just told was completely apocryphal. "Now, we've taken up far too much of your time, and I apologize for the error and the inconvenience we've caused you. I'll see to it—"

"Wait a minute." She wet her lips nervously and blinked furiously. "You really do look attractive in that blouse."

"Thank you."

"I would suggest a brighter color next time. The fuchsia, perhaps."

"Do you really think so?" Brin asked obsequiously.

"I didn't catch your name, my dear."

"Brin. Brin Cassidy."

"Well, Brin, you've been such an absolute doll that I've decided I'm going to do this tired little interview after all."

Brin spread her hand wide over her heart, which at that moment was pumping with glee. "Oh, Ms. Hunn! What can I say? You're being far too gracious and forgiving."

"Please," the designer said, raising her hand as though granting a papal blessing. "That's part of being a professional."

By the time Brin led her into the studio, Pamela Hunn was practically purring. "Whitney, would you please get Ms. Hunn a cup of coffee? Cream or sugar?"

"Neither, my dear. We must watch our figures, you know." Brin laughed with her, while the crew looked on in stupefaction. "Sit here on this sofa, Ms. Hunn. So tacky, isn't it?" She looked toward the gum-chewing girl. "Careful how you attach her microphone. This blouse is silk." The designer missed the discreet wink she gave the girl.

Brin felt as if she had put in a hundred years rather than half an hour at her new job, but Pamela Hunn was situated on the set, wired for sound, and simpering under her adoration. It choked her to cater to an infantile ego, but if that would get this first interview on tape, so be it.

"How did you do it?" Whitney asked worshipfully as she led Brin to Riley's dressing room. "She called me a great, gawky girl totally without grace."

"At least she alliterated." When Whitney stared back at her blankly, Brin went on, "I stroked her ego."

Whitney stared at Brin with undiluted admiration. "You sure did a good job."

"Thanks. Speaking of egos, let's see what frame of mind Mr. Riley is in."

She knocked once on the door, but didn't wait for his permission before marching in. "We're ready for you on the set."

Riley was standing in front of the theater mirror, a towel tucked into his shirt collar. He was holding a sponge and a compact of base makeup in his hand; a small saucer of water and his coffee cup were on the dressing table. "You and I had better get something straight right now, Miss . . . what was it again?"

"Cassidy," she said tightly.

"Yeah, Cassidy." He turned from the mirror to face her.

"*I* run the show around here. Nobody else. I let you get by with some high-handed maneuvers this morning because it was an emergency. But don't think that just because you can push other people on the set around, it includes me. Is that clear?"

Without releasing her from a glacial glare, he moistened his sponge, dabbed it into the compact of pancake makeup and spread some on the tip of his nose to cut the shine under studio lights.

Unperturbed by his warning and his intimidating stare, Brin calmly said, "We roll tape in two minutes, Mr. Riley. If you're not on the set by then I'll make a formal complaint to the production manager. And by the way, you just dipped your makeup sponge in your coffee."

She slammed out before he had a chance to speak. But she had to hand it to him: Furious as he was when he stormed onto the set, by the time the cameras were rolling, he was all pro.

Charm oozed. His voice held just the right amount of confidentiality, which had won the hearts of housewives pausing to watch his program between cycles of the clothes dryer, and secretaries clustered by the dozens around office coffee machines to gossip about him. If he didn't listen avidly to every word Pamela Hunn said, if he didn't have an earnest interest in the sketches the designer displayed and expounded upon, then he was a tremendous actor.

As soon as the show was in the can and Ms. Hunn had been escorted out, Brin called a production meeting for everyone associated with *Riley in the Morning*. Some of the crew's surliness had dissipated. Her handling of this morning's crisis had won her their respect if not their liking.

During the meeting she laid down a list of rules, regulations, and assignments, and firmly made it known that she expected them to be adhered to.

"You can be replaced." She was smiling when she said it, but her voice carried a discernible trace of threat. "*Riley in the Morning* is number two in the ratings during its time slot. By the next rating book, I want us to be number one and stay there. If you don't want to cooperate, get out now. Nothing is going to keep me from realizing my goal." As though on cue, her eyes slid to Riley. "I'd like to see you now in your dressing room, Mr. Riley."

Her heels tapped on the concrete floor as she left the studio and the properly subdued and silenced production crew. She was waiting in the hall outside his dressing room door by the time Riley caught up with her. He opened the door, bowed, and swept his hand wide, indicating that Brin should precede him. He followed her in and, without offering her a seat, flopped down on the sofa, working at the knot on his necktie. Brin remained standing in the middle of the room.

After consulting a notebook she said, "Every morning after the taping session is finished, Whitney will bring you a file on the next day's guest. Study the compiled information overnight. And from now on I won't tolerate any of your temper tantrums."

"You won't, huh?"

"No. I won't. And stop terrorizing Whitney."

"Dim Whit? She's used to it."

"For reasons I can't fathom, she adores you. But if she were a St. Bernard instead of a sensitive, impressionable young woman, I wouldn't let you talk to her the way you did this morning."

"You wouldn't *let* me?"

"What time did you go to bed last night?" she asked, as though he hadn't spoken.

"What?"

"You heard me."

He stared at her for a long moment. She watched his frown slowly reverse itself into a sly smile. "To *bed* or to *sleep*?"

She gave him a tired look and sighed. "I couldn't care less what goes on in your bed, Mr. Riley."

"Oh, no? Then why ask?"

"You force me to be blunt. You look like hell." She was rewarded by his dumbfounded expression. Apparently he wasn't accustomed to having his looks unfavorably criticized. "From now on get a good night's sleep before coming in to videotape the shows. And no wine the night before. It makes your eyes puffy."

He shrugged off his insouciance and sat up straight. "What the hell—"

"And if your eyes have bags under them anyway, I suggest you hold an ice pack on them for at least fifteen minutes every morning after you get up."

He wagged his index finger at her. "Let me tell you what you can do with your ice pack."

"I think that's all," she said, snapping her notebook closed.

"Not quite." He bounded off the sofa and caught her as she reached the doorway, gripping her by the shoulders.

"Release me."

A grin tugged at one corner of his lips. " 'Release me'? Didn't you forget the 'you cad'?"

"Let me go, Mr. Riley, or I'll—"

He burst out laughing. He laughed long and hard. His eyes were sparkling as they moved from the top of her head to the tips of her toes and back up. Jon Riley looked at his new producer, really looked at her, for the first time.

He saw a head of short, dark, curly hair, bobbed to just below her jaw. Dark brows arched gracefully over eyes the color of aquamarines, shot through now with sparks of anger. A pert nose. A kissable mouth. Oh, yes, a very kissable mouth, with a sulky lower lip he'd love to capture in a playful bite.

And most interesting of all, a shallow vertical cleft that nicked the edge of her chin and made it look damned impudent. She was cute and sexy and fiery, and if he hadn't made it an ironclad rule never to mix business with pleasure, he would see just how hot that fire inside her burned.

"You pack quite a wallop, don't you, Miss Cassidy?" he asked huskily after his laughter had subsided. "A tiny package of woman chock full of explosive dynamite. This is going to be interesting."

She worked herself free of his hands, and knew she succeeded only because he chose to let her go. She opened the door. "I'll see you in the morning, Mr. Riley."

"I wouldn't miss it for the world, Miss Cassidy."

The sound of his laughter had followed her down the hall that day. She had all but run from it, from him, because she had known, even then, that after having been touched, emotionally and physically, by Jon Riley, she would never be the same. . . .

CHAPTER THREE

"Earth to Brin. Come in, Brin."

"What? Oh, I'm sorry. I was—"

"I'll say. How can you daydream during a party? Some of us are ready to leave, but didn't think we should until we sing 'Happy Birthday' to the boss."

"Of course," Brin murmured, trying to pull her thoughts back into the present. "I'll speak with the caterer to see if the cake is ready."

She glanced at Riley on her way into the kitchen. He was still behind the bar, still dispensing drinks and grins, but his eyes were on her as she moved across the room. And from the intensity with which they burned, she suspected he knew where her thoughts had been.

Stewart was in the kitchen, already preparing to light the

candles on the birthday cake. "I guess it's time for the cake," Brin said.

"I guess so," he said, snidely implying that he thought it was past time.

When all the candles were lit, Stewart held the swinging door open. Brin pushed the small wheeled cart into the dining room. Everyone turned and began applauding when they saw the spectacular cake. There followed a rousing chorus of "Happy Birthday" and Abel Winn was pushed forward through the crowd to blow out the candles, which he successfully accomplished in one breath.

He accepted everyone's hearty birthday congratulations and laughed good-naturedly at the jokes made about advancing age. Holding up his hands and begging for silence, he made a short speech.

"Thank you all for coming tonight and sharing my birthday with me. Those of you who have to work tomorrow . . . tough," he said bluntly, and everyone laughed. "There'll be no excuses for hangovers. You'll have Brin to blame for your excesses tonight. She is a hostess without equal." He turned to her and kissed her cheek affectionately.

Flustered, she asked Stewart to slice and serve the cake. Abel accepted the first slice, but drew Brin aside when everyone crowded forward to sample the dessert. Abel set the plate of cake on an end table when they managed to reach a semi-private corner of the room.

"I meant what I said. Tonight's been special."

"I'm glad."

"And it's because of you, Brin."

Brin was aware that Riley was glowering at them from across the room. She smiled up at Abel brightly. "Thank you. It was my pleasure."

"I know this isn't the time to discuss business, but—"

"No, it really isn't, Abel," she said hastily as, from the corner of her eye, she watched Riley round the end of the bar and start making his way toward them.

"Please let me finish. Before you give me your answer tomorrow, I want to embellish our offer. How does forty thousand a year sound?"

"Extravagant." Too late. Riley was standing just behind Abel, looming over him like a dark bird of prey. Brin wondered why Abel didn't feel hot breath on the back of his neck.

"Perhaps it is a bit extravagant," Abel said, chuckling. "But I'm prepared to pay it to seduce you into accepting this job."

"You're too generous, and it sounds wonderful, but I still haven't decided." Didn't Riley have enough manners not to eavesdrop? Why didn't he go away? Why had he shown up at all, tonight of all nights, when her future hinged on this decision? She certainly didn't need Riley cluttering her mind.

"The second year you'll get a raise and start earning a percentage of the profits. Naturally, the company will cover all your moving expenses."

"I'm not too keen on moving to Los Angeles."

Winn frowned, thinking. "I want you to be happy. The company owns several houses down there. You can rent one from us for the cost of the utilities. There's one near the beach you might enjoy."

"Abel! I can't let you pay for my housing. Please, let's not talk about it any more tonight."

"But I must have your answer by tomorrow, and I want to entice you into accepting. Tonight's my last chance."

"If I turn down the job, it's not because you haven't made the offer attractive enough."

"Very well," he said, looking disappointed. "I can see that you're a woman of integrity, who can't be bought. Talking about money unnerves you."

What unnerved Brin was seeing the malevolent expression on Riley's face. Abel must have noticed her absorption with something over his shoulder, because he turned around. "Oh, Mr. Riley. I'm trying to talk Brin into making a career change. You weren't very smart to let her go, you know."

Abel Winn smiled pleasantly into the threatening face frowning down at him, but the smile never reached his eyes. The atmosphere between the two men was as hostile as that between two male beasts competing for the favors of a female.

At last Abel said, "Brin, there's a group at the door waiting to say good night. Shouldn't we move over there?"

Without waiting for her compliance, Abel took her elbow and guided her forward. She had no choice but to go with him, and as hostess she should have been at the door anyway as the crowd began to thin out.

Still, she felt bad about deserting Riley, who looked so brooding and angry. And that sentimental feeling made her impatient with herself. Why should she care what Riley thought? She had left him months ago. In all that time he hadn't made any effort to contact her. Until tonight he'd been indifferent to their separation.

He was out of her life. Out of her system. And she was determined he remain out of both.

"You'll think about all I've said?" Abel asked as she held his coat for him half an hour later.

"I promise."

"And I'll have your answer tomorrow?"

"Yes."

Everyone but Stewart and his crew had left. She and Abel were alone at the door. He clasped her hands between both of his. "I know you'll give me the one I want," he said like a man accustomed to getting his way. "Good night, Brin. Everything was splendid." He kissed her cheek again, and she got the uneasy impression that with the least encouragement from her, he would have turned it into more than a fraternal peck.

Lord forbid! She had been down that road once. Mixing professional and personal relationships was deadly to the nerves, not to mention the heart and emotions. Never again. She had lived with one super ego, and, as much as she liked Abel Winn and respected his business acumen, she recognized an ego that would never enjoy sharing the limelight with anyone, especially a woman. Just like . . .

Riley? Quickly her eyes scanned the room. It was empty. Where was Riley?

She bade Abel a final good-bye, locked the front door, and went into the kitchen. Stewart was packing up the last of his supplies. The back door was standing open. Steve and Bart were loading a panel truck parked in her driveway.

"Have you seen—"

"The hunk?" Stewart finished her question for her. "No. We were just lamenting that. He must have slipped out without even saying good-bye. Bart's simply crushed."

"Oh hush!" Bart mouthed as he hefted a crate of dishes to his shoulder.

Their bickering wasn't doing Brin's headache any good. She only wanted to be left in peace. And blessed silence. As she wrote out the check to cover Stewart's bill, she swore she wasn't disappointed that Riley had left just as abruptly as he had appeared.

"You forgot to deduct the fee for the bartender," Stewart said, looking at the amount of the check.

"Consider that your tip."

"You really are a doll. I hope we'll work together again." Stewart squeezed her shoulder before going out the back door and closing it behind him. Brin locked it and turned to face the littered kitchen. Stewart's fee didn't cover cleaning up her own dishes, and nothing was where it belonged.

She sighed, knowing she would never rest if she left the mess till morning. But before she tackled it, she was going to change her clothes. She hauled herself upstairs and entered her bedroom.

At the door she came to an abrupt standstill. Riley

was stretched out on the bed, his head propped up against the headboard, casually thumbing through the latest issue of *Broadcasting*.

"Everybody gone?"

"What are you doing here?"

"Resting. Do you realize I was on my feet for almost four hours straight?"

"You know what I mean," she cried angrily. "What are you doing here? In my bedroom. On my bed. I thought you'd gone home."

"Home?" he asked, tossing the magazine aside. "I don't have a *home*. I have a *house* that used to be a home . . . when I shared it with my wife."

She turned away from him, kicking off her shoes. Facing the mirror, she ran her hands through her hair. "I'm tired."

"You look it. Come lie down." He patted the space beside him on the bed. In the mirror he looked as tempting as the apple must have looked to Eve, and just as dangerous.

"Not on your life."

He laughed. "Why? Because you remember how much fun we had when we used to come home from parties?"

Exactly. And if she did cross the room and lie down with him, they'd make love, and then she'd be in the same rut as before. She couldn't survive the climb out of it again. The first time had nearly killed her. "I don't remember."

"Yes, you do. That's why you're afraid to lie down beside me. I wonder why it's so much fun to make love after a party. Is it because you're relaxed and usually in a good mood? We had some of our best times in bed after a party."

"Why won't you leave me alone? I've told you I'm not going to talk about this tonight."

"Do you still have that black lacy garter belt you wore when you dressed up?"

She whirled around, wondering if he could see through her clothes. "No."

He flashed a knowing smile. "Liar. You've got it on now."

"I do not!"

"Prove it."

"No."

He started laughing, and she ducked into the bathroom to keep him from seeing her own smile. "What are you doing?" he called.

"Changing clothes."

"That's silly, isn't it?"

"What? Changing clothes?"

"No, taking cover to do it. I've seen you, you know. There's not an inch of your glorious skin that I can't describe in vivid detail."

In the bathroom, Brin unzipped her dress and peeled it down. She glanced at the garter belt around her hips and smiled. It had always stirred him to passion, though he'd never needed much titillation. The evocative words he called through the door brought a rosy blush to her skin.

"I'll bet you're wearing those panties that match the garter belt, aren't you?"

She shoved that very scrap of satin and lace down her legs and stepped out of the garment. "No."

"I can just imagine you standing there in those sheer black stockings."

She rolled them down her legs with careless speed. Cursing herself for a fool for even playing this childish game with him, she finished stripping until she was naked. Hastily she pulled on another pair of panties, an old pair of jeans, and a sweatshirt. After shoving her feet into a pair of moccasins, she went back into the bedroom.

"Charming," he said blandly.

"If you don't like my attire, you can leave." She stalked past the bed on her way to the door. He lunged off the bed and caught her by the seat of her pants. She screeched, but couldn't escape his grip in time, and found herself thrown across the bed on her back, with him stretched above her. He was grinning as he pinned her down.

"Let me up."

"Uh-uh. You get a certain glint in your eyes when you're feeling prissy and need to be taken down a notch or two. Give you an inch and you'll take a mile." He nuzzled her ear. "I'd like to give you a lot more than an inch, Brin."

"That's vulgar."

"Damn right, and you used to love it. The naughtier I talked, the better you liked it."

"I—Oh, stop." He had started tracking her ribs with his fingers. She was extremely ticklish. "Riley, I mean it now, stop!"

"Say please."

"Please," she gasped. "Please."

The tickling subsided, but his hand slid beneath the

sweatshirt and stroked her stomach. "Bet you do have on those panties."

"Bet I don't."

"What do you bet?"

"Name it."

"A kiss?"

Sure of winning, Brin said, "You're on."

His blue eyes speared down into hers. She grew very still. He unsnapped her jeans and pulled the zipper down. His eyes skated down as he pushed the cloth aside.

He didn't see the black satin panties, but another pair just as sensuous, made of light blue silk. He closed his eyes as a wave of longing swept over him. When they came open again, he touched the smooth, soft skin of her abdomen.

"I win," Brin whispered shyly, suddenly submissive under the thoroughly masculine heat in his eyes.

"I welsh."

His hand slid over the silk panties, then inside them to the silk beneath. Making a low growling sound deep in his chest, he lowered his head. He kissed her navel, wantonly, hotly, relishing it with his tongue.

Brin was transported back, back to so many moments of passion such as this. She felt the familiar tendrils of desire twine through her system. Before she realized what she was doing, her hands were tangled in the silver-frosted strands of his hair, clasping and unclasping in a tempo that matched the gentle but thorough lashing of his tongue.

Her body was totally compliant, but her mind clung to a remnant of reason. "No, Riley, no."

"Oh, yes."

"No." She groaned with a mixture of frustration and arousal as he manipulated the spot he knew to be the most sensitive. "No!"

He lifted himself over her until his breath was striking her face in warm gusts. "Why? You want me."

"No."

"You *do*. You're my wife."

"Not anymore."

"There aren't any documents to that effect."

"It's not official, but—"

"All right, so you walked out. I let you go. I gave you space. Distance. Time. How long is this game of yours going to last, Brin?"

"It's not a game!"

"You won't let me make love to you?"

"No."

He rolled away from her, flopped onto his back, and covered his face with both hands. For long moments he lay there, breathing like a bellows, his chest heaving. He was still aroused. One glance at his tight-fitting jeans testified to that. Brin tore her eyes away, afraid that even now she might give in to what she wanted more than anything in the world, to have Riley inside her again. To hell with pride. She wanted Riley.

But he removed his hands from his face and rolled to a sitting position on the side of the bed. "No, I guess it isn't a game. A few hours, overnight, several days. That might be classified as a game. But not seven months. Whatever the reason you left me, it was serious, wasn't it?"

"Yes, very." She struggled to a sitting position and refastened her jeans, looking at him with troubled eyes. His smile was gentle and sad. He touched her cheek with the back of his finger.

"Let's go clean up the mess."

Taking her by the hand, he led her down the staircase. "I wish you would just go, Riley."

"Not yet."

"Please." Too many more scenes like the one upstairs and her icy resolve would thaw. It was dangerous to be around him. That was why she had made the separation quick and clean and absolute.

"Why do you want me to leave? Do you expect Winn back?"

She yanked her hand free of his. "No. I told you there wasn't anything like that between us."

"I saw you playing kissy-face."

"We weren't playing kissy-face."

"I saw him kiss you at least half a dozen times."

"Oh, for heaven's sake. He kissed me on the cheek a few times. Tiny tokens of appreciation."

"Yeah, well," he said, dumping ashes from a crystal ashtray into a plastic trash bag he'd taken from the kitchen, "I don't like other men kissing my wife, no matter how much they 'appreciate' her."

"Coming from you I find that laughable."

"What's that supposed to mean?" He loaded a tray with dirty glasses from the bar while she scooped up napkins and paper coasters and crammed them into the trash bag.

"It means that you've kissed your share of other men's wives. I don't remember a time we were out in public that some woman didn't come up and throw her arms around you. You always kissed back."

"That goes with my job."

"You didn't seem to mind it."

"Wait a minute!" He snapped his fingers as though a light had just come on inside his head. He looked at her with genuine disbelief. "Is that what this is all about?"

"What?"

"The separation. You saw some broad kiss me, and that provoked you into moving out?"

"Don't be ridiculous, Riley," she said, vexed that he could think her so petty. "If that were it, our marriage wouldn't have lasted the fifteen months it did before I left."

Brin didn't want to pursue that train of conversation, so, as they entered the kitchen carrying the party debris, she asked, "Are you hungry? You didn't have much time to eat."

"I nibbled, but I could stand something." He opened the refrigerator and pondered its contents. "By the way, you never did thank me for saving your neck tonight."

She paused in the act of tying shut the filled trash bag. "Thanks, Riley," she said with soft sincerity.

He glanced over his shoulder and winked. "Just so you appreciate me." He came up with the makings for a ham sandwich. "I was glad to do it. And it was fun. I only wish it hadn't been a party in honor of Abel Winn. And another thing," he said, slapping a knifeful of mustard on the slice of rye bread, "I didn't like what he said about my letting you 'get away.' What was all that about moving expenses and rent-free housing? What kind of job is he offering you?"

"A very good one," she said honestly. "Did you try any of this shrimp?" She popped one into her mouth.

"What kind of job, Brin?" He wasn't going to let her change the subject.

"As producer of *Front Page*," she admitted quietly, not meeting his eyes.

Riley laid his sandwich back on the plate without having taken one bite. Going to the back door, he gazed out the window at the skyline of one of the most beautiful cities in the world. Tonight he didn't even see it. Sliding his hands, palms out, into the back pockets of his jeans, he whistled softly. "That *is* a very good one."

"I haven't accepted it yet," she said hurriedly. She felt an almost maternal need to protect him. Why, she didn't know. But she felt that this piece of information might bruise his ego irreparably.

"Why not?" he asked, spinning around.

"I'm still considering it."

"What's to consider? *Front Page* has been written up in every trade publication. It's being touted as the hottest thing on television since *The Tonight Show*."

"It's got a long way to go before it gets there. It's not

even in production yet. It's still on the drawing board. The concept hasn't been clearly defined. Talent hasn't been selected. They're not even market-testing people yet." She said that to let him know that he hadn't been entirely passed over as a possible candidate for a host position on the new show. "Abel is projecting that it'll be early next year before it goes on the air. And it'll be syndicated. There are no guarantees that stations will buy it."

"They'll buy it. It's got Winn's megabucks backing it. It'll be a slick package they'll scoop up like popcorn." He looked at her closely. "And he wants you to be its producer."

"One of several. A Hollywood veteran has been named executive producer."

"I repeat, what's to consider?"

"I like what I'm doing now," she said evasively.

"That two-bit radio show?" he asked incredulously.

"*I* don't think it's two-bit."

"For your talents it is. Anyone fresh out of a college communications course could handle it. You outclass that program, and you know it. Besides, you should be in television. Why are you stalling Winn? Holding out for more money?"

"No."

"Then I don't understand."

She moistened her lips. "I'd have to move to L.A., for one thing. You know I love San Francisco."

"It would mean leaving behind more than the city."

"Yes." She fiddled with the hem of a dish towel. "My parents."

"And me." Her head snapped up and her eyes clashed

with penetrating blue ones. "Were you going to skip out of town without a word?"

"No. I was . . ." She swallowed hard. "I was going to ask for a divorce."

The silence that descended was deafening. When Riley broke it, his words sounded brittle enough to break. "Is that why you haven't asked for a divorce before? Because no job offer has been attractive enough until now?"

The accusation stung, but it was justified. That must be what it looked like to him, and Brin didn't blame him for jumping to that conclusion. If only he knew that he had been the main reason she hadn't accepted Winn's job offer immediately. She couldn't quite bring herself to think about making a final, irrevocable break with Riley.

She had lived without him for seven months, but they were still legally married. They still shared the same city, the same name. Taking the job with *Front Page* and moving to L.A. would end the state of marital limbo they were in and make divorce a necessity.

"I swear to you, one has nothing to do with the other," she said.

He came toward her slowly, searching her face, looking for clues to the problem that still perplexed him. "Why did you leave me, Brin? And why, if living with me and being my wife were so intolerable, why haven't you asked to be free of me completely?"

He cupped her face in his hands and tilted her head up. He stroked away her tears with the pads of his thumbs. "*Why?*"

"I don't know," she groaned. "No reason. A million reasons. It's all muddled up in my head."

He pressed his lips against her forehead, drawing her close and squeezing his eyes shut against the pleasure and pain of holding her, but not having her. "You haven't asked for a divorce because you don't want one. You don't want to be rid of me any more than I want to be rid of you. And I don't think you want that job, either, or you would have jumped at the chance."

"Don't you think I can handle it?"

He put space between them and smiled down at her. "I know you can. Do you think I've forgotten what you did for *Riley in the Morning?*"

Three months after she started working at the television station, they got the results of the rating period. *Riley in the Morning* hadn't quite made it to the number-one position in its time slot, but it was gaining substantially.

Brin allowed the crew one celebratory coffee break before calling a production meeting. She was a slave driver, a taskmaster, but instilled in all her subordinates a zeal for what they were doing.

Perhaps that was a skill she had learned from her father, a Navy man whose last post had been in San Francisco. The Cassidys had liked the cosmopolitan city so well that when Admiral Cassidy retired, they decided to stay. After having been moved all over the world during her childhood, Brin was allowed to attend her last three years of high school in one place.

The people she worked with knew little about her other than that she was a bundle of energy who pestered them with details until everything was perfect. Innovative ideas seemed never to be in short supply. The crew listened, fascinated but incredulous, as she suggested that they do some of the programs live and on location rather than restricting the show to the studio.

". . . with a live audience," she finished, her face expectant and excited.

"Live?"

"With an audience?"

Riley's response belonged on the piers.

"Well, why not?" she demanded, put off by their lack of enthusiasm for the idea.

"It's never been done before."

"That's a real good reason," she said dryly, giving the floor director a scornful look. "Thank God they didn't say that to Phil Donahue."

"All right, you've made your point, but what about money? It'll be expensive to transport all the studio cameras to an outside location. Not to mention the overtime it'll cost for engineers to set it up."

"Leave that to me," she said confidently. "If I can work out the details with management, are all of you game?" They nodded. The enthusiasm she had generated was infectious. "Riley?" she asked.

Their first few weeks of working together had been rocky. He'd scowled. She had looked through him. He'd grumbled. She had turned a deaf ear. He'd shouted. She had shouted back. Sometimes they had raised the roof with their arguments, but he had come to respect her judgment. She might look like a doll, but she was far from dumb.

"If you could get that freak with the pink hair to eat out of your hand, you can accomplish anything."

Four weeks later found them broadcasting the fifth and final show of the week live from a new shopping mall. Each morning they had drawn a live audience of several hundred. Everyone at the studio from the lowliest gofer to the CEO was high on the success of Brin's idea.

It had been a terrific week. Viewers had loved the change of pace, as their calls and letters testified. Everyone in the sales department was doing handsprings, because sponsors were calling them, wanting to buy commercial time on *Riley in the Morning*.

Brin and Riley had been working closely together. She had ceased being strictly his producer and had become his wardrobe consultant, makeup artist, scriptwriter, and general right hand.

"Brin?"

"Hmm?" She was concentrating on placing the lavaliere microphone in just the right place on his necktie. It was only a few minutes before air time. Everyone else had cleared off the set. Brin had jumped up from her high stool behind camera one and bounded up on the dais to adjust the microphone more to her liking.

"If a union boss catches you doing that, he'll have your rear."

"Then let's hope no one catches me."

"Yeah. I'd sure hate to see anything happen to such a cute behind."

She took the compliment in stride. Such comments from coworkers were easy to come by and didn't mean anything. "I won't be but another second."

"Take your time. I rather like the feel of your fingers in my chest hair."

That meant something. And she couldn't have taken it in stride if her life had depended on it.

Her eyes sprang up to meet his. She was alarmed to find his face so close to hers. And her fingers *were* in his chest hair. She had slid them between the buttons of his shirt in order to adjust the mike cord so that it would remain as invisible as possible. Nervously she wet her lips with her tongue and noticed that he was watching her mouth as she did.

"There, I'm done," she said thickly, withdrawing her fingers quickly.

"Lunch?"

"What?"

"Lunch? Today? When we get finished here?"

"Uh, I don't think so, no."

"Dinner?" He grinned. Winningly. Boyishly. She heard someone in the front row of his audience sigh. A woman no doubt. As a result of his smile, Brin felt her thighs grow weak and fell prey to a melting sensation that was delicious . . . but alarming.

"Definitely not."

"Breakfast, then."

"I don't ever eat breakfast out."

"Neither do I." The soft emphasis with which he spoke set off a chain of explosions in her middle. Her eyes locked with his and there was no mistaking what his invitation to breakfast implied.

"Hey, Brin, baby," the head cameraman called out, "we've got a great view of your tush, but unless you want that to be our opening shot, you'd better haul your buns off the set. Counting down from thirty seconds."

She turned and ran. Literally. And not just to get off the set in time. But to escape the captivating power of Riley's eyes, his compelling voice, his seductive insinuations, and her treacherous susceptibility to all three.

For the last several weeks she had felt that she and Jon Riley had finally reached an understanding, had established a reasonably good working relationship, had even formed some kind of grudging friendship. And yes, in quiet moments, when she wasn't being observed by either him or the crew, she had looked at him as most women would and had seen an attractive, sexy, virile male. What woman wouldn't notice and admire?

But *this*! *This* was out of the question. *This* was to be avoided at all costs.

Still, after the broadcast, she secretly hoped he would seek her out and continue the forbidden conversation. She would never accept a date, of course, but it was nice to be pursued.

But as soon as the cameras were shut down, he was surrounded by adoring fans, all clamoring for his autograph. One aggressive female fan nearly wrenched his neck in her effort to smack a kiss on his mouth. He only laughed and let her indulge herself.

"Brin?"

"What?" She was unaccountably furious, and spun around at the sound of her name. Whitney Stone jumped back in fright. Only then did Brin realize her fists were clenched at her sides. "I'm sorry, Whitney. What is it?"

"I'm spreading the word. We're all going to lunch together as soon as everything's packed up. Daddy's footing the bill on behalf of the station. It's a celebration." She named the restaurant and Brin nodded in agreement.

But she didn't go. She told herself it was because her desk was piled high with papers, that she had mounds of work to do back at the station, phone calls to return, letters to answer. But actually it was because she was fuming, boiling mad, and she couldn't say why. Or, rather, she *could,* and that was the real reason behind her anger.

She refused to believe she was jealous of every woman who made a fool of herself over Jon Riley. *She* would certainly never fall into the ranks of his adoring fans.

Her mood didn't improve when Riley came crashing into her office without even knocking. He slammed the door behind him. "Where were you?"

She catapulted out of the chair behind her desk and faced him belligerently. They squared off like two fighters in the ring. "If you need me for something having to do with the show, I'd appreciate—"

"Where the hell were you? Dim Whit said she told you where we were meeting for lunch."

"She did. I chose not to go." For no good reason, she slammed a file drawer shut. It broke her nail, and she cursed.

"Why?"

"I didn't want to."

"*I* wanted you to."

"I doubt you even missed me. I'm sure there were plenty of fans there drooling over you."

He stared at her for a moment, then slapped the heel of his hand against his forehead. "My God, she's jealous."

"What!" Brin shrieked. "Me?" Her eyes narrowed to slits. "Why you pompous, conceited, arrogant buffoon. I wouldn't give you—"

A gentle push sent her up against the wall. His shove had enough impetus behind it to knock the breath out of her and give him the advantage. He trapped her between himself and the wall.

"What you give me is a hard time and a hard—" His hips pressed forward, making his meaning abundantly clear. "You're the most maddening, aggravating, infuriating female I've ever had the misfortune to meet. The most irritating, exasperating"—his voice lowered—"exciting . . . oh, hell."

His mouth came down hard on hers. She fought him like a wildcat, squirming and wriggling, clawing and slapping when she could get her hands free.

He was stronger. He was male. Unrelenting in his purpose. Driven by need. His lips twisted over hers, parting them. His tongue plunged inside.

Brin's squeals of outrage eventually softened to whimpers of defeat, then, at the coaxing of his tongue, to sighs of desire. When she stopped struggling, he lifted his hands to either side of her face and tilted her head back. His mouth gentled considerably. His lips tempered from plunder to persuasion. His tongue no longer thrust bruisingly, but sank with delicious leisure and thoroughness into the silky heat of her mouth.

They kissed forever.

And when finally he raised his head, he looked down into eyes as confused and cloudy as his. "Dammit, Brin," he whispered hoarsely. "What did you do to me? What's going on here?"

CHAPTER FOUR

The silence in the kitchen was so profound that the drip in the sink sounded like Niagara Falls.

"That first kiss knocked me for a loop," Riley whispered huskily in her ear, knowing that she had been sharing his memory whether she ever admitted it or not. "I had never tasted anything so delicious as your kiss. I couldn't get enough of your mouth. I'd had climaxes that didn't affect me nearly that much."

"Riley, please." Brin felt herself weakening again. Damn his glibness! He was a master at ad lib. He knew what to say, and how to say it seductively. No wonder that honeyed tone and lilting inflection had kept him king of the morning talk shows for years. His female audience couldn't resist them.

But he wasn't an image on a television screen and she wasn't an audience of one. This was real.

"Thinking about the past isn't doing either one of us any good." She pushed him away and busied herself at the countertop.

"Coward."

She turned on the hot-water tap full force. A cloud of steam blossomed around her as she glared at him. "I'm not a coward."

He laughed. "You wouldn't have made Admiral Cassidy very proud of you that day. He would have shot any man in his Navy who showed such cowardice."

"I wasn't afraid of you, Riley."

"Not of me." He touched the tip of her nose. "Of yourself. And of what was happening to you on the inside. Here." His finger slid down her front and softly poked her just below the navel.

She swatted his hand away. "I merely left the office."

"You ran like a scared rabbit."

"If you'll remember right, I was called away. I got a summons from the station manager." Viciously she squirted a stream of liquid soap into the sink.

"Yeah, I remember. Dim Whit knocked on your office door with the message just as I touched your breast. I never have forgiven her for that," he said wryly.

"I thank heaven she timed it so well. I don't know what came over me."

"*I* would have if she hadn't interrupted." His mischievous

grin and the expression in his eyes left no doubt that the double entendre was intentional.

Brin was suffused with heat, as though her body had been stroked by the devil. "Nothing like that would have happened at work. We both have better sense than that."

He began placing dishes in the dishwasher after she had rinsed them in the soapy water. He chuckled. "Brin, honey, you're still an innocent. Write this down as fact. If Dim Whit hadn't knocked on your office door at the precise moment she did, I would have done my damnedest to get inside your clothes, to get inside you. Right then. Right there. I didn't even know where I was. And it didn't matter. I had to have you. Had to kiss you. Yes, I have better sense than to do anything like that at work, but common sense was shot to hell the minute I touched you."

He turned to her, and she was consumed by the blue flame in his eyes. Beneath the heap of bubbles in the sink, her hands fell still. "I was so angry because you hadn't joined us for lunch that I could have wrung your neck. But I simply had to kiss you. It wouldn't have mattered if the sky had opened up and rained down fire on me, or if Satan had reached up out of Hell and grabbed me by the ankles, I had to kiss you."

She dragged her eyes away from his. But she couldn't close off her ears. When he spoke again, the words descended on her like velvet caresses. "I knew I was in love with you after that first kiss."

He stepped away from her, and the emotional vise squeezing her chest relaxed. She admonished herself for letting him get to her this way. He played with her emotions. She mustn't let him. For whatever reason, he had decided he needed her, after seven months. But as soon as his ego was soothed, as soon as she had served his immediate purpose, she would be right back where she'd started.

"You didn't finish your sandwich," she remarked, hoping to distract him.

"I'll get around to it," he said offhandedly, as though his mind were elsewhere. He was sitting on a kitchen stool. The heels of his shoes were hooked over the bottom rung. "I think that's when you knew you loved me too."

Her diversionary tactic hadn't worked. He seemed to have a one-track mind. Well, if he could rehash their past without its causing him unbearable pain, couldn't she? If she avoided talking about those golden days, wasn't that as good as an admission that she still cared? Damned if she would let him think that.

"How did you reach that conclusion?" she asked with studied nonchalance.

"You started avoiding me after that."

"Hardly. I saw you every day."

"In production meetings and on the set. But if we so much as accidentally met at the coffee vendor, you scuttled away."

"I've never scuttled in my life."

"You know what I mean. You wouldn't risk being alone with me for ten seconds."

"Because every time we were, you tried to grab me."

"You enjoyed being grabbed."

She blushed, knowing there was no sense in denying that. "Someone could have seen us."

"I had to chance it. I was desperate to get my hands on you."

"Oh, sure. As I remember it, you were squiring that football player's widow at the time."

"I had to keep up appearances. What did you expect me to do, have it leaked to the press that Jon Riley had the hots for his producer? Besides, if I had asked you out, you wouldn't have gone. Right?"

"Right. But you got around that, didn't you?"

He shrugged. "I had no choice but to trick you."

His grin was so disarming, she had to smile back. "I should have seen straight through your ruse."

"I think you did," he suggested smugly.

"No I didn't!" She denied it vehemently, though she had often wondered if she had known what he was up to that day he called. . . .

"Hello?"

"Hi, Brin. What are you doing?"

The nerve! The conceit! To call and not even identify himself. "Who is this?" she asked perversely.

"I'm sorry. This is Jon Riley," he said formally. She heard the amusement overriding his tone and wished she had held her tongue. She'd only given him rope to hang her. "Are you busy?"

"Yes."

"Doing what?"

"Cleaning my apartment."

"Can it wait?"

"No."

"I want you to meet me."

"Now?"

"Sure, now."

"Forget it."

"Why?"

"I don't want to."

"But I have a terrific idea that won't wait."

"It'll have to. This is Saturday. I'm off on Saturdays. We'll talk about it at the production meeting on Monday."

She made herself sound piqued and impatient, but her heart was chanting, "Don't hang up yet, don't hang up yet," and her fingers were nervously twisting the phone cord. Her pulse was drumming double time and her palms had grown moist. And those were only the physical manifestations she allowed herself to acknowledge. Others were too embarrassing to think about.

"I'm in the park." He said it as though that explained everything.

She glanced out her window. "The park? On a day like today? It's cold, and I think it's going to rain."

"Nonsense. How soon can you be here?"

Tell him to go to hell, her better judgment warned her. "I haven't agreed to meet you."

"Do you want to hear this idea or don't you? What kind of producer are you?"

"An underpaid one."

"You just got a raise. You were given three months to prove yourself. When the last rating book showed a marked increase in our viewership, you got a raise. Want me to be really gauche and tell you how much it was?"

"How do you know all that?" she asked, aghast.

"Dim Whit overheard her dad talking about it."

"Does she report everything to you?"

"As you said, she adores me." His arrogant grin transmitted itself through the telephone.

"You really are a manipu—"

"How soon can you be here?"

"I haven't said I'm coming."

"But you are, aren't you?"

No. No. No. But her mouth seemed incapable of forming that simple one-syllable word. Instead she heard herself grumbling, "Oh, all right. But only for a while. Where are you?"

Every step of the way she told herself to slow down; she didn't want to be early or seem too anxious to see him. In spite of her determination to appear unhurried, she arrived at Golden Gate Park in record time, breathless and expectant. But he wasn't at the appointed place, a public telephone booth, where he had said he would meet her. Damn him! Well, she certainly wasn't going to loiter about as though she were waiting for him.

Her attention was called to a spontaneous frisbee-throwing contest being held on one of the famous park's grassy fields.

One contestant was matching the skills of his Doberman with those of a red Irish Setter. The agile dogs and their masters had drawn quite a crowd. Brin wandered through it, willing her eyes not to search every face to find Riley's.

"*Pst!*"

She turned her head, but quickly continued on her way. The man who had so rudely addressed her was unshaven and had a slouchy fedora pulled down low over his brow. He was wearing opaque sunglasses in spite of the gloomy clouds overhead. If he had been wearing a trench coat instead of the leather bomber jacket he had on, Brin might have thought he was a flasher. As it was, he was merely a creep.

"*Pst!*"

Glancing over her shoulder, she was alarmed to see that the creep was following her. "Get lost." A woman alone wasn't safe anywhere these days!

"Playing hard to get, Brin?"

She stumbled on her own two feet as she whipped around and peered at the face behind the hat and beard stubble and sunglasses. "*Riley?*"

"Shh." He flipped up the sunglasses long enough for her to see the eyes that could only belong to him. "It's me." He took her hand and steered her away from the crowd, still watching the frisbee contest.

"What are you doing? Why are you dressed like that? I didn't recognize you."

"Which is precisely the point. When I go out on Saturday mornings I don't want to be recognized."

He was hustling her across the grass so fast she could

barely keep up with his long stride. "I thought you were a masher."

"I am," he said, grinning down at her. "I got the girl, didn't I?"

"Where are we going?"

"Into the woods."

She tried to stop, but he dragged her along. "I thought this was a business meeting."

"Who told you that?"

"You did."

"No, I didn't. I said I had an idea to discuss with you."

"Well, that could only mean—Ouch! Slow down. I got the backlash of that branch."

"Sorry. Now, what were you saying?"

"I said"—she panted—"that you mentioned a great idea that couldn't wait till Monday. Can we rest, please?"

"Okay. It's starting to rain, anyway. Let's duck under here." He ran down a shallow ravine. She had no choice but to scramble after him. He pulled her beneath a footbridge just as the clouds opened up to release a soft, fragrant silver rain.

"Terrific," she said, staring out at the water-washed landscape. "I told you it was going to rain." Turning, she looked up at him with aggravation. "So here I am wasting a good day off by standing under a bridge in Golden Gate Park with you. Now, what brilliant idea of yours got me into this situation? And for heaven's sake, would you please take off those ridiculous glasses so I'll know for sure who I'm talking to?"

He took off the sunglasses and put them in the pocket of his jacket. "Thank you. Now let's hear that idea."

"I think we should turn this into a meaningful relationship."

She stared at him blankly. Her expression didn't change. Her face didn't register the slightest emotion. When several seconds ticked by and she still didn't say anything, he said, "That's it."

"That's it? *That's it?* That's what you dragged me out of a nice, warm, dry, comfortable apartment on a Saturday morning to say?"

"Yeah!" he replied with a happy grin. "What do you think about it?"

"I think you're insane." She spun on her heel and took a step into the pelting rain, but he grabbed the hem of her jacket and jerked her back. His arms went around her securely, and she found herself locked in an embrace that felt too good not to terrify her.

He was strong, lean, hard, masculine. Her first impulse was to wrap her arms around him and get as close to him as she could. But that would be foolhardy, so she resisted the temptation. Instead she inclined away from him. He was having none of that and only drew her closer by tightening his arms around her.

"I think the idea merits some discussion, at least."

"It won't matter if we discuss it from now till doomsday, Riley. It's impossible."

"Nothing's impossible."

"This is."

"Why?"

"It would never work."

"Why?"

"We're business associates."

"So?"

"So we should keep it strictly business."

"Shut up."

"You're—"

"For once, Brin Cassidy, just shut up."

He bent his head low and captured her lips with his. And hers clung. She couldn't have denied herself that kiss in a million years, because his whiskers were about the most exciting thing she had ever felt against the delicate skin of her face. His lips were warm and moist as they moved to part hers. His tongue was darting and playful, and slow and deliberate, and thoroughly erotic, as it first skimmed the inner lining of her lips, then dipped far inside to fill the hollow of her mouth. He tasted like peppermint toothpaste and smelled like expensive cologne and rain . . . and man . . . and sex.

"God, Brin, I thought I'd die before I had a chance to kiss you again." He buried his beard-roughened face inside her collar and kissed her neck.

"This is crazy. Crazy." But even her own assessment of the situation didn't stop her from taking full advantage of being held in Riley's arms. She knocked the hat off his head onto the leaf-strewn ground. She nuzzled his ear and brushed her lips through the dark, silver-streaked hair just above it. "We shouldn't be doing this."

"But we are and it's fantastic."

"Hmm."

"Isn't it?"

"Hmm."

Their mouths fused again, and she marveled over the evocative powers of his kiss. She felt that kiss all the way down to her toes. It swirled around her breasts, through her belly, and into her thighs.

She slid her hands into his jacket, around his waist, and flattened them on the supple muscles of his back. "If we should be seen . . ." she said with a moan when their lips drifted apart to flirt with each other.

"We won't be. And even if we are—Ouch!"

"What's the matter?"

"Something . . . the zipper on your jacket, I think . . . There. Yes, that's better. Like that."

She sighed contentedly as he opened her jacket and pressed her against his chest.

He kissed her with a wildness that was thrilling, his head moving from side to side, his tongue probing as though searching for an entrance into her soul. "I want you, Brin. So damn much."

He cupped her bottom and lifted her off the ground, settling her against him in a way that banished any doubt as to his need. He fit their bodies together as nature had intended. The provocative grinding of his hips robbed her of breath.

"Please, please." She wasn't sure what she was begging for, but the words seemed to slip from her lips each time his mouth released them.

She lost count of the kisses they shared. Greedily her hands caressed him, and he took liberties with her until she was almost frantic with need. But somehow each of them retained a modicum of reason.

At last he let her slide down his body until her toes touched the ground again. She rested her cheek on his chest and heard the thudding of his heart. His hands moved lovingly in her hair. His lips brushed petal-soft kisses on her temple. The air was fogged with the moist vapor of their breath. . . .

"Sometimes I can still hear the way the rain sounded on that bridge overhead," he whispered now.

Emotionally overwrought, Brin leaned against the kitchen countertop, her arms stiffly bracing her up. Riley stood behind her. Close. So close she could feel his body's response to the memory of that rain-shrouded afternoon under the bridge. His hands rested on her hips, lightly, but with enough strength to hold her bottom against his front. His breath was warm and misty on her neck as he spoke softly.

"I wanted to make love to you right there. Lying in the leaves, standing up, any way I could. I wanted you so bad I ached." He kissed the back of her neck, opening his mouth and sponging her skin with the tip of his tongue. "Maybe I should have." His hands slid around to the front of her thighs. He moved them up and down, stroking soothingly, until they climbed to the top. His thumbs nestled in the grooves that funneled toward the vibrating heart of her femininity.

"Maybe I shouldn't have let you talk me into taking things slow." His thumbs moved, and she gasped.

Breaking away from him, she put necessary space between them. "That was the only way it could be," she said in a trembling voice. "Then and now. You can't come sailing into my life after seven months of separation and pick up where we left off. I need space, time to sort things—"

"Oh, bull!" he shouted angrily. "All that space and time didn't do you any good the first time. You laid down the game rules and, like a puppy on a leash, I obeyed them. You insisted on only one official date a week. No hanky-panky at work. 'Keep it strictly professional at the TV station,' you said, and I did."

"Because you knew as well as I did that we couldn't compromise our jobs."

"Right. I agreed with that. But I went through weeks of pure hell until you finally admitted that you wanted me just as badly as I wanted you. You're so damned stubborn, Brin. I knew from that first kiss that we would be a perfect team, in bed as well as out. And in the long run I was proved right." He started laughing. "Of course you were *shocked* into admitting it."

"If you're referring to—"

"That's exactly what I'm referring to."

"Come in," Brin called out.

Whitney stuck her head around the door to the producer's office. "Hi. Sorry to bother you, but we've got a problem."

"Just one?" Brin said, smiling. "What this time? Don't tell me Monday's interview has canceled."

"No, but Riley's already left, and he forgot to take his homework with him."

"Forgot?" Brin asked skeptically. He was so good at improvising during interviews that she had a heck of a time getting him to study pertinent facts before the cameras rolled.

"Well, in any event, I found the file on the set and he's split," Whitney said. "I'd take it to him, but I'm flying to Palm Springs with my folks for the weekend as soon as I get off work."

Brin took the file reluctantly. "I guess I could drop it off at his place." One of her stipulations had been that they avoid spending time in each other's homes. She didn't know how much longer she could hold out without going to bed with him, but she was bound and determined not to be just another notch on his infamous belt.

She waited until late that Friday evening before driving to his address, hoping that he would already have gone out and she could leave the folder in his mailbox. How she would bear the torment of learning that he was out with someone else, she didn't know.

His sports car was parked in the driveway, however, and Brin moved toward the front door with the weak-kneed trepidation of a music student approaching the piano at her first recital.

She rang the bell, once, twice. She was just about to leave

the file in the mailbox and make a mad dash for her car when the door swung open.

"Oh!" Her hand flew to her chest, but she managed to avoid covering her eyes.

"Brin!" His delight couldn't be masked. "What are you doing here?"

"I, uh, brought you this." She thrust the file at him as if it were a hot potato. "Were you taking a shower?"

"No. I always walk around wet with a towel around my waist when I'm at home." His grin was heart-stopping. He looked devastatingly handsome, even if his hair was plastered to his forehead in sodden points. "Come on in," he offered, stepping aside.

Like a somnambulist, she moved inside. She was dazzled by his bare chest. The muscles dipped and curved appreciably, without looking grotesque. Last summer's tan had soaked into his skin, for there was still evidence of it. The network of hair covering it was dark and beaded now with drops of water that she could imagine catching on her tongue and swallowing. She avoided looking at the square of terry cloth that covered his loins, but his legs were long and lean and as athletically proportioned as the rest of him.

When her eyes finally returned to his face, her tongue felt too thick to form words. "I can't stay."

"Don't be silly. Besides, I'd like you to see my house."

At the risk of appearing rude at best and a prude at worst, she made no further move to enter, gazing instead at the spacious, tastefully decorated, plant-filled hallway, which had a skylight. When Riley closed the front door, the finality of that clicking, metallic sound brought her around as surely as smelling salts.

"I'm sorry for the intrusion," she said in a breathless rush. "I know you must be getting ready to go out. If it hadn't been important that I bring over the file, I wouldn't have bothered you on a Friday night. But you've got two very serious interviews to do on Monday and one of the topics you'll be discussing is abortion and you know how controversial that is, so I've compiled a lot of information and it will be necessary—"

"I love you, Brin."

She was stopped dead in her tracks.

Mutely, she stared up at him. She didn't speak, didn't even smile. It didn't strike her as ridiculous that he was standing in a puddle of water he'd dripped onto the floor. She was mesmerized by his eyes and the sincerity she read in them. For once, she merely stood there and listened.

"I'm not getting ready to go out. I was getting ready to spend a quiet evening at home, alone, thinking about you. Which is what I do to occupy just about every minute of the day."

He laid the folder she had given him on a table and took the steps necessary to bring them nose to nose. "I love you." Pressing her face between his hands, he granted her the sweetest kiss she had ever known in her life. Passion smoldered just below the surface, but this was a kiss of devotion, a tender expression of newfound love.

Calmly, almost with detachment, he unbuttoned her coat and slipped it off her shoulders. Unheeded, it fell to the floor.

He touched the front of her blouse, lightly, barely skimming it with his hands. Then, without asking her permission, he unfastened the buttons. He was in no hurry. When all the buttons were undone, he spread the fabric wide.

His eyes made several rapid sweeps, then slowed to make a leisurely search, drinking in every detail of texture, shape, and color. He unhooked the fastener of her brassiere. She didn't deter him. The lacy garment came free, and he peeled it away.

Brin felt him stiffen. She saw him swallow hard. Saw him blink away tears. Saw him lower his head. Then she felt his mouth, warm and wet and loving. Loving her.

"I love you, I love you," he vowed against the silky skin of her breasts. His lips planted deep kisses into the lush fullness and tugged on the nipples, which pearled against his tongue.

She whimpered and clasped his head. "I love you too. I do. I didn't want to, but I do."

Their mouths came together hungrily. She had never known a feeling like that of his bare damp chest against her breasts. Mindlessly she rubbed herself against him and that electrifying carpet of hair.

There ensued an orgy of kissing that was interspersed with incoherent love words and sighs of immense pleasure and groans of building need.

"Brin, darling, my towel . . ."

"Yes?"

"It fell off."

Her arms were linked tightly around his neck. Her face

was buried in the hollow of his shoulder and she could feel the warm pressure of his sex against her middle. "It did?" she asked in a small voice.

"Um-hm." He put enough space between them to look down into her face, waiting until she raised her eyes to meet his. Then he lifted one of her hands from around his neck and kissed the palm fervently, sending a trill of sensation spearing pleasurably into her belly.

Slowly he carried her hand down. "Touch me."

He placed her hand in the general vicinity, but left the choice up to her. She could have refused, and he would have let her. But she loved him, and at that moment nothing seemed so important as demonstrating that love.

She flattened her hand on his abdomen. Slid it down. Her fingers sifted through the coarse hair, then encountered the velvety tip of his sex. Shyly she investigated it. With a sharp intake of breath he let his head fall forward onto her shoulder, and his whole body shuddered. He moaned audibly when she took him in a small, tight, gentle fist.

"Oh, my God . . . Brin . . . Sweet . . . I want . . . Ahh . . ." He kissed her with unleashed passion. Then he pressed his lips against her forehead and repeated again and again, "Be my lover. Be my lover. Be my . . ."

CHAPTER FIVE

". . . lover."

It wasn't an echo from the past, but a heartfelt plea in the present. He held her tight. His lips moved against her cheek. "Be my lover, Brin. Be my wife again."

The doorbell pealed.

As though wrenched from a dream, Brin jumped away from him. Her face was flushed, her eyes glazed. The doorbell's chime had acted like a dash of cold water on her mounting desire. It had brought her to her senses, but she didn't know whether she was thankful for or resentful of the intrusion.

She turned and rushed into the living room. Riley was right behind her. She opened the door, sheltering her body behind it. "Abel?"

Brin hoped the man outside the door couldn't hear

Riley's muttered litany of profanity. She could imagine the way his brow was beetled with fury, but she dared not glance at him and give away his presence in the house. It might be difficult to explain. Her voice was as shaky as the hand she combed through her tangled hair. "This is certainly a surprise." That line was straight out of a B-movie script, but she hoped Riley believed it.

Riley could only hear Brin's half of the conversation. Standing ramrod-straight, his muscles rigid with rage, he strained to catch every word.

"No, I wasn't sleeping. . . . I would invite you in, but it's awfully late. . . . Of course I'm thinking about it, but I haven't reached a decision yet. . . . I said I'd tell you in the morning. That's what we agreed on. . . . I know, but please give me time. . . . Yes, I promise to tell you then. Good night." Quietly, as though she were afraid of rousing a potentially dangerous beast, she closed the door.

But the beast was already roused, as she found out when she turned to face Riley after Abel's car had driven off.

"Is it his habit to come courting after midnight?"

"No. And he didn't come courting."

"I'd like to know what the hell you call it."

"Nothing."

"How often does he do this 'nothing'?"

"Never. Tonight is the first night he's been here."

"You expect me to believe that?"

"It's the truth!"

"Why tonight?"

"He wanted to say thanks for the party again." Riley

muttered something under his breath, and Brin was glad she hadn't caught all of it. The few key words she had heard were graphic enough. "He wanted to know if I had reached a decision about the job yet." She headed back toward the kitchen. Riley tracked her like a trained hunter. He was through the swinging door before it had time to close behind her.

"He said morning, didn't he? Well, didn't he? Wasn't that your deadline? Why is he badgering you about it tonight? Huh?" He was furious, and Brin knew his temper was something to dread. "I don't know where this guy gets off, even being as rich and powerful as he is, coming on to *my wife!*"

Riley slammed his hand down on the countertop. He didn't see the glass, didn't hear the crunching, splintering sound of it when it broke, didn't even feel the pain until Brin covered her mouth to stifle a scream. Puzzled, he looked down to see that the meaty part of his hand just beneath his thumb was pumping blood.

"Well, I'll be damned," he said softly.

Brin, petrified at first, sprang into action. She lunged for the sink and turned on the cold water. "Riley, oh, my God, does it hurt? Here, hold it over the sink, oh, Lord, it's bleeding, Riley." She blotted the wound with a dish towel, but her attempts at staunching the flow did no good. The red stain spread until the towel was soaked with it. "Oh, Riley," she said, sobbing. She crammed her own bloodstained fingers against her lips, and tears flooded her eyes.

Calmly Riley sponged the deep cut that ran from his

thumb joint almost to his wrist. "I think I'll need a few stitches," he said with remarkable composure. "Will you drive me to the emergency room?"

"Yes, yes. Let's see. What . . ." She raised a hand to her forehead as though trying to arrange her darting thoughts into some semblance of order. The man she loved was bleeding profusely. She hadn't lived with him for seven months, but that thought never entered her mind. His pain was hers, and she would have laid down her own life at that moment to take away his hurt. "You'd better take your jacket." She swung the windbreaker over his shoulders. "Let me wrap up your hand with a clean towel."

She did so with fingers that operated automatically. If she had thought about the blood being Riley's, the torn flesh being his, she would have been totally ineffectual. "There, maybe that'll stop the bleeding until we get to the hospital. Where are my keys? Oh, here they are," she said, reaching for the hook by the back door where she always left her car keys.

"Careful, darling," she said, leading him down the back steps as though his legs were injured, and not his hand. "No, no, let me get the door for you. Are you in pain?"

"No," he lied with a brave smile.

"Don't lie to me, Riley! You are too. Your lips are white. I always know when you're in pain because your lips turn white. Remember that time you hurt your back playing softball? I knew you were in agony even though you swore you weren't."

She tucked him into the passenger's side and buckled the seat belt around him. Within seconds the Datsun was tearing through the hilly streets of San Francisco toward the nearest emergency clinic.

"Maybe you should elevate your hand just a little, darling. There, isn't that better? Why don't you lay your head back? I'll have you there in no time."

"You'll make a terrific mommy."

"What?" She whipped her eyes off the road for only a fraction of a second. The speed at which she was driving wouldn't permit more than a momentary distraction. "A mommy?" she asked in a high, light voice.

"Yeah. I think we should have a couple of kids, don't you?"

"Well, I . . . I haven't thought about it lately."

"I have. They'd be terrific."

"Children are a big responsibility."

"Don't get me wrong. You wouldn't have to give up anything to have my baby. Selfishly, I'd want you to work producing my show for as long as you wanted to."

"I wouldn't want just one baby. I was an only child. You were too. You know that wasn't much fun. I'd want to have at least two."

"Then you agree that we should start a family?"

"Can't we talk about this later?" she asked absently. Blood was seeping through the towel wrapped around his hand. She touched his thigh in that unconscious, comfort-giving way a woman has with her man. "We're almost there."

She turned the car under the porte cochere of the emergency clinic and parked illegally. A policeman came up to her just as she was opening the door for Riley.

"Sorry, miss, but you can't leave your car here."

With a hand under Riley's right arm, she helped him alight and then turned to face the policeman. Since she had been married to Jon Riley, Brin had made it a cardinal rule not to use his name to secure the best tables in restaurants, or to obtain theater tickets when none were left to be obtained, or to demand special attention from anyone. Now, without even thinking about it, she broke that rule.

"This is Jon Riley. I'm his wife. He has hurt his hand and it's bleeding badly. I'm taking him in."

The policeman looked at Riley. "Well, whadayaknow! It *is* you! Me and the little woman wouldn't miss your show. I work nights, ya see, so I'm home in the daytime. It just wouldn't be morning without Riley. That's what we say."

"Could we just . . . ?" Brin edged around him, nudging Riley forward.

"Sure, sure. Get him right on in there, miss, I mean Mrs. Riley. If you'll give me your keys, I'll park your car."

"They're in the ignition," she said over her shoulder.

She felt Riley shaking and glanced up worriedly, afraid he was about to faint from blood loss. The grin on his face revealed that his tremors came from laughter, not lightheadedness. "Didn't you always say you'd never act like a star's wife? That you'd never throw my name up to people?"

"This is an emergency," she said primly.

His burst of laughter drew attention to them. As soon as

the admitting nurse recognized him, she hustled them into an examination room, where they were immediately joined by a team of nurses. One unwrapped his hand and began to wash out the deep cut with a vigor that made Brin's stomach roil. One stuck a thermometer in his mouth. Another took his blood pressure. Brin, feeling useless all of a sudden, stood in the background.

The doctor strode in, saying, "I hear we have a celebrity in our midst."

"You'll forgive me for not shaking hands," Riley said with a wry grin as he extended his right hand for the doctor's inspection.

The doctor's vocal assessment of the wound was a series of grunts and "hmms" that had Brin shifting impatiently from one foot to the other while gnawing the inside of her cheek. Had the glass severed an artery? Was the muscle affected?

"It'll require some stitches. Should hurt like hell for a few days, but it'll be all right in a week or so." The doctor slapped Riley on the shoulder. "I'm gonna drink a cup of coffee while the nurse anesthetizes it and—"

"A shot?" Riley asked, paling for the first time.

"Several, I'm afraid."

"In my hand?" His voice quavered.

Brin pushed her way through the crowd of nurses, most of whom were sightseers. Riley reached for her. "He doesn't like shots. Needles."

"He'll like them even less if I sew up his hand without deadening it."

She put her arms around Riley's shoulders and held him close, smoothing the hair off his now-damp, pasty-gray forehead. "It'll be over soon, darling. I'll stay with you."

And she did, through it all, through the five deadening injections in his hand that coaxed sweat from every pore in his body, through the seventeen stitches, through the careful bandaging. She shushed him when he cursed, quipped jokes about hunks with no guts when he blanched at the sight of the syringe, and hugged him fiercely when the needle pierced the flesh around the angry cut.

The obliging policeman insisted on bringing her car up to the door as they left the building. Once on their way, Brin didn't have to suggest that Riley rest his head on the back of the seat. The effects of the accident were beginning to tell on him.

"I'm not really afraid of needles," he said drowsily, rolling his head to one side to watch her as she drove.

"You big liar. I remember when you had strep throat and had to get a shot of penicillin. The nurse you terrorized had to fetch me out of the waiting room before you'd cooperate and drop your pants."

"I think she only wanted a glimpse of Jon Riley's buns."

"As I recall, she wasn't impressed. I don't think anyone's buns would have impressed her. Try another lie."

"I only wanted a good excuse to pillow my head on your lovely breasts. And that's not a lie."

"You raised a ruckus that had us forever banned from that doctor's office just for that?"

"It was worth it. Just like tonight. Did you notice when I pecked a little kiss on the tip of one while no one was looking?"

She shot him a withering look. "Save it for someone who'll believe you, Riley. You're a crybaby."

"But did you notice?"

"Yes, yes, I noticed."

He chuckled at her exasperation and glanced out the windshield again. "Where are we going?"

"I'm taking you home."

"*My* home?"

"Yes," she said doubtfully. "What did you expect?"

"I expected you to let me spend the night at your place. This is my right hand, you know," he said, lifting the bandaged hand as though to remind her of it. "I could get a fever. I could go into shock. I could—"

"All right, all right, spare me the horror stories." She executed a U-turn at the next traffic light. "But don't read anything into this. I'm just doing what any compassionate human being would do for a fellow man."

"I understand. And don't think I don't appreciate it." He said it solemnly, but she sensed the amusement behind his words. They rode in silence for a few blocks, before he said, "Know what this reminds me of?"

"What?"

"The night we got married."

The car swerved and Brin swore. "Pothole," she said by way of explanation for her carelessness.

But Riley knew she was thinking about the night she had become his wife. "We just dropped everything and set off for Lake Tahoe. Remember?"

How could she ever forget? "You dropped everything, literally."

"My towel?"

"Yes."

"Lord," he groaned as his memory carried him back. "Your hand was on me and I was dying. I said, 'Be my lover, Brin.' And you said . . ."

"No, Riley. I can't." She pushed herself away from him. She cast her eyes down, then quickly up again. Oh, he was beautiful.

"Can't?" he rasped.

"Won't."

"You said you love me."

"I do," she moaned. "I do. But I won't be just another of your groupies. I know about all the scalps dangling from your belt. Your sexual exploits are a favorite topic of conversation around the coffee machine at work. I don't want my name to be bandied about with all the others. And when you got tired of me and broke off the affair, we could never work together again."

"You're saying you won't go to bed with me?"

"That's right."

Gently he laid his hands on her shoulders. "You don't believe me when I say I love you?"

"I believe you believe it. But—"

"You don't think what I feel for you is different? That it's something permanent?"

She caught her lower lip between her teeth and shook her head.

"I do love you, Brin. And I want to make love to you. What do I have to do to get you into bed with me?"

Her answer was flippant. "Marry me."

"All right."

She almost dislocated several vertebrae in her neck when her head snapped up. *"What?"*

"I said, 'All right.' I'll marry you. I was hoping that would be your condition. It saved me from going down on bended knee. Do you realize how ridiculous a naked man looks on bended knee? And what if you said no? There I'd be, naked to the world and humiliated all at the same time."

"B-but I was only joking."

His brow arched over his frowning eyes in the way that made the women in his audience swoon. "Do you always play with a man like this, joke about marriage?"

"No, but—"

"Will you marry me, Brin?"

She got lost in the deep, cerulean pools of his eyes, and never quite remembered saying yes.

"This is crazy," she said a half hour later as they sped toward the Sierras and Lake Tahoe.

"I'm crazy about you. Crazy, and in love for the first time in my life." His free hand was taking liberties at the front of her dress.

"We're going to be the two craziest people ever sealed in caskets if you don't keep your eyes on the road and . . . uh, your hands on the wheel."

"Want me to stop?" he drawled close to her ear as his fingers lightly brushed her nipple.

"Hmm, no." Her hand crept higher up his thigh. She squeezed him gently.

He cursed softly and removed his hand from her bodice. "Fair's fair, and you've made your point."

She settled back in the car seat and said dreamily, "My folks will be so disappointed. Mother always wanted me to have a church wedding, long white dress, the works. She's wasted a lot of money by subscribing to *Bride* all these years."

"We'll call them tomorrow morning and invite them to fly up for the rest of the weekend. Separate suites, of course," he added. "Will they like me?"

"Only a few weeks ago Mother *very casually* remarked that I should settle down and marry a 'nice young man like that Jon Riley.' That I should have a family, a house with a yard and a dog, and stop concentrating on a career."

"And your father?" There was a trace of uncertainty in his voice. Brin had talked about her father and his stern, military bearing. "What does the admiral think about me?"

"He grunted something about your hair being too long. But then, he thinks everyone's hair is too long. If that's his only criticism, you're in like Flynn. What about your mother?" She knew that Riley's father was deceased, but that his mother lived in San Jose.

"I'll call and invite her up too. We'll turn it into a real family affair and try to make amends for not inviting them to the wedding."

"But will your mother like me?"

"Are you kidding?" he asked, turning his head to look at her. "She thinks I'm a smart aleck and has been telling me for years that what I needed was a good woman who would take me to task."

Brin laughed and snuggled against him. "I just want to take you."

During the long drive they exchanged bits and pieces of themselves, filling in the years they hadn't known each other, getting acquainted as lovers do.

Brin had expected to be married in one of the tacky wedding chapels that sprouted up like weeds along the highway the moment they crossed the state line into Nevada. Invariably these chapels had gawdy neon lights that boasted low rates, advertised the fact that no blood tests were required, and bragged that they were open twenty-four hours a day. Organ music and artificial flowers were available at extra cost.

But Riley braked the car in front of a quaint church nestled in a grove of pine trees. It had a steeple and stained-glass windows with a glowing, mellow light shining through them. He assisted Brin out of his low, sleek sports car and guided her up the steps and through the arched front door of the church.

Brin gasped with pleasure and surprise when she stepped

inside. The entire chapel was lit with candles and decorated with flowers, real ones, all white. At the head of the carpeted center aisle, in front of the altar, stood a bespectacled minister who looked like he'd stepped out of a Norman Rockwell painting. A buxom woman, probably his wife, was smiling angelically from her place at the organ, which filled the chapel with traditional wedding music.

"You don't happen to be Catholic or Jewish, do you?" Riley asked with a concerned frown.

"No."

"So a Protestant service is okay?"

"Yes, it's . . ." She choked up. "When did you arrange this?"

"I called from your apartment when you went in the bedroom to change and pack. Are you pleased?"

"Pleased?" she asked with a soft smile, reaching up to touch his cheek. "You are so dear. I love you."

"I love you too," he said huskily, bending to kiss her fervently. Moments later the minister tactfully cleared his throat to break them apart.

After the meaningful exchange of vows, Riley drove Brin to a resort hotel at the base of one of the ski lifts. "I've never been here, but I understand it's five-star-rated."

As well it should be, they noted the moment they entered. An elevator swept them up from the lavish, antique-furnished lobby, complete with a grand piano and an enormous fireplace, to a suite that made Brin gape like a girl straight out of the sticks. There was a small kitchenette and wet bar between the sitting room and bedroom. A redwood hot tub gurgled in one corner of the bathroom. A fireplace was situated in the bedroom opposite the king-sized bed.

"Ready to cut your wedding cake?" Riley asked as she surveyed the suite, taking in every well-thought-out convenience and luxury.

"Wedding cake?"

The cart that the deferential waiter wheeled into the sitting room contained, not a cake, but a soufflé, rising a good two inches above its white baking dish and looking as fluffy and light as a giant marshmallow. It was nestled in a stiff linen napkin folded to represent a swan. The "swan" was swimming through a pond of white flower petals. Brin surveyed the epicurean artwork through tear-blurred eyes and only prayed that, if this were all a dream, it would last till morning.

"It's lovely."

After checking with Riley to see if they would be needing anything else, the waiter withdrew. Riley divided the rich vanilla soufflé, smothered Brin's portion with creamy Grand Marnier sauce, and served it to her. They fed each other bites, licking each other's fingers when they got wonderfully messy.

Champagne followed. Feeling as bubbly and golden as the wine, Brin let Riley lead her from the sitting room into the bedroom. Taking her champagne glass from her, he set it aside and faced his bride. His hot blue gaze rained down on her face. "Well, here we are," he said softly. . . .

•   •   •

"Here we are." Brin braked the car in her garage and pushed the button to close the door behind them. "Were you asleep?" she asked as Riley lifted his head and blinked his eyes open.

"No. Just thinking about our wedding night."

She had been thinking about the same thing, but she wouldn't allow herself to enter into a conversation about it. Not now. Not when Riley's eyes were darkly ringed with fatigue and his face looked gaunt and pale from loss of blood. Not when she was feeling maternal and caring and protective toward him. Not when he was spending the night with her.

She ushered him inside, cautioning him to avoid stepping on the broken glass that had showered the kitchen floor. "Would you like anything?" she asked as she lifted his jacket off his shoulders. "To eat? To drink?"

He shook his head, and without another word she led him upstairs to the bedroom. "Does your hand hurt?" she asked sympathetically as she flung back the covers on the bed.

"No, it's numb. It would be my right hand, wouldn't it? It probably won't be much use to me for the next few days."

"You'll have to take it easy. You lost a lot of blood."

"I'm just glad I didn't need a transfusion. I'm not sure I could stand having a needle in my arm that long." He slipped out of his shoes and dropped to the edge of the bed to peel off his socks. When he automatically lifted his right hand to unbutton his shirt, he realized just how incapacitated he was.

"Here, let me." Brin hurried to his aid. Taking his arm,

she pulled him to his feet. He stood before her, his arms hanging loosely at his sides. With deft fingers she unbuttoned the first few buttons. It was only when the backs of her knuckles brushed against the soft, springy hair on his chest that her movements became clumsy.

Suddenly she became aware of just how intimate the procedure of undressing him was going to be. A reflection of days gone by. Of nights when they had made a deliciously naughty game of undressing each other. Or, in a sweet rush of passion, had nearly ripped the clothes from each other's bodies.

She pulled the shirttail from the waistband of his jeans and exposed his chest. It was so achingly familiar, as familiar to her as her own face in the mirror. The dark forest of hair, the taut, tanned skin, the flat coppery nipples, which she knew responded to the merest touch of fingertips or tongue. He was lean enough that every rib was visible. His stomach was flat and corrugated with muscle, his navel deep and hair-whorled.

As casually as possible, she tossed his shirt across the chair. "Do you, uh, want your jeans off?"

"I don't usually sleep in them."

Her head was bowed. She wondered if he knew she was feeling dizzy and breathless. To ward off the vertigo, she closed her eyes until she was able to continue. Her hands had to be forced to move to his belt. The metal buckle was cool against her fingers, but the skin beneath the snap was warm as she fumbled to open it.

She pulled the zipper down slowly, stretching the cloth as far away from his body as it would go. Which wasn't far, since he wore his jeans as snug as decency would allow. It was impossible to pretend that the firm evidence of his sex didn't exist or that she couldn't feel it against the backs of her fingers.

When the zipper was all the way down, she slid her hands into the waistband of the jeans at the sides of his hips and eased them down over hard, trim thighs. She went down on her knees in front of him and drew the pants past sinewy calves until he was able to step out of them.

"I don't usually sleep in my underwear, either," he said thickly.

She tilted her head far back, gazing up the entire length of his body to meet his eyes. His rawly masculine image seemed to sway in front of her like an erotic mirage. She wanted nothing more than to rest her cheek against the strong columns of his thighs, to hug his hard frame against her. To kiss the hair-roughened skin. To taste—

Realizing where her thoughts were taking her, she surged to her feet. "Well, you'll have to suffer tonight." She virtually shoved him down on the bed. As soon as his head hit the pillow, she raised the sheet and blanket over him as though she couldn't bear to look at him a moment longer. And it wasn't because he repulsed her.

The bathroom door slammed behind her as she retreated like a cowardly soldier seeking respite from the battleground. She stripped for the second time that night and pulled on a cotton knit panty and tank top. She loved sleeping in them for their form-fitting comfort. They were a designer's copy of masculine underwear, but the way Brin's figure filled them out left no doubt as to her gender. Over the matched set, which was robin's-egg blue, she pulled on an old robe that Riley had once claimed worked better than a headache as a turn-off.

Switching off the light, she reentered the bedroom. "Do you need anything?"

He had lowered the covers to his waist. His left arm was folded beneath his head. His bandaged right hand was resting on his lap. "Only some tender, loving care. I'd like to continue our discussion about having babies. You know, Brin, living apart as we are is going to make it damn hard to make . . . What are you doing?"

"Getting down covers," she answered from the closet.

"What for?"

"For the bed I'm going to make on the couch downstairs."

He sprang to a sitting position, obviously annoyed. "Oh, for heaven's sake, Brin."

"No, for *my* sake and yours. We can't muddy up this issue any more than it already is by sleeping together tonight. I hope that's not what you had in mind when you asked to spend the night here." His glowering frown made it clear that that was exactly what he'd had in mind. "Good night, Riley. I'll see you in the morning." With all the imperiousness of a queen, she swept out of the bedroom, trailing the end of a blanket behind her like a royal train.

She heard his terse expletive and smiled to herself.

But the joke was on her. Even though the sofa was long enough to accommodate her and as comfortable as any bed, she couldn't sleep. Damn him for reminding her of their wedding night!

It had been as enchanting as a fairy tale. Romantic. Sexy. And as she tossed and turned on the sofa, her thoughts seemed bent on returning to it. . . .

"Well, here we are," he said softly. The ivory satin sheets beckoned them from the bed. A fire was burning in the gas fireplace for effect. Its flickering light projected their shadows on the walls and was reflected in their eyes. "Would you like to try out the hot tub?"

"Maybe afterward."

"Afterward?" he asked, raising his brows teasingly.

Her cheeks grew pink. "Later," she amended.

"Does that mean you want to get in bed as fast as I do?"

"Yes, please," she said politely. "Besides, it's nearly dawn." She laid her hand on the placket of his shirt. "If we don't hurry, we won't have a wedding *night*."

"We sure as hell can't let that happen, can we?" He nuzzled her throat, his arms sliding around her waist. "Would you like a few minutes alone?"

"Not necessarily," she breathed against his neck.

"Then, do I have permission to undress you?" He waited for her answer, and when none was forthcoming, he raised his head and looked down at her. Her eyes were smoky with desire, her lips moist and inviting. She nodded her head and stepped out of her shoes, taking several inches off her height and making her seem more feminine than she already did.

The jacquard silk dress was monochromatic tones of white. One shoulder had a row of pearl buttons, which Riley dexterously unfastened. He reached beneath her left arm to slide down the side zipper. The dress shimmied down her body. She was left standing in a champagne-colored slip that robbed Riley of breath. Her breasts amply filled the stretchy lace cups, making a brassiere unnecessary.

He slipped his thumbs beneath the satin straps and eased them off her shoulders. "I don't know whether to kiss you or look at you," he murmured.

"Why not both?"

After a kiss that left them dazed, his eyes drifted over her lazily. She held her breath as he lowered the slip to her waist. Her breasts held his eyes captive for a long time. Then, with the same blend of tenderness and passion that he had demonstrated before, he cupped her breasts in his hands and made love to them with his mouth.

"Riley." She sighed and clasped handfuls of his hair between her fingers as his tongue played upon her with undivided attention and nimble expertise.

He lowered his head farther and kissed her stomach, then sank to his knees and pressed his face into the softness of her belly. Her slip was removed by unhurried hands. He gazed at the pale stockings and lacy garter belt with a mixture of excitement and impatience.

He carefully unhooked the garters and rolled the stockings down her legs, taking precious time to measure the fit of her calves in his palms. When the veil-sheer stockings had been removed, he slid his hands up and down the backs of her legs from derriere to ankles. She shivered and made faint mewling sounds that brought a smile of pure male arrogance to his lips. He unfastened the garter belt, and it dropped from her hips.

The sheer panties hid nothing. His eyes moved over her rapaciously. But when he removed that last airy garment, he reined in his passion and savored her nakedness with an attitude of worship.

He enfolded her in his arms. Pressing his fingers into the fullness of her buttocks, he drew her close. He feathered light kisses across her abdomen, leaving the skin damp with caresses. Finally his lips melted into the soft dark cloud of hair. He used his tongue to express his joy in her.

Brin uttered a soft cry as her knees gave way and thumped against his chest. She would have collapsed had he not stood, caught her against him, and carried her to the bed. Before she had opened her eyes fully, he was naked, too, and lowering himself over her. She welcomed him, pulling him close, arching against him as their mouths came together.

He tested her preparedness with loving fingers that parted and stroked until she was moving restlessly, her legs sawing wantonly against his. Sensations swirled through her lower body. The flower of her sex bloomed open, and she ached for his possession. Then he was there, warm and hard and full. Sliding into her. Uniting them.

He raised his head in surprise and started to ease away. Brin wouldn't let him; she tightened her limbs around him.

"I love you, Riley," she whispered, her lips moving against his nipple. "I love you."

It took a long, lusty time, but his body patiently rocked hers to fulfillment. He nestled inside her after he was spent, reluctant to leave the small, tight warmth she gloved him in. Dawn crept through the draperies, bathing their sweat-dampened bodies with rosy light. "My sweet, sweet bride," he said in a voice that told her she was cherished. He kissed her ear, her neck, her mouth, her breasts. "I love you, Brin."

"I love you, Jon."

Lifting his head, he looked down into slumberous aqua-marine eyes. "That's the first time you've called me that. Sure you've got the right guy?"

She smiled sleepily and drew his head back down to her breasts. "I've got the right guy. Jon, Jon, Jon . . ."

Brin shifted uncomfortably on the sofa. Sleep stubbornly eluded her. When she heard a noise on the stairs, she sat up abruptly and spoke aloud the name that had been echoing through the chambers of her mind for hours. "Jon?"

CHAPTER SIX

Brin switched on the lamp. Riley, who was groping his way downstairs, was blinded by the sudden light, and blinked against it. "What did you say?"

"What? When? What are you doing out of bed?" She flung off the covers and rushed to the foot of the stairs, thinking he might need assistance.

"You called me Jon."

"Did I?"

"Yes. You never call me Jon except when we're making love."

"I must have been dreaming."

"Must have been a helluva dream."

His insinuating smile poured over her like warm honey.

Her body's tingling response to it vexed her. "You haven't said what you're doing out of bed."

"You didn't ask."

"I did so."

"You did? Hmm. I must have been shell-shocked by hearing you call me Jon."

He took the remaining stairs and came to stand above her on the last step. Only then did Brin fully realize that he was as scantily dressed as she. He was wearing nothing more than what she'd last seen him in, a pair of cotton briefs . . . *brief* cotton briefs, which rode low on his narrow hips. She loved that spot, an inch or two beneath his navel, where the satiny stripe of hair began to unfurl. He loved being kissed there too. Loved—

She jerked her eyes up to his face and caught his mocking smile. Uncomfortably aware of the brevity of her costume, she crossed her arms over her chest. The ugly robe had been left behind in her hurry, leaving her in nothing more than the bikini panty and tank top, which clung like a second skin.

"You've got great legs," Riley whispered roughly.

Months ago, when they had lived together as husband and wife, neither of them had exhibited a trace of modesty. Nakedness had never been awkward. Now, with the stillness of the night closing around them, with the specter of their separation looming between them, with his intense blue eyes boring into her, Brin felt more naked than ever in her life. Exposed. Vulnerable.

Any small animal whose weaknesses have been exploited will lash out at its predator. In this case, Brin's only weapon was hostility. "You came all the way downstairs, woke me up, to tell me that?"

"No, but as long as I was here . . ." He shrugged. "The anesthetic is wearing off."

Her animosity vanished and her brow puckered with concern. "Your hand hurts?"

"Like hell."

"The doctor said it would when the deadening began wearing off. He gave me some pain pills for you to take. They're in my purse in the kitchen. I'll get them."

She turned in that direction, but Riley grasped her wrist and stopped her. "I don't want a pain pill."

"But if it hurts—"

"I'd rather have a brandy. That'll numb the pain, but won't knock me out. Join me in one?"

With his fingers still loosely clasped around her wrist, he pulled her across the room to the bar. She padded after him docilely. The lateness of the hour lent a surrealistic quality to the occasion. Were they actually walking around in the middle of the night, in her friend's extravagantly decorated living room, in their underwear? It seemed impossible, yet it was so.

He deposited her on a stool and circled the end of the bar. His search through the stock turned up, not one, but two brands of brandy. He selected the more expensive and poured a hefty portion into a snifter.

"None for me, thanks," Brin said, curling her toes over the rung of the stool.

"A liqueur? Bailey's? I know you love Bailey's."

"Nothing."

"Then, cheers." He tipped the snifter toward her before taking a sip. He closed his eyes as the burning liquor slid down his throat, through his chest, and into his stomach, where it spread its welcome fire through his belly. There was a taut white line outlining his lips. His nostrils were pinched.

Brin touched the bandaged hand. "It really does hurt, doesn't it?"

"I'm all right," he said with that air of masculine superiority over pain that drives women to distraction.

"Why can't you just admit that it hurts?"

"Why whine about it?"

"Because when someone doesn't feel good he's entitled to a little sympathy, that's why. It's natural and normal."

"Does that apply to women too?"

"Certainly."

He started laughing.

"What's funny?" she asked.

"Is that why you always went to bed when you got cramps?"

"Cramps hurt," she said defensively. "If you had had to suffer them a single day of your life, you would have carried on something terrible. Any man would."

He reached out and put his palm against her cheek. "I

know they hurt." His thumb stroked her lower lip. "But we discovered a no-fail cure for them, didn't we?"

Brin swallowed hard. She lowered her eyes. She shifted restlessly on the stool.

"And our method beat Midol all to hell," he added raspily.

"I don't remember."

"Yes, you do."

"How do you know what I remember?" she challenged.

His eyes slid down her throat to her chest. She followed his gaze down, but she already knew what had given her away. She could feel her nipples straining against their soft confinement.

"Take your brandy upstairs," she said quickly, sliding off the stool. "I'm going back to bed."

She returned to the couch and made a production of fluffing up her pillow. It didn't need it, but the activity gave her something to do so she wouldn't see the knowing look in his eyes.

She lay down and pulled the blanket over her shoulders, turning on her side and pretending that sleep was imminent. She felt the sofa sag with his weight as he sat down on the end opposite her head. He lifted her feet into his lap. With an annoyed sigh she rolled over and looked at him.

"You said you were taking your brandy upstairs."

"No, *you* said I was taking my brandy upstairs. You're sure having a hard time keeping straight who says what tonight. Could it be that you're flustered because I'm here?"

She made a scoffing sound and closed her eyes in feigned

boredom. "All right, stay. I don't care. Only be quiet so I can sleep." She sighed deeply and closed her eyes again. But seconds later she jackknifed into a sitting position. "And stop that!"

"You always did have sensitive feet." His left hand was beneath the covers. His thumb had gone straight for the spot where the ball of her foot met her big toe. A mere touch, much less a rotating massage of his thumb, had always elicited a reaction from her.

"You're not going to let me sleep, are you?" she demanded.

"How can you sleep when I'm suffering?"

"The brandy's not helping?"

"Not yet." He held up the snifter. He hadn't drunk but a third of it.

"All right," Brin said tiredly. "I'll baby-sit you. But if you become drunk and rowdy instead of sedated, I'm packing you off home. You can drive with your left hand."

"You should know," he said with a lazy grin.

Heat surged through her as she recalled all the times he had done just that while his right hand was otherwise occupied. She rebelled at her own tendency to remember the past; she certainly didn't need his less-than-subtle reminders of it. "Stop making lewd insinuations, or I'll send you upstairs."

"I was surprised to discover you were a virgin on our wedding night."

"Riley! Didn't you hear what I just said?"

"That wasn't an insinuation. That was a simple statement of fact. I was surprised."

"Why?"

"There aren't many virgins your age left."

"My age? You make me sound ancient. Like a relic from the past."

"How old were you? Twenty-five? Come on, Brin. How many twenty-five-year-old virgins do you know?"

"Maybe they should all be rounded up and herded into museums."

"You sound piqued. I only said I was surprised. I didn't say I was disappointed." He was stroking the high arch of her foot with an indolent thumb. "In fact I liked it very much," he said softly. "It would have driven me crazy if I had had to imagine who'd been with you before me. I couldn't have stood the thought of other men making love to you."

The unrelenting caress on her feet was lulling her into a trance. She was remembering all the times his tongue had performed that same ritual, turning her bones to butter and her blood to simmering, liquid desire. That he still had that hypnotizing effect on her was something she resented. Unwisely she spoke aloud the first retort that flashed into her mind.

"There are other ways of making love."

His thumb came to an abrupt standstill. Brin felt the angry tension in his fingers as they closed more tightly around her foot. She watched his dark brows pull into a harsh V above his nose. "What's that supposed to mean?"

She wished for all the world that she hadn't opened her mouth, that she had weighed his reaction to such an oblique boast before speaking aloud. But there was no backing down now. "Just that I never said other men hadn't made love to me. Because my virginity was intact you assumed as much."

"Meaning you played around a lot, you just never went 'all the way'?"

She shrugged.

"With whom?"

"Oh, honestly, Riley. What difference does—"

"I'll tell you what difference it makes. It makes a helluva lot of difference to me, that's what difference it makes."

"Why? Why now? It didn't matter when we were married."

"When we were married you didn't flaunt your former lovers in my face."

"I didn't flau—"

"Who were they? Men you knew in college?"

He was making her mad. His stupidity and obstinacy were fanning her smoldering anger into a wildfire. "Of course. I went to Berkeley, you know."

"Oh, of course. That explains a lot." His eyes narrowed to fine blue slits. "High school?"

"Some," she said with a toss of her head.

"Junior high?" When she only glared back at him defiantly, he whispered, "My God." His eyes raked down her body as though seeing it for the first time. "Did you lead all those men a merry chase the way you did me before we married? Tease them until they were nearly crazy? How far did you let the poor bastards go?"

"This is ridiculous."

"How far?" he shouted. "Did you let them see your breasts? Touch them?"

"I won't—"

"Kiss them? What about your thighs?"

"Riley—"

"Did they kiss your thighs? Between them?"

"Stop this! I won't listen to any more!"

She tried to extricate her feet from his grasp, but his left hand seemed to have assumed the strength of two. He imprisoned her ankles in an iron grip and firmly tucked her heels into the notch of his lap. "Oh, yes, you will. You'll listen to it all. You brought this up, now I want to thoroughly exhaust the subject."

"There *is* no subject. There were no men."

"Did you love them back? With your hands, your mouth? How did they love you?"

"They didn't! *There were no other men!*" Her shout finally penetrated the red mist of jealous rage that fogged his brain.

His bare chest was heaving with each ragged breath. She saw him visibly pull himself together, though he didn't release his hold on her feet. "Who was your first lover? Who?"

"You were." She strained the two words between her teeth. Her whole body was vibrating with humiliation and fury.

For several ponderous moments they stared at each other, then Brin flopped back onto the pillow. Wearily she raised one forearm over her eyes. "There. Is that what you wanted to hear?"

"You hadn't ever—"

"No, Riley, I hadn't ever." She lowered her arm and looked at him. Both of them were surprised by the tears forming in her eyes. "Couldn't you tell? Didn't you know? Is your ego so fragile that you had to have me spell it out for you?"

He laid his injured hand in the valley at the center of her rib cage and, with the slightest movement of his fingers, stroked her tummy. "Why did you say there had been other men?"

"To provoke you, I guess," she admitted listlessly.

"Why did you want to provoke me?"

"I don't know. Maybe because of the other women." The tears were dried now. Her eyes were as deep and turbulent as the bay during a Pacific storm. "The women before *and* after we were married. You've been going out. I read the newspapers."

His hand became still, then was completely withdrawn. He reached for the brandy, which he had set on the end table, and took a long sip. When he returned the snifter to the table he said curtly, "You've been out too. Winn's been squiring you around for weeks."

"How do you know that?"

"I have my sources."

"I've explained Abel to you. There's nothing romantic about our friendship."

"The same is true when a woman accompanies me on a personal appearance."

She looked at him skeptically. His face drew into a self-righteous frown. "You know what those social events are like. I'm expected to attend them on behalf of the TV station. I'm also expected to have an escort. Those dates don't mean anything. Nothing happens."

"I know better," she said, springing to a sitting position again. "I remember the time we went—" She broke off in mid-sentence. "Never mind."

His mouth tilted up at the corner. "Come on. Finish. You remember what time?"

"Nothing. I forgot."

"Could you be referring to the night I spoke at that Marin County shindig? The night they sent the limousine for us?"

The fiery blush that spread across Brin's cheeks was as good as a signed confession. . . .

"How did we rate this?" Brin asked.

The limousine that had come for them at the appointed time was long, black, and luxurious. The chauffeur seemed to sit at least half a block away from the backseat, where Brin rode with Riley.

"You rate it because you're with me. And I rate it because I'm a famous television personality."

"And such a humble, self-effacing one," she said with amusement and affection. Leaning forward, she kissed him on the cheek.

"Hey, look at this," he exclaimed with boyish enthusiasm as he discovered the button that operated the electric moon roof. "And there's a stocked bar, lest madam get thirsty." He showed her the panel that slid open to reveal the bar. "And there's a color TV in case you don't want to miss an episode of *Dallas*."

He played with all the gadgets and buttons. "Just don't break anything," she cautioned. "We couldn't afford to have it repaired."

"You're not to worry your pretty little head about this family's finances," he said in the chauvinistic manner he knew irritated her. He grinned when he got the expected baleful look. "My agent's just negotiated a new contract. It embarrasses me when I consider what they're paying me."

"I'll bet," she said dryly.

"And I've been informed by inside sources that my producer is up for a big raise too."

"Who told you that?"

"My wife. Who has an inside track with my producer."

"Just don't forget that one doesn't overlap the other. Your producer was recommended for a raise because of her brilliant handling of *Riley in the Morning* and the substantial increase in its rating points."

"And what reward does she get for her brilliant handling of Riley?" he growled close to her ear.

"Hmm, just more of Riley, I guess." She purred seductively and curved her hand around the back of his head as he leaned over to kiss her.

"Have I told you how delectable you look tonight? Is that a new blouse?"

"No and yes, in that order." Her lips sipped at his. "You look pretty tasty yourself, Mr. Riley. I happen to become wild and irresponsible where men in tuxedoes are concerned."

"I wish you'd told me that before." The conversation was momentarily suspended by a lengthy kiss. "Know what I just realized?"

"No, what?"

"That I haven't seen you all day."

"You saw me for hours at work."

"But that was work. And once we got home you were busy getting ready for tonight and put me to work planting those bedding plants on the patio."

"Did you miss me?"

"I missed this." He thrust his tongue deep inside her mouth and his arms closed more tightly around her.

When they finally pulled apart she murmured, "I'm flattered. We've been married ten whole months and you're not tired of me yet."

"Not a chance," he whispered against her neck. "In fact, if you'll lower your hand a few more inches, you'll see just how tired of you I ain't."

"Riley!" she said, giggling.

"Sorry. Just how tired of you I'm not."

"Shh! The driver will hear you."

Reaching behind him for the panel of buttons, he found the one that raised a partition to separate them from the chauffeur. "There. All taken care of. Ever made love in a limousine?"

"No, and . . . ah, darling . . . behave, now. The chauffeur . . . hmm . . ."

Unconsciously she slipped off her high-heeled sandals and rubbed her stockinged foot against his calf. Her arms folded around his neck as he lowered her into the plush corner of the limousine, which received her like a velvet embrace.

"I really like this blouse." It was black, sheer organza, and the rhinestone buttons cooperated with his busy fingers. "I like the way it rustles. Ever notice how sexy the sound of rustling clothes is?" She wore a black lace teddy beneath the blouse.

"Riley, we really shouldn't." Her protest was weak because he was already massaging her breasts, lifting and re-shaping them within his hands. "Three hundred people are waiting for you and . . . hmm . . . you'll forget what you're supposed to . . . to, uh, oh, Riley . . . say."

"I bet you taste as good as you look."

He slipped his hand inside the webby lace cup and lifted her breast free. His thumb finessed the crest into sweet arousal, then he lowered his head and took it between his lips. He worried the tender peak with his tongue, flicking crazily and stroking sinuously until Brin was almost delirious with pleasure. She blindly tore at the studs of his tuxedo shirt until his chest was bare and her hands could thrill to the feel of his skin, his chest hair.

The black moire skirt she was wearing to the formal affair crackled appealingly as his free hand slipped beneath it.

The skin of her upper thigh was soft, silky, and his fingertips derived as much pleasure from their caress as they gave. His fingers tiptoed up the suspenders to the satin garter belt, then stroked the warm skin above it.

When his hand slipped inside the matching panties and cupped her femininity, they both gasped softly. "Jon, that's . . . oh, yes."

"You're so sweet. And wet. So wet. I love touching you like this. And like this."

His fingers explored. Deliciously. Her throat arched and her head ground into the velour upholstery. She bit her bottom lip to keep from crying out her ecstasy.

Her response enflamed him. He withdrew his hand and frantically opened the zipper of his trousers. His possession was swift. They were frenzied by the impropriety of what they were doing. The threat of discovery, the ruination of the fine clothing that was bunched between their straining bodies, only served to heighten their excitement. His hands opened wide over the fleshy part of her bottom and drew her up hard against him. His hips ground into her, rolling and thrusting madly.

The crisis came quickly, like an explosion that shuddered soundlessly through them simultaneously. He buried his face in her neck and released his groans of completion in a hot torrent of breath against her fevered skin. Replete, her arms fell away from his neck.

And just as simultaneously, they began laughing.

"Oh, my gosh, Riley. What have we done? You'd better get off me and let me assess the damage."

He raised his head and peered out the window—which was tinted, luckily. "You'd better hurry, sweetheart. I'd say we have three minutes at the outside."

"Oh, no," she squeaked. Her clothes were put in order swiftly enough, but one sandal couldn't be found until she got down on all fours on the floorboard and groped beneath the seat.

"I can't find one of my studs, Brin," Riley said in near panic. "Oh, here it is . . . no, that's part of the seat belt."

"Ouch, damn! Here it is. I just found the little devil with my heel. It's probably put a run in my stocking."

He inserted the stud, tucked his shirt in, and replaced the cummerbund. "Don't forget to zip up," Brin said.

"Thanks." His bow tie was crooked, and Brin took time out from recombing her hair to straighten it. Swift fingers reattached the decorative comb in her hair, and she checked her compact mirror for damage wreaked on her makeup, with which she had taken great pains.

Through the tinted windows they could see that a small welcoming committee was waiting to greet them beneath the awning of the exclusive country club. "How do I look?" Brin asked anxiously as the limousine glided to a halt.

"Like you've just made love."

"Riley!"

"Well, you asked." Laughing, he took her hand and squeezed it. "Look at it this way, all the women will be jealous of you and all the men will be jealous of me. I doubt many of them had a tumble on their way here."

She began laughing. "I love you."

"And I love you." His face grew almost fierce. "Swear to God I do."

The chauffeur came around to the back door of the limousine and opened it. Much to the amusement of their welcoming committee, Mr. and Mrs. Jon Riley were caught kissing. . . .

"Admit it," Riley said softly. "It was fun."

"I never said it wasn't fun." Brin was plucking at a loose thread on the blanket. "You were always fun." Her eyes drifted up to his, and she looked at him through a thick screen of lashes. "How much fun have you had with other women since I left? Taken any limousine rides lately?"

He gently lifted her feet off his lap and, taking up the brandy snifter, leaned forward and propped his elbows on his knees. He swirled the snifter with his left hand as he stared down into its contents.

"I was mad as hell when you left, Brin," he began quietly.

Suddenly Brin didn't want to know. Why had she provoked him into telling her? She didn't want to hear his confession. But it was too late. He had made up his mind to tell her.

"Without a word, you were just gone." He turned only his head, but it swiveled toward her so abruptly, she jumped, and recoiled from the laser action of his eyes. "Do you blame me for being hurt? What if I had just moved out on you without one word of explanation, recrimination, regret, remorse, anything?"

"I guess you had reason to be angry," she conceded softly.

"Damn right I did." He tossed down a draft of brandy. "Until I got your letter in the mail, I was crazy with worry."

"But I left you a note."

"Oh, sure. Five words. Big deal. 'Don't worry. I'll be fine.' Don't worry, with perverts walking the streets. And there are plane crashes and car accidents happening every day." His agitation mounted with each word. "Lakes and oceans to drown in. Mountains to fall off. I thought of them all." He drew a deep breath, which calmed him. " 'Don't worry.' I swear, if I could have gotten my hands on you that night I would have strangled you!"

He shot off the couch and began to pace. "Then, when I got your letter, which instead of giving an explanation, only told me to stay away from you, I got mad. Fighting mad. Spitting mad. I wasn't too friendly a fellow to be around. Couldn't and wouldn't work. When the station manager called and told me either to shape up without you or get out for good, I regained my sanity. Why should I let you ruin my career, my life? So I went back to work. And that's when the indifference set in."

"That's when you started seeing other women," she said dully.

"Well, why not? How did I know you weren't dating? How did I know you hadn't been having an affair the whole time we were married?"

She gave him a dirty look and he relented. "All right, I never really thought that, but it crossed my mind. So I started dating. And the younger and sweeter and more obliging they were, the better I liked them."

She buried her chin in her chest. She wouldn't cry. She wouldn't! After all, what had she expected? Nobody had to tell her how potent Riley's sex drive was. He was sure to have sought an outlet for his frustration.

"Some women will do anything to make sure a man asks them out again," he said tauntingly. "And at the risk of sounding boorishly conceited, I didn't have to go far to find the most cooperative ones."

Having stood all she could, Brin threw back the blanket and lunged off the couch. "I think I'll have a drink now." She strode toward the bar.

"There were plenty of women at my disposal, Brin."

"I have no doubt of that," she threw over her shoulder. "But spare me the salacious details. I don't need to hear any more." She slammed a highball glass onto the bar and held a bottle of Bailey's over it.

"But I didn't sleep with any of them."

Brin's hand froze in the act of pouring the cream liqueur from the bottle. Her eyes riveted on his, across the room. Her heart bumped against her ribs, and she felt the sting of sudden tears. She felt like crying because she believed him.

"I haven't slept with another woman since I married you. In fact, since the first day I kissed you."

"You haven't?"

"I guess I'm a sucker when it comes to marriage vows."

The bottle of Bailey's thumped on the bar. She had almost dropped it from lifeless fingers as she watched him move toward her slowly. As she stood transfixed, he reached over the bar and took her hand. With gentle pressure, he guided her around the end of it until she stood directly in front of him. Then he laid his good hand on her shoulder and pressed down on it until her fanny touched the high stool behind her.

She was grateful for its support, because she thought she might faint, both with relief at what he'd told her and with love. Oh, she could deny it, but when she drew her last breath she knew she would still be loving Jon Riley.

He parted her thighs and stepped between them, bringing their bodies close. She could feel his chest hairs against the clinging fabric of her tank top.

"In my misguided youth I thought sex was all for kicks. I was greedy, but aloof, you know?"

"Yes. I think so."

"It wasn't until I had made love with you that I knew what it was all about. And when you left me, mad as I was at you, I just couldn't bring myself to cheapen what we had shared. With anybody else it would have been a parody of the real thing."

He took a step closer. "Why would I want another woman, Brin, when I had you? Why would I even look for another woman, when I had loved the best? That isn't it, is it? Did you think I was being unfaithful to you?"

"No."

"Did someone tell you an outrageous lie about me and another woman?"

"No."

"Then what was it, sweetheart?" He lowered his head, bringing his face close to hers. His lips feathered over her neck, her earlobe. The bar caught her in the middle of her spine as she leaned back to give him access. "Why did you walk out on me?"

He kissed her mouth, but held back the passion that pulsed between them. He played at her lips with his, but restrained himself from claiming them in the way they both yearned for.

He raised her arms to the back of his neck and crossed them. Then he traced the undersides of her arms downward, loving the involuntary moaning sound she made at his touch. His thumbs made a suggestive pass through her armpits. His hands paused, hovered, before the heels of them began to rub the sides of her breasts.

"What was it, Brin? Money?"

"Of course not."

He pressed into the fullness, forcing her breasts forward until the nipples made contact with his chest. Reflexively her thighs gripped his more tightly. The hair that sprinkled his legs tickled the smooth insides of her thighs.

"Work?"

"No."

"Then, what?"

Their lips finally met with the passion that had been promised. She caressed his tongue with hers as it delved into her mouth. His hands moved to the bottom of her tank top and began inching it up. Up, baring her navel. Up, baring her midriff. Up, baring the undercurves of her breasts. Up, until her breasts were flattened against the solid wall of his naked chest.

A low, mating sound rumbled in his throat as their kiss deepened. His hands splayed wide on her back. He drew her as close to him as possible, lifting her up until she stood on the lowest rung of the stool and was eye level with him. His lips were ravenous, his tongue rapacious, his hands unyielding. Their thighs pressed, rubbed, shifted against each other in a hungry desperation to gain ground.

Her womanhood tipped forward, instinctively seeking his hardness. His arousal was solid and hot as it pushed against his briefs. He plowed his hands into the waistband of her panties, covering her derriere with demanding fingers that urged her ever forward, ever closer. He gave in to the wildness streaking through him.

And then his tongue touched her nipple and her whole body went rigid with alarm.

No! She couldn't—*wouldn't*—let it happen. She'd have no ground left to stand on. The last seven months would mean nothing. If she made love to him, she would start eroding again.

She pushed him away and almost fell off the stool in her haste to escape his embrace. Turning her back, she leaned against the bar, bracing herself against it with straight arms while she gulped in air.

Riley stood behind her, his breathing just as labored as

hers. He stared at her back, still bare because her top was hitched up. He tried to penetrate her brain, tried to understand the incomprehensible.

"*That's* it, isn't it?" Riley asked in a wheezing voice. Brin said nothing. "All right. So now I know." He took her by the shoulders and turned her around. Catching her cleft chin in his hand, he tilted her head back, forcing her to meet his eyes. "What went wrong with us in bed?"

CHAPTER SEVEN

The telephone rang.

Had it been a bolt of lightning it couldn't have been more intrusive or electrifying. The moment was charged with emotion. Tension crackled like old paper.

Brin was the first to move. She pulled down her top with one swift tug and took a step toward the phone.

"Don't touch it," Riley barked.

"This is *my* house, *my* telephone. I'm answering it."

"You can't hide behind a telephone. We're going to have this discussion whether you answer that phone or not. And I swear to God that if Abel Winn is on the other end of that call, I'll tear the damn thing out of the wall!"

She glared up at him as she raised the receiver to her ear.

"Don't you dare bully me," she commanded him through clenched teeth. Then she said sweetly, "Hello?"

"Uh, Brin, were you asleep?"

"Whitney!"

Riley let loose a string of scathing profanities. Mentally Brin flinched. "Dim Whit?" he spat. "It's Dim Whit? I'll kill her." He curled his fingers and pantomimed choking somebody.

"Shh!"

"What?"

"Not you, Whitney."

"Is somebody with you? Golly, Brin, I'm sorry, I—"

"No, nobody's with me." Riley's ferocious scowl deepened and he reached for the phone. Brin dodged him in time. "Actually there is somebody with me, but . . . Oh, never mind, Whitney. It's a long story. Is something wrong?"

"Well, sort of."

"You'll have to speak louder. I can barely hear you. It's awfully noisy in the background." Brin turned her back on Riley, who was making vicious slicing motions across his throat with his index finger. Even if she hadn't worked in television she would have been able to interpret that hand cue.

"I'm at the airport," Whitney informed her.

"The airport! It's four o'clock in the morning."

"I know, and I'm sorry to be calling you now."

Brin dropped onto one of the barstools and propped her head in her hand in the posture of someone who doesn't know when the next brick is going to fall. What next? People didn't call from airports in the middle of the night for a friendly chat. Calls originating from airports at four in the morning usually portended disaster.

"I went to New York to see my former roommate from Smith. I took the red-eye home. I got on the plane okay and . . ."

Riley nudged Brin's elbow. She looked up at him. Wearing an inquiring expression, he waggled the bottle of Bailey's in front of her. She shook her head. He shrugged, took up the brandy bottle, poured himself another generous draft and drank it down in one swallow. The potent liquor must have felt like a branding iron when it hit his stomach, because he made a comical expression of pain. He poured another two inches into the snifter and began to sip it slowly.

". . . and now I can't find it." Whitney Stone had just concluded her tale of woe, and Brin, having been distracted by Riley, had missed the essentials of it.

"Can't find what?"

"My purse. Say, Brin, are you sure you're okay? You sound funny. You weren't doing it or anything, were you?"

Brin's eyes slid up to Riley. He was watching her with the single-minded concentration of a cat on a trapped mouse. "No, nothing like that," Brin said uneasily. "You lost your purse?"

"Yes. It's gone. I can't find it anywhere."

Brin massaged her throbbing temples. She closed her eyes and wished for once that people didn't always count on her to be dependable, good ol' Brin.

"What's going on?" Riley demanded in a terse whisper.

Covering the mouthpiece Brin said, "She lost her purse."

"Brin?"

"Yes, Whitney, I'm still here. I'm trying to think. Did you check with the flight attendants?"

"They helped me search the plane after everybody got off."

"Somebody could have taken it."

"I don't think so. I don't remember getting on the plane with it."

"How could you get on an airplane without your purse?"

"Because she's d-u-m-b," Riley said, tapping his forehead with his index finger. "A space cadet."

Impatiently Brin waved her hand and mouthed "shut up" at him. "Weren't you carrying your boarding pass in it?"

"Don't fuss at me, Brin. I already feel like a fool."

Brin was immediately ashamed of herself. The younger woman was obviously close to tears and in need of help. Brin shouldn't have been so impatient with her. It certainly wasn't Whitney's fault that Riley was standing near-naked in front of her, looking like he was about to take a big bite of her. "All right, calm down. Crying won't help. What can I do?"

"Could you come get me?" Whitney asked in a small voice.

"At the airport? Now?" Brin asked in a high, reedy tone.

Now it was Riley's turn to wave his hands. He did it with considerably more gusto than Brin had. He waved them both, crisscrossing them in front of his body like a flagman aborting a landing attempt on an aircraft carrier. "No, no, no!" he hissed loud enough for Brin to hear. "Nix. That idea is out." She ignored him.

"I know it's asking a lot, Brin," Whitney was saying.

"What about your parents?" Brin asked hopefully.

"They went to Carmel for the weekend. Besides, if they find out I've done something this stupid, I'll catch hell."

"Do you need a place to stay? You can stay—" She slapped away Riley's left hand as he reached across her for the disconnect button on the phone. ". . . can stay . . ." They were engaged in an all out hand-slapping contest now. "Hold on, Whitney." Brin covered the mouthpiece again. "So help me, Riley, if you don't leave this telephone alone and mind your own business, I'll—"

"This *is* my own business."

"She called me, not you."

"If you invite her over here—"

"I repeat. *This is my house.* You can't tell me what to do." She stared him down, then returned to the girl on the phone. "Do you need a place to stay?"

"No. The housekeeper is at home, but she won't drive after dark, and even if she did, no one would ride with her. I think she's certifiably blind. And if I ask her to pay for a taxi, she's sure to tell my parents. Do you mind too much, Brin?"

Mind? Why should she mind? Already tonight she had bickered with a recalcitrant caterer, dealt with the sudden appearance of her estranged husband, who had had the unmitigated gall to crash her party, diplomatically avoided the attentions of a man she wanted to work for but whom she did not want to become romantically involved with, rushed a bleeding man to the emergency room, played nurse to him while his hand was being sutured, and deflected his sexual advances while at the same time facing the dilemma of their crumbled marriage. What was one more catastrophe in light of all that? It was as if she were living through a bad episode of *The Twilight Zone.*

"Where are you?" She tried not to let her weariness and despondency show as she told Whitney to be watching for her car within the hour.

"You can't be serious," Riley said when she hung up and headed for the stairs.

"Don't badger me, Riley. She needs help."

With considerable emphasis, he set the snifter down on the bar. "I need help. You need help. Our marriage needs help."

"Our marriage has been on the back burner for seven months. One more hour won't hurt it."

He was right on her heels as she entered the bedroom. She went into the bathroom and pulled on the same jeans and sweatshirt she had worn earlier. Riley's blood had dried on them, but she was too tired to notice.

"I'll be back—What are you doing?"

"Trying my damnedest to put on my pants," he said from the edge of the bed, where he was seated, struggling to hold the jeans with one hand while he pushed his legs into them.

"You're not going anywhere."

"The hell I'm not. Do you think I'd let you drive out to the airport alone at four in the morning?"

"I don't need your protection."

"Don't pull a feminist act. Be reasonable. Anything could happen. You could have a flat tire."

She propped one fist on her hip. "You're the one who should be reasonable. If you can't even put on your pants, how much help do you think you'd be with a flat tire?"

"All right, Brin. Stand here and argue with me." He stood up, wriggling, trying to work the tight jeans over his hips without using his injured right hand. "But every second you waste here leaves Dim Whit out there alone with whatever perverts are lurking around the airport."

"You're actually concerned for her safety?"

"No, I'm concerned for the perverts'."

He had a point. And as she stood there ruminating on it, he managed to get into his shirt. "Button me up?"

He looked so damned adorable with his hair mussed and that boyish grin with the dimples at each end, Brin didn't know whether to kiss him or rake her nails down his face.

"Oh, all right," she said grudgingly. "Besides, I don't trust you here alone. No telling what you'd do while I was gone. You're worse than a three-year-old who has to be watched every second." She virtually shoved the buttons through the holes, as though punishing them.

"Unless you want me to be exposing myself to Dim Whit, you'd better zip up my pants too."

She turned back and her gaze dropped to his fly. True. It

was gaping open. In nervous reaction she wet her lips with her tongue.

He chuckled. "Gee, I'd like for you to, Brin. But I don't think we should take the time right now."

His joke made her mad. She drew her face into a taut, stern, no-nonsense mask and reached for the tab of the zipper. She yanked it upward.

"Ouch! Damn, Brin, be careful. You'll have to, uh . . ."

"No way."

"What's the matter?" he taunted. "Scared?"

"No!" she denied vehemently. "Aggravated. This wouldn't be a problem if you didn't wear your jeans so indecently tight."

"I never recall your complaining before. Come on, just a little pressure—"

"I know, I know." She nervously wet her lower lip again, daring him with her eyes to make another lewd comment. Then she thrust her hand between the folds of soft denim and pressed until she could easily slide the zipper up.

"There. See? No sweat." She felt his warm breath on the crown of her head, heard the amusement in his voice, and stepped away from him quickly. Turning on her heel, she proudly stalked from the room and down the stairs, not checking to see if he was following. He was. By the time she reached the back door, he was right behind her, stumbling down the back steps.

Stumbling?

She whirled around and peered up at him closely. His eyes were unnaturally bright. His smile was a shade crooked, and sappy. His lean cheeks were flushed. She reached up and put a hand on his forehead, but he didn't feel feverish.

"Whash a matter?" he asked.

Her eyes went round, then narrowed suspiciously. "You're plastered!"

He made an attempt at sobriety by pulling himself up straighter. "I am not. Jush a little, teeny-weeny bit woozshy from losh of blood." He held up his unsteady left hand, but had difficulty showing a fraction of an inch between his index finger and his thumb.

"Oh, for heaven's sake." None too gently Brin packed him into the front seat and fastened his seat belt.

By the time they were under way, his head was lolling on the back of the seat and his eyes were closed. "I must be crazy," Brin muttered to herself. "It's four o'clock in the morning. I'm driving through the streets of San Francisco with a drunk man while on my way to rescue a dimwit!"

To her surprise Riley chuckled, though his eyes remained closed. He reached across the interior of the car and patted her thigh. "You're a fine woman, Brin. A fine woman."

And because it felt so good riding there, she let his hand stay.

Brin saw Whitney before the younger woman spotted the car. She honked the horn, then stepped out onto the pavement and waved her arms, shouting Whitney's name. The girl came jogging toward her, lugging a suitcase.

"Brin, you'll never know how much I appreciate this. I don't know—Is that *blood*?"

"Uh, oh, yes."

"What happened?"

"It's a long story. Do you mind riding in the backseat?"

"No, sure." Whitney opened the rear car door and tossed her suitcase inside, scrambling in after it. "Were you hurt, Brin? Did you have an accident?"

"No, I—"

"Who's that? *Riley!*" Whitney shrieked.

Riley swore expansively, having been jarringly roused from his nap. He popped erect and bumped his head on the ceiling of the car. "Dammit!" His mumbled cursing continued as he turned to glower at the passenger in the backseat.

When he raised his hand to examine the bump on his head, Whitney cried, "Your hand! Did you hurt your hand? There's a bandage on it."

Riley shot Brin a look that said, "That's probably the most brilliant deduction she'll ever reach." To Whitney he said, "Yes, there's a bandage on it. And now I might have to get one on my head, thanks to you."

"I'm sorry, but I didn't see you sitting there. What happened to your hand?"

"It's a long story."

Whitney's round face puckered in perplexity. "That's what Brin said."

"I cut it on a broken glass and had to get stitches." Riley sighed and faced forward again, glad to have laid that matter to rest.

"Hmm," Whitney said. "Were you at Brin's house when it happened?"

"Yes," they chorused, looked at each other, then fell silent as they once again stared out the windshield.

"Were you two in bed when I called?" Whitney asked bluntly. Brin braked sharply. Riley laughed. Whitney clapped her hands together. "You *were*? You guys are back together? Oh, I'm so glad. I always said—"

"No, we're not back together," Brin interrupted. Maneuvering like a demolition driver, she swung the car onto the freeway.

"Oh." Whitney was obviously crestfallen. "Then why were you in bed together?"

"We weren't!" Brin cried. She now wished she had let Riley talk her into staying at home and letting Whitney fend for herself.

"Well, it sounded like it," Whitney retorted defensively. "I heard all this scuffling and whispering and just, you know, *felt* like I had called at a bad time."

"It was a bad time because we *weren't* in bed together," Riley said.

After a short silence Whitney said, "Oh, I see."

"No, you don't." Brin looked in the rearview mirror to meet Whitney's eyes. "Riley and I are not getting back together," she said emphatically.

"Why not?"

"That's what I'd like to know," Riley chimed in, straightening from his slouch and looking at Brin's profile.

"It would be best for everybody if you two would reconcile your differences," Whitney said.

"Amen."

"Be quiet. You're drunk."

"He's *drinking* now?"

"I slept it off."

"You weren't asleep that long, and no, he's not *drinking.*"

"I thought Riley had more character than to take to drinking."

"He hasn't taken to drinking!"

"Well, make up your mind, Brin."

"Yeah, make up your mind, Brin. You're the one who said I was drunk."

Brin emitted a short, loud whistle. "Look, guys, if we're going to take this show on the road, we're going to have to smooth out the dialogue." She had regressed from an episode of *The Twilight Zone* to an Abbott and Costello routine.

"If you two got back together it would certainly help the show," Whitney went on, obviously undaunted by Brin's shrinking supply of patience. "After what Daddy told me I can see why Riley would want to mend his fences."

Brin's head came around abruptly. "What about the show?"

Brin had stayed in contact with Whitney only because Whitney had assumed other responsibilities at the television station soon after Brin resigned her post as producer of *Riley in the Morning*. She couldn't have remained a confidante of Whitney's if the girl were still working in Riley's shadow. Not that Brin didn't trust her. She didn't think that Whitney Stone would maliciously carry tales about her back to Riley. But she knew how enamored Whitney was of him and how his charm could have swayed her into selling her own mother.

Brin's incisive question elicited diverse responses. Riley jerked as if he'd been shot, and snarled, "Nothing."

Whitney scooted forward so that she was sitting on the rim of the seat cushion, and folded her hands on the back of the front seat. "The show is in trouble."

"It's not in trouble," Riley countered.

"Well, Daddy says it is. Serious trouble. He said that ever since Brin left it's been sliding into the toilet. And that's a quote."

Brin hazarded a glance at Riley. He was looking at Whitney with murder in his eyes, but Whitney was so caught up in the subject that she didn't notice. It wasn't often that people looked to her as a source of valuable information. Now that she had an audience intent on hearing what she had to say, she was going to expound on her topic and enjoy every minute of the attention.

"What do you know about it?" Riley asked belligerently. "You're not even working on the show any longer. For that matter, what does 'Daddy' know? He's not back there. He doesn't know what I have to put up with to get every show on tape. Ineptitude. They've surrounded me with morons and expect me to overcome that."

"You could try harder to get along with people," Whitney said bravely. "You yell at everybody. Browbeat them until they're scared to death of you. I should know. And those producers—"

"Producers, plural?" Brin asked.

"He's run off three since you left."

"They were incompetent," Riley shouted. "One broad

they hired wore earrings that dangled down to her shoulders and a ring on every finger. I think she was into devil worship. I was interviewing gurus, fortune tellers, and witches every other day."

Brin bit back a laugh.

"Then they hired this jerk who had just graduated from Cal Tech with a degree in television. Hell, he'd never even seen the inside of a television studio. But to hear him tell it, he knew everything there was to know. He was telling engineers and technicians who had worked in TV for over twenty years how to do their jobs. And who did they bitch to? You got it. Me! The next one—"

"She ran out of the studio in tears," Whitney interrupted enthusiastically.

"What happened?"

Riley opened his mouth to speak, but Whitney got there first. "I wasn't there, but if what everybody said was true, Riley was horribly cruel to her. And I didn't think she was *that* fat."

Brin looked at him with incredulity. "You called a woman fat? To her face? Riley, how could you?"

"I didn't call her fat," he snapped.

"Not exactly, no," Whitney conceded. "What he said was, 'Why don't you just park a battleship in front of the floor director when he's trying to give me time cues? I couldn't see around it any better than I can see around you.'"

"I sent her two dozen roses later, by way of apology," Riley grumbled. He slumped down in the seat, crossed his arms over his chest, hunched his shoulders forward, and looked like a little boy who was settling down for a long pouting spell.

"He hit a cameraman," Whitney reported.

"Hit?" Brin cried. She turned her head and stared at Riley. Finally he met her accusing stare.

"I didn't 'hit' him," he mumbled. "I just sort of . . . pushed him."

"Have you lost your mind? What's wrong with you?" Brin asked him. "Why would you hit *or* push anyone?"

Riley didn't see fit to answer, but Whitney did. "Because the guy told Riley that he would hand-deliver you to his bed if that would bring you back to the show and improve Riley's mood."

The silence in the car was thick. Whitney's eyes flew back and forth between the two of them. She adored them both, mainly because their lives seemed to contain the drama so lacking in hers.

Neither Brin nor Riley moved. They stared out the windshield, straight ahead. Whitney hadn't known what to expect when she imparted that last bit of information, but she was mildly disappointed that something drastic hadn't happened.

"This week Daddy told me that the station manager called Riley in on the carpet and told him he'd better get his act together. No pun intended. He told Riley to find a producer he can work with and bring the ratings of the show up to where they should be . . . or else."

She didn't need to explain what the "or else" was. "Or else" could only mean cancellation. Professional death.

"Why isn't anybody saying anything?" Whitney asked

after a ponderous silence. "You're not mad at me are you, Riley?"

He drew in a long breath and released it on a sigh. "No, Whitney. I'm not mad at you."

"Brin is still your wife. She should know what's going on in your life. You two are my favorite people in the whole world. I want you to be happy. Living apart like this is silly."

"I . . . we appreciate your concern," Riley said quickly. He gave Whitney a soft smile, which ordinarily would have made Brin love him even more. "Be sure to notify the credit-card companies tomorrow that your purse was lost."

"I will, Riley, I will," Whitney said worshipfully.

"You must learn to be more careful. There are some bad characters roaming around who prey on absentminded young women. I'd hate like hell for anything to happen to you."

"You . . . you would?" she sputtered.

"Of course. What would I do without my Dim Whit?"

The smile Whitney gave back to him was radiant.

Brin brought the car to the curb outside the Stones' impressive house. She hadn't had to ask directions. She and Riley had come here to a company Christmas party. "Do you need any help with your bag?" Brin asked Whitney. She tried to appear calm and unaffected by all that Whitney had said, but it was difficult.

"No, thanks," Whitney replied, opening the door and climbing out, dragging the suitcase with her. She bent down and spoke through the window in a soft voice. "Brin, you're not angry with me for speaking my mind, are you? You know how I feel about you. I think you're super. You're the only person who ever treated me like I wasn't a doormat. And even though Riley has yelled at me on occasion, I know he really likes me."

"Yes, he does. I know he does." Brin patted Whitney's hand reassuringly.

"I didn't mean to butt in. I just want you two back together because I know you love each other."

"It's not that simple, but as Riley said, we appreciate your concern."

"Well, thanks again for the ride."

"Good night."

"Good night."

Brin kept the car idling at the curb until they saw that she was safely inside and in the housekeeper's care. Then Brin turned the car homeward. Riley had either fallen asleep or was pretending to be. In any event, they didn't speak on the trip back. Brin was fighting a battle not to cry. She was angry. Furious, in fact. And hurt. The pain of humiliation ate at her vitals like a carrion bird.

When they were several blocks from their destination, she said, "I'm going to drop you off at your place."

"*Our* place," Riley corrected her sourly. "And you can't do that, because my car's still at your friend's house. Besides, I told you this predawn expedition isn't going to keep us from having our discussion."

She tried not to let him know how furious she was, but as soon as the kitchen door was closed behind them, she unleashed her wrath.

"You bastard!" she began without preamble. "When I

think about . . ." Too angry to continue, she marched the length of the kitchen, then back. Her shoes crunched on the broken glass. "Now I know why you didn't want me to see Whitney tonight."

If there was a remnant of brandy-induced inebriation left in Riley, it was burned away by her anger. He assumed an arrogant stance, one knee bent, hands on hips, head cocked to one side. "Just what the hell are you talking about? What has Whitney got to do with anything? I want to know why when I kissed you—"

"You were afraid she would spill the beans."

"Beans?"

"And you should have seen your face when she did."

"What?" He was getting angry in his own right.

"Since you showed up here unannounced and unwelcome, you've been whining about how you've missed me. How you love me. How you want me back." She rounded on him, her cleft chin jutting forward. "Tell me, Mr. Riley. Do you want me back as your wife or as your *producer?*"

If she had socked him in the gut he couldn't have seemed more surprised. His breath whooshed out, and an expression of absolute disbelief came over his face. "Is *that* what you think this is all about?"

"Yes!"

"Well, you couldn't be more wrong."

"Am I? *Am I?*" She began pacing again, thumping her clenched fists on her thighs as though barely preventing them from striking out at something; namely, his handsome face. "When I think what a fool I've been, when I think about how close I came to being lured into your web again, I could scream."

She bristled with anger as she faced him. "You don't want me back because you love *me*. You want me back because you love *yourself*. You want me back to save your skin. Your all-important career is on the line and you want me to save it for you.

"You don't want me back in your bed nearly as much as you want me back in your studio handling petrified or petulant guests, keeping the crew in line, taking care of the million and one details of producing a daily television talk show. The mighty star can't be bothered with such piddling details, so he becomes a penitent for one night. That's what all this has been for, hasn't it, Riley? It wasn't just coincidence that brought you to me on the night I was making an important career decision."

He denied her allegations so softly, it was unsettling. "You're wrong, Brin."

"I don't think so."

"You are."

"You expect me to believe that if *Riley in the Morning* were doing well in the ratings, if everything were just super-keen at the television station, if your job weren't in jeopardy, you'd still have come here tonight begging me for a reconciliation?"

"It's true."

"Oh, I'll bet. Tell you what, Riley, you can choose." She tossed her head back haughtily. "Do you want me to come back as your producer? Or do you want me as your wife?"

"Both." He closed the distance between them and took her shoulders between his hands, even though he winced with the pain it caused his right hand. "What's wrong with having both? We were a good team in the studio. A better one at home. A terrific one in bed." The focus of his eyes sharpened, and they seemed to drill into her. "Which brings us back to our original argument. What happened to all that fantastic sex?"

"I don't want to talk about it," she said tightly, growing stiff beneath his hands.

"Well, that's just too damn bad, because I do and we are. That's the crux of the problem. That's what went wrong with our marriage, and I don't intend to deny or ignore it. I want to know why. Why? Why wasn't it good for us anymore? I remember the first night I noticed that something was wrong. It was the night of the Press Club's award program."

As painful as it would be, Brin knew he was going to make them run this gauntlet. He wasn't going to leave her alone until they talked about that night and the ones that had followed. . . .

CHAPTER EIGHT

Oh, Riley!" Brin gripped his knee beneath the table when the master of ceremonies announced that the Press Club had voted *Riley in the Morning* the best of local television programming.

Grinning from ear to ear, Riley leaned over and kissed her, then stood and made his way through the banquet tables that filled the largest ballroom of the Fairmont Hotel. On the dais he accepted the coveted award, to a standing ovation.

"Mr. Mayor, fellow members of the media"—he drew in a deep breath and released it on an unsteady laugh—"this is terrific!" His speech was endearing and self-effacing. He publicly thanked the management of the television station, his crew and technicians, most of all his producer.

"I guess all those ideas we talked over in bed paid off, honey." Everyone laughed and glanced in Brin's direction.

And that was the last time that evening that anyone looked at her, or even acknowledged that she existed, much less that she was the mastermind behind the show's innovative programming.

Riley was photographed until he held up his hand in front of his eyes and said, "You've all turned purple." Everyone within hearing distance thought that was hilariously funny and commented that his spontaneous wit was no doubt one reason for his success.

Though everyone else seemed to have forgotten that Brin and Riley were a team, he hadn't. He called her forth out of the crowd to meet the mayor. "Mr. Mayor, I'd like to introduce my producer and wife, Brin."

She extended her hand, but instead of shaking it, the mayor clasped it warmly between his and patted it. "This is a pleasure, Mrs. Riley. Riley, you've got a mighty pretty little lady here."

"Thank you. I think so." Riley's arm went around her shoulders with proud possession. Apparently he didn't notice her rigid posture or strained smile. Probably because at that moment he was called away for another round of picture-taking.

"Wow, what a night," he said once they were in their car and on the way home. He loosened his tie and unfastened the collar button of his shirt. "She's a beauty, isn't she?" With his free hand he held up the gold statue of a woman. His name and the date were engraved on the shield she held in her hands at waist level.

"Yes, she is," Brin admitted. She hated herself for harboring these resentful feelings. But she was hurt and felt overlooked, inconsequential, and insignificant. Had she truly been slighted, or was her ego making her feel as though she had been? Was this as important as it seemed to be, or was her imagination blowing it way out of proportion?

Riley didn't notice that she was unusually quiet. He chatted on about the evening, about who had been in attendance, others who had won awards in various fields of journalism, the banquet food, the emcee's stale jokes.

Not until they were in bed did he get an indication that something wasn't right. He was tipsy on champagne and happiness and reached for her beneath the covers, ready for a private celebration of his success.

She went into his arms willingly enough. She even kissed him back with all the fervor in her heart. But he didn't notice that when he drew her closer against him, and she rested her head on his shoulder, she squeezed tears from her eyes.

His hand moved caressingly over her breasts. "I'm sorry, darling," she said quickly, lifting his hand away, "I don't think I'm up to it tonight."

He raised his head immediately and looked down at her with concern. "Brin? What's the matter? Are you sick? Why didn't you tell me? Do you need anything?"

"No, no, I'm not sick." She touched his chest, but immediately removed her hand. "I just don't feel very well." She couldn't bring herself to say she had a headache. She wasn't about to resort to that cliché.

He smiled in understanding and pressed his hand against her lower abdomen. "Having your period?"

She shook her head, biting back the groan of pleasure that issued up through her throat at the touch of his hand. "No. I just . . . would you mind if we didn't tonight?"

"Of course not. I'm not a surly beast." He kissed her mouth softly and turned her so that her bottom was tucked against his lap and his thighs were supporting the backs of hers. His arms wrapped around her, and his breath stirred her hair as he whispered, "Just let me hold you. You're so cuddly and warm. I love just holding you." He kissed the back of her neck. "I love you."

"I love you too."

And she did. That was why her shame at what she was feeling tasted so brassy and bitter on her tongue. . . .

"Professional jealousy?"

Genuine disbelief was stamped on Riley's features as he gazed up at her from the foot of the bed, where he was sitting. As they had reconsidered that evening, which had represented a major turning point in their happy marriage, they had moved from the kitchen, through the living room, and upstairs to the bedroom, as though migrating toward the source of their problem.

"You left because you were jealous of my success?"

"I knew that was what you would think." Brin turned her

back on him and went to the dressing table, sitting down and gazing at her reflection in the mirror. She was mildly surprised to see that she was still wearing the diamond studs in her ears that she had worn for the party. They were a laughable contrast to her bloodstained sweatshirt.

Her face was lined with fatigue. She was extremely tired, and knew that most of it was mental weariness. She had been thinking too much and too long tonight. Picking up a hairbrush, she dragged it through her hair. "That's why I didn't want to talk to you about this, Riley. I knew you'd dismiss it as jealousy and consider me a fool."

"I could never consider you a fool, Brin. And I'd hardly 'dismiss' the decline of my marriage."

"For seven months you did." Her tone was sharper than she had intended.

He seemed almost ready to refute her accusation, but he closed his lips and let his head fall forward. "You've got me there, Brin. I should have come after you sooner. I wanted to. There hasn't been a day when I didn't have to talk myself out of coming after you and dragging you home—by the hair on your head if necessary." He raised his head and met her eyes in the mirror. "I was too damn mad at first, then too damn proud."

"A big television star doesn't go groveling to his estranged wife, begging her to come back to him."

"Something like that, yeah." He got up and began pacing the width of the room. She saw him unconsciously nursing his right hand.

"Does your hand hurt?"

"Yes, but that doesn't matter."

"Why don't you take one of those pain pills the doctor sent home with me?"

"Because I don't want my brain to be dulled. I want to get to the bottom of this. I need to understand it." He rubbed his eye sockets with the thumb and index finger of his left hand. "Let me get this straight. You were turned off sex that night because I won the award. Right?"

"Wrong." She laid the hairbrush aside and swiveled around on the dressing-table stool to face him. "Don't you know how proud I was of you?"

"I thought so at the time."

"I was. I still am. I guess I resented the fact that I didn't share the award. I felt at least partially responsible for the success of *Riley in the Morning*. Call it proud, call it selfish, call it presumptuous, but that's how I felt."

"So did I, Brin! You were responsible. I recognized you from the podium during my acceptance speech. You *were* the brains behind the show's comeback. Didn't I make that clear? Did I make you feel otherwise?"

"No, but everyone else did. You were the one photographed and interviewed. You—"

"You mean that if some photographer had asked to take your picture that night, my marriage wouldn't have broken up and we wouldn't be having this discussion right now?"

She counted to ten slowly. "Please don't insult me, Riley. Of course it's not that easily explained. That night was only the culmination of many. Every time someone looked past me to see you, I felt a bit of myself chipping away. I felt myself diminishing."

"Public recognition goes with my job, Brin," he said softly.

"I know that, and I wasn't disturbed because fans weren't clamoring for my autograph. There was room for only one star in the family and you were it. I didn't want to be the star. I didn't want to share the limelight. It's just that I didn't want to be invisible, either."

She got off the stool and needlessly began straightening the covers on the bed. She needed activity, movement, or she was going to explode. Besides, when she looked at him, she found it near to impossible to voice her thoughts.

"After months of diligent, hard work, after the ratings had been pulled up, and after *Riley in the Morning* had become a show the competitors had to contend with, I was reduced to being Mrs. Riley. Not Brin Cassidy, producer. But only an appendage of yours. A virtually useless, invisible one, I might add."

"You are my wife, Brin. You shouldn't have agreed to marry me if you didn't want to be Mrs. Riley."

"I *did* want to be. But I am a *woman*, not merely a wife. I wanted to be your wife and your producer, recognized as both, not only as the pretty little lady standing just outside your spotlight."

"I never thought of you that way. Sometimes I act chauvinistic just to get a rise out of you, but you know I'm not really that backward. You know better than to accuse me of that."

"You didn't think that way, but everyone else did."

"And that's why you started freezing up in bed? Not because of what I thought, but because of what other people thought?"

"How was I to compete?" she asked, rounding on him, frustrated at his obtuseness, his inability to see her point.

"Compete? I don't understand."

"You should see yourself in public, Riley. You revel in celebrity. You love the attention and the acclaim. And the louder the applause, the better you like it."

"You knew that about me before you married me. At this late date am I supposed to apologize for that aspect of my personality?"

"No. I love that part of you too."

"Then what are we fighting about? Heaven above, I must be getting as dense as Dim Whit!"

Brin drew a deep breath, hoping that she could make her feelings clear to him. "That night when we got home, you were higher than a kite. Drunk on celebrity. You had basked in all that adulation. Your enjoyment of it was almost orgasmic."

"I was happy. Wasn't I supposed to be?" Impatience made his voice louder.

"Yes, of course."

"Then why should you feel threatened?" he nearly shouted.

"What could I do to you in bed that would make you feel that good?"

Stupefied, he stared at her. Gradually he lowered himself

to the bed. "God." He covered his face with his left hand and dragged it down over his features until one by one his fingers trailed off his chin.

When he looked up at her again, his eyes were bleak. "You thought sex with you wouldn't be as good as winning some damn statue?"

"What could I do to top it?"

His shoulders slumped defeatedly, and he shook his head in bafflement. "That's comparing apples and oranges, Brin."

"It didn't seem so at the time. I felt thoroughly inadequate."

"You make me sound like an egomaniac, who made impossible demands on you."

"I don't mean to," she said, her tone and expression softening. She came to stand close to the foot of the bed, where he sat. "Oh, you have a healthy ego, all right, but this was my problem, my psychological trauma, not yours."

"It's *our* problem, Brin. Why didn't you tell me any of this? Why didn't you discuss what you were feeling?"

"Because I knew it would sound like sour grapes. I knew you would think I was just jealous of your high public profile."

"And you aren't?" he asked teasingly.

She laughed softly. "Not in the way you mean. I resented it sometimes."

"What times?"

She could tell that he had a sincere wish to know. "Your audience sees you only when you're perfect. Perfectly groomed, perfectly happy, perfectly everything. But I saw you when you looked like hell, when you got out of bed, before your first cup of coffee, when you slouched around the house in grubby clothes. I held your head over the commode that time you got a stomach virus. I washed your dirty socks."

"But I folded them," he said, holding up an index finger. Her smile never quite reached her eyes. "I see your point, though," he said softly. "I'll admit I never thought of it that way."

"I guess I resented everyone thinking you were perfect when I knew better. Sometimes, in my most paranoid moments, I thought that you saved your perfection for everyone else and I got the leftovers."

"I was never as good as when I was with you, Brin." He reached for her hand and squeezed it. With a gentle pressure, he urged her down on the bed beside him. They sat there, shoulders touching. "Think back to that first day you reported to work. As you so impolitely pointed out, I was a mess. I had bags under my eyes; I was doing shoddy interviews. I had grown placid, which is death for anybody on television. You whipped me into shape. And if no one, me included, gave you credit for that, we were at fault."

"Is that all I wanted? Credit? Yes, I suppose so," she said, answering her own question. "Now that sounds so crass and selfish, so shallow."

"You wanted sensitivity from your husband, which is what any woman has a right to expect. John Q. Public is basically a stupid animal. Don't blame him for being insensitive. Place the blame where it belongs. With me.

"I should have realized what you were feeling and done

something about it. I *am* a conceited, self-centered bastard. There I was, soaking up the glory, while you were hurting. In this case, ignorance was not bliss. I should have come to you on bended knees, in gratitude, thanking you for what you'd done for me. Instead I crawled into bed that night expecting you to give even more of yourself to me, to make yourself accessible for my pleasure and well-being." He touched her hair. "No wonder you were turned off sex."

"I was never turned off sex."

"You could have fooled me."

"Don't you see, Riley? I was afraid I wouldn't measure up. You had thousands of women idolizing you. But you were no idol to me. I knew you were fallible." She spread her hands wide, palms up, as though giving him a humble offering. "I merely loved you. In spite of your imperfections. I loved you so much it hurt. So much that I didn't want to fail you. And if I couldn't match that high you got from your adoring fans, that would be my failure."

"So you stopped trying."

"I guess that's right."

He stood up and ambled around the room as though looking for a place to light. It was a familiar tactic he used when trying to arrange his thoughts. Brin sat where he had left her, waiting for him to speak.

"I couldn't figure it out. At first I thought I was just catching you on off days. Before, we had always laughed about it when one or the other of us was sexually out of sync. You weren't laughing any longer."

He paused in front of her dressing table. He picked up

the hairbrush she had used minutes earlier, and lightly slapped it against his palm. "Finally—sometimes I'm not too astute and have to be hit over the head with a two-by-four before I catch on—I realized that you weren't interested in sex at all. Zilch. Zero."

"I wasn't sure you even noticed."

He laughed mirthlessly. "Oh, I noticed, but I pretended not to. I was shaking in my boots. Scared . . . well, scared. I didn't want to face what was so painfully clear."

"Which was?"

"That I couldn't make my wife happy in bed." He was facing the mirror. Now he raised his eyes to meet her reflection. "You seem surprised," he said when he saw her expression.

"I'm stunned. How could you think that?"

He turned around. "Brin, when a man touches a woman and she cringes, it's a pretty good indication that she doesn't either like or want his touch."

"Did I do that?" she asked in a small voice.

"At first your turn-off wasn't so obvious. You just became this brisk, businesslike creature who never slowed down long enough for me to get my arms around, who never had time for a kiss, whose conversation centered around *Riley in the Morning* or there wasn't any conversation at all, who was so exhausted from the way she was driving herself that when we did get into bed she fell asleep instantly. Or pretended to."

"You make me sound like a machine."

"That's what you were, a machine who looked and sounded like Brin, beautiful, sexy, intelligent Brin. But I didn't know you anymore. And I was lost. I didn't have an instruction booklet on how to operate this new machine. Nothing I did seemed to work."

He laughed ruefully as he toyed with the perfume decanters on her dresser. "The happy-go-lucky approach fell flat, because your sense of humor seemed to have evaporated. The romantic approach was hard to pull off, because I couldn't even get near you without the invisible barriers going up. And once, when I tried the caveman approach by reaching around you and covering your breasts with my hands, you fought me off and made me feel like I had a contagious disease."

Brin's eyes were brimming with tears. She looked down to find that her fingers were threaded together tensely in her lap. "I wanted you to touch me, Riley. I wanted to make love with you. But I just couldn't risk it."

"Do you have any idea what it does to a man when he thinks he can't please his wife?"

"I imagine it's terrible."

"Hell on earth."

"It couldn't have been good for your star's ego."

"It would have been just as devastating if I'd been a ditch digger. I tormented myself for hours analyzing what was wrong. Was I too passionate? Not passionate enough? Did I want sex too frequently? Not frequently enough? Was our bedroom scene too kinky? Not kinky enough? Did my body revolt you? Was I too small to satisfy you?"

"Oh, Riley," she said, shaking her head and laughing scoffingly.

"Well, that's what goes through a man's head!" he cried defensively. "All I had to go on were the signals you were transmitting. And what I interpreted them to mean was that you wanted nothing to do with me in bed."

"Why didn't you ask me what was wrong?"

"Do you think I wanted to hear you say that I was too small?"

For the first time in months, they laughed together. It sounded good. It felt good. But when the laughter subsided Riley said seriously, "For two people who have made careers in the communications field, we certainly didn't communicate, did we?"

"No. We didn't."

"I was afraid to broach the subject for fear of what I'd hear."

"And I couldn't broach it because I thought you'd ridicule me for being jealous and petty. And I swear to you, Riley," Brin said with complete sincerity, "that wasn't the reason."

"Clarify it for me one more time. I want to be sure I understand why you left."

"I was afraid that if I stayed with you I'd continue to lose ground, that I would eventually become no more to you than a shadow, that I would lose all sense of my own identity. Before long I'd become boring to you and therefore dispensable. When I went to work for *Riley in the Morning,* the show needed me. You needed me. Once I put you on top, I was afraid you wouldn't need me anymore, professionally or otherwise."

"You were wrong. Very wrong."

"Whether I was or not, that's how I perceived the situation, and we generally act on our perceptions, not on actualities."

Slowly he walked toward the bed, and crouched in front of her. "So where does that leave us?"

She sighed. "I don't know."

"Are you going to accept Winn's job this morning?"

"I don't know that either," she said with a note of desperation. "But if I do, I want you to understand one thing, Riley. There has never been, or ever will be, anything personal between Abel and me."

He looked chagrined. "In light of our recent conversation I think you can see why I suspected that there might be some passion simmering there."

"Never. At least not on my part."

"He's reputedly a hotshot in boardrooms and bedrooms."

"So are you."

His eyes lit up. "Yeah?"

"Fishing for compliments? Don't expect me to stroke your inflated ego, Mr. Riley."

"Could you?"

"Oh, yes," she answered after a cautious pause. "I certainly could."

"How, Brin?"

She must be awfully tired. Because she rarely wept except when she was very tired, and she was dangerously close to tears now. Reaching out, she brushed the silver-tipped hair off his forehead. "I could tell you that no man compares to you, that I've never been attracted to another man the way I was to you from the very beginning, that your kisses are to die for." She smiled a gamine smile and leaned forward to whisper, "Your body is nothing less than magnificent and you certainly aren't too small!"

"Whew! That's a relief."

Laughing softly, they bumped foreheads, then noses. They stayed like that, exchanging breaths. At last he tilted his head to one side and grazed her lips with his. It was a kiss as gentle as a spring rain.

"Do you know what it felt like when you left me?"

"I wasn't proud of the way I went about it. I took the coward's way out."

"You had stayed home from work that day, saying you were sick. I called several times during the day to check on you."

"I didn't answer the phone."

"Which worried the hell out of me. Then when I came home and found all your things gone and your note . . . well, it was like I'd been hit by a Mack truck."

She pinched her eyes closed and shuddered as she inhaled jaggedly. "I'm so sorry."

"That night I was in a stupor. I kept asking myself what I'd done wrong and made grandiose plans about how to win you back. But the next day when I got your letter saying you weren't coming back no matter what, I flew into a rage."

"What did you do?"

He joined her on the edge of the bed. "I went out on the patio and, bent on destroying something, uprooted all those plants you'd had me set out."

"Those things cost five ninety-nine apiece!" she cried.

"At that point I didn't care. Made a helluva mess. Then I got blind, stinking drunk."

"So did I."

"You did?"

"Not blind, stinking, but morosely so."

"I got angry enough to wait you out, to defy your desertion. You walked out? Fine, good, see if I care." He shook his head sadly. "But life just wasn't fun anymore. You'd taken all the color with you. Everything was gray. From time to time I'd forget what had happened and would turn to you to share a comment about a book or a movie or a TV show or a flavor of ice cream. Only you weren't there, Brin, and I would lose all pleasure in it."

He combed his fingers through her hair. "I wanted you back at any cost, but my damnable pride kept me from coming after you. And each day that passed made it harder to come begging."

"I missed you too," she confessed quietly. "It was scary. Suddenly nothing in my life was familiar, not my job, or where I lived. But I couldn't come back, either. In the first place I wasn't sure you wanted me back. And if you did, what would have been the point of leaving? What would I have proved?"

"And now? Have you proved what you wanted to, that I can't or don't want to live without you?"

"That wasn't my intention. I set out to prove that I could be a whole, viable person without Jon Riley."

"You always were, Brin. God forgive me for making you

feel that you weren't." He cupped her face between his hands and stroked her lips with his thumbs. "Abel Winn is offering you the moon. I hate the bastard for being capable of doing that, but that's life. You'd be crazy not to take that job."

"It's not morning yet. I haven't made up my mind."

"That's the advantage I'm pressing. He's not here with you tonight. I am. You're still my wife. I want you back in my life. I love you. So stay with me tonight. Share my bed. Lie with me. No sex. Just be near. I think we owe that much to each other."

"And what will happen in the morning if I do accept Winn's job?"

"I'll let you go and wish you well. I swear it."

Why did she hesitate to give him an answer? She believed him. He would live with her decision. Why, then, was she terrified to share a bed with him for the remainder of the night?

Because she still loved him. And because love sometimes paid no attention to wisdom.

Granted, she was seeing their marriage from a different angle. Riley was still her husband. She *did* owe him this night. And she owed it to herself, because she had to be sure. If she did decide to take the job in Los Angeles, which would be tantamount to divorcing Riley, she had to be certain that she was emotionally, as well as physically, free of him.

"All right, Riley," she said softly. "Let's go to bed."

They undressed slowly, watching each other. As bodies were unclad and skin was uncovered, they had a difficult time keeping libidos under control.

"I think you'd better stop there," Riley said thickly. She was down to the tank top and panties.

She nodded in agreement and was glad he had left on his briefs. He switched off the lamp. Habit placed her on his right side. As soon as the covers were pulled over them, they rolled to face each other, as they always had.

"Be careful of your hand."

He rested it above her head on the pillow. "It's practically well by now."

Brin knew he was lying. His lips were still rimmed with that telltale fine white line. "Sure you won't take a pill?"

"And miss any of this? Not likely." He wove their legs together and inched closer.

She laid her hand on his neck. "You should get some sleep."

"I don't want to." His protest was belied by his eyelids, which were struggling to stay open. The events of the night had exacted their toll. He was putting up a valiant battle to stave off their effects.

"But you need to rest," Brin whispered. She curled her hand around his head and pulled it down to her breasts.

He nestled there, butting his head against the soft flesh until he found a familiar spot. "You don't play fair," he mumbled sleepily.

"Shh." Her fingers sifted through his hair. "Go to sleep."

Within minutes she could tell by his even breathing that he had lost his fight and was asleep. But Brin lay awake. She had only a few hours to make up her mind and she still didn't know what her answer to either man would be.

The job with Winn was tantalizing. The money was more than adequate. It would be exciting to get in on the ground floor of a new, nationally syndicated show. She had never been able to resist a challenge like that.

But she didn't really want to move to Los Angeles. Money wasn't everything. *Riley in the Morning* had never failed to stimulate her creative juices and keep her excitement level at its peak. What could be more challenging than making a successful marriage?

And she loved Riley.

She rested her chin on his head and hugged it tight against her. She loved Riley. At that moment she couldn't think of anything more tantalizing than sleeping with him every night. He was more fun to be with than anybody she'd ever known. He acted a bit petulant at times, but that ornery streak in him appealed to her maternal instincts. And she could be a real bitch when she put her mind to it. He'd always handled her darker moods with uncanny tolerance, patiently coaxing her out of them with laughter.

She wanted *Riley in the Morning* and she wanted Riley.

So what was keeping her from committing herself to that decision? Only one thing: Why had he chosen tonight to seek reconciliation?

Was it because he couldn't stand another day without her, or because he'd been handed down an ultimatum? Did he want his wife back? Or his producer? Was his marriage more important? Or the future of his television show? Whom did he love the most, himself or her?

Did it matter?

Her fingers closed around a handful of his precious hair. Whom had *she* loved the most when she'd walked out on him? Whom had she been preoccupied with? Whose well-being had been foremost in her mind?

Yet he had swallowed his monumental pride and come after her. He had recognized and admitted that they were far better off with than without each other. Certainly there were problems inherent in any two-career marriage. If Riley had the courage to meet them head-on, didn't she?

Brin kissed the top of his head, his shoulder. But he didn't wake up. Not even when she left the bed and crept downstairs.

CHAPTER NINE

B rin?"

"Hmm?"

"Did you get up?"

"Yes. I went downstairs for a while."

"What for?"

"I got the coffee ready and set the timer."

"What time is it?"

"Early. I'm sorry I woke you up."

"It's okay. I'm glad you did."

As she resumed her spot beside him, their legs automatically interlaced. She snuggled close to his chest, burying one hand in his armpit. His left arm went around her waist.

"Does your hand hurt?"

"Maybe," he answered dreamily. "I can't feel anything

but you." For several moments nothing disturbed the dawn-quiet silence in the house except their gentle breathing. Then he said, "You feel so good against me. You always did."

"I'm glad you think so."

"One of the first things I noticed was how physically compatible we are."

"I noticed that too," she said, smiling against his chest. The soft, crinkly hairs tickled her lips.

"God, I've missed holding you. Just holding you. It feels so good." He tried to draw her closer, though that was impossible. He rubbed his cheek against the crown of her head. When he relaxed his hold a fraction, she tilted her head back in order to look up at him.

"It feels good to be held."

A spasm of emotion flickered over his face. His deep blue eyes burned into hers. They took in her delicate complexion, which the first morning light only made more pearlescent. Her hair formed a wreath of tangled, inky curls around her face. The long lashes surrounding her aquamarine eyes were dark and luxuriant. Her lips were rosy and moist and looked ready to engage in any activity suggested. As always, the cleft in her chin bewitched him. She looked wanton. Willing. Tousled sexiness incarnate.

He whispered her name huskily before his mouth moved down to hers. Lips touched. Parted. Touched again. And again. Then clung. His tongue shyly pried her lips open. Investigated.

Brin, yearning and pliant, arched her body against his and curved her hand around the back of his head. He needed no further encouragement. His tongue spiraled down deep into the hollow of her mouth. It wasn't hurried or abusive or plundering. It wasn't apologetic or timid either. But questing, seeking, reacquainting itself with every sweet nuance of her mouth.

He whispered incoherently as his lips skittered over her face, brushing airy kisses on her forehead and eyelids and cheeks and nose. But always his lips came back to hers. He nibbled at them, catching her provocative lower lip lightly between his teeth, worried it gently, then soothed it with damp sweeps of his tongue. He tasted the smile that tugged at the corners of her lips. His kisses were wild and controlled, rowdy and tender, capricious and lazy, playful and passionate. Ever changing, ever evocative.

"You have the mouth I fantasized about in my youth," he growled softly.

"What makes it special?"

"Everything. The taste, the shape, the way it responds. I love it."

He kissed her again until they were both breathless.

"You're an excellent kisser," Brin murmured drowsily, as though his mouth had siphoned all the energy out of her. "Every woman should know what it's like to be kissed by you at least once."

"What's it like?" His lips rubbed against hers.

"Like being made love to."

"The very act?"

"The very act. Your kisses say that you're definitely the man, I'm the woman. No matter the tempo, they're never sloppy. Always thorough. Your kisses leave me weak, yet terribly aroused."

He raised his head high enough to gaze down at her. A groove formed between his brows as his index finger circled her mouth where the skin had turned rosy. "My beard—"

"It doesn't matter." As though it weighed a thousand pounds, she lifted her hand and stroked his chin, where a morning stubble bristled, shadowing the lower half of his face. "It's rather piratical. And I've always had a hankering to be taken by a pirate."

"Why's that?" The backs of his fingers strummed the column of her throat.

"I'm not sure. I think it has something to do with his sword."

He suspended his love play to angle his head back and look down at her cynically. "His sword, huh?"

"Um-hm." She smiled suggestively.

He touched his lips to her ear and whispered something naughty. She giggled, then swatted his bare shoulder playfully. They engaged in a skirmish of slapping hands and harmless nibbling teeth. When it ended, their mouths were hotly fused again and both considered themselves the victor.

Playfulness gave way to passion. With a low groan, Riley stretched out his legs. Taking the subtle cue, Brin straightened her knees. They moved together until they were toe to toe, shin to shin, thigh to thigh. When their loins met, the heat spread up through them like spilling lava.

She gasped his name.

He sighed hers.

He crooked one arm around her neck and bent her head back over it while his mouth savored hers. His other hand splayed wide over the small of her back, anchoring the yielding feminine delta against his swollen sex.

Moans of mutual satisfaction welcomed the first pinkish rays of light that filtered through the shutters into the room.

"I missed you, Brin." His breath was hot against her neck. He poured love words into her ear like a healing elixir. "I missed this. I missed having you in my bed, missed your passion. Sometimes I thought I would die if I could never hold you like this again. I needed you so much I wanted to die. Missing you was a physical illness. Make me well," he ended on an urgent plea. "Make me well."

His hand slipped inside her panties. Strong, warm fingers kneaded the firm flesh of her derriere, urging her closer. She wedged her hand between their bodies and curled her fingers into the elastic waistband of his underwear. She felt him stop breathing. Time stood still for a moment while their hearts thumped together.

Then her hand moved. Peeling the briefs down, she freed him. He let his breath go with a sound that was part sigh, part moan. He was hard and smooth and velvety against her thighs.

Impatiently his hand grappled with her panties and worked them down past her hips. She kept her legs pressed together tightly because she knew he loved a challenge and because his probing against the downy cleft at the top of her thighs was immensely pleasurable.

Instinctively she turned onto her back. An urge as old as mankind directed him to follow, to cover. His hands scoured her restlessly, almost desperate in their need to touch her flesh. Mindless of the bandage that wrapped his right hand, mindless of the painful wound beneath it, he caressed her.

With a wild recklessness, he took the hem of the tank top in both hands and pulled it over her head. He flung it aside viciously. With legs pumping as rapidly as pistons, he shoved his underwear down his legs and kicked it away. Levering himself above her with straight, rigid arms, his eyes devoured her naked body.

Then, only then, did he regain his senses. He blinked to clear his eyes of a passion-induced blindness.

"Don't stop there, Riley," she gasped.

He laughed softly. Gradually he relaxed the muscles in his arms, and lowered himself down onto her gently. He kissed her mouth softly, then pressed his face into the fragrant, satiny, warm hollow between her shoulder and neck. He rested there until his heart had ceased its pounding and his breathing had slowed down.

"I don't want it to go that fast." His voice was a soft, rumbling vibration against her throat. "I want it to be good. Better than it's ever been. The best."

She cupped the back of his head and tunneled all ten fingers into the thick strands of his hair until they pressed against his scalp. "I told you that that was *never* the problem. It's always been good."

"I know. But I want this to be as special as the first time. I want us to remember this." Lovingly, adoringly, he smoothed the wayward curls off her flushed cheeks. "I love you, Brin Cassidy. I want you to know how much."

He moved far enough away from her to view her entire body. Smiling, he finished removing her panties, which were bunched around her knees. Then his eyes wandered up the entire length of her body. "You're so beautiful," he whispered.

Laying his hand first on her ankle, he let it travel everywhere his eyes had gone, stopping to examine everything that struck his fancy.

The back of her knee . . .

"That's so soft."

"And I don't even shave there."

The light scar on her thigh . . .

"What happened here?"

"I fell onto a broken bottle at the beach."

"How old were you?"

"About six."

The mole beneath her right breast . . .

"That's beautiful."

"It's ugly."

"Not to me."

The cleft in the edge of her chin . . .

"I love this."

"I asked my mother about that once. She said before God sent me down to earth, He pointed at me and said, 'You're my favorite little angel.' That's where His finger touched me."

Riley chuckled. He took one of her hands in his and

studied the patterns of veins, the dainty bone structure, the long, tapered nails. Lifting her hand to his mouth, he ardently kissed the palm, delving in its center with his tongue. She squirmed. "That tickles, but it's delicious."

"*You're* delicious."

His tongue touched the pad of her middle finger, and she reacted with a violent jerk. His eyes narrowed with the discovery. Slowly he bathed the pad of each of her fingers with that agile seducer.

"Riley," she groaned. Her back arched off the bed and her eyes fluttered closed.

They flew open when she felt her own hand being lowered to her breast. She gazed up at him with a question in her eyes. He remained silent, still, staring back at her. She wet her lips. She was suddenly shy, and terribly aroused. "You want me to . . ."

The breathless question dwindled to nothingness. He nodded. His eyes shone a brilliant blue, and his arousal was transmitted through that light. It seemed to go straight through her.

"But you never . . . said . . . never mentioned . . ."

"I think it would be beautiful to see," he said gruffly, tracing her finger where it lay against her breast. "Your fingers are still moist from my mouth."

Her feelings were ambivalent. She was timorous, yet aware of a tingling excitement deep inside her. Boldness won out over bashfulness. Loving him, wanting to please him, she began to move her hand. Then her fingers. Lightly, softly, provocatively.

A groan issued out of his throat when she had made herself ready for him. He bent down and took one sweet, ripe crest between his lips. Kissing her breasts with a mouth that seemed fashioned to give that caress, he suckled her nipples lovingly, then flicked his tongue over them repeatedly, until Brin thought she would explode from the pressure building within her.

Gauging her mounting desire, he slid his hand over her belly. His fingers sifted through the dark tuft of hair, then insinuated themselves between her quivering thighs. She closed her thighs against his hand, trapping it there, moving against it.

Tenderly he parted the velvety petals of flesh to find the wet silk they protected. He stroked her with maddening leisure. Sensitive to her needs and desires, he brought her to the brink of oblivion time and again without letting her slip over.

He kissed his way down her middle, over her tummy, her navel, her belly. His dewy lips nuzzled the V that pointed the way to the heart of her femininity. With swirling thrusts and circling strokes, his tongue expressed his unselfish love.

Modesty abandoned her. Nothing mattered except getting closer, having more, giving all. In that instant, she knew what it was to love. Her soul opened up, and all that was Brin Cassidy belonged to Jon Riley, exclusively and forever. Her spirit showered him with fragments of herself until it had all poured out. And conversely, she didn't feel empty, but full to overflowing. With love.

"Jon, no, please." She felt that her body was about to

experience the release her heart had already undergone. "I want you inside me."

He let her lift him up, let her hand guide his body into the snug arbor of hers. He sank into her, deeply, as far as he could go, then reached high, higher. Trapping her head between his hands, he kissed her with all the passion pumping through him.

"Can you feel how much I love you, Brin?"

"Yes, yes, yes," she chanted in time to the driving motions of his body. "I love you, Jon. I love you."

Her climax came only seconds, heartbeats, before his. He watched her throat arch, her head toss, her face shine. Then he released his own torrent of love. It jetted into her womb and straight to her heart.

"You succeeded."

She lay draped across him. Their posture was indolent, exhausted. Idly she plucked at his chest hair. Frequently her lips puckered enough to kiss his chest.

"How's that?" he asked. His eyes were closed. He was perfectly at peace for the first time in months.

"You said you wanted us to remember this time. *I'll* never forget it."

"Forget what?"

Brin wound a clump of hair around her index finger and yanked on it hard.

"Ouch!" he exclaimed. "I'm sorry, I'm sorry. Can't you take a joke?"

Laughing, he wrapped his arms around her and rolled her to her back. He gnawed at her neck with comic enthusiasm, making the guttural sounds of a hungry jungle predator. When their lips finally made contact, the kisses they exchanged were tender and love-laden.

"I want to be your wife again, Riley," she whispered when he eventually lifted his lips from hers.

"You've never stopped being my wife."

"You're going to make me spell it out, aren't you?"

He grinned, his eyes twinkling devilishly.

"Very well." She sighed. "I want to move back into our house."

"And into our bed?"

"And into our bed." She touched his mouth. "Definitely into our bed."

"And share our lives?"

"Until we grow very old."

"What about babies?"

"What about them?"

"You didn't exactly pounce on the idea when I brought it up earlier."

"You were bleeding all over my Datsun!"

"Oh."

"Besides, we weren't officially back together then."

"It was only a matter of time."

"Don't get cocky or I won't tell you that I accidentally forgot to 'protect' myself."

"Accidentally?"

"I warned you not to get cocky."

His grin was the essence of cockiness. But he became serious when he asked, "Are you sure, Brin?"

"About the babies?"

"About it all."

There was no hesitancy in her answer. "Absolutely, positively sure."

"And what about the job with Winn? I hate asking you to give up that opportunity."

"I already have."

"You already . . . *What?* When?"

"This morning. I went downstairs and called him."

"Damn," he said softly. "Why didn't you tell me?"

"You didn't ask until now."

"What did you say to him?"

"That I was flattered by his offer, but that by accepting it, I would have to give up something far more important to me. My marriage."

"Bet he didn't take kindly to that." Riley couldn't disguise the pleasure in his voice.

"Considering that I called him before daybreak and got him out of bed, I think he took it as well as could be expected. In fact he sounded glad to hear from me so early."

"He thought you were calling to give him the good news."

"And I was," she said, snuggling against him. "It's just that my good news wasn't good news to him."

"Did you mention that you had a randy husband waiting in bed for you?"

She pecked his chin with a kiss. "Some secrets are just too delicious to share." She linked her arms around his neck. "So now are you happy? You've got your wife and your producer back."

"That sure is going to come in handy"—he kissed her—"especially if I ever get another TV show."

"Hmm, it sure—" She broke off in mid-sentence. Her head plopped back down on the pillow as she looked up at him dumbfoundedly. "What did you say?"

"I said that if I ever get another TV—"

"Okay, skip over that part and tell me what it means."

He rolled off her and lay on his back, resting his head in his left hand and propping his bandaged right one on his chest. "Dim Whit had *most* of the facts straight."

"Which ones? Is *Riley in the Morning* in trouble or not?"

"You'll be glad to know that it has gone to hell since you left it," he said, giving her an arch look. "Basically because the star of said show didn't give a damn about it anymore."

"How badly did the ratings slip?"

"Let's just say that management was justified to call me in and issue an ultimatum. Their answer to our dilemma was to get you back. Pronto. And I was assigned the job. I was to use any means, fair or foul."

"I see."

"That's when I told them that my marriage was already in trouble and that I wasn't about to jeopardize it further for the sake of any TV show, and if that was what they expected, they could take the show and . . . I think you get my drift."

He stared at the ceiling for several moments, afraid to

know her reaction. Finally he garnered his courage and turned his head. Tears were standing in her eyes. "My God, Brin, why are you crying? Are you that upset?"

She shook her head, sending crystal tears splashing over her cheeks and onto the pillow. "You did that for me?" She knew that *Riley in the Morning* meant the world to him. It was the most important thing in his life. Yet he had been willing to give it up for her. His plea for reconciliation hadn't been for the sake of his career.

"Does it bother you that you're no longer married to a star?"

"I'd love you no matter what you were."

He reached for her hand. She laid it in his left palm and he squeezed it hard. "I always knew we made a terrific team." Steeped in love, they stared at each other across the pillow.

Finally Brin found enough voice to say, "Now the crucial question. Will you make it stick?"

"What?"

"Don't play dumb with me. Your resignation. You've quit at least a dozen times that I know of and you always go back."

He laughed, then sobered. "They might not take me back this time."

"They would if they thought you were going somewhere else," she said in a sing-song voice. "They'd probably offer you a fat new contract to entice you back and guarantee that you stay."

He propped himself up on one elbow and looked down at her. "What's going on in that clever brain of yours?"

She giggled. "It stands to reason that if we get back together, make our reconciliation public knowledge, and let it be known that I've been offered a spot on *Front Page*—"

"Yeah, I follow so far."

"That they'll assume you're going over to the Winn Company as host, with me as producer of *Front Page*."

"But I'm not."

"They don't know that!"

"And by the time they do—"

"They'll already have begged us to come back."

"You're not only sexy, you're smart." He smacked her bare fanny with his palm and kissed her hard. They were laughing when they fell apart. "The bluff might not work, you know."

She shrugged. "Then we'll do something else. Something totally unrelated to television."

"You have that much faith in me?"

"I have that much faith in us." Her eyes became lambent, reflecting the mellow golden light of the new day. "I pulled a foolish, juvenile stunt by walking out like that, Riley. It was stupid, and I'm embarrassed about it. I've discovered what it really means to love, and I love you more than ever for forgiving me. Let's not ever let something fester between us like that again."

"Come here," he growled, hauling her close. "If we start comparing the stupid, juvenile, foolish things we've done, we'll waste precious time."

They kissed with newfound love, a love that was stronger than what they had known before. She was smiling when they drew apart. "Precious time away from what?" she asked in a sultry voice. She raised herself over him and dipped her head low on his chest, kissing and nibbling.

"Food, for one thing." Her tongue sponged his nipple, and he sucked in his breath sharply. "I never did, uh, finish that . . . that, uh . . ."

"What?"

"What?"

Her tongue was at his navel, behaving with impish impropriety. "What didn't you finish?"

"That, uh, ham sandwich. I, Brin . . . Brin?"

Her lips whispered through the thatch of dark hair above his sex. "Hmm?"

"What does a guy . . . good, merciful heaven, I'm dying . . . a guy have to, uh . . . ah, yes, like that, just like that . . . have to do to get . . . uh, breakfast?"

"I'm keeping you in bed for a good long while yet, Riley," she purred as she positioned herself above him. "I discovered a long time ago that morning is your prime time."

ABOUT THE AUTHOR

SANDRA BROWN began her writing career in 1980. After selling her first book, she wrote a succession of romance novels under several pseudonyms, most of which remain in print. She has become one of the country's most popular novelists, earning the notice of Hollywood and of critics. More than forty of her books have appeared on the *New York Times* bestseller list. There are fifty million copies of her books in print, and her work has been translated into twenty-nine languages. Prior to writing, she worked in commercial television as an on-air personality for *PM Magazine* and local news in Dallas. The parents of two, she and her husband now divide their time between homes in Texas and South Carolina.